Praise for 'A Divide

'Filled with suspense, accuracy, real- _____ ___ _____,
A Divided Inheritance will satisfy even the most
discerning of history buffs.'
The Examiner

'Impeccable research, layers of intriguing plot line, an
understanding of the complexities of 17th century politics and the
sheer power of descriptive prose...a classy, compelling adventure
story and a true journey of discovery.'
Lancashire Evening Post

'Achieves what all stellar historical fiction must: through the voices
of imagined characters, important lessons from the past linger and
haunt long after the book is finished.'
Ann Weisgarber, Orange Prize nominee

'A multifaceted tale about the consequences of religious intolerance,
the expiation of guilt, the importance of family, and the appearance
of unexpected love.'
Sarah Johnson, Reading the Past

'I was thoroughly gripped until the end of this exhilarating book.
And I would highly recommend this swashbuckling tale of lace,
swordsmen, Spanish dancing, spice and romance.'
Sixtyplussurfers magazine

First published 2013 by Macmillan
This edition Quire Books 2018

This is a work of fiction and is the production of the author's imagination.

This book is written in UK English with UK spellings.

A Divided

Inheritance

For John, with love

A Divided Inheritance

Deborah Swift

Au coeur vaillant, rien n'est impossible
Motto from 'Academy of the Sword' by Girard Thibault

QUIRE BOOKS

Part One

Chapter 0

London, September 1599

Magdalena dare not sleep in case she did not wake. She was thinking of her sons; of Zachary in particular. How to convince him. There would be a chance, if only he'd sit still long enough to listen.

She struggled to push herself upright in her bed. Her nightdress was damp with sweat, though she shivered with cold so much she had to drag the tangle of covers right up to her neck. No matter that it was autumn and mild, and flies still buzzed lazily round her ale cup. Death hovered near, like the onset of winter. She put the vapour pipe to her lips again and inhaled deeply.

A picture of Zachary rose up in her mind; his darting eyes, his restless energy. He had grown wilder this last year now that she was confined to her chamber and there was no one to father him. And as for Saul and Kit, they had no patience with him, never did have. They sensed he was different to them, God knows how, but they did.

When they pinched him, thinking she could not see them, it used to make her come running to chastise them with slaps. That was when she could reach them, but now she resorted to harsh words, shouting and cursing at them like a shrew, but it was no use. The wily scoundrels – they knew she could do nothing. Not lying here stuck like a sow in a stall.

How in God's name would Zachary fare, once she was gone? The dread for him rose up within her. Absurd, she thought, when he was almost grown now and a youth – no longer the wiry babe in arms who suckled at her breast. Still, she feared for him.

She warded off another spasm of coughing by draining the lukewarm ale and lay back on the pillow. She stared at the peeling plasterwork on the ceiling, hearing the street cries outside and the clop of hooves passing by. Her breath came heavily now, with memories of Zack's tears, and the too-innocent faces of her elder boys.

How terrible to know this of your own sons – to see so clearly their cruelty and malice. She had never thought she could despise her own children, but Kit and Saul had defeated her. Their venom came from nowhere, mysterious, risen in them like bile. As if their blood somehow remembered their father and his fists, although they had been only mewling babes when she had left him.

It shamed her, that she loved them, despite it all. These ugly hearted sons. They would never change, and she was dog-tired of pretending that they would. Nobody sees the truth of their children as a mother does. So, she must do what she could for Zack. She pushed the opium away, prepared to bear the pain if she could only scrape her thoughts back together, and keep her wits one last night.

It was almost dark when she heard the door latch click, but she knew it must be Zack for he was always a few hours ahead of his brothers. He liked to enjoy a little time with her alone, before Saul and Kit came in with their ale-breath and swagger.

She heard his weapons and his night's pickings drop outside her door with a clatter. Too tired and sick to use the bedchamber, she slept in the main chamber now, on a pallet piled with sheepskins and old cloaks, for she could never seem to get warm.

Soon some other family will lodge here, she thought, and I will be just a half-sensed presence, a scent of poppy left hanging in the air.

'Zack!' she called out, mustering her strength.

His dark curly head appeared round the door. He tiptoed in, although it was clear she was not asleep. She followed him with her eyes as he came, seeing him as if from a distance. Small and skinny, his legs poked out from under an oversized cloak, a new one, by the look of it, of damson-coloured wool. He closed the open window, and lit the sconces with a taper, and then paraded before her, swishing the cloak, grinning, showing off its green silk lining.

'*Qué bonito!*' he said, in Spanish. 'Can you believe it?' he crowed. 'The gent hadn't fastened it properly, so I had it whisked off in a trice. Had to run like a hare afterwards, though. Fine, isn't it?'

'Yes,' she murmured, 'it surely is. But come, sit a moment.'

'Why, are you worse? What is it?' His eyes were wide with concern.

'Not worse, no. But I need to tell you something.'

He sat, unhooked the cloak and threw it over the bed, smoothing it with his fingers. His hands were none-too-clean as usual. He lifted a corner and brought it up to her face for her to see. 'It will keep you warm, Mama. Look how tight-woven it is. I chose it specially, and the—'

'Yes, yes.' She dismissed it with a small gesture and took hold of his hand to keep his attention. He squirmed a little, unused to this, but did not withdraw. There was fine dark down growing on his upper lip. She was about to reach up to touch it but her eyes blurred. Unshed tears that she would not see him become a proper man.

She swallowed and took a deep breath, hoping her voice would hold. 'In Spanish, eh? It's easier for me.' He nodded. 'Nathaniel Leviston, whom you called uncle. You remember him?' The English name seemed strange amongst the Spanish words.

Zack was very still now, seeing her tears and recognizing something different in her tone. She pressed his hand, 'Well, he has no sons. It could be he will be glad to take you in, and—'

'What do you mean, Mama?' He never let her finish, always wanted to be ahead of the conversation.

'When I am gone, he will come to find you. I have written to him. I pray I have not left it too late. But Zack, he is wealthy and, who knows, he thinks you are his kin, and he might be prepared to help you if . . .' she paused, trying to think of the right words, 'if your brothers do not prove kind.'

He was already protesting. 'But you aren't going anywhere,

Mama. You're staying right here, until you get well. Wait, I'll fetch you some more of your draught.' He tried to pull away, but she clung tight.

'No. No more poppy,' she said, breathless with the effort of speaking and of holding him. 'Not tonight. I need to be clear in my mind. I need you to understand. There is no money. I have nothing to leave you. Promise me. Promise you'll go with Uncle Leviston. He will—'

'Hush, Mama. You're not making sense. It's the physic. But I'll promise to go with him if that's what makes you happy.' He stroked her forehead with his hand, and she fell back, defeated, unable to summon the energy to insist more.

He did not know how serious she was. He promised as though it was of no account, like his promises to look twice before crossing the street, or his promise to wash his hands before eating. She had so much more she needed to tell him; how to be a man in this world, what the important things were – faith, tradition, following your heart.

'Come lie up here next to me, then,' she said.

She drew him close, inhaled the smell of the dusty London streets and the outdoors from his hair. He let her, though she knew it was the last thing a twelve-year-old boy really wanted to do. He was always on the move, never still. She pillowed his head in the crook of her arm.

She knew how to manoeuvre him to listen, so she squeezed him and told him of the time he was born, when he was so scrawny she had almost given up on him.

'You were the size of a screwed-up fist, that's all,' she said, reverting to English, to draw him in.

It had been his favourite story when he was little. The tale of how he was so small she did not think he would survive, but she prayed to Our Lady to let him live, and her prayers were answered. Zachary made no sound that he was listening, but his fingers closed round hers, so she knew she had his attention. She pulled him a little closer.

'You were a proper little fighter,' she said.

'And one day I'm going to have my own school of the sword, just like Savioli.'

'But before that, when . . . I've been trying to tell you, Uncle Leviston will come for you. He thinks he is your father,' she said. 'And it is his money that has kept us all these years.'

'But why? I don't want him as a father. He's dull and smells of old clothes. Why does he think that? He's not my father.'

'He was one of my gentlemen friends. He paid me for my company.' She brushed lightly over the truth. 'I'm sorry, pigeon, but I had your brothers to think of.'

'I know, Mama. I know what you are.'

'I had to do something. Spain and England were at war, nobody in London wanted a tutor any more, or to learn the Spanish tongue.

I had to make a living somehow. Leviston liked the fact I was a Catholic. That's why.' She paused, 'You will listen to him, and let him help, won't you?'

Zachary was mute.

She touched him on the arm. 'Did you hear me?' No answer, just stubborn silence.

'He's a respectable man – despite me. When I am gone I hope he will father you if he can.'

Zachary still said nothing. It was as if she had extinguished a light in him. Of course she knew that dry Uncle Leviston was no sort of father in a young boy's eyes. Not any sort of hero – not handsome, or dashing, or easy-natured. But he was wealthy, and more decent than the rest, that at least.

Zachary turned to look at her just once, his expression so full of hurt and grief it made her wince. 'Don't leave us, Mama.'

She could not answer so she just shook her head. Zachary rolled on to his side and his back came between them like a wall. She reached out to wind an arm round his waist. Just enough time to feel his skinny ribs through his shirt before he leapt from the bed and ran off without a word.

'Zack!'

She would have liked a kiss, a moment of tenderness as a keepsake. Tears seeped from the corners of her eyes. The effort to talk had sapped her willpower and finally she gave in and reached out for the opium. The pain was worse, she could hardly take a breath. Had she made him understand? She did not know. Pray God it would end soon.

Dreams came, of her childhood in Granada, of the red-hot sun and her mother's fragrant rabbit stew. Of the noise of the cicadas, and the smell of burnt earth, and the braying of donkeys. Of when she was a child the same age as Zachary, light and free and dancing on her bare brown feet. Through these pictures the opium did its work and she slept.

The clang of St Mary's bells woke her. There were pale-breasted swallows lined up on the eaves preparing for their flight. She had seen them in Spain, admired their red throats, their swooping, elegant dances. She wondered where these English ones flew to in the winter. Someone had told her they buried themselves in the mud at the bottom of the lakes until spring.

The cold had spread through her flesh now, as if she lay buried in dark silt herself. She remembered her dream and imagined what it must be like to have Zachary's legs, his energy, and his whole life stretching before him like an untrodden road. There was no sign of him still, but she listened out for him with every ounce of her strength, even though each little sound made her bones ache.

The door banged open. The noise of two pairs of boots. There was a smell of strong liquor as Kit bent to look over her.

'Mama.' And then a whisper. 'I think she's worse.'

'No, she's not. She's the same,' she heard Saul say. Even over this they contradicted each other.

'Please don't argue.' She propped herself up on her elbow a moment and croaked to Kit to fetch the quill and ink. He grumbled and then clattered about the room searching for it until Saul snapped, 'Not over there, you bumpkin, in here.' She heard the scrape of the desk drawer opening. The room was blurred, as though she looked through a fog.

'She hasn't written to anyone for weeks. It's a bad sign,' Kit whispered. Then loudly, next to her ear, he said, 'Shall we send for someone?'

She shook her head. Finding a willing priest could take time, and be dangerous, though she knew she would need one soon enough.

'If you're sure?'

'No, no one.'

'Mama, what do you need the writing things for, then?' Saul asked.

'Just put them by me in case I have need of them.'

Saul was still insisting to Kit, 'If she's well enough to write she's better than yesterday.'

She had thought to draw them both into an embrace, like when they were babes, to feel the warmth of their bodies against hers, but now she knew she had not the strength. They seemed too big for the room with their bluster and argument.

Just go, can't you? She willed them to leave, feigning sleep.

'She's sleeping again,' Saul said, from close to her face, his breath damp on her cheek.

A sudden cool disturbance of air brushed her cheek, and she heard Kit hiss, 'What's that you've got?'

'A cloak. Rat-face must have got it for her. A fine one, too.'

'Hey, let me look.'

'Let go!'

'She'll notice. And we'll get into trouble.'

'Nah, she won't. Look, she's asleep.'

And so it was with relief she heard them stumble to their beds. The new cloak had gone. She imagined Zachary's disappointed face and it made her angry. The anger seemed to light a fire inside her. She must make him understand. She hauled herself up to lean on the wall behind her and took the quill to write. Over the next quarter hour she pressed the parchment against her knees, applied the quill to it in determined but querulous strokes.

It was almost five bells when she felt Zack slide in next to her, wind his arms around her waist and nuzzle into the back of her neck. She was floating with the effects of the opium and could barely move to embrace him, but she let out a long sigh of pain and joy. Her boy had come home. Her letter to him was under the pillow. It was as though those few scrawled words contained the last of her heat and warmth, the last of Andalusia. She clasped hold of his hand and wound her fingers into his.

When morning came, his hand was still in hers.

Too cold; the thought drifted by, too cold now to move. The chill crept into her bones until it rattled the windows of her breath.

On the opposite roof the line of swallows clustered together, dark shapes edging the eaves. She was as light as they; all feather and bone. All at once they took flight, wings beat past her window, the flash of pale belly and black forked tail. So it was time; time to go home. She let something in her lift, and wheel, and soar into the sky.

Chapter 1

May 1609

Elspet Leviston leaned over the desk, squinting at the reference she was writing for the lacemaker's girl who wanted to become a housemaid. Her quill scratched over the paper in brisk efficiency for she had several more letters to write for Father after this one, and she enjoyed the task. She hummed a madrigal as she did so, enjoying the hiss as she stamped the seal into the hot wax. Every now and then she sighed and said, 'Give over now,' good-naturedly to the two dogs at her feet who were thumping their tails on the ground, demanding her attention.

Finally, she succumbed, and went to get her cloak and hat along with the leashes. She rang the bell for Martha the housemaid to accompany her, and called the dogs, although there was no need – they were already panting beside her, ready for their afternoon outing.

'Come, Jakes.' The setter jumped up at her skirts, its ears flapping. The other one, the terrier, tried to chew her feet, tail batting back and forth, little barks escaping in his excitement. 'Diver, you little tinker, leave go!'

Finally, she had the clips fastened on the pair of them. Both dogs began to bark excitedly and to pull at their leashes. 'Stop it,' she chided them. 'We're going. Just wait whilst I get my gloves.' She handed both dogs to Martha and put on her gloves.

At last they were off, both dogs scampering ahead on the familiar path alongside the wall of the Convent of Westminster, and away from London town. Elspet and Martha passed the brewers, screwing up their noses to each other at the smell of yeast, and then tugged the dogs back so that they could peer in the window of the little silk-weaver's with his guild sign of the silk-flies and loom. He waved at them through the window before they headed out into the countryside. Once the track gave way to grass they let the impatient dogs off the leads and they sprang away.

Elspet watched the dogs nosing in the verges and inhaled the smell of the pasture, glad to be away from the city stink. 'What a lovely day, Martha!' she said.

'It is that, mistress.'

'And nice to be outdoors. I'd almost forgotten what it was like to stretch my legs. And this is the only time I will have this week to get out into the air. Father will expect me to go into the offices with him again to write up the ledgers. One of the clerks gave notice.'

'Is that so, mistress?'

'There's always something. But at least it is not some infection. Not like when the business nearly went under and they had to burn the lace for fear the plague would spread. It was six years ago next week, Father was saying. Can you believe it?'

'I didn't think it was that long since,' Martha said.

'And what a waste. No wonder Father was so ill. Thank goodness those days are past.'

'He's lucky to have your help, mistress. Everyone says so.'

'Tush. But he's doing very nicely now, everyone wants his Flanders lace, it's so pretty. Oh look!'

Jakes was scrabbling and growling at the underside of a hedge, his liver-coloured flanks shaking. He was strong as an ox when he caught sight of any small creature – cats, rabbits, mice or birds – if it moved, he would chase it.

'Is it a rabbit?' Martha asked.

Jakes emerged with a stick between his teeth, his tail wagging furiously.

'Some rabbit!' They laughed as he dropped it right in front of Elspet's feet.

'He knows, doesn't he?' Martha said. 'Sometimes I think he's almost human. Shall I throw it?' She lifted it and hurled it down the path, and they both watched as he sped off like a flying shuttle with Diver the little terrier bounding after him, yapping excitedly.

After an hour they were back at West View House, unlacing muddy boots in the hall. Elspet hung up her cloak, and heard the door creak open behind her. She paid it no mind, accustomed as she was to the servants coming and going with coals for the grate.

But a hand on her shoulder made her swivel round, startled.

'Father!'

He was never back from work this early. From the corner of her eye she saw Martha dip a ragged curtsey, both dogs were growling and barking and pulling at her.

'What a din,' Father said. 'Martha, take those wretched dogs out the back, to the stables.'

Martha bobbed and pulled the dogs away. Elspet heard Jakes barking all the way to the back door.

'Elspet, may I introduce your cousin, Zachary Deane.' It was only then that she saw him; the stranger hanging slightly back in the doorway, his eyes casting quick, sidelong glances about the hall.

'Oh,' she said, pulling off her muddy gloves in haste and putting them aside. 'I wondered what was the matter with the dogs.'

'You're too soft with them,' her father reproached.

'They look like fine animals,' Zachary, the young man, said. He placed one hand on his sword as he made a small bow.

Father's fingers pulled nervously at the edge of his robe. The newcomer was still bent over and she saw his hair was tangled and damp with perspiration. He swung back to upright with a brisk wave of his hat.

Father nodded to her to prompt a response.

'Oh – your servant,' she murmured, dipping her head first to the newcomer, and then to her father, 'Forgive me, Father, you caught me by surprise.'

She tried to catch the young man's eye and smile, but he glanced away, finding something of interest in the yard.

'Zachary is my sister's boy,' Father said in a rush. 'But Magda—', he broke off. 'I mean to say, Zachary's mother and I have been estranged for some years. Unfortunately, she has passed away.'

Zachary smiled thinly at Father, his lips compressed, and then looked at the ground.

'I did not know she was gone,' Father said, 'and Zachary and I have only just found each other.'

'My condolences, Cousin.' Elspet's first impression was that Zachary did not look like a man in mourning – not wearing that shoddy rust-coloured doublet and cloak worn to grey at the hem. She wondered if he was ill-fed; his hose sagged at the ankles.

'With his mother gone, it is right and fitting we do our duty and look to our own,' Father said. 'Zachary will lodge in the lower chambers, and I know you will make him welcome.'

In the distance Diver was yapping. Elspet gathered herself. She regretted not being warmer or more welcoming, especially as her cousin had been bereaved. He must think her lacking in courtesy. She smoothed her ruffled hair and said, 'What a terrible thing. I am so sorry to hear of your loss, I hope you will feel at home here.'

Father turned to him. 'The lower chambers are not much, but —'

'They will be better than I am used to, I'm sure,' Zachary interrupted him. 'Do not go to any trouble on my account.' His voice was pleasant and neutral, though his eyes darted restlessly round the hall.

Father patted him on the arm sympathetically. An unusual gesture, for he was never much given to outward shows of affection. He must be trying hard, Elspet thought.

'Good.' Father exhaled a long sigh. 'I'll take Zachary down, and Coleman will help him fetch his trunk from the carriage.'

'No need,' Zachary said. 'It's paltry few things. I can do it myself.'

'Coleman will assist you. No point having servants else.'

Zachary was about to speak but then closed his mouth. Instead he gave a curt nod. He cast Elspet a long appraising look before turning and going back out of the door.

When he was out of earshot, Father said, 'You will grow to like him, I know you will.'

'I like him already.'

'No you don't. It is written clear as clear on your face. You looked him up and down as though he were a servant you were about to hire.'

Indignation rose up in her. Father had described exactly the way Zachary had looked at her.

'Come now, he has lost his mother and, by all accounts, his greedy elder brothers have taken his inheritance and left him with nothing but what he stands in. You must be kind, as I know you are.'

'I'm sorry if my manner gave offence, Father,' Elspet said stiffly. 'How long will he stay?'

'As long as is needful.' Father was impatient, 'Besides, he's only just arrived.' He tapped her on the arm, to take his leave of her. 'I'll go and enquire if he has everything he wants.' He hurried away, and the uneven fall of his footsteps passed through the hall.

As soon as they were out of the door she hurried over to the window and drew the curtain aside. The lining flaked dust into her fingers. Moths had made a feast of the drapes and she had talked to Father about it, but he never noticed these things. His free time was spent crouched over his tracts in his chamber, or down in the priest cellar like a badger in his lair. She had lost count of the number of times she had asked for more linen for drapes.

Who was he, this cousin? Where had he come from? Father's complexion had turned pink as a pig and he had been all a-fluster, most unlike his usual self. He had touched Zachary's arm with such warmth. It gave her a pang; since Mother had died, Father had never shown much fatherly fancy to her except in the matter of teaching and correcting. Her family was never demonstrative, Father thought it improper, but perhaps it was what her cousin was used to.

Elspet peered out into the yard, tilting her head to the greenish glass. The carriage was right below her window. Nobody was there yet; the horses were idling, back legs cocked and resting, heads low. The unsettling thought crossed her mind that perhaps Father considered Zachary to be a suitable match for her. She sincerely hoped not.

The outside door swung open and Cousin Zachary appeared in

'Mistress,' Turner said.

'Goody Turner,' she squatted down next to Jakes where he was spreadeagled on the floor having his stomach rubbed, 'we have a new cousin.'

'Look, he found the only puddle in London,' Turner said, holding out the muddy cloth. Elspet took it and scrubbed at Jakes's stomach. 'He's just arrived. He's called Zachary. My cousin.'

'That's nice.'

'He's going to stay awhile, Father says. He's in the old nursery.'

Goody Turner's eyes lit up. She used to be their nursemaid before she was their cook. 'How old is he?'

'Old. I mean he's grown. Sorry. About the same age as I am, I should think. Maybe a little older.'

'Oh.' Goody Turner sighed. 'Will he be wanting his midday meal, then?' She pushed Diver away from his stick with her foot. 'If he is, I'll be needing these dogs out from under my feet.'

'Sorry, I'll take them up. Where's Martha?'

'Set to mending the fires, like as not, if your father's got visitors. Happen it will be nice for Master to have some male company. He's had a house full of women and maids all his life.'

'I'm sure we've been company enough, though.'

'Hmm.' Turner did not say it, but Elspet knew what she was thinking. Every Catholic father wants a son, and Mother had done nought but produce girls or stillborns until she died birthing Lydia. But this was something no one ever dared speak of out loud, even Goody Turner.

Elspet sat down on the floor and scooped Diver into her arms, more to reassure herself than to pet him. Strands of grass still clung to his white fur. She breathed in the familiar comforting smell of warm dog and wondered about whether Cousin Zachary's mother had died in childbirth. He had lost his mother too, just like she had, but of course men were better at hiding their emotions than women.

She remembered the night Mother died as clearly as if it were yesterday, though it was nine years since. She could never forget the sight of Goody Turner blundering past her door, cheeks running with tears, her hands full of bloody cloths. The terrible animal noises from her mother's chamber. When the screams finally stopped, her father's voice echoed, desperate in the sudden quiet, 'Can nothing more be done?'

More silence.

'What of the babe? My son, does he survive?'

The midwife's answer came back, 'God be praised. A beautiful girl.'

A loud crash. 'I'm to lose my wife for a girl?'

The way he said 'girl' stuck in her mind like a thorn. Elspet rushed on to the landing to look, and saw servants were sweeping up the remains of a broken vase. They kept their heads down and low. When she cried out, Father did not turn, but she saw his back as he flung open the front door and staggered into the squally weather outside with no coat. There was thick silence then, the servants quiet as mice, her mother's moans all finished, the new babe too afraid to cry.

It was a whole month before Elspet took the courage to name her. Lydia. A lovely name, like music. She thought Mother, Lord rest her soul, would have liked it. But Father was not interested to look upon Lydia. He let the choice of name stand, and after much persuasion by Goody Turner, she was duly baptized.

Father was lost without Mother, he could not settle to his books. Once, at prayer, he told Elspet God was punishing him, and that was why Mother was taken. Punishing him for what, he refused to say. In the dark days after her death he just kept confessing over and over, in the priest cellar below. All the confessing in the world was no use, though. Lydia, too, died of the smallpox only two months later. Or perhaps because her father would not love her.

Elspet shuddered and hugged Diver tight, kissing the top of his hairy head as he squirmed and panted in her arms. She'd sworn to mend her broken family, and prove to her father she was as good as any son.

'This new cousin, will you bring him to see old Goody Turner?' The old nursemaid broke into her thoughts.

'Of course I will,' Elspet said. 'But you will meet him soon enough anyway. Did Martha manage Jakes yesterday?'

'No, mistress. She had to come back after only a quarter hour.

She said her arms were stretched as long as beans with his pulling.'

'Then I will take him out again. He needs more exercise. He can have a good run, and I need to get out into the fresh air.'

'I don't know – you've just come back! It seems to me you're never happy unless you're out tramping the fields with those dogs. It will be dark soon, mistress. Master would not want you walking abroad at night, even with the dogs. They're soft as cotton, the pair of them. No earthly use as guard dogs, the great daft things. If you hold tight, I'll ask Martha to go too, and I know Broadbank the groom would be glad to walk out with you.'

'Don't fuss, Turner. Diver can stay here. We won't go far. Just into the gardens and the courtyard. I'll go fetch my cloak.'

After another pleasurable half-hour on the terraces throwing a wooden ball for Jakes, she went to the stables to look at Father's new horse. A fine-boned chestnut, with laid-back ears, it skated around in its stall, hooves churning up the straw, flanks crashing against the wooden walls. She pulled Jakes away; he might get between its legs, the halfwit dog, if she let him into the stall. She reached over to quieten the horse, but it rolled its eyes and nipped at her arm. What on earth was Father thinking of, to buy such a horse at his age?

It was turning twilight as she came back across the yard, but she caught the glint of something fly, and heard a small grunting sound. It was Cousin Zachary, wielding his rapier, practising his cut and thrust. He was bare-armed and the rapier pierced the air in a series of darts and strikes. His curling hair was stuck to his forehead with sweat, his face grim.

She pulled on the collar to draw Jakes closer. Jakes let out little barks now, straining at the leash, anxious to join in with the game going on in the yard. Her cousin ignored her and lunged towards his imaginary opponent with renewed venom, his feet skidding and scraping in the dirt. His breath exploded in short exhalations as he leapt to throw his bodyweight behind the sword.

'Heel, boy, heel!' she hissed under her breath, dragging Jakes away, keeping under the overhang of the house. Anxious to get in where it was warm, she thrust the dog in through the door ahead of her with a slap on the behind, but then paused.

Someone else was watching her cousin's practice, over in the kitchen window. It was Father. So taken up with Zachary was he, that he did not once glance her way. Even Jakes did not scamper over to greet him as he usually did. Father stood like a simpleton in the lamp-light of the kitchen, a look of beaming pride on his face.

Chapter 2

The next morning when Elspet went downstairs there were two empty plates already on the table. One was Father's – he always placed his knife like that, across the plate. The other had a scatter of crumbs about it and the remains of a half-eaten rind of cheese.

There were great gouges in the butter, unlike Father's thin scraping. She called Martha. 'Where is Father?'

'He went out early, mistress. With Master Deane. They've gone to Mr Bainbridge's.'

'Master Deane? Oh, you mean my cousin. Did he say when he would be back?'

'No, mistress.'

She sat down at the table. Usually Father would show her the mail and news from the city, and she would tell him about the household business, and how the women lace-makers were getting on with their orders. Of course Father never really listened properly; he always had half an eye on the broadsheet. But, with no company, the knife rattled loudly on her plate and her small meal was soon finished.

Father had never invited her to go with him to Mr Bainbridge's, because she was a woman, and Bainbridge did not trust women's tongues. Bainbridge was of the Roman Church like themselves, and held a secret morning Mass in his house whenever their priest, Father Everard, was able to be there. Ever since Guido Fawkes and his fire-powder plot, it had become more dangerous for them to hide their travelling Jesuit priest, Father Everard, and so Bainbridge sometimes hid him for them. A shame, for she liked Father Everard's company, and he liked her. He was a good tutor, and his bright-eyed enthusiasm for culture and for other countries knew no bounds. How she loved his French and Spanish lessons, and hearing him talk of the romance of Paris and Madrid!

She picked up the broadsheet and untied the ribband, but let it lie on the table. She had no heart for reading, for she was picturing her father and Cousin Zachary at Mass together. She knew Bainbridge had a fine statue of the Virgin and a high table bedecked with Leviston's lace to serve as an altar. The lace had been hand-picked by her father; the best from his stock. Father's lace business was famous, but despite his generosity to Bainbridge, their own altar had to make do with no lace at all.

'Bainbridge risks his own neck, like us, for the sake of his soul,' Father used to say. 'It is the least I can do.' But he had never invited her to Bainbridge's, even though her tongue was safe enough.

No point in sitting moping like this, she thought. She stood up, brushed down her skirts and descended purposefully below to make her prayers. The chill damp of the cellar made her shiver, and she hoped Father and Zachary were warmer at Bainbridge's. Was it brave or foolish to continue holding Masses at home, she wondered? Father said Protestant spies were everywhere, and the thought of it made her stomach swoop.

She closed her eyes and began an *Ave*, threading the ivory beads through her palm with her thumb. No matter that Cousin Zachary and her father might be worshipping at a proper altar with a proper priest, she was determined her own soul would not be one jot behind theirs.

When her *Aves* were done and the *Pater Noster* too, she prayed for her father and for the souls of her dead sister and mother, and for her king – that he might find some peace in his heart, so that Catholics might live unmolested in this great city. She prayed for Joan, her elder sister too, who was in France. Dear Joan. She was a nun, and probably did not need her prayers, being full of the holy life as she must be by now, but she always included her. She had fond childhood memories of her throaty laughter and still missed her, from the happier times when Mother was still alive.

Teeth chattering, Elspet stood up, but then, as an afterthought and because it was her duty to include all her family, she reluctantly knelt back down again and said a hurried prayer for Cousin Zachary.

Prayers done, she bounded upstairs to check that the dogs had been fed and fetched some warmed milk and honey from the kitchen, and a plate of cinnamon toast. It was always chill until the fires took properly, and her feet were numbed from kneeling for prayers. On the way back she passed by the old nursery – Cousin Zachary's door.

Was he in there? She paused outside, as if hooked by an invisible thread, and put her ear close to the jamb. There was no sound from within – so it was true, he had gone out with Father.

In a trice she had put the tray down on the boards outside and lifted the latch. The door creaked open in the draught. She looked over her shoulder. No sign of a servant. She'd peek in for a few moments – just to see what sort of a man he might be. After all, last night he had not even joined them for their supper, but had eaten a tray of cold meats and pickles in his room, and then father had taken him into his study. Their muffled voices had told her nothing, though she had heard her father's laugh once or twice.

It struck her that it was a sound she had missed, one she had not heard since her mother was alive.

She stepped inside the old nursery and pulled the door so it half closed behind her. The shutters were only open a fraction, so it was moistly warm; the remnants of a wood fire had settled to ash in the grate. She tiptoed over to the kist at the foot of the bed where lay her cousin's travelling trunk and clothing, and yesterday's discarded worn russet-brown doublet and breeches. She fingered the fabric. Just as she thought; not hardwearing, not proper quality. So he was not from a well-to-do family, nor one of rank. And his garments were thrown here all in disarray, so he was not a tidy person either. Martha must be busy, no servant had yet been in to put his things away.

She looked to his trunk. Did she dare? Feeling guilty already she hooked open the lid of the trunk with the tip of her index finger, just an inch. A few lawn shirts and undergarments lay crumpled and none-too-clean, as if they had been thrust inside in a hurry. She could not see much, so she lifted the lid away from her until it was fully open, her breath loud in the empty room.

She stared a moment. No prayer book or tract that she could see – usually they were at the top when someone was travelling. But there were no religious keepsakes at all, only a battered pewter hip flask, a corked pot of what was probably shoe-blacking, and a pair of riding gloves thick with horse grease. She moved them aside carefully. What was she searching for? She did not know, just something to tell her a little more about him, she supposed. About his family, where he had come from. Father had told her nothing, and it was only natural, wasn't it, to want to know? She suppressed the prickle of conscience.

The edges of some papers were sticking out from underneath a soiled shirt and she eased these out. But it was only a treatise on fencing – stiff-looking woodcuts of men with guarded expressions, their swords brandished aloft. Disappointed, she slid it back. She prised open a case to find a pair of daggers, the usual sort that gentlemen carry, and something wrapped in a velvet cloth.

Dice. So he was a gambler. She hurriedly wrapped them up again, patting the papers back in place on top, aware that she had gone far further than she had intended. What in heaven's name was she thinking, becoming so engrossed in her cousin's things? She quickly put everything back in place and shut the lid. The muffled peal of the city bells striking the half caused her to glance fearfully over her shoulder again but, thank the Lord, there was not a sound in the corridor outside.

She tiptoed back towards the door. So he had only the one trunk, and that seemed to be all his possessions. How strange. Except that against the corner of the wall were propped a frightening number of swords, all resting in their scabbards, their belts trailing on the ground. But there were no miniature portraits, no heirlooms. No clue as to where he had come from, or who his family might be. She paused, her hand on the door.

A satchel dangled there on the coat hook. It was almost as if it called to her. She couldn't. It would surely be a sin, and she had just finished her prayers. She stood a long moment, weighing it in her thoughts. But it was too much of a temptation. No sooner had the thought come and gone, then the satchel was in her hand. She felt through the contents speedily: a kerchief, something damp that made her withdraw her hand in revulsion – a mouldy apple-core. She pulled out a tinderbox and a blackened grindstone and placed them quietly on the table, listening intently for sounds outside as she did so.

But here at last might be something. A handwritten letter, folded into a tight square. She opened it out and eased it flat. The writing was shaky and indistinct, and the edges furred, worn away with age so that long holes made the writing even harder to decipher. It had curled, leaning-back capitals in a flamboyant hand. It was dated 25th September 1599. She made a calculation – ten years ago, when she was only thirteen. She took it to the window to hold it to the light.

Dearest Zack,

By the time you read this I will be gone and you will have to face the future without me. Pray do not grieve too long – life is short and precious and the world will be a worse place without your sunny smile. You must listen to your Mama now.

I have written to Uncle Leviston and he will . . .

The noise in the corridor came too late.

'Mine, I believe.'

She twisted round, horrified, the open letter dangling slack in her hand. Zachary was right behind her, his face white. He snatched the letter away with such speed that the paper near scorched her hand. Turning his back, he folded it and stowed it in his doublet. The tension in him made her afraid. She stepped back towards the wall.

'Wait, I can explain . . .'

But no words would come. How could she explain? She felt her face flame red. Meanwhile, he was gathering up the tinderbox and whetstone lying on the table, pushing them back inside his satchel.

He whipped round to face her. 'Did you touch anything else?'

She could not move. 'No, I—'

'My swords, you did not touch them?'

'No, I only . . . it was just—'

'Is this your usual idea of hospitality? To pilfer through a guest's possessions?'

'Cousin, I'm sorry…' she faltered.

'Just leave.' His expression was stony, full of contempt.

'I was only—'

'Get out.'

She hitched up her skirts and fled out into the corridor, her face hot with shame. The tray was where she had left it, the milk cold in the cup, a wrinkled skin on the top, the toast waxy with grease. She stooped to pick up the tray and the door slammed shut a mere thumb's width from her face. She slunk away then, mortified that he should have caught her. Heaven help her if he told Father. She would not blame him if he took the rod to her, though she was a grown woman. What would he think? That she had taken leave of her senses, like any reasonable God-fearing man might?

She took the tray back to the kitchen, and left it for Goody Turner to deal with. She knew one thing, recriminations would not be long in coming. Father would no doubt want to know why she was spying on her cousin, and truth be told, she had no proper answer. She should have learned by now, some things were best left alone. She remembered other occasions from her childhood when she had been caught listening at the door. It seemed women were excluded from everything important.

Father had been angry at her eavesdropping. 'Has she nothing to occupy her?' he asked, but had Mother just smiled in a placatory way and said, 'tush, leave her be, she'll grow out of it.'

Elspet could not concentrate any more on her book-keeping. She kept expecting Father to arrive at any moment and demand an explanation. She knew the men were in the house somewhere, but she kept to her chamber and every time one of the servants passed by, her stomach lurched. She did not dare go to Father's chambers as she usually did to go through the day's figures, but set to needlework instead.

A noise alerted her that someone was in the yard, but she kept away from the window in case Zachary thought she was spying on the yard followed by Coleman and his stable boy. Zachary was right below her as the servants climbed atop for his luggage. He was somewhat short in stature; she supposed she was as tall as he. Kind folk called her stately or handsome, but nevertheless, she mused, he was still short for a man. He had nice hair though, curling dark hair just like her own, but not so unruly. Zachary reached up to help with the bags, but Coleman shook his head emphatically at him and Zachary turned away. He folded his arms and scrubbed at the dirt on the drive with one foot.

Surprisingly, he had only one small trunk, a sword case for his arms, and a leather satchel – a pitiful amount for a gentleman. Father had said he had been disinherited, and she felt a moment's sympathy for him. As she pondered this he looked up and saw her face at the glass. He raised one hand in solemn greeting. Instinctively, she scurried back behind the drapes, but then chided herself; he had clearly seen her watching, after all. Feeling foolish she went back to the window to return his wave, but the yard was already empty; they had all gone inside.

She paced the floor then, wondering what might be taking place in the lower chambers. So many questions. Why had she never been told of her cousins? She had the impression there were other brothers older than Zachary. Father said they had stolen his inheritance. What did that mean? She had never heard of any kin on Father's side. Mother, God rest her soul, had a brother, Edward, but he had married a Frenchwoman and they had settled in Paris. Father's family was a whole new mystery.

She could not imagine her father having a sister. In fact, she could not imagine Father had ever been a child at all, that he had ever played or chortled or skipped down the stairs, the way she and her sister Joan had when they were children.

She smoothed down her skirts and hastened out of her chamber and down to the kitchen to tell Goody Turner the news. When she pushed open the narrow door, Goody Turner was towelling Jakes with a dishclout and Diver was chewing on the stick now that Jakes had discarded it. Diver jumped up wagging his tail for his pat on the head before returning to the fascination of the splintery stick.

him again. But even from across the room she could see him through the aperture, his wiry figure practising his parry and thrust, despite a deluge of rain that sluiced from the sky and turned the surface of the yard to a quagmire. He lunged and stabbed as if it were the weather itself he was broiling with.

She could not forget the look on his face when he caught her reading his letter. It was from his mother, she imagined. Yet she had been given to understand that his mother had only just died. From the few words she was able to decipher, the letter suggested she had possibly been dead for some years. She hadn't just died at all.

It was confusing, and she tussled with it. She would never dare to broach it with her father, at least not until she had apologized to her cousin. By evening, she was jittery when it came to dressing for the evening meal, so that Martha despaired of lacing her properly into a clean gown. When the time came she sat quietly in the dining hall looking into her lap, dreading the whole subject arising.

A place had been set on her father's right for Zachary, and she was to sit, opposite her cousin. The dogs were lying quietly under the table, they seemed to have grown accustomed to the idea of Zachary's presence already. Jakes sprawled at Zachary's feet, his nose practically on his boots. She suppressed a twinge of jealousy that her position had been usurped so quickly.

That night for supper Zachary had changed into a showy doublet and hose, with too much gold braiding on the sleeves. She recognized it from his trunk because it looked new, but the thought that she now knew all his possessions caused her to cringe with embarrassment.

Father poured him a cup of small beer. 'I think, after all, you will come with me to the quayside tomorrow,' he said.

Zachary smiled, 'Thank you, sir, I would be interested to see just how the business is run, now that I have heard so much about it. But will I not be in the way?'

'No, no. New blood is always good. There comes a time when the older generation have to pave the way for the younger; am I right, Elspet?'

She nodded politely and made a vague noise of assent. Zachary looked smug. He helped himself to the roast partridge plated at the centre of the table before Father had taken his, but Father merely looked upon him indulgently. 'That's right, you must keep up your strength,' he said. 'I saw you training last night in the courtyard barely a half-hour after you had arrived, and I saw you were out there again today.'

'A man must keep himself fit for purpose. To miss a day would mean my body is not prepared.'

'What are you preparing for, Cousin?' Elspet asked mildly.

Father cast her a disapproving eye.

'London's full of villains. A cut-throat from behind, coneycatchers in the alleyway, highway thieves. A man must defend himself.'

The answer seemed more for Father's benefit than for hers.

'My daughter has had too much female company, and does not understand the obligations of men,' Father said. 'At your age I was the same, always with the fencing master.'

'Is that so? Who was your master?'

'Now then . . .' Father looked discomfited. 'Ah yes, an Italian, I think.'

'Was it Bonetti?'

Father shook his head.

'Master Saviolo, then?' Zachary pressed.

'I can't remember,' admitted Father.

Zachary smiled. He had caught him out. Elspet was sorry for her father and a little irritated. Until yesterday Father had believed that there was no further need for fencing since the advent of gunpowder, but now he seemed to be changing his mind.

'Anyway,' Father blustered, 'I will take you to the chambers tomorrow and show you the ways of the lace trade.'

Zachary smiled, then nodded, chewing over his food.

'Tell me about your family,' Elspet said, looking deliberately at Zachary. 'You have brothers, my father said?'

'I have no dealings with them.'

'But—'

'Elspet,' Father chided, 'finish up your meal before it cools. Leave your cousin to eat in peace.'

She cut her meat slowly then, aware of an uncomfortable silence in the room, as if all ease had been stifled. The servants also seemed to feel it; they crept in wordlessly to take the savouries away and returned equally silently with the sweetmeat platters.

When the repast was over, Father invited Zachary to his study for more wine. It was the custom in their house, when there was company, for the men to retire to Father's chambers whilst the women remained companionably at table. That way the men were not disturbed by the servants clearing away. But it was quite a different thing when there was no other female company present and Elspet was left suddenly alone at the long expanse of board with only the leftovers for company.

She rested awhile, an empty feeling in the pit of her stomach despite the meal, before she wrapped her mantle deliberately about her and descended the stairs to the kitchen.

Confound them both, she thought. She would sit with Goody Turner and fuss the dogs. Zachary Deane was just a novelty; Father would soon tire of his company. Give him a few days, and Father would return to his usual custom of sitting in the oak-panelled chamber, his books open on his knee before the crackle of the fire, whilst she wrote up the day's trading figures and listened to him rail against the Scottish king.

She had no idea whether Zachary could converse with Father on his favourite subject – how Isabella should have been Queen, or how much he knew about Dante's *Divine Comedy*. He would not last long with Father if not, she thought dryly.

Chapter 3

Zachary stifled a yawn. He must make himself look interested. He cocked his head to one side and opened his eyes wide. He would act a bit. After all, he was getting free bed and board and it always served you well to butter the palm that fed you.

Old Leviston's offices were exactly as he had predicted – old-fashioned, musty, and full of surly staff who bowed and scratched before him, but sniggered behind his back when he wasn't looking.

Leviston pointed to a long column of figures in yet another ledger and began explaining about yardages. Zachary kept his expression of interest, but let his attention wander. He marvelled that he was there at all. But it was not a case of choice, his mother would have called it *el destino* – fate.

'So you see, there's much more profit in Flanders' lace,' Leviston said.

'Oh yes, yes I see,' Zachary said, not understanding one jot.

After Leviston had showed him, in flea-like detail, the prices of grades of lace he was nearly wall-eyed. Thank God, the old man finally took him down to the warehouses. Now this was more like it. A shipment had just arrived, and there was all the hustle and bustle of unloading and packing to horse.

'Bring that one over,' Leviston shouted, and the bow-legged man with the bolt of lace over his shoulder veered towards them. He dropped his load with a thump on the table and stood respectfully to one side, cap in hand. Leviston jammed his eyeglasses on the bridge of his nose, picked up the shears attached by string to the bench, and slit open the bale with a practised hand. He extracted one of the hand-tied parcels within and shook it out before him.

'Look,' he said, 'this is how we check the yardage.' And he demonstrated how the men measured the lace by stretching it out over the counter. Old Leviston looked quite lively. He was even perspiring. After, he showed him how it had to be reeled in before it could be wound on to cards.

Leviston dismissed the red-cheeked apprentice who was tugging at the delicate stuff in his big white gloves, and took hold of Zachary's wrists, pushing his bare hands under the lace.

'See, Zachary, how fine the work is. Only in Flanders do you get such fine work.' Leviston's eyes were alight.

'Fine indeed.' And, true enough, he had to admit that he could grasp the skill of it. He had never paid lace much attention before. He gazed a moment at the delicate white strands draped over his skin, trying to understand the movement the bobbins and needles must make – thousands of tiny parries and thrusts for one handspan of lace.

Leviston smiled at him, the stiff smile of a man unused to smiling. 'I knew you'd have a feel for it,' he said, 'it's in the blood.'

Zachary forced himself to beam back, and Leviston clapped him awkwardly on the shoulder. The apprentice gawped like a bedlam fool from one to the other, but Zachary glared at him. His uncle's sudden affection disconcerted him. The apprentice sidled away, brushing the flecks of cotton waste from his sleeve.

The warehouse, one of many, was the size of a large stable, with bays of shelving stacked with brown and green oilskin-wrapped parcels. If this was all lace, then it represented the flying hands of thousands of working women. A fleeting memory of his mother's face came to mind. She would have been amazed to see it. But as far as he knew, Leviston never deigned to bring her here.

He glanced over to where Leviston was now talking with the overseer, a man introduced to him as Wilmot. Wilmot was a solid dull-looking man, with a long pale jaw, wispy yellow hair and a beard shaped like a spade. He was listening hard, hands propped on a measuring cane, leaning forward slightly to catch his employer's words. They were discussing shipments and prices.

With all this, Leviston must really be a rich man. So it begged the question, why had he let his house get so rag-a-tatter? Zachary scanned Leviston's unfashionable doublet, which was almost threadbare, and wondered why his gangling daughter had been dressed in such an uninspiring faded green wool, with the elbows worn thin. Zachary shook his head. If he owned all this – well, he'd be choosing new suits every week; fine slashed velvet, gold-tipped lacing, and all the new fashions from France.

Wilmot and Leviston were still deep in conversation. When they'd done, Leviston said, 'My apologies for that. Just a few bits of business to clear up. Come, I'll take you over to the tavern and we'll have something to eat and a warm ale. It is always draughty in the sheds when the ships come in, and they'll be another hour or two unloading.'

'That sounds fine,' he said. 'It's all been most interesting.' He put on his gentleman's voice, to sound more learned.

His friend Gin Shotterill always used to say, if you speak like they do, they'll think you're one of them. Otherwise they'll think you a fool.

The twelve-penny tavern was cold and cramped, despite being the haunt of gentlemen, and they had to wedge themselves side by side into a seat with no window. The back door partition was behind them with its whistling draught.

Zachary had no wish to continue a conversation about grades of lace, so after they supped what was put in front of them and exhausted the small talk about the dubious quality of the ale, Zachary told him he would like to meet up with a few of the fellows in Hanging Sword Alley for some fencing practice, before returning to West View House.

'Of course,' Leviston said. 'I will tell the kitchen hands to wait the evening meal until eight, shall I?'

'If that's not too inconvenient, sir,' he said. 'I wouldn't want to put the household to any trouble.'

'Not at all, not at all. I'll arrange it. We will have a chance to talk business afterwards. There are some new samples of gold-point I'd like to show you – from Brussels. Not bad, some of them. There's a good profit margin in them, though the weave is not as dense as the French. An ounce of gold will go further, I think.'

Zachary nodded, though he was not much enamoured of spending a whole evening poring over women's fancies – a waste of good gold, in his view.

He was mulling over better uses for gold when Leviston suddenly said, 'Is your mother often in your thoughts?' His voice was gentle.

Zachary was momentarily nonplussed, not understanding. Then he realised. Leviston had taken his staring into space for melancholy.

'Not so often now,' Zachary replied guardedly, twisting his head sideways to look at him. He feigned a nonchalance he did not feel. 'After all, life goes on. It is ten years since and I have seen many neighbours and friends go since then, and in the end, death is not such a strange thing.'

'But different, surely, when it is your own kin, and her so young.'

'True.' He could sense a conversation coming that he did not want to have. He could think of nothing to say that did not give away his feelings, so he offered a platitude. 'Death keeps no calendar.'

'Indeed no. And you are aware that it is some years since I lost my wife.' Leviston waited for Zachary's reaction, but Zachary kept silent. He would offer no condolences, out of respect for his mother.

They sat for an awkward moment, each waiting for the other to speak. Leviston did not seem to know what to say next, but he cleared his throat several times before taking another gulp of ale. Someone else came in and the bitter draught shivered up Zachary's neck. Leviston shrugged an apology to Zachary with a rueful look as the door banged closed behind them. Finally, he said, 'Your mother was a beautiful woman, you know.' His voice held a kind of plea, but he was looking down, as if the ale in his tankard had suddenly become interesting.

'Yes.' Zachary was tight-lipped. He was damned if he would absolve him.

'We were . . . close, once.'

'Yes. She told me.'

'What did she tell you?' Leviston slid to the edge of the bench and turned sideways to look him full in the face.

Zachary paused. He knew what Leviston was implying, but he must be careful. Act surprised. He was supposed to think that Leviston was his uncle until he was told otherwise. He replied, 'I know that she had a high regard for you, as a sister might.' That much was true at least.

'Then you might think well of me?' Leviston wiped a bead of sweat from his brow, despite the draught from the door.

'Of course. Family is family. I remember you from when I was small. I am delighted to have found my uncle again. I am in your debt, sir, for seeking me out after all this time, and for offering me your hospitality.'

'She did not . . . I mean—' Leviston swallowed before going on. 'She did not speak of me as . . .?' Zachary waited, watching his discomfiture, as if he was a fish-fly on a hook. Leviston's mouth worked a little before he could blurt out the words. 'I am not your uncle, Zachary. You are my son.'

Zachary feigned shock, jerked back in his seat. 'What do you mean?'

'I have never been your uncle. I am your father.'

'My father?'

'I am sorry if this comes as a shock. There is no easy way to broach it, I'm afraid. But you are of age, so I feel bound to treat you as an equal and tell you I am no relation to your mother. Your mother and I were lovers. When I stayed with her she called me "Uncle" so that you would feel comfortable in my company.' His pale grey face had become mottled with red. Zachary pitied him; it was a hard confession to make.

Zachary shifted uncomfortably on the seat; he was no longer sure he wanted to hear about his mother and this balding man before him. She surely couldn't have loved this man. Not his beautiful Mama. But he had no choice; Leviston was continuing. 'We were lovers until she fell with child. But I was already married, you see, and my wife . . .'

To his surprise, a spurt of righteous anger filled him. Zachary found he had stood up. 'Are you telling me you cast my mother aside? With never a second thought for either of us?' He balled his fists, shocked at how agitated he felt.

'No, Zachary, it was not like that. Not as simple as that. It started as a business arrangement, but as it became more frequent, well, your mother grew in my affections. Things became complicated. Then you were born and . . . God knows, I wanted to be with her, with you both—' Leviston paused. His fingers clawed at his collar and to Zachary's horror he could see his eyes were swimming with water. Leviston pulled off his eyeglasses and wiped a hand over his eyes. 'But you have to see I had a duty, a duty to Agnes my wife. She told me she was expecting a baby herself. I was caught. I could not abandon Agnes then. It tore me apart. You must understand that I—'

Zachary cut him off. 'You chose, Uncle. You chose between your wife and my mother. You played no proper part in my childhood, and yet you expect me to accept you now as my father! Well, it is too much to ask.' Zachary faced him with difficulty in the confined space. 'Pray pardon, sir, but I need time to think.'

He picked up his sword belt and girded it on with deliberate movements.

'Please, Zachary, don't go like this, let me try to explain—'

'There is nothing more I want to hear.' And with that he clattered out of the tavern and away up the street.

He did not know where he was going, just away from Leviston. It was too uncomfortable, listening to him talk. He did not want to know about his mother's liaisons with this man. The thought made him sick. He buttoned his cloak against the wind and lowered his head, to try to stop the thoughts crowding in. He strode away down the street, dodging other passers-by.

He had only a hazy memory of what his mother had said the night she died. He had been only twelve, so the words in his head were vague, although he had repeated the scene over and over to try to fix it there. In the morning he had found her lucky talisman – the finger-sized piece of Calvary wood she said was from Christ's cross – still under her pillow. And with it the letter. He had kept them both all this time. Even when he had wept and cursed her for abandoning him. They were the last of her, and even when Leviston never came, he could not let them go.

His mother had meant well, of course, she was like a dog who would fight wolves for her pups. And Zachary had not been surprised that Leviston never appeared, and he had been glad.

Neither had Zachary bothered to look for him. Leviston had always seemed too stiff and formal; Saul and Kit had mocked him, called him Uncle Carbuncle. At least his brothers were familiar, and much as he hated them, he loved them too, though he would never have owned it. So he had tried to stick with his brothers with never a thought for Leviston, even when he was so hungry he had cried. Even when his ribs were so black and blue from his brothers' beatings that he could not stand.

He paused on the street corner, and leant against a wall. Would he go back to West View House? He had almost forgotten about Leviston entirely until a week ago. Until that piece of paper fluttered down in St Paul's. He had passed those notices nearly every day and had hardly given them a second glance. Had it not been for the fact that the wind had gusted through the open door and the damned thing had fluttered to his feet, he would not be here now.

Nathaniel Leviston seeks his nephew, Zachary Deane, he had read with astonishment. The strangeness of the way that paper came into his hand, like a message from above, meant he could not ignore it, it was surely a sign from heaven. So he had taken himself to Leviston's notary as the paper suggested, and from there to a meeting with Leviston himself, and to West View House. All in the space of a few days. Smooth – as if his life was all of a sudden sliding on greased pulleys.

And now, he had probably ruined it all, the one chance he'd ever had to better his lot.

He set off walking again, but stepped aside to avoid the scarred beggar with his rattling pan, blinking away the image of his cut-throat brothers who were adept at whipping the pans from men such as these. Lord knows, he'd tried to make his way like them, through petty thievery and gambling. It kept the wolf from knocking at his door until he was grown enough to make wagers on his sword-skills. For, if he said it himself, he was a neat hand with a blade.

He walked on up the road, blowing on his hands to warm them, and feeling unaccountably angry. Damn Leviston. Why could he not have just accepted him as his nephew? The only reason he'd agreed to go to West View House at all was that he needed proper training now from a real master of fence.

He dreamt of the day he would whip his brothers. Take revenge for the years of beatings and bullying. But for proper training he needed more money than he could get from his usual 'trade'. He had thought to take a few things the Levistons would not notice once he had got inside the house, and sell them on, but now it would be awkward. Leviston was so honest, and had taken such an interest in him.

He stopped to let a street-hawker with a tray of bread-cakes pass. Perhaps he should abandon the whole idea of living at West View House. The daughter was obviously suspicious – she'd been going through his things. And he wasn't sure he wanted to go through life as Leviston's son, it would be a hard task to sustain and, besides, it was becoming clear that Leviston would be hard to stomach as a relation.

A voice calling from behind him made his heart sink. He turned reluctantly.

'I'm sorry.' It was Leviston, arriving breathless and hatless. He had obviously followed him up the road. 'That was clumsily done. I'm no use with sweet words.' He twisted his hat in his hands. 'But it is out now, and I cannot withdraw it. I am a fool in matters of the heart, I know. Pray forgive me.'

Zachary paused and waited, his satchel clasped in front of his chest like a barrier. Nobody had ever apologized to him before like that. He did not know how to respond.

Leviston stuttered on, 'I meant you to know the truth of it. It seemed only fair. But it would be an embarrassment – an embarrassment for us all, were it to be generally known.'

But you do not know the truth, thought Zachary, guiltily trying to organize his thoughts.

Leviston was still talking. 'And you must get to know Elspet better before I tell her. That is, if it suits you, I was going to suggest that we ignore what I have told you and continue to call each other "Nephew" and "Uncle".'

Zachary grasped at this. 'I cannot call you "Father".' He was adamant.

'But "Uncle"? Surely you can keep calling me "Uncle", just as you used to when you were a boy?'

Leviston looked so open, standing there, all innocent, big eyes pleading, that Zachary's nod had happened before he had time to think.

'Uncle, then,' Leviston said, patting him on the arm. 'Come, let us take the carriage home.'

'But I—'

'Enough work for one day.' Leviston linked his arm in his. 'Let's get home to the house. I can go through the rest of the figures with you there.'

Zachary was not sure if he was disgusted with himself or relieved. What on earth had he done? He would have to go on pretending. But now it was worse; he'd missed his chance to tell the man the truth. As they strolled together up the street he consoled himself by thinking that if only his mother could see him now, side by side with the sober-cloaked Leviston, she at least would be smiling a proud smile.

Chapter 4

Elspet knocked at the door to her father's study. Zachary had been in there for more than an hour and she had grown tired of waiting for them to emerge. Father opened the door and gestured her in. She squeezed in past the trunks piled high with books and the baskets with samples of lace.

'Pray pardon, Father, but I wanted to talk with you about this month's figures before we go in to the chambers tomorrow.' She held out the thick ledger of bound vellum.

'Ah.' Father looked uncomfortable. 'Come in a moment and sit.' He cleared some cards of dusty cut-work from the only other chair. Zachary was sitting in the one near the window, the low-backed upholstered chair she usually occupied, a tankard of small beer on the sill next to him.

She sat, and Zachary looked her over.

'We were just discussing the new bobbin-lace from Milan,' Father said. 'It has been selling well, much better than the needle lace.'

'That's because it sits flat, Father, Elspet said. 'The new soft collars demand something that will lie close. Ruffs with picot edges are no longer *à la mode*. Can I see?'

He handed her a fall of airy lace, almost transparent, but edged with tiny scallops and florets. 'Oh, yes, it's beautiful. I can imagine this round a silk collar. How much?'

'Ten pence a yard. Not much profit, I fear – many bones, you see, for the making of it.'

'If there's not much profit in it coming all the way from Milan, is there no way it could be manufactured here in England?' Zachary asked.

She smiled at him, thinking that obviously he understood nothing of the lace trade. 'No,' she said. 'The English specialize in tape lace and needle lace. Here, lace-making is a craft for the poor; it keeps them occupied. In Milan, there are whole factories of makers, almost like a proper guild.'

'Well, no reason we could not do that here,' Zachary said, picking up a bone bobbin from the desk and juggling it through the fingers of one hand.

She looked to her Father to catch his eye and garner some support. To set up a factory like that would be an undertaking quite beyond him. He was not as strong as he had been since his narrow escape from the plague. And his eyesight had deteriorated. Sometimes she had been obliged to quietly instruct Wilmot to return shoddy lace that would never have got past Father in earlier years.

But he looked away from her, and seized on Zachary's words with enthusiasm. 'Now there's an idea worth thinking about. Expansion. Yes, I like the sound of it.'

'But, Father, there is enough to do already. We can barely keep up with the orders as it is.'

Zachary was still juggling the bobbin with distracting deftness. 'Then we need more supply, I would say, to meet demand.'

'Quite right. It's an excellent notion. I'll run it past Wilmot tomorrow.'

'Yes, Father,' she said, 'we'll do that.' No point in her objecting, but the overseer would soon throw cold water on Zachary's impractical idea.

Father paused, ruminating. 'I was thinking, I don't think it necessary for you to come to the chambers tomorrow, Elspet.'

'Tush, Father, I always come with you on Fridays.'

'And I'm sure there are other more productive things you could be doing than sitting in my chambers hunched over the figures. You should be socializing, calling on other young ladies, practising your music.'

She glared at Zachary. He was still playing nonchalantly with that infernal bobbin, and ignoring her. She wished he would go, she did not want to argue with Father before him.

'But how will you manage the figures, Father? Your eyesight is not what it was, and you hardly have time—'

'There is nothing whatever the matter with my eyesight. I have perfect eyesight. But you should be at home more. The servants need more supervision. Though I'm not saying it was not pleasant to have your company. But you are not making your way much in society, and you should be able to do things other women of your age do, as Zachary has pointed out. He is quite right, it is selfish of me to keep you closeted in my chambers.'

Zachary put down the bobbin. 'I didn't mean—'

'And there is no need, I shan't lack company, Zachary will assist me,' pronounced Father.

Zachary jumped to attention, 'If Cousin Elspet wants to carry on, then I see no reason why she should not, I was only saying—'

'It will be a pleasure to have your company, and I'm sure Elspet will fill her time perfectly well with women's crafts.'

'But what about my fencing?' Zachary was frowning now, sitting forward in his chair.

'There'll be time enough for that, never fear.' Father beamed uncharacteristically at them both. 'So it's all settled.'

The next day, Zachary bent his head against the wind and hurried away towards the square stone tower of St Paul's. Another morning with Uncle Leviston had almost finished him. However did Elspet Leviston stand it? He'd told his uncle he was going to his fencing training but, truth be told, he had yet to find a legal Master of Fence to take him on – at least, one who had served his proper state apprenticeship, not just a twopenny charlatan. He had hankered after studying with a certified master for so long now that the ache had taken up permanent residence in his bones.

Leviston had given him a purse for his first lesson, and today he felt like escaping the warehouses and finding a bit of fun. His uncle's company, though solicitous, already stifled him.

Zachary shook the wet off his hat, crossed the threshold of St Paul's and swaggered inside. The big church was a place he knew every inch of, especially the stone-vaulted ceiling. When he was small he used to nip and foist there with his brothers – that is relieving country folk of their purses, and taking the pickings back to his mother. She never asked any questions about where their trimmings came from, but accepted them as a gift, as if they were farm cats bringing back a mouse.

Out of habit he looked at people's shoes to see where they hailed from. Country folk were the best pickings. When he was younger, he'd pretend to faint, and you could always tell the country folk by the way they rushed over to see what was amiss. As they bent over, a quick chop would let the moneybag fall like a plum, and up he'd leap and scramble away. A small paring knife was his first weapon, and it still had a place in his armoury even now, tucked up the lining of his sleeve.

To mark himself out as a gentleman, he threw his cloak over one shoulder to flash its green silk lining, strode down the aisle and looked about for any acquaintances who might fancy a fencing bout or two. But not his brothers; he didn't know where Saul and Kit were now and he didn't want to know. They'd gone off to find their ruffian father, Ben Hagget, and now they were on the dub with him, like as not. Ben Hagget had beaten them all, his mother included, until they'd fled. And as they grew, it became obvious his sons were rent from the same cloth; like father, like son.

Inside the church it was bustle as usual; Paul's Walk was less like a walk and more like a dodge. It was not long before he spotted John 'Gin' Shotterill, already in the company of two country squires. Gin was trying to persuade them into one of the nearby ordinaries for a game of dice.

'Hey, Deane, over here!'

Zachary sauntered over to his friend.

'Allow me to present Mr Ashley and Mr Walker.'

He bowed low to the gentlemen, who seemed relieved to see a diversion.

'Pleased to meet you both.'

'We're just going over to the Green Man for a game of dice,' Gin said.

'Good plan. I'll join you.' Zachary turned to the one called Ashley, whose woollen stockings and iron-soled boots shouted 'country'. 'Been in town long?'

'Since yesterday,' answered Walker for his companion. Ashley looked a little uneasy, but he let Gin lead them and Zachary brought up the rear. It was for all the world like herding sheep. If he and Gin had a pen, he thought, he bet they could get them both into it, easy as winks.

'Just one game, then,' Walker said, 'and we'll be on our way. We have another appointment to keep.'

'Do we?' Ashley said.

'Yes, we do,' Walker cut in tersely.

Zachary grinned to himself. 'Oh well, better be just a quick one, then,' he said.

They wended past the tract sellers and bookmen huddled under canvas in case it should rain, and into the Green Man. Supplied with a jug of ale, Gin and Zachary dropped their dice on to the table. Ashley lowered his be-whiskered face close to the table to inspect them.

'Let's use mine,' Walker said, fumbling in his satchel.

'Fine,' Zachary said. 'You look like a trustworthy fellow.'

Walker relaxed a little then, thinking his good honest dice were in play. After he and Ashley had lost three rounds, Zachary said,

'Lady Luck is smiling on us today.'

'Give me the dice.' Walker was suspicious. Gin put on an innocent face and passed them over. Walker weighed them in his hands, examined them an inch from his nose, then waved them at Ashley, who nodded. Reassured they were his own, Walker blew on them to bring good fortune.

They played another three rounds. Gin and Zachary let them win the first one, so as to give them confidence, but after that the men brooked two more losses.

'I say!' Ashley slapped his hand over the dice. 'We've lost nearly two pounds! Best stop now.'

'No,' Walker said, 'our luck is about to change, I can feel it. A few more rounds, just to see if we can break even. These gentlemen won't mind another couple of games, will you?'

They shook their heads emphatically. Gin caught Zachary's eye and had to press his lips together to keep from laughing.

'But what about our appointment?' Ashley looked uncomfortable.

'What? Oh, that. It can wait,' Walker brushed him off. 'Three more rounds, I say. Whose cast?'

'Mine,' Zachary said and rattled the cup.

'Another half-crown on the number one and three,' Walker called, sliding his coin in.

Zachary threw the dice from the cup on to the table to roll and land six four.

'Hell fire and damnation, you win.' Zachary raked in the winnings.

'One more.' Walker was desperate now. His face had turned pale as gruel.

Gin and Zachary glanced at each other. Gin's eyes had the familiar triumphant glint Zachary knew so well. They were a team, both well-practised at the sleight of hand necessary to change the gulls' dice for their own. Zachary's set were 'bristles', made with a horse hair glued to one dot to make it fall to the six or four. Gin's were 'gourds', hollowed out and skilfully weighted to fall to the three or five. By artful juggling between the honest set and theirs, they never failed to relieve ignorant folk of their excess coinage.

Walker and Ashley never stood a chance.

Zachary did not consider it cheating, as it needed a genuine skill and training to master it. It had taken years of practising casting those dice to get them to fall pat as he wanted. Zachary had no interest in any ruse that did not require intelligence and a deftness of touch.

They were about to leave the two country sots four pound the poorer when there was a commotion at the bar, and a shout.

'Look to your swords!'

Zachary's hand shot to his hilt. Gin swiped the remaining coins from the table. A quiet game of cards at the other end of the tavern had turned over into a brawl.

'What's to do?' Ashley grabbed Zachary's arm, and hastily put himself behind him.

'Leave go, man,' Zachary said, shaking off his clinging hand and craning his neck to see.

Everyone in the place was standing now, and a circle of heads surrounded the disturbance. A sound of smashing crocks and then an audible exhalation as the whole crowd of men surged backwards. Zachary was knocked back into Ashley, who tottered backwards into the stools. His balance went and he slumped like a sack of coals against the wall behind.

'Outside! Take it outside. I'll have no duels in here!'

The landlord's disembodied voice was ignored. A blade whipped through the air over the heads in front and the crowd pressed to the side.

The door banged open and cold air rushed in. Zachary was jostled out of the door by the throng, where he elbowed his way past the taller men amid curses to get to the front. Two men were fighting on the rutted road. One was a sinewy yellow-haired youth, slashing and hacking at his opponent's sword. His face was red as a beet and he sprang from foot to foot as if he had ants in his shoes. He leapt to the side to parry away the point of the other man's sword. But it was the other, the swarthy man in the dark doublet, with hair white like a frost, who held Zachary's attention.

'Who is he?' he asked the man next to him. But the man just shook his head, his eyes glued to the unfolding duel.

Never had Zachary seen a man fight like this. He was completely arrested by him. The fluidity of his movements made him hold his breath. A bolt of envy and admiration shot through him. It was not just the swordsman's technical proficiency, it was as if his whole being was the sword. He did not fight with the sword, he was the sword. The blade simply swooped in the air like a bird.

The crowd was silent but for the noise of the lad hacking with all his strength and might. He blustered and lunged, groaned and slashed. And the other swung his arm easily, his blade arcing, moving against every attack as if it were nothing, a horsefly to be brushed away.

Finally, as if tiring of the game, the man in the black doublet aimed a swift dart and the lad was on his back in the dirt, a flesh-wound to his thigh spurting a red jet of blood.

The other sheathed his sword with one, sleek movement and wiped his hands on his doublet. 'I am sorry,' he said. His accent was slight, but noticeable.

'To the death!' the lad cried, sitting up and trying fruitlessly to stand. He was brave enough, Zachary thought, he would give him that.

'No,' laughed the foreigner. 'I would not have the dishonour of a young man's death on my hands.' He picked up his hat from the ground and turned to go.

A young woman rushed in to tend the lad's wounds, but Zachary only dimly noticed her. He leapt after the man who was walking away. The swordsman placed his low-crowned hat back over his white hair as if nothing unusual had happened. The crowd parted for him as if he were royalty. There was something in his mien that made men give him space.

Zachary arrived breathlessly in his path. 'Are you a fencing master? Do you have a school?' His voice came out less politely than he had hoped.

The man had no option but to stop, for Zachary was blocking his way. He looked Zachary up and down in slight surprise. 'No. Not in London,' he said.

'But who taught you? I have never seen fencing like that. Zachary Deane, sir, at your service. Please, won't you tell me from whom you have the skill?'

'The skill, yes.' The man laughed. 'You are right. It is a good translation. *La Verdadera Destreza*. It means the true skill. You might call it, mastery. I learned it from Carranza – in Seville.'

'Can I—' His words were cut short by a thud and a sharp pain in the side of the head. He grunted and his knees cracked as they hit the ground. He sprang straight back on to his feet, and spun round. The street wavered before his eyes, a pulse throbbed in his ear.

Walker and Ashley. Both were bouncing in their shoes, fists raised before them like prize-fighters from a penny chapbook. Walker's fist had blood on it. Zachary brought a hand to feel his ear where he had been hit.

'Bastard!' he said in disbelief as he saw blood on his hand.

'Cheat us, would you, you beggar?' Walker yelled. The crowd closed in on them.

'We picked up your dice.' Ashley was red in the face. 'Thought we were too stupid to notice, did you? They're rigged.'

'Not my dice.' Zachary held up his palms and shook his head, 'must be Shotterill's.'

'He says they're yours,' Ashley said.

'We'll settle this by combat,' Walker said, puffing himself up.

The crowd let out an 'Aah', followed by a general murmur.

'By the sword,' Zachary said.

'No, by God,' said Walker. 'None of that nonsense. Man to man. By the fists.'

'Duel by s—' Zachary began to protest.

Walker pushed his fist up to Zachary's nose. 'Seven o'clock, I'll fight and Ashley will be my second.'

Zachary viewed the stocky figure of Walker with consternation. He was a thick-set bugger. Word was, these northern men were used to wrestling, and it was something of which he had little experience. 'You will lose,' he jeered, with false bravado. His head throbbed.

'Don't bank on it,' Walker said.

'Where?'

'Lincoln's Inn Fields. At the lightning ash.'

'Is it far?'

'You'll find it.'

'Your friend Shotterill seems to have left you hanging,' Walker said. 'We expect to see him as your second. If not, we'll be calling these good folk to witness you tried to cheat us and would not give us fair dealings.' The staring crowd of onlookers hooted and heckled.

'I can't stand a bad loser,' Zachary said, goading him. 'We beat you fair and square. As we surely will tonight, if it's a fair fight.'

'And we will prove you wronged us, sir – by the grace of God, and my fists.'

'Till tonight, then,' Zachary said. He had intended to be back at

West View House by nightfall. He hoped the bout would be a quick one, and he could be back before curfew and in time for supper.

As for Gin Shotterill, he knew exactly where the crafty snake would be hiding. By hook or crook, he'd make damned sure he joined him at the lightning ash.

Chapter 5

Elspet waited by the window. True to his word, Father had taken Cousin Zachary with him to the Exchange and his chambers. But when he returned in the evening, he rode alone, trailing the new horse which tossed its head and rolled its eyes. She hurried out.

'What has happened? Did it throw him? Where is Zachary?'

He clambered off his gelding, saying, 'Nothing's amiss. Don't fuss so.' Broadbank, the groom, had appeared at the sound of hoof-beats so Father handed him the horses and said, 'Come inside. Don't loiter out here, it looks bad. You should be at your music.'

'Your hands are cold,' Elspet said, reaching out to rub them between hers. 'Where are your gloves?'

He pulled his hands away. 'I know, I know,' he said, 'but somehow I am always in the saddle before I remember to put them on, and then it's too late – the reins are in my hands and I'm trotting off.'

'I will have to tie a ribbon to the reins to remind you!'

'You will not. My horse would end up like a blasted maypole. Come along, let's get within.' Broadbank led the horses away and she took Father's cloak and hung it up in the chilly hall.

'What about Cousin Zachary?' she asked, 'Did he not go to the chambers with you?'

'He's…' Father paused, frowning. 'He's gone to meet with some fellows for some fencing practice. Hanging Sword Alley, I think he said. He'll be back to eat with us.'

She took his arm and squeezed it. He patted her hand briskly in reply and disengaged his arm. In the oak chamber jugs of warmed wine stood steaming on the stone hearth which framed a struggling fire. Exhaling, he sank into his usual cushioned chair and she settled into hers.

'So how was it at the Exchange? What's new? Has the rest of the consignment from Brussels arrived yet? I need some more of the shell edging for the pillowslips I'm making. But I've taken the dogs out . . . and I have been studying, working on my music and Latin.' She knew that would please him, but he only nodded distractedly.

'Pliny the Elder,' she went on, 'humankind and nature, as you suggested; I'm enjoying it. The description of Hannibal and the elephants is most extraordinary, don't you think?'

Father did not answer; he was looking pensively into the fire, with its single blue flame. To gather some response, she asked, 'And how did Zachary like sorting the consignments today?'

'Well enough,' he said, between sips of wine. 'Give me a moment before you start with your chatter.'

'I was only asking—'

'He is very quick. Asks all the right questions and I can see he's sharp as a nib. Of course, he's a little rough around the edges – he'll need training.'

'You mean, you are thinking of hiring him?'

'Hiring him?' He laughed. 'No, you goose. A man needs a younger man to learn his trade, and I can see he will do very well. He is family, and we must do right by him.'

The shock must have shown in her face for he got up and came to stand before her, offering her a cup of wine.

'You need not fear,' he said. 'I have it in hand, to make sure you have a suitable match. I know you have supported me with the business very well, better than I could have hoped. You have a good head for figures and it is to your credit.'

The cup was in her hand, but she set it on the floor to protest, but he carried on over her, 'And don't think I have not been grateful for that whilst you were still a child. But you are grown now, and will marry as all women will – and have your own sons to keep you busy.

You need to develop more womanly tastes. Besides, the lace trade is a cut-throat enterprise, despite its appearance – no business for a gentlewoman. No, I will go this week and draw up a dower agreement with the notary. Do not fret, there is ample provision to secure your future.'

At first she was so taken aback that she could say nothing. He continued to nod and smile until it hit her like a slap. He was serious. She got to her feet. 'Are you telling me that I am not to assist you any more? That you are to entrust Leviston's Lace to Zachary? Why, we know nothing about him. He is a stranger—'

'He's not a stranger, he is our flesh and blood. Though if you need distraction, I'm sure he will find work for you to do, to occupy your idle hours.'

'Is that how you view it, Father? Idle hours? That I was merely filling idle hours?' She could barely get the words out. 'Have you educated me and provided me with book learning about the world so that I can converse only with kitchen hands and maids?'

'You go too far, Elspet. Remember yourself, pray. Do not make me have to chastise you.'

She pressed her lips together, tried to calm herself. This could not be happening. She walked to the window and took in some deep breaths. At length she turned and addressed her father, with the thought that had been festering all day, 'Do you intend that Zachary will stay here for good, Father? Is that what you have in mind? Is he to live here with us?'

She saw the answer on his face before he opened his mouth. She looked away, her fists clenched under her folded arms.

'Do not take it thus,' Father said. 'I know it will take a little getting used to. But he is a good boy at heart, a good Catholic boy, and it is best that I groom him and make him fit for business. He has had a somewhat unconventional life. My . . .' He hesitated, chewed his lip as if searching for the right words. 'My sister was an unusual woman. She has not brought him up the way she should. But he is yet young. He will need some tuition, and take some time to adapt to our ways, but then his success will bring further prosperity to us all.'

She bit back the words; she did not think Zachary would be as easy to mould as her father clearly did. He was no wet-eared youth, but a grown man. There was silence in the room, except that outside she could hear Diver whining and scrabbling at the door to get in.

'Stop it, Diver!' Father yelled at the door.

Elspet turned back to face him. She felt as if she was begging for scraps herself. She asked him the burning question too sharply, as if she was merely asking what provisions she should order for dinner.

'You have someone in mind, Father?'

He looked sheepish. He knew exactly what she meant.

'There is someone I think might be a good match,' he said. 'A fur trader. He is a fine man – most devout, of our own persuasion. He fought for the Catholic cause with the Wright brothers in the Essex Rebellion.' He rushed on, caught in his own enthusiasm, despite her stiffness and lack of response. 'Father Everard could not speak of him too highly, and he is looking for a wife. It would be a good alliance – lace and fur – and would mean our family would have the chance to expand into that trade too, should we choose.'

Zachary. He meant Zachary. She was to be married off to supply a cousin she barely knew with opportunities for trade.

'And what is his name, pray?'

'Hugh Bradstone. A good solid family.' She had never heard of him.

'And he is very well connected,' Father said, oblivious to her, stooping to refill his wine cup and waving it expansively in the air. 'The family has a four hundred-acre estate in the country near Tockton. Hugh's just begun to take control over it with his father's blessing. And perhaps he may wish to keep a house in London when he's in town. He knows this house is to come to you. It will be a fine match.'

'And tell me, where is Tockton?'

'Yorkshire? Lancashire? Somewhere in the North, I think.'

'And you are happy with this arrangement? That I should be shipped off miles away from you, to a place I've never heard of?'

Father looked baffled. 'I would have thought you'd be glad. I believe he's quite personable.'

'What do you mean?'

'That he looks decent enough. Tall, broad. A fine figure of a man. You'll like him. Besides, I've invited him to dine with us next week.' He sat down again as if the matter was closed.

Her mind was in turmoil. 'But what about the dogs?'

'I expect Broadbank will take them out, if you don't wish to. What does it matter?'

'No, I didn't mean that. I meant, if I am to be married, who will care for them?'

'Why, Broadbank of course, or Coleman, or the other staff.'

She ran over to him then and crouched at his knee. 'But Father, they're nothing to them; they care for them because we pay them to, but it's not the same as a master's love. Does Mr Bradstone like dogs?'

'I've no idea. What an absurd question. I know you love them, of course you do. But they are dogs. That's all, just dogs.' He sighed. 'Try to find some perspective, Elspet, you cannot remain unmarried for ever. No, I have a good feeling about Hugh Bradstone – it will be a useful partnership, I am sure of it.' He took up her hand where it rested on his knee, and held it as if unsure what to do with it. 'This alliance – I know Rome will smile upon it, two old families like ours, both steeped in the Faith. Though of course it has to be said, if Bradstone takes you north, I shall probably miss you about the place.'

'Not as much as I shall miss you,' she said, clinging to his hand, choked at this unusual admission of affection.

'Now then,' he said, looking discomfited and withdrawing his hand, 'nothing is set in stone. You have to meet the gentleman first. Brace up, and go and make sure Turner knows to wait supper for Zachary. And tell Coleman to fetch me directly he arrives. We will eat at eight of the clock.'

'Yes, Father.' She walked unsteadily out of the door and went straight to her chamber. She needed time to think. Her head was reeling with all the sudden changes that beset her. She was to be married to someone she had never met. That hateful cousin Zachary was to live with them and be trained to take on Father's business – her business, that she had helped him with all these years since Mother died. Had she scrimped on stuffs for her own clothes so that her upstart cousin could squander the savings? Why, Zachary knew nothing whatever of the lace trade. But in her heart she knew he could learn. Father was determined to train him, and he taught well. It was the thing Father did the best. But perhaps she could put him off the idea, if she tried hard enough.

She had always thought Father's stinginess was to preserve her inheritance. She thought she had proved her worth over and over. Evidently not. She reached up to the window to pull the curtains tight shut and threw herself down on the bed.

The embroidered coverlet made by her mother was faded, the colourful blue birds and yellow flowers bleached by the sun over the years to a drab brown. She hauled it up and wrapped herself in it like a protective cloak. She imagined Mother coming into the room, bowing her lace-capped head to listen in the way she always did when something had troubled her children. Elspet inhaled, trying to catch the faint rose scent her mother always wore in the pomander at her waist. But there was no trace of it.

She had stupidly assumed she would stay in London. That she would be married, yes, but to a London man, a husband from the city who would love West View House as she did, who would want to restore it and keep it in their family for their children or future generations. Never for one moment had she thought she might be wed to someone who would take her out of town to some place – Tockton? It might as well be the New World, for all she knew about it.

Martha the maid's arrival with hot water aroused her from her thoughts. She did not feel like dining with them, but knew she would go hungry if she did not. She washed and changed her day dress for more suitable apparel, a pale lemon skirt and bodice with tied sleeves, and let Martha tame her dark springy curls into a knot at the nape of her neck. The gong for supper resounded in the hall, and smoothing her cheeks with her palms again to cool them, she descended the stairs. She did not want her cousin to realize how flustered she really was.

But when she entered the great hall there was no sign of Zachary, and her father was pacing the floor.

'Tell the kitchen to hold the meal,' he snapped as the kitchen maid tottered in with a tray bearing three bowls of steaming leek soup. The maid hesitated a moment, unsure what to do. 'For heaven's sake. Put the tray down first, then go and tell them. I'll send word to fetch the other courses up when my nephew is home.' She did as he bade her and retreated downstairs.

'I thought he'd have been here by now,' he mumbled to himself.

'I'm sure he'll be along any moment,' Elspet said, to soothe him, repressing the shameful hope that he was lost somewhere and would never return.

'Yes, you're right.' Time passed by and, despite Father's walking up and down, they both heard the thin bell of the time-piece ping the quarter, and then the half.

'Come, Father, let us eat anyway,' she said. 'I'm sure he will smell his food and arrive directly.'

'Till the next bell,' he said.

'Pray heaven he is not caught up in any trouble,' she voiced a concern for him that she did not really feel. The worry was for her father, not for Zachary. It bothered her, her father going to Mass. 'It's hardly safe for us Catholics to be abroad these days,' she said.

Father sat down on the dining chair, but then immediately stood up again, a crease of worry lodged between his eyebrows. 'Bainbridge knows what he is doing.'

She saw him chew his lip, and knew it was she that had sowed the seed of worry in him. She instantly regretted it.

'I wonder if I should go to look for him?' Father said.

'I'm sorry. Take no heed of me. It was thoughtless of me.' She hastened to comfort him. 'I'm sure it is not anything to do with our faith. He's safe, I'm sure. Perhaps he has simply forgotten the time, as folk do when they are engaged in an activity that attracts them. Many a time I have forgotten the hour whilst making a new design for a chair cover.'

He looked at her as if her talk of chair covers was somehow an insult. 'You don't understand,' he said.

'What? What don't I understand?'

He sighed. 'Nothing. It is not your fault, it is mine.' Then, after a little rumination, he said, 'You're right, my dear. Let's eat. I'll send down to the kitchen.'

He shook the bell and the food was duly summoned. They left the soup, which had gone cold. When the hot platters arrived the beef was dry and the cabbage had disintegrated into greenish water in the dish, but by that time Elspet was so hungry that she did not care. After a perfunctory grace she set to eating with relish.

Father tutted. 'Try to be a little more dainty, won't you, Elspet? Hugh Bradstone will be expecting a lady of manners.'

'And he will have one,' she said pointedly, 'provided that Cousin Zachary sees fit to keep good time, and does not keep the whole household waiting.'

Father did not answer but pursed his lips and, with a gloomy expression, helped himself to more of the dripping cabbage. Their meal was finished in silence.

Whenever there was a noise outside, Father kept jumping from his seat, and when there was still no sign of his errant nephew, he sat back down again. She said nothing, for to do so would be to reproach him again, and the loud tick of the hall clock did that task well enough.

She picked up her napkin and wiped her mouth and hands. 'I will be in the oak chamber as usual,' she said.

He nodded impatiently, as though her voice interrupted his listening.

So for another night she sat alone with her wool-work. A small part of her felt slightly pleased that Zachary was proving to be what she thought he was, a lazy good-for-nothing. The front door banged shut, and she paused with her needle. Almost curfew time.

Through a chink in the curtain she spied Father standing on the doorstep, still waiting. Her heart went out to him. The foolish old thing; he must be worried that something had befallen Zachary. It pained her to see him thus, standing out in the cold.

Curse Zachary. Why couldn't he keep to his agreements? She found herself uncomfortably torn between hoping Zachary hurried on home, and hoping he would never come back. She heard the servants go to the dining room next door to collect the rest of the dishes, and in the quiet she could not help but hear their whispered conversation.

'Not back yet, then?' came Martha's reedy voice.

'No. Mr Leviston's in a rare old lather over it.'

'Shh. He might hear.'

'No. He's gone out to look for him. I heard the door go.'

Elspet paused in her sewing and strained to catch their conversation. Of course her mother's warnings that those who eavesdrop hear nothing good about themselves came instantly to mind, yet still she could not help herself.

'You know what they're saying, don't you?' The kitchen maid.

'What?'

'That he's not his nephew. Master Zachary. That he's his . . .' Here the sound fell into a whisper.

'Never!'

'Ssh! I heard it from the apothecary. I was at his counter as they passed by this morning, and I said to that nice Mr Hollis, "Look, there goes Mr Leviston's nephew." He says, "No, miss, it can't be." He says he's seen him afore and he's a ruffian. Says he's a cloak-snatcher from St Giles. Can you believe that?'

'No. That can't be right. He must have got the wrong lad—'

Elspet was on her feet without thinking. She threw open the door so that it banged against the wall. Both maids jumped, their eyes wide with shock.

'Have you finished clearing the table?' she asked.

They nodded dumbly in unison.

'Then stop your gossiping out here and return those plates to the kitchen.'

'Yes, mistress,' they bleated in chorus, and dived below stairs.

Elspet's heart was thudding behind her wooden stomacher. Heaven forbid Father had heard any of their scurrilous nonsense. To conjecture, well, that was natural. But to spread malicious gossip, that was quite another matter. She would not brook servant chatter about the family, not even about Zachary, whatever her own personal thoughts on him were.

She pulled the front door open and called impatiently from the threshold, 'Pardon me, Father, but I think you will do him no good standing out there. Why don't you come inside? If something has happened, someone will surely come to tell us of it.'

'They may not know where he lodges,' he protested.

'But I fear for you; your chest is still weak after your fever. Far better to wait indoors than stand out there in the cold.'

'I thought he would be back.' His face was crestfallen, like a small boy.

'Where did you last see him?'

'At the Dog and Bucket. He was going to the fencing master.'

'Then let us send the stable lad to Hanging Sword Alley to see if he can discover where he is.'

'Do not fuss. But perhaps you're right. I'll send a lad out.'

But the stable lad could find no news, and it was the early hours of the morning before Zachary returned. A rapping at the door made Elspet sit up sharp in bed, confused with sleep. She listened and caught the sound of something clattering. Then curses and the noise of metal scraping on the wall.

She reached for her shawl, grabbed the night lantern and stumbled out on to the gallery. She peered down the stairwell into the shadowy hall. A servant had obviously opened up, despite her father's express command that after night curfew the house be barred to entry.

Zachary was slumped against the wall, still wearing his sword and, by the look of it, drunk. A flickering candle sconce cast a yellow glow over his crumpled form. He sported a black eye, a bloody ear and a deep gash to his forehead. His hair was wet and matted to his scalp.

Father must have lain awake all night, for he had been far quicker than her to the hall, and he was still in his nightgown, his face gaunt as Death himself. The manservant and her father struggled to haul Zachary to his feet, but he resisted them.

She ran down the stairs, but Father waved her away.

'Go back to bed, Elspet. We can manage.'

'Shall I—'

He hunched his body over Zachary and shouted urgently over his shoulder, 'Back to bed, I say!' He was trying to shield her from the sight of her cousin. It struck her that he was ashamed. He did not want her to see Zachary like this. 'Back to bed!'

It was an order, and she obeyed. She watched from behind her chamber door on the upper gallery as they hauled Zachary by the armpits, half stumbling, his boots dragging on the floor and round the steps to the lower nursery. She was horrified. Father was a penny fool if he intended to put his business in the hands of such a gin-soak. And what if the servants were right? She hardly dare contemplate what that would mean.

The soles of Zachary's boots disappeared round the corner and there was a whump as they threw him on to the bed. A shout of protestation, and Father's voice urging, 'Lie down.'

'The bastards jumped me,' came Zachary's voice, slurred and hoarse. 'It wasn't a fair fight.'

A few minutes later Father stepped back into the hall, grey-faced and grim, and ascended the stairs to his chamber. He would not catch her eye. Instead he grasped her door handle, and banged the door closed so hard it was enough to make the lock rattle. She was shut out again. Father clearly thought this was no business of hers.

Chapter 6

Elspet could not fathom it. Even after the drama of the night before, Zachary and Father continued with their usual routine of early repast, Mass at Mr Bainbridge's house, and then a day at Father's warehouses and office. Of course she was obliged to wait at home. It was probably because they did business together afterwards. It rankled; she wondered what they were planning, but she pushed away the resentment as she watched them return together at night from her upstairs window.

Her father was talking animatedly, looking more vibrant than she had seen him in many months, hanging on Zachary's words. And when Father replied, Zachary cocked his head to one side, listening, his face all bruised like a prize-fighter. To her chagrin, any disagreement between Zachary and her father had obviously been mended.

The servants whispered to each other as Zachary went by, and cast sidelong looks at each other. She frowned at them, of course, but said nothing. It was hurtful that Father had not taken her into his confidence about her cousin's injuries.

Their routine persisted all that week, but Father no longer brought her the books from the business, or asked her advice. She missed going up into town. Things were happening behind closed doors that she was no longer privy to, and she became consumed with curiosity to know what passed between her father and her cousin.

In the long evenings, whilst the men hid out in her Father's chamber, she sat before the spitting fire in the kitchen, with Goody Turner and the dogs for company, needle in hand. She was attempting to adapt one of Mother's rose-coloured silk suits into a tolerably fashionable style. It was difficult enough to persuade Father to pay attention to the household expenses, let alone pay any mind to how she was dressed. For a lace importer he had scant idea of how lace should look ruffled around a sleeve, or as a trim on a boned bodice. To him it was just so many yards of profit.

Earlier in the week she had asked him, 'Might I have a few pounds to buy stuff for a new gown, Father? Summer is coming and I'm still in last year's winter wool.'

'Your apparel seems fine to me, Elspet. But are you going someplace where you will have need of it?'

'No, Father. It's just that Mr Bradstone—'

'I'm sure Bradstone would prefer a sensible wife – one who does not fritter away his hard-earned coin – to a wind-brained woman in the latest gown. You are already a handsome looking girl without needing any assistance from the draper.'

So that was that. But it preyed on her mind. The house looked down-at-heel, and it injured her sense of pride. It was not even that she wanted Mr Bradstone to like her – indeed, she rather hoped he would not; the last thing she wanted was to be married to some boorish northern fur-farmer. But she would like to look as though she was worth marrying, at least, and not to be subjected to his humiliating scorn.

So now she sat painstakingly unpicking and re-seaming the stiff silk sleeves, feeling the cool material slide through her fingers as she sewed. Diver sat on her lap, with his tousled head in the way as usual. she fondled his ears and smiled; she had not the heart to move him.

Her enforced solitude gave her plenty of time to think. She pondered over the gossip about Zachary. It couldn't be true, could it? Did not Father say he and his sister had been estranged? Perhaps that was a good reason why they had led such separate lives, that she had fallen into some unspeakable low-life. But no, it was too ridiculous. No relation of her straight-laced father could be involved in any criminal profession; she refused to believe it.

Martha laced her into the rose-coloured bodice and tucked in the ends. 'You look beautiful, mistress,' she said, 'like a flower in a garden.'

'Thank you, Martha. I'm glad you did not say which flower. Loosestrife, probably; they're the ones sticking up above all the rest.'

'No, mistress. A rose. The pink suits you. Just your hair to dress now.'

'You flatter me. Anyway, no need to spend too long with my hair. Father seems to think Mr Bradstone is a pious recusant who doesn't want a wife interested in gowns and so forth.' She sighed. 'And anyway, he's from out of town, where they'll have no idea of fashion.'

'Hmm.' Martha's grunt was disapproving.

She swivelled round. 'Oh Martha, don't tell, but I'm not sure I even want to meet a dull furrier from some out-of-the-way town I've never heard of. He'll probably smell of old pelts and the tannery. Truth be told, I hope to put him off.'

'Let me just pin the lace cap in place, at least. You'd best look respectable.'

She fidgeted as Martha pushed her head back round, then pulled and pinched at the back of her hair.

'Done,' Martha said. And it was just in time, for the big bell was ringing and she heard the manservant answer the door. Her father's falsely genial voice followed, then Zachary's slightly nasal tones.

She raised her eyebrows at Martha, who said, 'Best get on down.'

'I suppose I have to?'

'Can't say, mistress, but Mr Leviston, well, he don't like to be kept waiting.'

Elspet sighed and tied her shawl tightly around her shoulders. It was not yet summer, and there was a draught blowing in from the bluster outside. She would certainly have need of a wrap in their hall – Father had asked for the fire to be lit only an hour ago, as usual, despite their guest.

As she descended the stairs with Martha behind her, men's laughter drifted up. She pushed at the door and Father turned in greeting. But her eyes were fixed on the other two men. Zachary was dressed in a showy crimson doublet with gold-coloured slashing, surely new. She wished she did not know every item in his trunk. He was pointing out something in the yard to the green-clad stranger, who had his back to them. Her first thought was, 'Praise the Lord, but he's tall.' He towered over Zachary, and had to stoop to follow the line of the smaller man's arm.

'Mr Bradstone, this is my daughter Elspet.'

Mr Bradstone turned around and smiled. She let her knees bend and heard the rustle of Martha's skirts as she dipped behind her. Blood rushed to her face. It was as if she was all at once on fire. For he was surely the finest-looking man she had ever seen. And fashionable. She felt instantly the faded shabbiness of the room, and of her home-sewn gown.

'At last. Your father has told me so much about you.' Mr Bradstone smiled and bowed elegantly, removing his feather-trimmed hat and showing a crop of glossy brown hair.

'Has he?' she stammered, staring up at him like a fool. He was much taller than she.

Why had not Father told her? But of course, he would not notice. He'd said he was fine-looking, but Hugh Bradstone was not just attractive, he was impossibly handsome. She felt caught, like a goose in a pen, with all the men staring at her discomfiture. She managed to stumble out a greeting and a curtsey.

'So it's finished, is it, Cousin Elspet?' Zachary said, nodding at the gown.

'Yes,' she said, with embarrassment, wishing her cousin would not draw attention to it.

'Well, it took long enough. But it is a fetching colour on you,' he said. His tone made her feel as if it certainly was not.

'Thank you, cousin.' She twisted her hands together, unable to move, for now everyone was appraising her gown. She hoped to goodness the unpicking marks did not show.

'Elspet always fills a gown well,' said Father. 'She's a careful housekeeper; she has fashioned the gown herself from an old one of my wife's.'

She cringed inwardly. Oh Father, she thought, for heaven's sake do not tell him it is a second-hand gown; what will he think of us? As it was, she was sure Mr Bradstone already thought them quite behind the times with their chilly chambers and lack of wall-hangings. And she was surely not pretty enough for a man such as he. She could think of nothing to say; she was shrinking with shame.

'A seamstress, then? It is very well done,' Hugh Bradstone said politely to break the silence.

She was of course well aware that he had no option but to say this. Zachary sat down in his chair, looking amused, as if they were putting on a show just for his entertainment. She cast him a cold look.

Mr Bradstone, however, continued, 'And is the trim Leviston's lace?'

Father nodded, and puffed out his chest. 'Finest anywhere, that. Elspet, come here so Mr Bradstone can see.'

Obediently she approached Mr Bradstone and held out her sleeve.

'May I?' He lifted her arm and turned it this way and that. She was aware he must be looking down on the top of her head and the hastily pinned cap. 'Very fine,' he said, and caught her eye. To her surprise, the look contained a twinkle of amusement and plainly said 'We must be indulgent to your father'. When she withdrew her arm the heat of his fingers still lingered on her skin.

The talk turned to ships and colonies and where the imported fur originated. The men seemed to have forgotten she was there. She fanned herself with the lace ends of her cap to cool her face. It seemed hours until they all sat down.

At last the maidservants bustled in with the platters and the board was soon filled with dishes of meats and fowl. She was seated opposite Mr Bradstone. He was just as striking close up, with a small, neat beard above his white ruff. He spoke in a cultured voice, his eyes were very pale blue and she noticed that the irises were almost white at the centre.

When he saw her looking, he smiled and her stomach lurched before she ventured what she hoped was a demure smile back. This might be the man she would marry. It sharpened her senses. She took in everything about him. Her hand strayed up to pat her hair. Why had she not heeded Martha and let her dress it properly?

'We cull mostly beaver,' he was saying. 'I employ about two hundred trappers out there.'

'Two hundred?' Father sucked on his lips. He was impressed.

'I think most of the London milliners have beaver-skin from Bradstone's now. And coney, and musquash. The New World gives us access to more plentiful skins than we could ever obtain in England. I just struck lucky and had ships ready at the right time.'

When he said 'struck lucky', she registered the slight Northern flatness to his vowels, but it only made his voice more appealing.

'Do you wear fur, Miss Elspet?' he asked.

'I haven't—' she began, but Father threw her a pointed look. 'Oh yes,' she blurted out, 'I love fur.'

And it was true; in the winter her fur-lined cloak was one of her most prized possessions. She loved the softness and warmth of its lining. But she had not had a new one for nigh on three years and it was rubbed almost bald from wear.

'Then I shall send enough pale coney to your dressmaker for a new winter cloak.'

She replied, 'Sir, you are too kind, there is no need—'

Zachary interrupted her. 'Cousin Elspet is skilled with the needle. Perhaps she will look to her father's purse and make her own,'

'Delighted,' said Father, thankfully overriding them both. 'You'll give him the name of your dressmaker, won't you, Elspet?'

'Of course,' she said, thinking to herself that she hadn't been near Taylor's shop for almost a twelvemonth and he would be mightily surprised to see her there after all this time.

Aware of Zachary's glances, she tried to fix him with a look which would deter him from giving Mr Bradstone any further humiliating details about her circumstances.

So the food was served, and her choice of dishes went down exceedingly well, though Zachary was always first to the plate again, notwithstanding they were entertaining. She tried to eat daintily, as her father had suggested, which was easier than usual, as her stomach was so fluttery she could barely touch a bite.

Taking courage, she asked Mr Bradstone, 'Are you often in town?'

At the same time Zachary enquired, 'Do you fence?' But Zachary's voice was the louder.

She hung on Mr Bradstone's answer.

'Passably well,' he said, pausing to chew. 'These days I carry a powder weapon for my own safety as well as a rapier. My days of fighting for the cause are over, however. I am concentrating on business now. And, you know, on board ship I've found it is as well to have a gun rather than a sword – such a confined space, you see.'

'What sort? I mean, who made it?' Zachary asked, leaning forward.

'I left them in the hall. They're a pair of Mitchison's pistols, from Goldsmith's Row. Nice walnut stocks. Actually, I'm quite pleased with them. You can come and take a look after dinner. What about you?'

'Zachary has a fine collection of swords, I've never seen so many . . .' Too late she realized her mistake and shut her mouth abruptly.

'Yes, you had a very good look at all my possessions.' Zachary spoke in a low and level voice. 'Without an invitation.'

'Is that so? What do you mean?' Father asked, obviously sensing something odd.

She pressed the backs of her hands to her face, now uncomfortably hot.

'Oh nothing,' Zachary said airily. 'Elspet and I were just getting acquainted.'

'It was a misunderstanding, Father,' she said miserably.

Father frowned and gave her a look she recognized as his 'I am ashamed of you' expression.

During this little interchange Mr Bradstone had been casting his eyes from one to the other of them with puzzlement. There was an awkward silence. Zachary raised his eyebrows at her.

Mr Bradstone was the soul of tact for, seeing her discomfiture, he changed the subject. 'This is a splendid house. How many chambers have you here, Mr Leviston?'

'Oh, there are a dozen,' Father replied with relief. 'Of course. I should have thought. You will want to see all that. I'll take you around afterwards. Zachary can keep Elspet company whilst I give you a tour.'

'I'll come with you, Father,' she said, hurriedly.

She must steer Mr Bradstone away from the upper chamber where the panelling had been eaten by the worm, and have him look at the fine portrait of her mother rather than the disintegrating drapes on the beds. Besides, she had no wish to be alone with her irritating cousin. God forbid. She would much rather find out more about Mr Bradstone.

But Father was firm. 'No. I have a few things to discuss with Mr Bradstone, and we will be better undisturbed.' He gave her a meaningful nod and smile, which Mr Bradstone could not help but see, but did his best to politely ignore.

'You have a house in Yorkshire, I believe?' she asked him.

'Yes,' he said. 'Several, actually. The chief being an estate of about four hundred acres. Mostly flax, some cattle. A fine deer park too. I have a good overseer to look to it while I'm away.'

'And how far away are you from London?'

'Four, maybe three days' ride in fine weather. A stone's throw from the city of York.' He seemed amused by her questioning, but answered with a frank gaze.

'It sounds very nice,' she said, regretting instantly such a feeble response. 'I have never been to York.'

'Then we must remedy that,' he said, and Father smiled.

'Come,' Father said to Zachary, 'let's take a look at Hugh's pistols before Hugh and I take a tour of the house.'

'Mistress Leviston,' Bradstone made a farewell bow and she dropped a curtsey again, lower than before. He met her eyes as she rose, and nodded to her. It was a nod of acceptance. She could not help it, but she beamed at him like a child. Father and Zachary followed him into the hall. As soon as they were gone, she rang the bell and sent for Martha.

'I know,' Martha said, before Elspet had said a word. 'You want me to dress your hair.'

'How did you—?'

'He's a fine figure of a man. Such good legs. And his clothes! Cut velvet and shoes made of Spanish leather!'

She did not chide Martha for her forwardness. 'I know. He's not at all what I had expected.'

'Your father has his head fixed on good and proper.'

'He's so tall. He looks down on me.'

'Now sit still and I'll dress your hair, I have the pins here.'

She fidgeted in the chair as Martha tugged and skewered her hair into place. Just as she had finished, Zachary returned.

'You may go, Martha,' he said.

'But she—' Elspet protested, but Zachary was giving Martha a look.

'I've finished, mistress,' Martha said, bobbing hurriedly to Zachary and bustling away.

Elspet turned to face the window, annoyed that he should be using his authority so freely in her house.

'You've changed your hair,' he said.

'Yes.' She turned. 'Martha noticed a few pins were loose.'

'If I were you, I'd be careful not to wear your heart too much on your sleeve, cousin.'

'I don't know what you mean,' she said, covering her embarrassment by brushing down her skirts.

'A man likes a chase. It is the hunting instinct.'

She could not believe her ears. 'You are too impertinent. It is none of your business.'

'Ah, but it is. Your father has taken care to find you a good match, and they are not so easy to come by. I would not have him disappointed.'

'He won't be disappointed.'

'Good, because the furrier has coin to invest in the business.'

'And do my feelings in the matter count for nothing?'

He shrugged.

She let out a long sigh, then took a deep breath. Perhaps it was her fault they seemed to always be at sixes and sevens. 'Look, cousin, I know we did not get off to a good start, but I want us to be friends for my father's sake. And I know I am at fault here; I did not bid you a proper welcome and I looked at your things without asking. My behaviour was unforgiveable. I'm sorry.'

He turned away, and for a moment she thought he was not going to reply, but then he said, 'Why? Why were you snooping in my room?'

'I was curious, that's all. Wouldn't you be? Father had never told me anything about you or your family, and he still hasn't. It's remiss of him, and the servants have started gossiping already, making up all manner of nonsense—'

'What? What have they been saying?'

'I dare not even repeat it.'

'Then why bring it up at all?' He glared at her.

The door flew open and Father and Mr Bradstone breezed in, laughing together at some joke. She remembered her manners, glanced helplessly at her cousin and went to greet them. Zachary moved nonchalantly to the side, as if the conversation had never happened, and sat down with one leg hitched over the other on one of the upright chairs.

'And this is such a fine position here, overlooking the river,' Mr Bradstone said.

'I have always thought so too,' she agreed.

'Mr Bradstone was asking whether you might like to accompany him to view his ships on the east docks?' Father said.

She opened her mouth to reply, but then paused. She wondered about Zachary's words, and decided to try to be more enigmatic. After all, she did want Hugh Bradstone to like her. 'I thank you, sir. If you tell me the date, I will consult with my diary and see how it might fit with my other engagements.'

'Other engagements?' Father was incredulous. 'What other engagements?'

'Oh, this and that.' They stared at her expectantly. 'I promised a friend I would meet her to look over some cushions she is embroidering, and then there are one or two supper engagements—' Damn Zachary, it was all much more awkward than she had envisaged. The three men watched her flounder, before she blurted out, 'If you send your manservant with the date I shall see if I am free. My maid will bring you my reply.'

'Very well,' Mr Bradstone said, seeming not to take offence in the slightest. 'I will send word with the time and place. I hope we will meet again soon.'

She made obeisance to him once more, her heart all a shiver. After that the men retired to her father's chambers and she was left alone again in the chamber.

Of course it was nigh-on impossible to settle to any of her usual activities whilst the handsome Mr Bradstone was just beyond the door, so she pretended to supervise the servants clearing the dishes, and hovered uncertainly at the fireplace, toasting her feet in the unaccustomed warmth and waiting for some sign that the men might re-emerge.

They would be talking of her, she was certain of it, and she dreaded to think what Zachary might be saying. She wanted Mr Bradstone to think well of her. Hugh Bradstone, her father called him. It was a good, old name. She liked the sound of it.

She reappraised their chamber with the battered panelling and the threadbare rugs. If only, she thought, imagining them replaced by fine tapestries and sumptuous carpets. She could do a lot worse, she reasoned with herself. They would make a fine couple. Hugh Bradstone was a good-looking, devout man of some means. And he seemed pleasant-natured too. Exactly what she had always hoped for in a husband. Except that she had not thought she was ready for marriage; that was all. It would take a little getting used to if her father was set on it. But then she glimpsed a sudden sense of freedom: she would be her own mistress, away from Father and his stinginess, away from this irksome cousin. Perhaps she would be able to be of use in the fur trade; after all, she had much experience to offer in business.

If Bradstone asked for her hand, she supposed she would agree. She felt a fleeting sense of loss, the sort of loss when a choice of a new hat is made and you suddenly realize that you can no longer have any of the other just-as-beautiful hats in the milliners.

Chapter 7

Zachary relaxed on his bed, arms tucked behind his head, and sighed contentedly. Perhaps his uncle had thought him so unused to the finer things of life that he would never notice gristle on the meat. But for once his supposed cousin Elspet had ordered a decent cut of venison, and there had been a plump braised partridge to go with it, not to mention a whole duck stuffed with onions and herbs.

All in honour of the Yorkshire fur-trader.

I could get accustomed to this, Zachary thought, easy as jacks.

When the conversation with Bradstone had got too dull, Zachary suggested that they played a hand or two of cards in Uncle Leviston's chamber, and his uncle readily agreed. Needless to say, Bradstone fluffed the bidding and lost without knowing why, and in the end Zachary had to deliberately lose so as to keep Uncle Leviston's face. Poor old soul, he was growing to quite like him.

Zachary undid the laces on his breeches to let his full stomach have a little more room, and pondered the evening's events. Bradstone was about as sharp as a feather bolster. Cousin Elspet was taken with him, though – why did women always go for well-wrapped fellows with nothing between their ears? It was a mystery.

When he told her to give Bradstone a bit of a chase, he wasn't expecting her to turn chilly so suddenly – he meant for her to tease him a little, not to turn cold as a trout.

He might be a bit short on stuffing, but at least Bradstone was keeping to the old faith and wasn't one of those who sway back and forth and never quite make up their minds. By the time Bradstone left, there was the beginnings of a match made, he'd stake his life on it, and it would not surprise him one jot if dear Cousin Elspet were to be wed and bedded before the end of the year. And God willing, it would fall sweetly for him too, then, for he could continue unharassed as Leviston's nephew.

He could get used to living at West View House, he really could. After Bradstone had gone home, Leviston confessed that Elspet was the child his wife had been expecting when he was born. His wife had tried over and over for a son, but the babes all died. When his wife had died after the birth of the last daughter, he had blamed himself.

'I felt God was punishing me,' he said. 'He would not give me a son with Agnes. And you haunted my thoughts. I visited you as often as I could, but after Agnes died I was so beset with remorse for my unfaithfulness that I simply could not search for you. Even though Magdalena... I mean your mother, begged me to.'

Only after his narrow escape from death by the plague had he begun searching, desperate to see how his only son had fared. 'I neglected you all those years,' he said. 'Now, I want to make amends.'

He looked at him with doting eyes. And Zachary could not help but warm under the glow of his affection, despite the feeling of guilt that niggled him. When his uncle left him, he took out the Calvary wood, worn smooth by his mother's touch, and rubbed it between his fingers. What would his mother think? That he had come upon his uncle so late?

From Elspet's earlier apology, and her conversation, he guessed she could not have had enough time to read his mother's letter. He felt for it now, where it was tucked inside the pocket of his breeches, out of sight of Elspet's prying eyes. He sighed, reassured. The parchment was still there.

Nevertheless, it would be as well if Elspet were provided for, and even sweeter if she were a few hundred miles away in Yorkshire. It was hard to keep a lid on his past, and she was sharp as nails.

A few days later, Zachary met Gin Shotterill in their old haunt, The Green Man, for the usual ratting. When the bout was over they watched the men lead their whimpering dogs away, tails curled like eels between their legs. Shotterill emerged from the crowd round the pit rails and handed over his winnings.

'Knew that brindled bitch was no good right from the start,' Gin said.

'Her ears were back even before she was let loose,' Zachary said. 'Still, that was a fine match with Thatcher's dog.'

'He peppers them beforehand. Makes 'em snarl. By the time they get in the ring they'd go for a bloody bear, if he'd let 'em.'

Zachary glanced to the corner, where the landlord of the tavern was bargaining over the dog, trying to do a deal. The dog was straining at its collar, teeth bared, eyes on the make-shift pit where a few pathetic rats still writhed on the bloodstained boards.

'Do you not fancy a dog, Deane?'

'No,' he said. 'Not for the moment, anyhow. Can't see Uncle Leviston abiding another dog. They've got two already.'

'What's he like, your uncle?'

'Niggard-pursed. Hard to get him to open his palm for decent food and beer.'

'Still, you've got a better billet than before. Can't complain, can you? I can't get over it, you being related to a man like that.'

'Hmm.' Zachary had told Gin the bare minimum. The less he knew, the less likely it would be he'd slip up.

'You don't seem very keen,' Gin said. 'What's the matter?'

Zachary weighed his words. 'Nothing. I suppose he's all right – if you like pulpit bashers. But I tell you, it's a strain having to mind my manners – not to spit or swear because there are ladies present, and to unbuckle and leave my swords in the hall every time I go in or out.'

'Ladies? What sort of ladies?'

'Not that sort. My cousin.'

Gin elbowed him in the ribs, and grinned, eyebrows raised in question.

Zachary warned him, 'Now don't get any ideas.'

'Go on, what's she like?'

'Too tall, too serious, and too attached to her rosary beads for you.'

'Oh. One of those.' They threw on their cloaks and made for the door, stepping around the crowded tables, and out into the fresh air. Immediately they were outside there was a high-pitched yell from a street trader. Zachary turned in irritation.

'Mounseer Lagardy, finest fencer in the whole of France!' A young lad thrust a handbill into Gin's grasp.

'What's it say?' He passed it to Zachary.

He glanced at the title. 'Hark at this! *Tonight at eight of the clock,*' he read, *'at Hanging Sword Alley, by the Signe of the Fish Hook, Monsieur Lagarde will demonstrate his Schoole of Defence: The Sword and Dagger, The Short Sword and Gauntlet, The Single Rapier and The Case of Rapiers. Fencers are invited to try their skill against Monsieur Lagarde and his fearless students on this Field of Honour.'*

'How's your mettle, Deane?'

'Not too bad. Been doing a few hours a day.'

'You going to have a go? He might be good.'

'What do you think?'

Gin slapped him on the shoulder and laughed. Without a word they set off towards Hanging Sword Alley.

The Alley was not the easiest place to find for those who didn't know it – it being just a crack in the wall near to Water Lane by the Thames. They had to press their weapons close to their sides to even get by. The sign of the Hanging Sword was jammed crookedly between the buildings at a perilous angle. It looked as though it might tumble at any moment and cosh someone, but as yet it never had.

Once through the needle's eye, though, the place seethed with young bloods, lounging against the walls or perching on the ale benches outside the taverns. On each house swung a sign with the fencing master's insignia – the fighting bull, the rampant lion, or swords crossed in diverse ways.

They walked past the sign of the fighting stags where Zachary's old master Signor Pietro had his school, and on to The Fishhook, where they turned right into a walled courtyard. Fish were unloaded and gutted there when it was not being used for fencing. The cobbles were slimy with fish entrails and the place stank enough to peel the inside of a man's nose. Two lads in twill jerkins were brushing over the yard with straw and sawdust. Zachary and Gin stood to watch them work, along with a few others awaiting the entertainment.

Gradually a crowd gathered. The wall sconces were lit against the approaching dark. A few men impatiently stepped from foot to foot, or circled their shoulders, warming their muscles.

'They don't look much.' Zachary nudged Gin, who made a derisive snort. Zachary recognized the hangers-on from other bouts. They were puffers, most of them, and despite this attempt to impress the onlookers, most were endowed with more brawn than wit.

A commotion in the crowd, was followed by a shout and a flourish as the man Zachary presumed to be Monsieur Lagarde strolled in, accompanied by two or three mealy-mouthed apprentices carrying his arms. Zachary took note of Lagarde's yellowish complexion and wispy beard, assessing his form. He was a man of about forty years old with two frown lines scored vertically between his eyebrows, presumably from screwing up his eyes too hard.

Lagarde bowed to the audience who stamped and clapped lustily. One of his youths stepped forward to introduce him, in a thick French accent, and relieved him of his cloak, before handing him a rapier. Lagarde leapt into a low stance and twirled and brandished the blade in a show of speed and bravado.

The crowd laughed and jeered, but he ignored them as he and one of his students began a match designed to show off his skill. Zachary sighed and shook his head. Lagarde fought well enough, but then so would he, if his student conceded every point and left himself wide open for his thrust.

'Hey, will you look at that!' Zachary protested, outraged. 'He let him win!' He turned to Gin. 'It's just a bloody dumb-show. Men like that make me mad. I could do better than that with one hand tied behind my back.'

'Calm down,' Gin said. 'What did you expect? A fight to the

death? It's entertainment. He's got to please the crowd, and he's a living to make, like all of us.'

In front, a man jumped forth from the crowd and spat on the ground. Lagarde, though a little breathless, accepted the challenge and Zachary and Gin pressed nearer to see what would come of it.

They fought noisily with rapier and dagger, neither with much skill as far as Zachary could see and, with a lucky strike, Lagarde thrust the point of the dagger through the challenger's shoulder. A cheer went up. Zachary groaned.

'The Frenchman prevails!' shouted someone.

'Not bad,' Gin said.

'Fake!' Zachary shouted. He could not help but remember the movement of that white-haired foreigner in the tavern near St Paul's, his swooping sword, and the strange Spanish technique he said was called *La Verdadera Destreza*. The words were embedded in his memory; he had repeated them so often lest he forget the name. It meant The Skill, and that foreigner would have whipped this bandy-legged Frenchman and not even broken sweat. It made him angry that charlatans such as Lagarde should take money from gullible folks for lessons.

'Who's next?' called one of the young men.

Zachary propelled himself forward.

Gin Shotterill's hand reached out to stop him but Zachary dodged it, and jumped into the open space. He paced round Lagarde, taking advantage of the breathing room, his rapier fixed steady between them. Now he could see the Frenchman's eyes, and they were narrow and determined. But Zachary riposted with his most penetrating stare, and Lagarde quavered. His eyes still on Zachary, he threw away his rapier and dagger and a youth ran up and handed him a long sword.

'Two-hand sword, is it, you want try?' Lagarde said.

'If you wish,' Zachary called back, coolly.

Lagarde was trying to catch him short, but Zachary called his bluff and he, too, threw off his arms.

Gin Shotterill appeared from the front row and gathered up Zachary's tackle. 'Be careful,' he called.

Zachary glared back at him. 'Someone hand me a long-sword!' he shouted.

A long-sword bobbed and danced over the heads of the crowd. Zachary grabbed hold of it to find it much weightier than his own, and badly balanced; the edge toothed as if it had been used for hacking wood. He hoped he could wield it. He wanted to make this Frenchman eat the dust.

He brought the sword up over his shoulder, and swung it around his head a few times. His arm muscles burned. The crowd gasped in excitement, for he was short, and the sword was a monster of a thing.

He and Lagarde circled each other. The Frenchman made the first pass and Zachary leapt nimbly out of reach. Whilst Lagarde recovered Zachary swung the blade overhead and let the momentum slice it towards his opponent's poll. With a grunt he hauled it back up at the last moment so the tip just touched Lagarde's head with a little tap.

Lagarde staggered backwards looking up, and placed his hand to his hair in puzzlement. The crowd laughed. Zachary turned to them, grinned, and waved his free hand in a flourish.

Lagarde was rattled. He lunged clumsily with the point of his sword, but Zachary dodged sideways and the blade struck forward into empty air. As he passed, Zachary was able to turn the flat of his blade and neatly spank him on the backside.

The crowd went wild, cheering and laughing. Lagarde turned to see where the blow had come from, making the crowd guffaw even louder. His mouth began to tremble and his breath escaped in a wheeze. He ran with a yell, all control gone, and sliced a glancing diagonal towards Zachary's shoulder. It clashed against Zachary's blade and sent a jolt like a lightning strike up into Zachary's shoulder. For a moment they tussled there, locked together until Zachary wrestled his weapon free.

Having the advantage, Zachary pursued him with the sword threshing side to side. But Lagarde backed away, fearful now, holding his blade out like a cross until his back was up against the wall. Intent on more sport, Zachary gave a trim flick and Lagarde's sword flew from his hand and clattered to the ground.

Zachary lifted Lagarde's doublet with his point, 'Hey, won't you take a look, his knees are knocking together!'

The crowd let out a cheer, but the cheer turned into boos, as a hand coiled around Zachary's neck and something stung him through his sleeve. He twisted round.

One of the French student had pushed his face right up against his own, ire burning in his cheeks. A dagger in his hand dripped blood. '*Arrêtez!* Enough!' the lad hissed, trying to prevent Zachary from humiliating his master further.

'You dog!' Zachary cried, looking in amazement at his arm where blood was soiling his sleeve. 'This was supposed to be a fair fight! You cut me from behind!'

A yell of protest from the audience. Straightaway, Gin and a throng of men from the crowd launched themselves forth and set to beating about the youth. From the corner of the yard more of Lagarde's students leapt to join the fray.

Zachary whooped. A fine battle had burst out, with each man desperate to see some of the action. The yelling and commotion drew folk from the rest of the alley and soon the whole yard was afire with everyone trying to whack Lagarde and his students. Zachary took on the nearest lad who was slashing wildly with a billhook. Just when he was about to pinion the lad to the wall, a shove from behind landed Zachary face down in the yard. The fish smell nearly choked him and he scrabbled to stand up.

His nose was bloodied and his doublet smeared with slime. The man he had been fighting was gone. Incensed, he darted about the yard looking for Lagarde, but he was nowhere to be seen.

He ran up to Gin, panting. 'The yellow dog. He's left his scholars fighting his cause. What a rogue. Look at his men, though, you can tell he's got no skill.' He pointed to where some of the French students lay groaning on the ground.

A warning volley of fire threw everyone into a panic.

'Quick.' Gin Shotterill grabbed his arm. 'Out through the tavern!' A group of the King's men had sealed off the yard.

They sheathed arms and dodged inside the fusty dark of the inn. They crashed past the tables towards the door, but when they got there it was barred by two more of the King's men. They turned tail and headed back to the yard but there were men bristling with pikes at the back door too.

An officer pointed a pistol at them. 'Drop arms! You are the cause of this, they say.'

'Not so, sir. It was Lagarde's boys – look, he went for me.' Zachary showed them the gash in his sleeve, the velvet mushed with blood.

'No matter, nimble Jack. You are under arrest. You will come with us to Marshalsea and the magistrate will decide who's at fault here. You too.'

'Good sir,' said Gin Shotterill straight off, 'I can pay. Here, my purse. I was innocent of blame. You can ask around. He is the one who fought with Lagarde, ask anyone.'

Zachary shook his head. Trust that turncoat Shotterill to blame him.

'What do you say?' The officer turned to one of Lagarde's men who was squinting round the tavern door.

'Yes. Not him. It was that one.' He pointed at Zachary. 'He fight with Monsieur Lagarde. He is the maker of the trouble. See what he has done to my face.' He touched a finger to a long wound down one cheek, and grimaced.

'All right,' said the King's man, taking Shotterill's purse. 'Get out of here.'

Shotterill slipped away like the devil.

'A thousand thank-you's to you too!' Zachary yelled after him. 'Bloody weasel.'

As Zachary was led away the crowd of young men doffed their hats to him. Like him, they knew skill when they saw it and, like him, they had seen too many rash claims and not a one proved in combat. Zachary had lost his rapier, but he held his head up high and saluted with a wave of his buckler, his righteous pride a keener sensation than the gash in his arm. He only wished his brothers could have seen him.

Chapter 8

'What is it, Father?' Elspet said.

His face was marble-white. He came back to the table and supported himself on it as he lowered himself down into the chair, the letter in his hand.

'Zachary. I thought I did not hear him come in last night. They've arrested him.'

'Are you sure? What for? What does it say?'

'*Your nephew Zachary Deane was arrested last night and has been taken to Marshalsea.* It's been written by a scrivener, and I can barely make out the signature – looks like *Shotterill* – whoever he is. Broadbank says the messenger boy ran off before he could question him.'

'You don't think—'

'I don't know what to think. But I must go there directly.' He scraped his morning correspondence into a pile and stood up.

'Finish your meat and bread first, Father.'

'No.' He paced the room. 'If he's been arrested because of the Faith, then we could all be at risk. Father Everard is with us this week, as you know.' Agitation had taken hold of him; he screwed up his napkin between his fingers. 'What if they saw us coming out of Bainbridge's? It could all be my doing. Martha, the shutters!'

Martha hurried over and closed them sharply against the day.

'Go and tell Father Everard to go to another safe house. Anywhere but here or Bainbridge's. And put everything into the priest hole,' he said. 'Quickly now. Martha, tell Broadbank to saddle my horse.'

Father hurried out into the hall, his sleeves still flapping as he hadn't had time to fasten them. A few moments later, she heard the sound of his boots and caught a glimpse of him as he bundled his cloak around his shoulders. The dogs barked in the hall at the sound of the door opening, and he shouted, 'Get back, Jakes! Leave it.' There was a yelp, then silence once more descended on the house.

Elspet hastened to Father Everard's chamber and knocked hard on the door. The priest opened it, and she began breathlessly, 'My Father says—'

'Oh no. Again?' Father Everard's face fell.

She shook her head. 'I'm afraid so. My cousin Zachary's been arrested and we don't know why. Best to be safe. Is there somewhere you can go? Not Bainbridge's, though.'

'I suppose I must try Lady Gawthorpe.'

'Here, I'll help you.' The poor man had not even broken his fast and already he was stuffing his tracts and papers into the panniers that stood waiting by the door. By the time he had taken his travelling cloak from the peg, Broadbank had appeared to help him lug everything downstairs.

'Oh, what a day for it,' Father Everard said, glancing out at the sheeting rain. 'I've never known such a wet spring.'

'I'm sorry,' she said, and embraced him. 'I'll miss our lessons whilst you're gone.'

'And I.'

'I hope you will be back with us soon. Father will write to you at Gawthorpe Hall.'

'My prayers are with your father, and with your cousin,' Father Everard said, bowing to her. 'I hope, for all our sakes, he has a tight tongue.'

Could Zachary be trusted? She did not know. 'God speed,' she said as the priest hurried away, 'and God bless.' But the priest was holding his hat to his head and did not hear her.

Poor Father Everard, she thought, always going from hearth to hearth at the least provocation, and with never a place to call home.

She passed the window on her way down to the cellar steps, and caught sight of the priest's bowed figure trotting away on his mule, face turned to the side against the rain and wind, one hand still clamped to his hat to stop it blowing off.

Elspet and Martha ran down to the cellar and bundled everything into a basket. She did not have time to fold the altar cloth but just used it to cushion the chalice and the other fragile things. Heaving aside the stone slab that formed the second lintel of the chimney was a struggle, and Martha, being the smaller, squeezed through the narrow gap.

Elspet thrust Martha the gold cross, the statue of the virgin, the candlesticks, and the missal on its cherub-carved stand. In her hurry they had become weights of wood and plaster, metal and paper, not holy things at all. Her heart beat fast as she climbed in with Martha to help her cover everything over with a dust sheet.

Was this all it was, their faith? How could it have become so reduced? From fine stone monasteries and vaulted aisles to a few paltry ornaments stuffed up a chimney?

She felt suddenly suffocated in the tiny space. The priest's hole was airless and reeked of dusty masonry. She pushed her way out of the gap and into the room, yet when she and Martha shunted the stone slab closed it was as though they were closing the door on their souls.

Martha looked up, like a frightened wren. 'They'll not come for us too, will they, mistress?'

Elspet gave a reassurance she did not feel. 'No, we've done nothing wrong. But we don't know yet what's afoot. We are taking precautions; that is all.'

'But what will happen?'

'Nothing, I hope. No one will have told anyone Father Everard was here, and he will be safe with Lady Gawthorpe. It will be a false alarm like we had once before, and we will all go back to our duties as usual.'

'But—'

'Thank you, Martha, you may go.' The maid shook her head and hurried away.

Elspet spent the day on the household orders, but was distracted by any little noise and the figures in the ledgers would not tally. Late in the afternoon, the sound of horses alerted her to Father and Zachary trotting into the yard.

'Thank God,' she murmured. The dogs barked, and scratched at the door. 'Only Father,' she shushed. She picked up Diver to fondle his ears and pulled back the drapes to look out of the window.

Father dismounted and led his horse towards the stable, limping as usual from his old hip injury which had turned aguey. Zachary slid clumsily off Father's new skittish horse and handed the reins to Broadbank. The horse tried to nip him but Broadbank hauled it away.

She moved away from the window. She had seen enough. Zachary was bruised again and a dirty blood-soaked bandage was tied around his upper arm. He walked as if he was an old man with a limp and stiffness in his joints. A night in the Marshalsea had obviously done him no favours. He did not turn to speak to Father, who was following him.

She bounded down to the hall to take her father's cloak. By the time she got down, there was no sign of Zachary; he must have gone to his chamber.

'You look terrible,' she said, taking her father's arm.

'It's all right,' Father said, waving away her concern. 'He was not arrested for the Faith.'

'Then why?'

'For fighting.'

She pressed her lips together. 'I thought as much. Oh Father. I sent poor Father Everard away, and now he's gone to Gawthorpe Hall. He had such a long-suffering face when I told him to go, like a dog put out of doors. And all for nothing.' She shook her head and hooked an arm in his to lead him to the drawing room where she had bade Martha light a fire.

Father sat before it and his fingers trembled as he unbuttoned his cloak. Obviously coping with Zachary was too much for him. Indignation rose in her. She fetched a glass of port wine and placed it in his hand.

'It's not to be tolerated,' she burst out. 'The whole household in turmoil, dreading the worst. Poor Father Everard feared for his life! And all for nothing, just that wastrel, brawling again. Zachary's running you ragged, Father. Is there no place else he can stay?'

'No, Elspet. He stays here.' He would not look at her. 'He is our kin, and I have a duty. I promised his mother.'

'Beg pardon, Father, but he takes no thought of you, he sends no message when he's to be late – he didn't even apologize when he failed to arrive for the meeting at the Lace Guild the other day. He was brought home half-drunk after a duel. And now he's locked up for brawling in the street. What will folk think of us?'

'It was not his fault, it was a Frenchman who started it.'

She let out an exasperated sigh. If he believed that, then he was more of a fool than she thought. 'What did the arresting officer say?'

'Nothing. I've already said, it was a general affray. Zachary says he was caught up in it, that's all.'

She felt suddenly as if she were the parent and he the child. 'You look tired, Father. You wait up for him every night, and he is always well after the watch. Is there perhaps some useful task you could put our cousin to, something for the business? Some education that will keep him occupied of an evening?'

The atmosphere changed in an instant as he snapped back, 'Do not be impertinent. What do you think? That we should lock him up here and give him a catechism to learn? Fie on you, Elspet. Let that be an end of it. He is settling, that is all, and we must learn to be tolerant. Young men get in the occasional scorching, it's only natural. Women don't understand. Now, leave Zachary to me and go and check that someone has walked those blasted dogs. They are getting out of control.'

She bowed her head and left him. There was no reasoning with him in this stubborn mood. Of course, there was still no word from Zachary himself, not a whisper of apology for the worry and trouble he had caused. Why, even the servants were on edge, thinking the whole household might be clapped in irons. Did Zachary give a fig for all that? Oh no, he was probably lying in his chambers like a king, sleeping off his ale-head.

84

A week later, Father called her into his chamber to talk. He had done nothing about Zachary's behaviour in all that time. Her cousin continued to keep his own erratic hours and have Father run after him like a serving wench. But she was glad she would have the chance to reason with Father once more. It felt good to see his cluttered desk again, his lace-stuffed drawers that would not quite shut, and his dusty, rolled parchments poking from overfull chests. She had missed his company.

'I have made a decision,' he said, once she had sat down. 'Perhaps I was a little hasty in dismissing your idea of an education for Zachary.'

Elspet clasped her hands in her lap and smiled at him. At last, he had seen sense and realized that she was right after all.

Father wrapped his fur-trimmed robe more closely around him. The fur was frayed at the collar. It made her think of Hugh Bradstone. She repressed the disappointment that he had not asked them to dine in return for their hospitality, even though the thought of that dinner made her grimace with embarrassment. She recalled her clumsy attempts at conversation, and how she had tried to follow her cousin's ill-conceived advice. It was hardly surprising Hugh Bradstone had not invited her out.

Father cleared his throat. 'This afternoon I met with my friend Tenter; we had some business to do and met in the Black Swan. He tells me his son is undertaking a Grand Tour. Apparently, it is part of a gentleman's education these days, to travel a little and see our neighbours and colonies, make contacts and learn other languages.'

Her heart leapt in hope. 'I, too, have heard people talk of this. So Will Tenter is going on a Grand Tour. Are you going to ask if Zachary may accompany him?'

'No, Tenter's son is quite unsuitable company.' Father looked at her as if she were crazed. 'He is only a mercer. No, I will send him. Zachary and I will plan the Tour together. He can go to Italy, to Rome. Even to the Vatican! And to Paris, for the Cathedral, and to visit the abbeys and monasteries of France. Perhaps take my greetings to Joan. It will strengthen his faith, round off his rough edges. And he can go to the Low Countries and to Brussels where we barter – it will give him an edge in society, prepare him for his life as a master of trade. And when he returns home to us, he will be more mature.'

She reeled from this list of destinations. Father had always been a bit of a miser. He could not help it. Her mother had always wondered where the money went to, since he paid a pittance to their servants and domestic staff. Now he was employing no tutor but the priest for her Latin and Spanish lessons, yet here he was, planning to spend what must amount to a small fortune on that ne'er-do-well of a cousin.

'But such a Tour, that will cost you dearly, will it not?' Her voice was unexpectedly choked.

'It will be expensive, yes. But I look upon it as an investment, to ensure the future of the business. And was it not your own idea? And a good one too. I have thought it over and you are right, my dear. All he needs is a little education.'

'But not this!' she burst out. 'Not this, where he is rewarded with such an undeserved gift. I meant something where he would work hard, be of some use!'

'He will work hard. He will be working for me.'

'But you will not be there, Father. You will not be there to see how he spends your coin gambling, whoring and fighting.'

'Enough.' He stood, and she knew with horror that she had overstepped the mark. It was as if everything was happening very slowly; time's wheel had stopped spinning. His tone turned icy. 'I will not hear such uncouth words from your lips. You disappoint me. I thought that I had raised an obedient and mannerly daughter. Would you had listened better during your own education; it might have made you less mean-tempered.'

She stiffened. 'Beg pardon, Father, I spoke out of turn.' She waited, pulling on the lace of her cuffs, but he drew himself upright and turned his back deliberately to her. Slowly he took down a ledger from his shelf. She tried again, 'I am sorry. It was unforgiveable. I spoke in anger, without thought. I apologize.'

She agonized for a few more minutes, but his back was still a wall between them and the bristling atmosphere remained, like a ditch of pikes. After a little while longer there was nothing to do but to tiptoe away. She closed the door. He did not call after her.

Of course, Zachary was like the cock of the roost when Father told him. He smiled, fit to crack his cheeks. It gave her a tight feeling in her chest to see her father's evident delight in his pleasure.

'Will you have me bring my embroidery down so we can sit together, Father?' she asked him, for they had barely exchanged two words since Zachary came out of Marshalsea, and she wanted to try to reason with him again. It was as if the sun shone only on Zachary, and she was left in the shadow.

'Not tonight,' he said. 'Finish your embroidery. I want to begin working out the best route through the cities of Normandy. Zachary will want to see the cathedrals. He will be leaving in less than a month and we still have so much preparation to do.'

She almost laughed. It was not Zachary who wanted to see those cathedrals, but Father. She would stake her life on it. Thank the Lord her cousin would soon be gone. By all that was holy, she could not wait for that day.

Over the next week, Father was like a man possessed, plotting with Zachary in his study, the heat of his enthusiasm perspiring on his brow. She kept her distance, but it was sad to see him living vicariously through Zachary, as though he could reclaim his youth just by being in the same room and rubbing shoulders with him.

And she could not help but note Zachary's barely disguised boredom when Father began one of his little lectures. Father loved to instruct, and make long soliloquies on the discourses of Greek philosophers, the science of the Italians and the great print-workers and bookbinders of Europe. And his passion was re-doubled now that he could talk of the architecture and cities where these men lived.

But still, she could not feel sorry for Zachary, however hard she tried. She'd lost track of how often he had kept them hungry. She was sure that when he was supposed to be trading for her father he was up to no good – the cuts in his clothes, his air of false nonchalance that told her he had been out with his good-for-nothing friends, not doing Father's business as he would have had them believe.

She was driven to distraction by their maps and papers, their talk of Paris and Antwerp and Cadiz. The board in the dining hall had a hand-penned map spread out in four sections, showing the pilgrimage routes of France and Spain. Next to it sat an itinerary in Father's tight hand detailing sea passages and coach stages, and the names of his business contacts.

Once, when the pair of them went out to the offices and the warehouses, she creaked open the great-hall door and went in to pore over their plans, to trace the routes with her finger on the map. She felt the raised ink where her father had scratched the route, and she recited the foreign names to herself. It was a kind of torture, like rubbing a wound, to put her finger on all the places she would never see, and yet she could not help herself.

She opened Father's ledger, and read out the long list of names like an incantation. Magical places, places she had heard of from the Spanish priest who had spent a long time living with them when she was a child. Father Pelé – she remembered his way of chanting Latin with his eyes upturned towards the heavens, his feet rocking slightly on to his heels. And his tales of the other Roman Catholic countries where the great feasts still took place under the stars on warm, balmy nights.

Nantes, Rennes, Padua, Assisi, Venice, Santiago de Compostela and Zaragoza, where Our Lady was transported to heaven by the angels. Father Pelé had told her of the street processions, the crush of the crowd as they shuffled along, the sweet smell of burning beeswax from the votive candles, the statues that wept real tears.

And Father used to sigh and his face turned sad. 'We had all that once here too,' he used to say, 'until that hatchet-man Henry dragged it down.'

Now Zachary would be part of it. He would see first-hand the stuff of her childhood dreams, be able to pray in frankincense-scented air, beneath soaring vaulted arches. She snapped the book shut. And she, Elspet, would be left reciting the empty words to the walls of the bare cellar downstairs. Still, it would soon be over. She exhaled a ragged sigh of relief. Zachary would take passage in a few weeks, she would get her Father back, and the house would return at last to normal.

Chapter 9

Miracle of miracles, Hugh Bradstone had invited Elspet to the theatre. When the letter came, she could hardly believe it. He said he was staying with a friend in London for a few days and wished to have the pleasure of her company. Martha dressed her in her second-best tawny silk and spent a long time braiding Elspet's hair under a jewelled cap – the only one she owned. She wore Mother's twisted gold and pearl drop earrings and for once she felt herself to be quite the lady.

The theatre was packed and the noise and stench of so many people was astonishing. She picked her way over the detritus of the previous afternoon's performance: plum stones, nut shells and discarded crumpled rags and papers. Mr Bradstone led her to a jute-curtained box overlooking the rabble, where they might enjoy the atmosphere and leave the noise and bustle below, where pie sellers and chapmen hawked their trade. She was on view to the crowd, and was proud to be in the company of such a good-looking man. The play was Dekker's *Mad Monk of Tomorrow* and very droll it was too. After checking that Mr Bradstone also found it to his liking, she laughed until her sides ached.

'Oh, look at that girl selling comfits,' she said during an interlude. 'She can hardly lift the tray.'

He did not offer to purchase any sweetmeats. 'They will be tainted,' he said, wrinkling his nose. 'I will take you afterwards to dine at a more reputable place.'

And so he did. He took her into an alcove out of view of the rest of the customers who were all men. The serving wench winked lewdly at him, and he told her not to be so impertinent.

As they dined on a simple meal of oysters and shin beef served on pottery plates, he talked of how much he was away, and of his estate. She had to do nothing but listen and smile and nod. He did not leave room for her to talk at all, so she listened, fascinated, to his descriptions of the hard life his trappers had, combing the frozen wastes of Quebec, and the easy lives of his men harvesting his acreage of barley in Tockton.

When they parted, he kissed her hand and then pressed it between his own. It amused her that Martha had watched them like a mother bird over her chicks. Martha remarked afterwards that he was 'quite the gentleman,' and it seemed a very apt description.

She had almost forgotten all about it until a few days later, when Father told her that Mr Bradstone had asked for her hand.

It was such a shock that she had to sit down.

'Now isn't that good news, Elspet dear? It is good to know you will be settled with such a suitable match.'

So soon? But she had met him only twice! She scarcely knew him. It gave her the most odd sensation, as if it were something happening to somebody else.

Eventually she said, 'Have you agreed it, Father?'

'Don't worry, of course I have.'

She nodded, amazed. A man such as Hugh Bradstone actually wanted to marry her. Why? She could not work out what possible advantage it gave him – except, of course, a share in Leviston's Lace.

For the rest of the day her heart seemed to flip in her chest whenever she thought of it, and everywhere she went folk smiled and bowed and offered their felicitations. Thanking them made her feel strange – as if she was thanking them for something to which she was not entitled. She had found Mr Bradstone an amiable enough companion, but she had expected a longer, more intimate courtship. This felt too quick, as if she was a basket of laundry to be handed over.

Father was, of course, delighted. He even broke open a dusty bottle of Malaga sack to toast her health, and she had to endure Zachary's smirking face as they raised their glasses to her good fortune and the alliance of Bradstone and Leviston.

Mr Bradstone, Hugh himself, wrote her a delightful letter expressing his 'deep happiness' that her father had agreed to the match. She spent a long time examining his narrow-shouldered writing, hoping it would tell her more about him. After she had read his words, she had a sudden urge to run away, but where could she go to? She could not even go to her sister Joan, for she had given up the outside world altogether.

She reasoned with herself; all young women must feel this. It was just the change of circumstances; that was all. Arrangements like this were common. She would get to know Hugh and they would grow closer, like all married couples did. Down in the kitchen, Goody Turner had some scones baking, and the smell drew her there. Such a homely smell. She lingered a while, petting Jakes and Diver and feeding them scraps of scone until Goody Turner looked so cross that Elspet had to slink away.

She did not expect to see Hugh again for a few days, as his letter said that he was going back to his estate in Tockton to make plans with his overseer for the summer planting and to prepare for their forthcoming visit. For now that the marriage was settled, Father had arranged for them all to travel to Tockton to meet Hugh's parents. She was aggrieved that Cousin Zachary should have to come too, but Father insisted he could not be left behind. Perhaps it was for the best – heaven alone knew what he might do if he were left to his own devices without Father's steadying hand. So – they were all to go, and she was consumed with curiosity about what her new home might be like. She was both looking forward to it and dreading it in equal measure.

By the middle of June, Father and Zachary were in a veritable lather of preparation. Maps and papers were scattered all over the house, whilst travelling trunks stood open by the back door for everyone to trip over. Their plans had advanced, as one of Father's ships was making a trade crossing to France the following week, and thank the Lord, Zachary had begged to be on it.

To impress their new in-laws, Father had allowed Elspet a bolt of dark blue dimity to make a new gown. In the candlelight it looked almost purple, a right regal colour. So involved in the sewing was she, that when the rap came at the door and Jakes ran to growl at it, she did not get up. Probably the costermonger, she thought.

Martha opened it, and Hugh's voice greeted the dogs, 'Get down, boy, get down, I say. Infernal nuisance.'

She jumped to her feet, 'Mr Bradstone! You must pardon my appearance,' she said, embarrassed, putting aside her work, 'I was not expecting you. I thought you had gone home to Tockton.'

'I delayed departing,' he said. 'There have been storms off the north-west coast from Ireland, and four vessels lost. I feared for my own, but thank God, it's safe. But I'm afraid I'm the bearer of bad tidings.'

'What's to do?' Father appeared from the door to his chamber, his cap askew, and his shadow, Zachary, at his shoulder.

'My apologies, Mr Leviston, Mr Deane, for this tardy call, but I've just heard four ships have gone down in the storm, the night before last. Can you believe this weather? I've never known a summer like it. Bainbridge's vessels were amongst those lost. Fifty-six men lost on his two ships, and two score more on the others.'

'Oh my Lord.' Father's face went white. 'Does Bainbridge know?'

'He's taken it very badly. All his Irish linen and hemp. His whole autumn stock lost. He was relying on it, and his trade will not survive another blow like this. He lost one in last year's spring bluster, did he not?'

'Is it really that bad?' Zachary asked. 'Bainbridge never struck me as being short of a silver penny or two.'

'They say he'd taken out a loan to fund it,' Hugh said.

'Really?' Father's voice sounded hollow. He swayed slightly on his feet.

'He was hoping it would make up for the last loss. Now he'll have to sell his house, like as not, and even that might not cover it.' Hugh turned to Zachary. 'Word's out that his creditors are already circling.'

'I can't believe it. Four ships lost, you say.' Father sat down, but almost missed the chair. Hugh rushed forward to assist him.

'Poor beggars,' Zachary said. 'Could nobody help them?'

'Elspet, leave us to talk,' Father commanded.

'I would rather stay.'

'Men's talk,' Zachary agreed.

When she did not go, Hugh looked up at her, surprised. 'I would do as your father asks, Elspet. These are tales and deeds unsuitable for a gentlewoman's ears.'

'Do not fret. I will send Martha to fetch you before Mr Bradstone departs,' Father said.

'Excuse me, then, gentlemen.' She curtseyed reluctantly. Hugh was only trying to protect her, for sure, but it was frustrating to be always on the wrong side of the door when something occurred. She banged it shut more loudly than she had intended.

Martha heard it go, and came up from the kitchen, a question on her face. Elspet put her fingers to her lips, in a gesture of silence. Martha grinned, putting her hand over her eyes to indicate she would see nothing and went quietly back below. Elspet crept back to the door and, holding on to the brass handle, put her ear up to the crack.

The voices were muffled but she could hear them well enough. She heard that the sea stood higher than the masts, that Bainbridge's master saw a light and thought it to be a warning. But the gale beat the ships on to the rocks, and that only three hands survived, clinging to barrels of potash. The light had been a Judas light, set by the wreckers to lure them there on purpose. When the sailors' broken bodies were washed ashore they were given no burial, but left to rot, whilst the wreckers filled their sheds with their pickings of tar and cudbear dye, linen and linseed.

Bainbridge had lost everything. The sea had claimed it all, and what the sea had not taken, the wreckers had. Bainbridge and his creditors would likely finish in the debtor's prison.

She leaned her back against the wall next to the door, lightheaded. This was not some unknown they were talking of, but a friend of Father's. It had come too close to home, this wrecking. It was the first time she had realized how precarious their business was. Everything lost, at the whim of the sea! She blew quietly through her mouth to calm herself.

'What of Mistress Bainbridge? How does she fare?' Father asked.

'I don't know. I could not gain admittance when I went to call,' said Hugh.

'She has sons to look to her, does she not?' Zachary's voice.

'Yes, but they are not at home,' came Father's wavering voice. 'They are in France. Bainbridge's whole stock gone . . . I can't take it in. Poor Margery. I feel duty bound to go tomorrow, to see if there's anything I can do.'

For once Zachary said something sensible. 'Leave it a few days. There were probably men on that ship Bainbridge knew and cared for.'

Elspet strained to catch her father's voice. 'I cannot bear to think of it. The Irish passage is the worst I know. Someone should go see if he has what he needs. And Margery Bainbridge will be distraught. I'll go tomorrow. What is Christian charity for, if it is not to stand by our friends in the Faith?' There was an uncomfortable pause.

'Without wishing to presume, Mr Leviston, Mr Deane is right. I really think it better to keep a distance,' Hugh said. 'We don't want to be caught up in Bainbridge's bad debts.'

Another silence. She could imagine her father's stubborn face. She wondered if he had turned his back on his guest.

The sound of footsteps moving in her direction on the wooden boards. She fled, sitting herself breathlessly before Father's desk. She swept up the household accounts ledger and pretended to study it. After what seemed an age, Martha arrived in a fluster.

'Oh there you are, mistress. I've been everywhere! Mr Bradstone is about to depart. They said to fetch you.'

'Thank you, Martha.'

'Excuse me, mistress, but what's to do?'

'Some ships have been lost in a storm, that's all.'

'Is it bad news? It's not the master's ships, is it?' Her worried eyes looked into Elspet's.

'No. Not ours. One of Father's acquaintances.' She was wary of telling Martha too much because the news would spread like wildfire in the servants' quarters below. Sometimes it was as though the servants were her children, and that she must protect them somehow from the burden of what she knew. She did not like this sensation; it made her feel sly that she could not simply confide in Martha. But Father always said that they must guard their business and keep it out of the servants' ears and eyes, so she stayed dumb.

Martha bobbed and went, and she hurried to the chamber where Hugh was preparing to depart, ready armed, with his cloak fastened on to his shoulders.

'Mistress Leviston. I know it is not a proper time to ask this of you – but I would be delighted if you would accompany me on a carriage ride tomorrow afternoon. Would you believe it, my servant had an accident in the old gig – a loose wheel overturned it. So before I trust myself to the long North Road home, I have had to purchase a new carriage. What do you say?'

She hesitated a moment, because she knew Father would be grieving for his friend's calamity. But Hugh pressed on. 'One of my friends, Mr James, has invited us to dine afterwards with himself and his wife Amelia. Please say yes.'

'That would be delightful.' She smiled up at him. She did not dare look at Zachary, who was watching the exchange with close attention.

'It is chilly, though, for the time of year, so wrap up well. Tell your maidservant to wear her winter cloak.'

'Never fear, I will.'

'I will call for you at one, then.'

She looked to her Father for his permission, but he was hovering, his eyes far-away, as if he was not really taking anything in.

Hugh turned to him. 'Pray do not get involved in Bainbridge's business. Wait a few days to see how circumstances fall out.' Father shook his head noncommittally. Hugh sighed, obviously realizing that it was a losing battle, and said, 'Well, then, I look forward to welcoming you all to Yorkshire soon. Zachary, there is fine hunting and riding there, and a good many birds to shoot an arrow at.'

'It sounds fine, but I'm afraid my plans for France have advanced. I will have set sail by then. I leave tomorrow on the early tide.'

'What a shame. Till tomorrow, then, Mistress Leviston,' Hugh said and took her hand, pressing it to his cool lips. 'Keep your Father home,' he whispered. 'He looks pole-axed by this news. And Mr Deane, I wish you safe travels and a speedy return.'

Zachary barely bowed.

Chapter 10

Well before dawn, Zachary heard Uncle Leviston barking instructions and servants crashing about with the luggage. He had packed the trunk he had come with himself, but Uncle Leviston had supplied him with a good deal more baggage. Last night he crammed a leather case so full of books and papers that it took two men to lift it even as far as the corner of the room. How on earth the old boy thought he'd be able to shift that Leviathan, with just a servant boy to help him, he had no idea.

After he had broken his fast as usual, he found his uncle in the hall, coughing and looking grey, but fussing over a further oilskin-lined trunk filled with rolled maps. He was stuffing it with papers about workers and lace-makers in Normandy, the place where Zachary was bound first.

'Pull harder,' his uncle told the servant hauling on the leather straps.

Cousin Elspet looked on sour-faced as Uncle handed him a new fur-lined cloak, and a purse full of coinage. He knew it must hurt; her father never gave her the means to buy new clothes. But with him, he'd been embarrassingly generous. He had even hired a coach to take them to the docks where his ship awaited them. The dogs barked and pulled at their leads on the doorstep as the carriage arrived. Elspet took control and handed them to Martha, who stood to attention with the rest of the servants. They waved briefly as he departed, in rain and wind that gusted sideways and blew into their faces.

When Zachary looked back at the doorway, the servants and dogs were gone and the door was shut against the weather. He would miss Jakes's lively eyes and wagging tail, and Diver's affectionate licks. His uncle and the dogs were the only ones who ever gave him a proper welcome. Cousin Elspet always looked disapproving, as though he smelt bad, and the servants whispered about him behind closed doors, but shut their beaks as soon as he entered the room.

Actually, he rubbed along with Leviston quite well. He'd got used to him. Leviston did not try to father him too much; he did not seem to know how. His idea of showing affection was to give him the benefit of his learning, and that was quite stimulating. He'd found out things from Leviston he knew little of before – philosophy, rhetoric, history. No, Leviston liked an audience, and Zachary had been more than happy to supply one in return for a soft life.

But there was no pang of regret at leaving, for although he wished it, it had never felt like home; he was too wary of being caught out. It had made him tense. He had always tried to change the subject when his uncle asked him about his previous life. He had not felt at home there. In fact, he had never thought of anywhere as home, he realized, not since his mother had died when he was only twelve.

He sat opposite Leviston, travelling backwards with Elspet beside him; she was pressed against the door as if to put a great distance between them. The servant boy travelled outside with the driver.

'What a day!' Leviston said.

He looked at Leviston and smiled. The old man patted him on the knee in return.

They were all soaked just from the journey from house to carriage. The hem of Elspet's dress was sodden, and her cloak dark on the shoulders. Leviston's hat dripped into his lap, for it was too windy to wear it. The news about the wreckings off the north coast hung over them like a pall. Today did not seem a good day to take passage.

Zachary put his misgivings aside. The odds were on his side, with ships lost so recently. And today he was off to France, where the weather would surely be better. And, what was more, he had heard that there was a craze for duelling over there, and he could not wait to try his hand.

Naturally, he hadn't told his uncle this. Best if he knew as little as possible about his real intentions – no sane man could follow the exhaustive itinerary his uncle had planned. Leviston was to join him next spring in Rome. The daft old fool, he could not resist it – the chance to preach and lecture him in the joys of Latin and the Holy Roman Empire. But he said he did not want to travel home again in the winter months. And who could blame him?

Zachary slammed down the leather blind as a squall of rain hit him in the face. Elspet brushed the wet from her skirt as if he was personally responsible for the weather.

When they reached the docks, an army of men were there to greet them and soon made short work of the luggage.

Leviston filled his ears with last-minute advice. 'Don't forget to call on M'sieur Corneille, and give him that sample I showed you.'

'I won't.'

'And you have the second map, the one that shows the—'

'Yes, yes. It's all here.' Zachary patted his satchel.

Leviston clapped him on the shoulder, and then in an awkward lunge reached out to clasp him to his chest. 'Go safe, my son,' he whispered.

'Goodbye, Uncle,' he said, out loud. 'See you next spring.'

Over his shoulder he saw Elspet looking on with distaste, as if she had swallowed something bitter, before she turned away to feign interest in the stevedores hauling bales of wool on to the pulleys.

'Say goodbye to your cousin,' Leviston said to her. He had still not brought himself to tell her that he was his father, much to Zachary's relief. To be cousin to Elspet Leviston was hard enough, let alone her brother. Especially when the whole damn thing sat on a lie.

'Goodbye, Cousin Zachary,' she said stiffly. 'I hope you will have a safe and speedy crossing.'

Yes, he thought. You cannot wait to have me gone. But he nodded and said, 'Give my regards to Mr Bradstone.' It was hard to keep the slight sting of mockery from his voice.

'Write,' said Uncle Leviston. 'Tell me everything.' His voice was almost a croak.

'I will,' Zachary called as he walked to the stairs. Damn; he was getting emotional.

Once aboard he stood on the deck to watch the men loading up the boat with crates of English pottery, cloth and ale. How much lighter the ship would be on its return, loaded only with lace and lavender from Brittany.

Leviston's cloak flapped in the wind, his white knuckles gripped his hat. His upturned face searched for Zachary in the crowd of those at the rails. Zachary dutifully brought out a kerchief to wave. There were many others on the quayside too, the wives of the officers and crew, all flapping their kerchiefs. Only Elspet was looking down, holding tight to her lace cap with one hand, keeping her hood up over her hair with the other. She stood stoically on the quay like an island. At last they departed. Elspet did not even look up, but turned sharply and headed towards the row of carriages.

For some reason Zachary felt insulted by this, until he caught sight of Leviston. Dear old Uncle. A wave of unexpected regret caught at his throat. There he was, jogging alongside on the quay, waving his pathetic little rag until he could go no further.

Zachary regained control of himself and breathed a sigh of relief. Freedom!

The servant boy came to tell him his cabin was ready, and the ship heeled against the waves. He staggered down to the cabin and peered through the wind-lashed port hole. Nothing but sea. He dismissed the servant and looked around the poky cabin at his fine new luggage and his polished leather arms case. Then he counted his purse, laying out the coinage in neat rows, amazed at his luck. Old Leviston was a good man, right enough. A good man but a foolish one. With a purse like this in his hand and a trunk of coin, not to mention all of the world at his feet, Uncle Leviston would be lucky if he ever saw him again.

Chapter 11

Elspet waited in the yard. With Zachary gone, the world suddenly seemed a more spacious place. Even the sun peeped out occasionally from behind the chasing clouds. When the carriage drew up, with its pair of matching bays, she smiled, enjoying the reactions of the servants to this new marvel. For Hugh's new carriage was indeed a beauty, built from ebonized wood on a red steel frame, and gilded with scrolls and fleurs-de-lis. The metalwork gleamed in the sun. Inside, it was furnished in luxury with comfortable goose-feather cushions. She congratulated herself; Hugh Bradstone was a man who, unlike Father, would not stint.

Even better, he had supplied a luxurious quantity of furs. Martha's eyes almost popped. There were sheepskins for under their feet and felt-cloth wraps lined in soft patched rabbit-skin. Such ostentation would never have been contemplated by Father, unless it was for Cousin Zachary, of course. She quashed a stab of envy at Zachary's good fortune and his uncanny ability to persuade Father to open his coffers.

Once in the carriage she chided herself for her uncharitable feelings, and counted her blessings – Zachary was on his way to France, and though she would never admit it to Father, she was heartily glad he was gone. Poor Father, she had left him grey-faced, roaming the house, picking things up and putting them down again with shaking fingers, as though unsure how he would occupy his time. She hoped Zachary would write as he had promised.

Hugh climbed in after checking that all was well with the horses. 'Are you comfortable?'

'Quite,' she said, as though she had been used to it all her life. She made up her mind to enjoy it all. It still held a sight unreality for her that she was to be married to this stranger, Hugh, who was even now smiling fondly at her from the opposite seat. His admiration for her was puzzling. He could have chosen someone dainty and pretty, the sort of girl who knew nothing of ledgers and never asked where the lace that trimmed her bonnet came from. Yet, instead, he had chosen her. She would please him by getting to know his business, and being a helpmeet there.

She glanced at him as the carriage moved off, at his even, sharply chiselled features and his well-cut breeches and doublet. She was curious as to what he was thinking. She wondered idly if he liked to read, or to play cards. Behind the façade of his good looks and his obvious good-standing in business, she knew little about him. But then she had noticed the same of all men, even Father. No matter how hard she tried, it seemed as though she fell into a void when she asked Father anything personal, as if she were asking him a conundrum he could not solve. Was it the same with all men? She was pondering this when Hugh smiled at her and pointed through the window.

'Look. They are ploughing manure into those sets already.'

She looked out. 'Oh yes,' she said, craning her neck as the ploughman receded from view. Though the wind was brisk, the sun gave a little tingling warmth to the side of her face. The journey took them into the countryside and it was delightful to see the little dabs of purple vetch in the verges, the tangle of dog-roses in the hedgerows. It was only then that she realized how free she felt without Father's criticizing presence. She stretched her lungs in a long, deep breath. Perhaps, after all, she would enjoy her new life in Yorkshire.

Hugh's friends, the Jameses, had a house by the river in Putney, close by the city, where after dinner the party could watch the craft go by on the Thames. Elspet had the disconcerting impression that Mr and Mrs James were weighing her up with every move she made, and it made her awkward and somewhat ill-at-ease, though she was sure they meant to be kind. Their house was highly polished. Everything was mint-new, with the plasterwork barely dry and not a speck of dust daring to make an appearance.

After dinner she and the mistress of the house, Amelia, retired to the marquetry-panelled parlour. Elspet examined with interest some flys Amelia was tying for Mr James's sport-fishing. She had a batch of tiny pigeon and woodpecker feathers in a hand-sized basket and showed her how she used small, bent wire hooks to fix them together in layers of grey and spotted.

'They are so pretty,' Elspet said. 'It seems such a pity to waste them on a fish.'

'True. I have a friend who has a sweet little bag covered in white swan-feathers, overlapped so...' and Amelia spaced a few out in a spiral shape. 'See. Though persuading them to lie flat is a lot of work, mind.'

'But worth the effort perhaps.'

They sipped at the warmed malmsey wine. Elspet tried to think of a suitable topic of conversation.

'Are you—?' They both spoke together.

'When are you two to be married?' asked Amelia.

'Oh, later in the summer, I think. The date has not yet been fixed.'

'Hugh is a sweet man,' Amelia said. Elspet picked up a slight sneer in her tone, as if she did not really think so at all. 'And he clearly dotes on you.' Elspet found herself blushing. 'But I feel I should tell you. You are not the first.'

'I did not expect I was.'

'No, you silly. I mean he has been actually engaged twice. Both times his father put his foot down. Said the girl was not good enough for his son.'

'But—'

And now Amelia leaned in, her eyes greedy, determined to tell her every last detail.

'Did you not wonder why he has not married? Why, he is over thirty! His mother tried her best, poor soul, but what can she do? The father puts his foot down at every suggestion. She despairs of ever having a grandchild. Such a sad thing.'

'I haven't met his parents yet. We are to go—' She paused and looked over her shoulder.

There was a disturbance in the hall. Amelia rose and put down the feather fly she was holding. But before she reached the door, it burst open and Hugh hurried in.

He grabbed hold of Elspet's hands. 'Elspet, your father . . . I think it might be best if I take you home.'

'What?' She peered out of the door, not understanding, half expecting to see Father there, but she saw only Broadbank, the groom; he was panting, with gobs of mud on his face and boots. 'Come in, Broadbank,' she called. 'What's the matter? Is he all right?'

'No, mistress. I mean, I rode as fast as I could, and the physician's with him, but—'

'Tell me!' She said this whilst Martha was already taking her by the arm into the hall and hustling her back into her cloak.

Broadbank followed after her, 'He went to see Goodwife Bainbridge and fell down all of a sudden; she had to send for the physician and they're bringing him home. The boy says...' Here he swallowed, and his lips worked but no sound came. She waited for the words. 'Sorry, mistress.'

She had no time to take this in. She let herself be moved like a puppet. Martha bustled her into the coach. Amelia James thrust her gloves through the window after her, where they landed on the floor. Hugh instructed the driver to push the horses and they lurched away through the darkening lanes back towards the Convent Garden. Nobody spoke. Hugh stared morosely out of the window as if uncertain what to say.

The black shadows of trees flashed past; the carriage jolted over the rutted track until she winced. One deep hole jounced her up so that she landed heavily and bit her tongue. She tasted blood as it flowed into her mouth but staunched it on her knuckles. Martha found her other hand and took hold of it, squeezing it tight as if to wring the pain away.

It was as if she was somehow suspended in a purgatory where the journey would never end, with the clatter of the wheels turning and the cracking of the coachman's whip in the looming dusk.

Amelia's words ran in her head too, like scattering mice at harvest when the scythe's coming. The idea of Hugh and other women had never crossed her mind. How ridiculous to be thinking of this at this time, when her father needed her. When finally she spied the lights of West View House, she almost wept with relief.

The carriage pulled up outside the house but the door was already standing open. She hardly waited for the wheels to stop before she was leaning out of the window trying to open the door. Broadbank, who had been galloping alongside all the way, wrenched it open and she half tumbled out and hurried within.

Before she had even crossed the threshold, she knew that Father was dead.

The servants were lined up in the hall, their faces grave. She had never seen them like this, and the passage was full of people. They bowed or curtseyed as she went past, and gestured silently upstairs. She ascended the stairs slowly now, quelling the desire to rush lest it seem disrespectful. She heard Martha sniffing behind her, but did not turn.

Father was laid out in his chamber still fully dressed. It was odd to see him lying on the bed with his best shoes still on, his good robe folded to cover his knees, his hands crossed over his chest. His white ruff pushed his beard up in a way she knew he would not like.

Hugh's head appeared around the door. 'Would you like—?'

'Go away.' Her voice sounded angry. She entreated him, 'Please, leave us alone.' Mercifully he went.

Goodwife Tyrwhitt from down the street got up from the dark recess in the corner and bowed her head.

'Was he shriven before . . .?' Elspet could not yet say the word.

'No, mistress. He was not.'

'Where is the physician?'

'We let him go, mistress. We had to, seeing as there was nothing more he could do, and someone came galloping for a woman in childbed. He didn't suffer, mistress. By all accounts he fell clutching his heart and it was mercifully quick. Won't you sit, mistress? We can pray together. We didn't know whether to fetch the parson, but we ordered the sexton to toll the bell.'

'No,' she said, rallying herself to give orders. 'No parson. I will arrange for prayers with one of father's friends.'

She nodded, as though expecting it. 'But for now, will you pray with me?'

Elspet moved away and knelt, and Goodwife Tyrwhitt got to her knees beside her.

She could not say the words. She heard them in her head, what she should say. *'Credo in Spiritum Sanctum, sanctam Ecclesiam Catholicam, sanctorum communionem, remissionem peccatorum; carnis resurrectionem, vitam aeternam . . .'*

I believe in the Holy Spirit, the holy Catholic Church, the communion of saints, the forgiveness of sins, the resurrection of the body, life eternal. She heard the sound of a dog whining downstairs.

St Joseph's bells began to toll to sanctify him, to ward off the spirits that might delay his flying soul. The sound of the passing bell was loud and terrible. She clapped her hands over her ears but it kept on tolling, as if to drum his passing into her head. His face was still and white and unmoving, despite the terrible din. It was then she knew he was gone, and she bent her head and wept.

Chapter 12

Father's funeral two days later was overshadowed by the memorial for Bainbridge's masters and ships' crews, held on exactly the same day. Most of Father's friends, anxious to watch the ghoulish entertainment of the sensation of the week, had decided to forgo his funeral and to go to the memorial service instead. So it was a depleted and sorry company that gathered to say their farewells and witness her father's final interment in the family vault.

Elspet had written to Joan that morning. She imagined her sister's sad face beneath her nun's veil, when she received the news. And she knew she must write to Zachary, Father would wish it, but at that time she felt she could not bear it. Besides, there was no urgency. Zachary was surely in France by now and could not have been reached in time to see Father laid to rest.

It was slow progress to the church with their sprigs of laurel and ivy. Of course the sun shone mercilessly that day. There were not enough men turned out to carry the bier, Father's coffin being made of walnut and heavy. Wilmot, the overseer from the warehouse, stepped forth, as did Greeting, Father's lawyer friend. Embarrassed, she went to ask Broadbank the groom and Greeting's manservant to act as the other pallbearers, unsuitably apparelled though they were.

Martha hurried to give them black gloves. They struggled to carry him forth, as Greeting had some infirmity and kept saying it really needed six, and they had to rest awhile every hundred yards.

She thought they would never get there.

At the church, Hugh was waiting in coal-black velvet with ribbons and a ruff starched to a knife-edge. He looked askance at the hastily assembled bier and the struggling pallbearers, and steered her down the aisle into the cold damp belly of the church. He opened the wooden gate and they slid into their family box pew, the pew they were obliged to keep by law.

He whispered to her, 'So few?'

She whispered back, 'The memorial service for Bainbridge's crews.'

'Oh. I see.'

The service was mercifully brief. She suspected it would have been longer had there been more in the pews. The sermon passed in a daze. She felt exposed in her front box with Hugh and she could almost feel the whispers on the back of her neck. She was under no illusions – the colleagues and servants who had pulled out their black wool and weepers to see Father buried were really there to get a glimpse of her future husband who would soon be in control of his estate.

When they arrived home, Martha had arranged full mourning duty so there were black gloves for all, which lay unused in a large heap on the hall table. Cakes and ale filled the board in the dining hall, yet even fewer came back to West View House for the repast. Mr Tenter, the mercer, had gone, and of Greeting there was no sign. The handful of mourners hovered around the laden tables picking at the food. No other relations were present, and few neighbours.

Father would have been distressed to see it.

Hugh approached Wilmot, whom he had met already. The conversation naturally turned to business, but she was too preoccupied to want to join their talk. She took a seat at the end of the table, feeling like a ghost herself.

Finally, Wilmot approached and said, 'I have closed the warehouses today as a mark of remembrance. You will wish the trade to carry on tomorrow as usual, will you?'

'I expect so. Do what you think is best. My father trusted your opinion.'

'You are most kind. I take it you will wish trade to continue –

under your orders, or those of your future husband of course.'

'Yes, yes.' It was as though she was thinking underwater. She agreed simply because it was easier than to organize her thoughts.

'Good. We will carry on exactly as if Mr Leviston were still there, until you are ready to instruct us. Greeting seems to be in somewhat of a hurry – he has invited all the beneficiaries of your Father's will to assemble at his chambers, so I will see you the day after tomorrow. As executor, he tells me he has written to your cousin already to inform him of your father's death.'

'How kind,' she managed. Wilmot continued to look at her, so she said, 'It is a shame Mr Greeting could not stay, for I see we have enough biscuit here to feed half the city.'

'Then if you don't mind me saying, why not do so? I know the custom of funeral dole is a little out of favour, but it would be better than it going to waste. And it would show generosity on your part and increase your father's good name.'

'I suppose so, it's just—'

'I know. It's too much to think of. Don't worry, I'll organize it. Show me to the kitchen.'

Elspet gave a nod to Martha, who led him below stairs.

Whilst he was gone, Hugh came to say his farewells for he was to travel that night for some business in York. 'Are you all right?'

'I'll manage,' she said.

'I'm sorry to leave you, but I'm afraid I cannot delay. It took my father six months to set up this meeting with the furrier's guild.'

She was disappointed he was leaving. She needed someone there, for what exactly, she did not know, just someone to be there.

'I will come back as soon as ever I can,' he said.

She went to the hall with him and he embraced her, holding her tight to his chest. She was aware that the whole assembly was looking at them through the open door from the dining hall, so she pulled away.

'Send a message when you have met with Greeting,' he said.

'Yes,' she said, 'the day after tomorrow, so I'll write perhaps the day after that. Soon, anyway.'

'God bless and keep you.' Hugh kissed her hand.

She took her handkerchief from her chatelaine, feeling somewhat tearful, and watched him head out of the front door to his waiting carriage. The chief of the mourners then made their excuses to be gone, seeming to take Hugh's departure as a cue.

But Wilmot was as good as his word. Before long, a trestle draped in black had been erected outside on the green with black escutcheons and drapes hastily pulled from inside. Great torches were lit against the impending dark. The servants, clad in their black gloves, cheerfully dispensed the dole to a great crowd, who had been drawn by the ringing of a large hand-bell. Even the poorest of them feasted on spice cakes and tit-bits of dried fruits washed down with burnt claret or Malaga sack.

Elspet saw the servants' flushed and merry expressions from the window, as they jested with their wives and neighbours in the light of the setting sun. Why do they never show *me* those faces? she thought.

As she watched, a straggle-haired woman from the widow-house nearby raised up her cup and shouted, 'A toast to Mr Leviston, a fine and generous gentleman as ever there was!' And she set to dancing, hitching up her skirts and persuading the next person to cling to her apron, till all were dancing in a long snaking line.

Elspet looked out, troubled. Pray God the stone was pressed safely down on the grave in the chancel, for if not, Father would surely be turning in it.

Chapter 13

'So sorry, my dear.' Greeting pointed vaguely in the direction of the vacant chair in front of him.

Elspet dipped her head to the assembled gentlemen and made her way past the knot of chairs and curious glances. She knew her eyes were still red with crying, but hoped the veiled cap shadowed her face.

There was little room to stop to exchange a word, for there were already a number of others bottled together in the stuffy upstairs room for the reading of the will. Why, half of Leviston's Lace must be there. Mr Wilmot raised his hat to her as she passed to take the chair at the front near Greeting's desk. Behind her, Martha sidled to the back of the room squeezing past the chairs to sit with the other servants.

Greeting made a eulogy to her father in which he portrayed him as a big-hearted, affable companion; 'as genial a fellow as one could hope to meet' – a portrait which she uncomfortably failed to recognize. Father's virtues were more subtle than that, one had to look hard to find them, buried as they had been under his books and his Latin and his somewhat laconic exterior. How he would have raised his eyebrow, had he heard himself described as a 'fellow'!

It bothered her that Greeting should have presumed to know her father in this way.

'Well gentlemen – and Mistress Leviston – we'll proceed,' he said.

He cracked open the well-sealed document before him. There were a lot of legal pronouncements at the beginning, and she half listened with impatience, waiting for him to reach the nub of it. Obviously, Father would have made provision for Wilmot as his second-in-command and, possibly, he would have left portions for the masters of his trading vessels. She knew, however, that he would not have thought to remember Goodwife Archer from Norwich who organized the English lace-makers. Men were apt to forget the women piece-workers whose craft skills underpinned their trade. She began to compile a list in her thoughts, tallying those deserving folk who served Father's interests and who should be rewarded.

A sudden hush in the room as Greeting's voice stopped talking. She looked up. He was staring at her with a quizzical expression on his creased face. He wiped his balding forehead with his sleeve. She glanced around the room. Martha had her hand over her mouth and a frightened look in her eyes. Everyone else was looking at her.

'Pardon me,' she was alerted by a quivering tension in the air, 'but would you be so good as to repeat that?'

Greeting's eyes flicked down at the document before him. Wilmot pressed his hand on her arm. 'Leviston's Lace goes to his son and you both,' he said gently. 'The estate entire. To you and to Zachary Deane.'

She heard the words, but could not make meaning from them. Son? What son? The bafflement must have shown on her face for Wilmot mouthed the words very slowly as if speaking to an infant. 'Mistress Elspet, you understand – Zachary Deane is not your cousin. He is your brother. Your half-brother. Wish it were not so, but there it is. The business is to go to you both. But not the house. Your father knew you were provided for, see. Read her that sentence again, won't you, Greeting, about her wedding?'

Elspet leaned forward to catch Greeting's voice. He read in a sing-song tone which made her father's words sound even less like they had issued from his pen. The room was totally still, everyone appeared to be holding their breath.

'. . . *as my daughter Joan has no need of worldly goods. My daughter Elspet is provided for by her marriage to Hugh Bradstone, so I bequeath to her the personal things as found in my chamber and twenty pounds as a gift to go to my first grandchild. The business is to be shared equally between said daughter and my only son, Zachary Deane. West View House to go to my son entire, in fitting recompense. May God forgive me for the wrongs I did him and his mother.'*

Martha gasped in the corner of the room. Elspet turned to look and Martha pulled out a kerchief and pressed it to her eyes.

She must have misunderstood. 'Are you saying that I am to share my inheritance with my cousin?' Her voice echoed in the room.

'My condolences, Mistress Leviston, I can see this is another shock,' Greeting said, 'but I am sure your cous—' he paused and licked his lips, 'your brother – will be delighted when he hears of his good fortune, and that you will be able to come to an amicable arrangement together . . .' His voice tailed away as he struggled to find something else to say.

She smoothed her skirts on her knee with a habitual gesture. She noticed her boots protruding from under her hem, the pattern of stamped holes in the leather. Everything was normal. And yet. She licked her lips, but no words would form. Her mouth was dry as tinder.

'We have sent letters to Mr Deane,' Greeting said hurriedly. 'As you are aware, he is on a Grand Tour. We have sent to France and also to Spain, where I am told he is next due to arrive . . . I am sure he will return as soon as he knows what a terrible misfortune has befallen your father, like a good son should.'

'A good son?' She almost choked on the words. Anger rose in her chest, as suddenly as a wound that spurts blood. She stood up. 'Oh yes, I am sure he will be back, like the bent penny he is.'

She approached the desk and was annoyed to see Greeting step back away from her. 'You had better fetch him home,' she said, hardly aware of what she was saying, 'because I will fight this. I am not giving away my home to some bastard brother.'

Greeting shook his head. 'It is watertight, Mistress Leviston. It cannot be revoked.'

'Who signed it?' She lunged for the paper, but he was too quick and swiped it away from her reaching hand.

'I did,' Greeting said. 'I and your father's friend, Mr Tenter.' He held the parchment aloft.

'Tenter.' She almost choked on his name. He was sitting behind her. She turned to him, 'You and Greeting cooked this between you. Why? Why in God's name? I thought you were a family friend. How could you have stood there and let my father sign this?'

' 'Tis not our business to interfere in a man's wishes. We must abide by what he thinks fitting, if he is the one with the purse, as well you know.' Tenter nodded around the room as if to garner support from the assembled men.

She rounded on them all. 'When was this? This is Zachary's doing. My father would never have agreed to such a thing without coercion. He pressed him, did he not?'

'On the contrary,' Greeting said, 'your father told me he was to know nothing about it. I regret to say, I think you will find it is all in order. He altered it only a few weeks ago. Your father was not to know his death would be so sudden. He thought you would be already wed to Mr Bradstone by the time the will would be needed, and that your assets would be enjoined to his. He felt it was a good alliance for all three. And I'm afraid it is binding. At least, as far as the law is con—'

Another voice interrupted, 'And have I understood correctly, the lace business – all the warehouses and the stock – they are not to go to his daughter solely, but to the son, Zachary Deane, as well?' Wilmot attempted to clarify the position.

'That is so. It belongs to both under the law of inheritance. Both must sign for joint ownership before the monies can be released, and before any workers can be hired or dismissed. There can be no disputing it as far—'

'—as the law is concerned.' Wilmot said this with contempt, but stood and swung his hat on to his head. 'I trust, Mr Greeting, that you will do all in your power to ensure that Mr Deane returns as soon as possible, and that he will allow Mistress Leviston to remain at West View House until she is married.'

'Well, I . . . yes, yes . . . of course.'

'Now, Mistress Leviston,' Wilmot spoke directly to her, 'I

suppose neither of us has any need to remain. I suggest you sign for your due settlement and whilst we await the return of Mr Deane, I shall escort you and your maidservant home.'

'If you think I am signing such a travesty, then you can think again. I will not consent to tie my good name to . . . to . . .' She fixed Greeting with a stony glare. 'Find my cousin and have him report to my lawyer.'

'Your lawyer's name?' Greeting asked.

She could not answer, for she had no answer. She simply wrenched her cloak from the pegs at the door and, ignoring Wilmot, ran down the stairs. Behind her she heard the 'tap tap' of Martha's wooden-soled shoes as she hurried after her, running to keep up. Elspet was breathless but did not pause until she was in the carriage. She slammed the door shut.

'Drive!' she ordered Broadbank.

'Where to, mistress?'

'Just drive, damn you.' He jerked into motion leaving Martha standing gawping on the road.

His carriage. It was no longer hers. Nothing belonged entirely to her any longer. It would all have to be marched past the eyes of Zachary Deane. A man she loathed and despised. She let the streets pass by her in a blur, before Broadbank, obviously thinking she had lost all reason, slowed and stopped. He climbed down and came and peered in at her through the window.

'Mistress?'

'Home,' she croaked, but the word near choked her. They passed Greeting's chambers again and stopped. An ashen-faced Martha dragged the door open and slunk into the opposite seat. Elspet could not look at her. As they approached the front door, she felt for the keys at her waist, like an intruder in her own home. The thought of Zachary ever lording himself in her chambers with his sack-swigging friends was too much to bear.

I won't let you get away with this, she thought.

Immediately, this thought was followed by a picture of her father's face, full of longing as he waved Zachary off. Oh Father, what in heaven's name possessed you?

Chapter 14

Time went by, and still there was no word from Greeting that her cousin – she would never call him brother – had any plans to return from abroad. She did not dare to hope that some miracle might have occurred and that Zachary had been killed on some foreign soil and would never come back.

During the weeks of waiting she continued to fulfil the household duties, take care of servants' needs, and listlessly prepare a trousseau for her wedding. She still had not written to tell Hugh. She did not know where to begin. A bastard brother was not something he would be glad she had inherited, of that she was sure.

The stonemason sent notes and questions about her father's memorial, but she was too bitter to think of it. Another query had just arrived. She stared at it blankly before tearing it into small pieces and dropping it into the fireplace.

Though the windows let in shafts of the morning sun, she was still cold. She rubbed her hands together to warm them. How could he have done this to her, her own father? She would never be able to tell Joan that Father must have gone with some other woman, whilst Mother had patiently waited at home. Greeting would give her no more information. But she knew Mother must have known.

And the thought that she had known, but borne it, twisted in her heart.

Father had become mysterious and unknown; the memory of him

as a faithful family man had disintegrated, like food turned to cinders. She heard Jakes scratching and whining at Father's chamber door again, as if to ask, where is he? She got up and went to look. At first she could not bear to move the dog away, her throat was wrung tight. But when he did not stop his whimpering and scratching at the threshold, she shouted at him until he cowered away, his tail between his legs.

She was instantly sorry, and fussed him and petted him until he licked her hand, looking up at her with his liquid-brown eyes. 'It's not your fault.' What am I becoming? she thought, and her eyes filled with tears. 'Come on, Jakes lad,' she said, fondling his ears. She grabbed the leads from the hooks and snapped his on to make up for it, and went to fetch Diver, who bounced up before her just as he always did.

'Will I come too?' asked Martha, appearing in the hall.

'No, no. I shall just walk to the common and then return. I need a little air. Jakes will guard me, won't you, lad?'

'Very well, mistress.'

She let the dogs pull her down the street. She passed a few people but they nodded politely or stepped out of her way with a raise of the hat. When she got to the common she let both dogs off the lead and let them race around after each other in the sunshine. Diver started immediately digging for moles, the earth flying up behind him. She barely saw them, for she was too deep in thought.

What on earth would Hugh say when he learned he was not to receive this house or business as dower, and that she must have that bastard Zachary Deane's say-so before she could so much as buy a new pair of bootees? With Father gone there was no man to fight her cause. It was strange, this feeling of rootlessness, as if without a man to vouch for her she was floating somehow unattached to the ground. She'd been led to believe that men had all the answers. That they would protect their womenfolk from all disasters. But it wasn't true, was it?

A message came to say Hugh was back in London, but Elspet's stomach was churning as Hugh's immaculate carriage drew up a few days later in the yard. He smiled and bowed low as usual on meeting her. He looked more handsome than ever and for a moment her heart lifted just to see him. Martha bobbed from foot to foot in excitement and cast her a complicit wink from behind the door as if to wish her good fortune.

He was far too much of a gentleman to ask directly after the will, but she knew she must tell him, so she sat him down, mustered her courage, and he listened carefully.

'I'm sorry, Hugh,' she said. 'The house is Cousin Zachary's alone, the business, and all his assets jointly held. We both must sign for them, and nobody can find him. It's a disaster. Only what is in Father's chamber is to come direct to me as a keepsake – and I think there is nought of value in it, just his books, his nibs and his timepieces . . .' Her voice rose as she spoke.

'But it will make little difference to us, surely?' Hugh said. 'Zachary is still family, is he not? And you and he were ever cordial, so I see no reason why our two businesses should not continue to grow together just the same. You will be able to visit with him here, whenever you like. And, in truth, I have land and wealth enough. Land and wealth, but no wife.'

His calm manner should have reassured her, but instead it only made her more agitated. She pulled on the fringes of her wrap. She did not know how to tell him why her father had favoured Zachary over herself. Hugh seemed to assume that it was the man's right to property, and that all families were as stable and settled as his own. He wrongly presumed the Levistons to be similarly safe and predictable stock.

Instantly she realized that she could never tell him that Zachary was not her cousin but her bastard brother. She could not even say that word to Hugh. She looked into Hugh's mild face and saw no reason to tell him Zachary had just appeared one day from out of the blue, like a cuckoo in the nest. Nor could she tell him that she hardly saw eye-to-eye with him.

'Besides,' Hugh continued, not noticing her discomfort, 'if I were your father, I would have done exactly the same. It is a man's place to take these responsibilities, not a woman's. Your cousin and I will get along fine, you'll see. And you need not worry, for there will be plenty to occupy your hand in Yorkshire. My house needs a woman's touch, I fear.'

'No, Hugh,' she said, 'you do not understand. I intend to contest the will. My father had always promised West View House to me.'

'Contest the will?' A look of puzzlement spread over his face. 'But why? I have property enough, surely? You can visit Cousin Zachary whenever I am in town. You would create trouble over a house such as this?' He held up his arms and gestured around him, his nose wrinkling. In an instant she took in the room's dear shabbiness. His reaction only served to make her more protective and all the more determined.

'It is mine, Hugh, and I shall fight for it.'

'Mistress Leviston – Elspet, is that wise?' He looked at her as if she was deranged. 'Surely it is not wise to provoke strife over a two-bit piece of land. Have a care now. We will think on it a while before doing anything hasty. We will be living in Yorkshire, but I daresay Zachary will be pleased to welcome you here at any time.'

No he won't, she thought grimly. But she said nothing. Hugh's family would never bicker over land; his father would never have kept a courtesan or have a bastard child hidden away for years without telling anyone. He was probably not even aware that families like hers existed.

She picked up the bell to ring for refreshments. 'Some chilled ale?' she asked, trying to maintain her composure, but feeling more and more out of sorts. She was uncomfortable that he was telling her what 'we' will do, meaning himself. It made her uneasy that she was to have no say in the matter. She felt herself resisting, like a horse in traces.

'Chilled ale would be excellent,' he said.

He must have caught her mood for he came over to where she stood near the window and took hold of her hand. His was large and soft and, for the first time ever, her own hand appeared delicate and dainty. He squeezed it gently, but she did not know how to respond. She stared out into the sunlit street where the shiny side of his carriage could be seen. There were so many conflicting emotions. She was awash with them all.

'The business, well, that is a blow right enough,' he said. 'I had thought to have sole control over that. But as long as your cousin is amenable to propositions, I'm prepared to write off the loss. It was a wife I was after, and if she is so much the poorer, well, I will just have to accept it. I can overlook it. I need to think of the future, of children. Though I think, if you do not mind, my dear, we will not mention the will to my family until after the wedding.'

She looked up at him, and tears formed in her eyes, not from grief, but because he thought he was being kind and she could not explain why his words disturbed her so.

'Take cheer.' He offered her a kerchief. 'I see no reason for us to stay in London any longer. We will shut up the house until Zachary returns. We need not delay. We can hie ourselves to Tockton immediately.' His arm crept round her waist, where she let it lie, sensed the comfort of it, almost gave in to it, but somehow could not. He dipped his head to kiss her, but she stayed stiff and unbending, frightened to let go in case she should break down.

He stepped away; he looked disappointed that she had not fallen into his arms. Perhaps he thought of himself as a hero, taking on such a dowerless woman.

'I will send word to Tockton to prepare a room for you in the guest wing,' he said, 'until such time as we are wed.' His tone said that the matter of the house was closed. 'Everyone is looking forward to meeting you and showing you how the estate is run, and there are ample servants to see to your needs.' His expression was stubborn, like a child insisting on sweetmeats.

'Perhaps that would be best,' she said, caving in, wanting to please him. 'I'm sorry, Hugh,' she said, 'I am not myself right now. . .'

He approached again and held her so tightly that she felt her ribs creak. 'I quite understand,' he said. 'To lose a father must be a terrible thing. I'd be lost without mine. It has been a shock, and it is natural to grieve. But your father was a fine man, and would not want you to have a falling out with your cousin, I'm sure. That is all he had in mind, to make your family ties the stronger. It is admirable.'

When he said 'admirable', a tear rolled down her face. She took a long shuddering breath and swallowed hard. If he knew the truth, the depth of her father's deception, perhaps Hugh would not find Father quite so admirable. But she recognized that he was right, perhaps Father had intended to draw Zachary and her closer together.

Foolish man, she thought sadly, the idea was quite impossible.

'Let's go straight back to Tockton,' Hugh said again.

She did not want to leave West View House. She felt that if she left she might never return. A tight sensation lodged in her chest, like a weight pressing down on it. She took a deep breath and regained control of herself. 'Give me a little more time, won't you, Hugh? I need to make arrangements for the dogs and pack up my personal possessions.'

'Do we have to wait? Cannot the servants see to the dogs and send your things on after us?'

'The servants are still bemused by Father's death. I need time to organize them until Zachary returns, and who knows when that will be. I cannot leave it to someone else or the house will run to ruin, and if I put someone else in charge, it will be too many changes.' She knew as she said it, it was herself she spoke of, she who'd had too many changes.

A fleeting expression of irritation crossed his face. 'Well, I suppose I could go on ahead without you. A month should be sufficient. Then I shall expect you at Tockton.'

A month. Only a few weeks more in her lovely house. And then Zachary would take control of it and she would be in Yorkshire, leagues away from everything she knew and loved. She should be grateful, for who else would take her now her dowry was tied to her cousin's whims? Hugh had saved her, caught her as she was falling. And he was the handsomest man in town, a man with a fine estate and a good reputation. Why, then, did she feel it as a sentence?

She was still grieving, she reminded herself; perhaps later she would allow herself to feel as fortunate as she knew she was.

Chapter 15

Seville, Andalusia

Zachary inhaled the tang of forged iron, the woody aroma of burning charcoal, and lifted his hat up and down to let the air waft his forehead dry. The smithy was wide open to the street and the heat of its furnaces rolled towards him in a wave, despite the sharp early morning sun. Above the entrance hung a cracked sign with a pair of crossed swords over a white dove and the name Guido de Vega. The name he was looking for. Beneath that sign was an even more decrepit and badly painted one, stained with smoke, which indicated a member of the sword-maker's guild.

'You want a blade?' The smith spoke in Spanish.

After two weeks of being in Spain, Zachary had remembered his mother's tutelage and replied in the man's native tongue, 'The finest you have.'

'It will cost.' The smith put down a dagger he had been working on and strolled over, wiping his hands on his leather apron. He looked Zachary up and down.

'I can pay.' Zachary bristled slightly and drew himself upright.

The smith spat sideways into the dust before going and lifting down a sword from the row that was hanging from the rafters like a display of shining silver teeth. His journeymen and apprentices stopped what they were doing to stare. He held out the sword on the flat of his palms.

Zachary took it and examined it, fingered the engraved mark of a feather near the top of the blade. 'No. One like that, I can buy anywhere. I'm after something special. A twin-edged sword – something light and, how do you say it? – skinny, like a rapier.' He mimed a whip-like cut, extending his sword arm in front of him in a swoop.

The man narrowed his eyes. 'A blade I can make you. But I will need to hear the clink of your coin first.'

Zachary pulled out a pouch. 'I fought three duels in France for this. And still I stand.'

The smith was impassive, unimpressed, but it was true. The craze for duelling had infected France like a fever. More were dead there from duelling than from the plague here in Spain, and Zachary had made his fair share of these conquests.

'Put it away,' the smith said. 'A blade can be made. But you must come here every day.' He moved closer, his bulk masking the heat from the fires. The tang of his sweat caught in Zachary's nostrils. He lowered his voice as if to tell a secret. 'A sword must have soul. It must be a part of the hand that wields it. You want to own your sword? And not have it own you? Then what will you give?' He went to hang the blade back up with the rest. 'Be here at seven night,' he said over his shoulder, 'and we will make a start.'

Zachary was dismissed. Did his ungentlemanly past show so clearly, then, that a smith felt he could order him around? Unable to think of a suitable retort, he shoved his pouch into his breeches and walked away. He heard laughter behind him. Devil fetch Guido de Vega. He did not like his attitude and there must be plenty more smiths in Seville. He walked up the Calle de las Armas, bypassing the hilt-smiths and scabbard-makers, examining weapons on display.

But the others he looked at were inferior, the blades soft or brittle. Or the smith too anxious to get hold of his purse, making unlikely promises of delivery the next day. But the truth of it was, he could not get Guido de Vega or his smithy out of his mind, for he had heard of his skill in Toledo and had followed him to Seville. He wanted a sword with Guido's feather mark, and he knew nothing else would do.

So it was that he found himself back in the same barrio that night. Walking in the Calle de las Armas was like a journey through hell. The noise of hammering, the glow of fires, the shouts of the smiths and their apprentices as they quenched the hot iron in belches of hissing steam.

The night air was thick, for close by were the potteries with their kilns, coughing out more soot. All the fire trades were here in Triana, where the river separated them from the main city of Seville, in case of an accidental blaze.

When Zachary arrived, Guido gave him a curt little nod of amusement, and handed over an apron without comment. It was blackened and scorched and heavy as armour. Zachary fastened it on, ignoring the apprentices' sniggering as it fell way past his knees.

'Pay no heed,' Guido said, handing him weighty gauntlets to match, and then tongs with a lump of grey matter between their teeth.

Zachary took the tongs and nearly dropped them. The metal was much heavier than he had expected.

Guido laughed, hoiked it back out of his hands, then plunged it into the furnace. Moments later, he extracted it, glowing orange, and dumped it on the anvil. Zachary watched Guido's forearms bulge as he wielded his hammer in long, swinging strokes. After a few moments, he rammed the flattened lump back into the furnace.

'Now,' he said, passing him the tongs. Zachary closed his nostrils as he drew the lump out again. The piercing heat almost singed his eyebrows and moustache, but he refused to look a fool before Guido's boys. The lump was a dull orange glow – like a sunset.

He lifted the hammer and, as it landed on the metal on the anvil, it jarred his arm, but he raised the hammer again and crashed it down. From the corner of his eye he saw one of the journeymen disguise a smile. He gritted his teeth and pounded even harder. He'd show them, the cheeky dogs. The sweat dewed on his brow and dripped on to the metal until it sizzled and disappeared.

The metal turned pale pink and suddenly there was a crack and the metal split asunder. He faltered and Guido was by his side in an instant. He clicked his tongue.

'You want to kill the steel before you have even begun? You must coax it, like a woman. Bring it up to heat, then work it. When you feel it become unresponsive, take it to the heat again. Use your eyes and your nose. Now, again.'

And a little irritated, he started anew. Three times he tried, but the metal would not shape for him as it did for Guido. Each time, just as it was almost flat, the metal cracked and the apprentices sniggered into their sleeves. By now his arm and shoulder were leaden and his face was wet with sweat. Anger rose up inside him.

'Devil take it!' he cried, dropping the hammer and peering into his palm. His hand was blistered from the handle and his head pounded louder than the hammer.

'Enough!' Guido called. 'Pick that up again and hang it back over there.'

Zachary deliberately left it where he had dropped it. 'I can't do it,' he said. 'I can't work with that stuff. You're giving me inferior metal.'

'Is that what you think? Not so. It is exactly the same as mine.' Guido's voice was level and reasonable but it only enraged Zachary more. 'Come, then, choose your own.'

Guido beckoned and strolled to the back where the iron from the bloomery stood on the sandy earth, waiting to come into the workshop. He gestured to it. Zachary looked, and saw a row of misshapen lumps of raw metal, each indistinguishable from the other. He knew he could not tell good from bad, especially at night, but he made a show of walking up and down and, finally, he pointed to one of them.

Guido gave him a tight smile. 'Fetch it in, then.'

Zachary lugged it in with his sore hands. It hurt, carrying this rough lump of metal, despite the fact that it was cool from standing in the night air. Zachary was determined not to show how much it cost him to bring it in and heave it with his blistered hands on to the work bench. As he stood and contemplated it, Guido dismissed the other artisans from the workshop. The tools were cleaned and put away, the fires damped. Work was clearly over for the evening. 'Tomorrow I will work with this,' Zachary said.

'Not tomorrow. Tonight. Juan, leave number two.'

Juan was about to put the lid on one of the furnaces, but now he stopped mid-movement, his eyebrows raised.

Zachary thought of a cool drink and his soft bed. He was more than ready to return to his lodgings. 'I think I'll wait till tomorrow, get a fresh start,' he said.

'No. Now. You do it now, or you do not come back tomorrow.'

Guido waved a finger at Juan, who shrugged, left the fire and went to dress in his doublet and cap. Catching Juan watching him, Zachary said carelessly, 'Fine. It makes no difference to me.' The tongs felt rougher than before and the metal a dead weight. He heaved the lump into the furnace. He was nauseous from the heat and his pounding head. Juan had left, but a waiting slave pumped the bellows and Zachary watched for the heat to infuse the metal and make it glow. This time, he thought, gritting his teeth, it would be perfect.

He could barely lift the hammer; his muscles were like water and his hands shook. He sensed the strings of his neck, tight as twisted cords. He swung the hammer down time after time, jaw clenched against the impact, shirt stuck to his back. The apron pressed against his thighs like a plank.

Nearly flat. He put the bar into the furnace one more time. When it came out he lifted the hammer and let it fall for a few more turns of the hour-glass. The metal was beginning to turn pink but one more hit should do it.

When the metal cracked again the sap drained from his body, the disappointment so sharp it took his breath. He hurled the hammer down and his whole body was shaking. He rushed to the edge of the street where he vomited into the dust. Bile splashed on to his boots. He was aware of passers-by stepping around him with disgust, but he bent double and heaved again. He propped himself against one of the wooden pillars that formed the overhang and panted for breath, trying to stem the water seeping from his eyes.

Guido appeared beside him and wordlessly helped him out of the leather apron. What freedom to be out of the weight of it! Zachary slumped uncaring to the ground, leaned against the post, wiping his eyes and mouth. Guido returned with his cloak, his hat and his sword belt and he struggled to his feet. It was humiliating to be helped him into them like an old man. His shirt stank of sweat and iron dust but he was too tired to resist, and besides, he could not look Guido in the eye.

'Tomorrow. Sunrise,' Guido said.

'Yes,' he mouthed. It had to be a jest. He had no intention of ever going back.

Chapter 16

The next day, Zachary was unable to stir from his bed. His back was almost bent double like an old ploughman's, his hands stiff and sore. He flexed his hands. Damn, they moved as if he were still wearing those thick leather gauntlets.

He had dismissed his English servant weeks ago, preferring to travel alone. But with his Spanish lodgings came a house slave, Ana, who had prepared a meal of chickpea bread, spiced sausage and peaches, and had served it up with a flagon of ale. When she slid the tray under his nose he had never seen anything so welcome. His mouth was parched, so he downed the ale in one draught. He leaned over the balcony to enjoy the view below, to see the black lace mantillas of the women going by beneath.

He was glad to be in the centre of the city. His lodgings were owned by the silversmith Luis de Ribera – a set of rooms with a grill-work balcony overlooking the bustle of the Calle de Virgenes. The place had been recommended to him by someone he had met in France who had also stayed there on his Grand Tour – and very airy it was too. He chortled to himself. Uncle Leviston would be speechless to see him, already in Spain, convinced as he was that Zachary was following his proposed route of lace producers and dusty Roman ruins. He crushed the feeling in his chest that made him feel guilty.

My God, but England seemed like a distant memory now. Was it really only a month ago that he had been shivering in those grey docks with Uncle Leviston and his old-fashioned, stiff-mannered daughter?

More than ever now, he sensed the Spaniard rising in him, his mother's blood. He was as dark and slight as they, their tongue submitted to his labours more and more every day. He loved the substance and beauty of Spain, the intensity of its colour. In comparison, France had been pale as whey, its people drab despite all their fuss and fashion. He chewed the spiced sausage, tasted the faint aroma of garlic, sank his teeth into the floury bread. When he cut into the peach it was fat and juicy, the flesh melting on his tongue, the flavour sweet and intense.

A flash of dark caught his eye and he looked up to see a swallow's forked tail dart under the eaves of the house. He loved the swooping of these birds, their flight somehow reminded him of a sword in motion. His mother had loved them too, said they reminded her of home. A sudden clamour of cheeping from the nest above his head announced the hunger of its occupants. He smiled; it must be their feeding time too.

His mood lifted. Bending forward, he rubbed his back hard with his knuckles. Perhaps it felt a little less painful than before. Guido's face floated behind his eyes. As if they had a will of their own, his legs stood, and he found himself thinking, 'I'm only a little late.'

He hurried down the Calle de las Armas, as fast as his sore back would allow. If he gave up on the blade now, then the sword had won. Even though it was not yet even formed, and was only an idea embedded in the metal, he must prevail, show it who was master.

Guido did not seem surprised to see him. '*Que llega tarde,*' he grumbled – you're late. He handed Zachary more metal and he set to work.

Today the metal flattened beautifully, he was learning to have a feel for it, to understand the texture and colour of it in the furnace. The apprentices and journeymen had stopped staring, as if he was old news. In his filthy apron he was one of them – at least for the moment. He listened to the talk around him, learning the Spanish for the different tools, repeating the words under his breath, *tenazas*

– tongs, *cepo de yunque* – the stock of the anvil.

At the end of the second day his ears buzzed like mosquitos but a blade lay in his hand, not much to see yet, just a long flat lump of steel marbled with a watery pattern where the layers had folded in on each other.

Guido looked it over, taking it to the lamplight and turning it in front of his eye, '*Muy bien.*' Zachary beamed. 'Once more, I think,' he mouthed, holding up one finger. 'Then Gabriel – he will show you how to shape the steel edges, and later the grinding and polishing.' Gabriel grinned.

At the end of the evening, Zachary called Gabriel over. He was the only one of the journeymen who had actually spoken to him, when he had passed a lighter jack-hammer and mouthed, 'This one – it is better.' Zachary asked if he could buy him a drink and they strolled over to one of the street-side eating places in the Corral de los Olmas and ordered ale and iced water to quench their thirst, along with the fruit jellies that were so popular here in Seville.

'Why are you doing this?' Gabriel asked, his big hands wrapped around his cup.

'Making a blade, you mean?'

'Yes. You could buy one finished already. If you don't mind me saying, you look as if you can afford one, yes?'

'I want something special. Ever since I first learned to fence, I heard men talk of the sword-makers of Toledo, their skill and craftsmanship. It's a dream, I suppose – the perfect blade – something strong as a cavalry sword, but narrow and flexible like a rapier. When I went to Toledo, they told me the best man still making swords was Guido de Vega. I went to find him but I was too late – he had moved here, to Seville.'

'A lot too late. He's been here over four years. Seville's like a beehive growing by the hour. You can't go a hundred paces without having to step round a scaffold or dodge a pile of rubble. The city's full to busting. But all the best craftsmen are here now. Stands to reason. But why not just pay Señor Guido to make it?'

'It was something he said, about the sword knowing the hand that . . .' Zachary wielded an imaginary sword in the air.

Gabriel understood and nodded.

'It was his idea, not mine. I know how difficult it is, and I was quite prepared to pay.'

'His idea?' Gabriel looked impressed. 'Well, I had to walk over hot coals to even get him to see me. We all did. Any smith worth his salt was fighting to get taken on by him. We thought he took you on as a jest, to knock you down a bit, take the wind from your sails. You looked that fancy.' He smiled apologetically. 'But anyone can see now you are serious. Touched in the head, maybe – you wouldn't catch many gentlemen with a hammer in their hands. But you just don't look the right size for a smith.'

'I'm not planning to make a profession of it! Just this one.'

'Watch out, you might get a taste for it.' They laughed. 'But I can tell you know a bit about the art of fence – are you a fencing master?'

'No, not me. Though I've seen some that are less skilled than I am, and men so fog-handed they can barely cut a loaf straight, yet still they offer their services. To tell true, I'm looking for a real master, someone who knows their game. I've been all over France looking for a good professor of fence. In France they all claim to have *'la botte secrète'*. The secret thrust, you know? But they're all talk, most of them.' He scooped up a spoonful of quince jelly and let it slip down his throat.

Gabriel grunted his agreement and took his cue to fish in his glass and slurp his jelly. He cocked his head to listen.

Between mouthfuls Zachary continued, 'I was supposed to go to Rome, but Spain was calling me somehow. My mother was from Cadiz. So I thought I'd come to Spain, get myself a custom-made sword, and a true fencing master. I saw a man fight once – he was a Spaniard. He was like nothing else I've ever seen. His sword was fluid – like silk ribbon, oh, it's no use! I can't describe it. And I'd love to find him again. He was from Seville.'

'You don't know his name, this master of fence?'

'Regrettably, no. Or I'd be camped on his threshold.'

'The best fencing master round here is Don Rodriguez by the Arenal Gate. He has never been defeated in any contest. But he is a fearsome fighter, well-known for his toughness. They say he sometimes takes on students, but he is not cheap. And he won't take *conversos*, so I don't know how he'd feel about an Englishman.'

'I'm only half-English. My mother was Spanish. How much does he charge?'

'I've heard as much as fifteen reales a day.'

Zachary blew through his mouth and shook his head. He might have to subsidise old Leviston's purse with a bit of thievery to be able to afford that. 'And you say he's good?'

'The best, by all accounts. He's the man who trains the constables for the Asistente.'

'Sounds like he could be the one. I'll go and search him out tomorrow.'

'Be careful. Don Rodriguez insists that his students are of a pure-blood lineage. His men are *familiares*, spies employed by the Inquisition, though they do not like to call them that now. As I say, he might not take kindly to an enquiry from one whose lineage cannot be checked. He might not take you. And he is not a man to cross by all accounts.'

'He'll take me, when he sees me fence.'

The stars were still bright pinpricks above the city and the cocks had not begun their crowing when Zachary got out of bed. He lit a wall-sconce and dressed awkwardly because of his stiff shoulders. How pleasant it was to dress in this balmy climate instead of shivering in the clammy dark in England. He girded on his sword and strapped on his Turkish daggers to make a good show, to look like a serious student. Today he was going in search of Don Rodriguez.

Better do a few moves and passes on the way, he thought, to make his body more pliant. On the balcony he stretched and inhaled the slight smell of citrus from the sprawling lime tree in the cracked terracotta pot.

When his exercises were done, he went down the stairs and saw two letters waiting for him on the hall table. He sighed; they were probably from Señor de Ribera about the rent. When he untied the first, he was stupefied to find that it had come all the way from

England. He took it back up to the balcony to the light to make sure. No, he was not mistaken. He turned it over in his hands, thinking how uncanny – he was just that moment thinking of how cold it would be in England, and now here was this letter as if he had conjured it himself.

He had to read it twice before he understood that Uncle Leviston was dead.

This would be the end of his hand-outs, the end of his life in Spain. But as well as the sinking sensation he felt something else. It was regret, a sudden sensation of loss. Just at that moment the cockerels crowed, the noise familiar yet disconcerting. A sound straight from biblical times, it pulled at a distant memory. He swallowed, knowing that the cocks crew for a day that had already begun without his uncle. Old Leviston would never be a part of this life again.

He sat back down, dazed. When his uncle was alive, Zachary had told himself he meant nothing to him, but now, standing here on the balcony looking down on the world, he felt his loss like a kick in the stomach. His uncle had loved him. But he had shown him no affection in return. And now it was too late. A shiver passed through him, the reminder that death is always present, hidden under the skin of things; and come this evening, any man could be a bag of bones like his uncle.

He shouted for Ana. She appeared silently, from where she had been asleep at the foot of the stairs, her big eyes in her dark face questioning.

'Can you bring quill and ink?'

She nodded and slid away. A few moments later she returned bearing a portable writing slope and a burning candle, which she positioned on the table. 'Thank you,' he said to her retreating back.

A little light-headed, he sat a moment on the balcony, and watched the pink tinge of the sun begin to brighten the horizon. He picked up the second letter now, saw it was also from England, and untied it. He read it and weighed each word. He read it again. And again. His heart beat hard in his chest, his hands were clammy, and only after the third time of reading did he allow himself a whoop of triumph.

He grabbed quill and ink, but paused, nib in hand. His mind whirled with new possibilities. He started to write but trembled with such excitement that his handwriting appeared on the page as a scrawl.

Everything was changed. He was rich – maybe he could afford to invest in some mercantile ships, or purchase a house. A grand villa! The thought of it was impossible to grasp. And even better, he would be his own man, beholden to no one. He wrote to Greeting and then, in a sudden desire to tell someone of his good fortune, he wrote gleefully to Shotterill. He laughed to himself – old Gin would never believe him, he'd think it some sort of monkey-trick.

Or, knowing him, he'd turn up here, the flea-bitten dog, hoping for the scratchings from Zachary's table.

'Ana!' he called, wishing to tell her to engage someone to have care of the letters and make sure they were delivered. But then he realized – she would have gone out to the bazaar as she did every morning.

So he sat with the pile of letters in front of him, and it was only then that he thought of Leviston's daughter, Elspet. What would he give to have seen her face when they told her the house was to come to him! He quashed the discomfort that the thought of her brought. The heat of the sun had already begun to pierce the morning haze, but he let it beat down on his bare head. Should he write to her? He baulked at the idea of it. His conscience was protesting but he refused to hear it.

He remembered the disdainful look Elspet wore whenever he was in the room, looking down her nose at him, as if he was never quite educated or gentlemanly enough for her. And as for the house – well, given a few more years it would just have crumbled to dust around their ears anyway. She wouldn't be needing it, he reasoned, she must be married by now and living in fine style on her grand estate in Tockton.

Tockton. Even the name sounded dull. He bet it was as chilly and damp as a tomb, and Hugh Bradstone too. Though happen that would suit Elspet Leviston well enough; she had no sense at all when it came to men.

The church bells pounded out the quarter. His news bubbled up inside. He was late, so he hurried straight to the smithy, the letters from England tucked safely into the pocket of his satchel, alongside the one from his mother. As he made his way through town to the bridge he kept stopping, to feel in the bag to check they were still there, that he had not imagined it.

'*Tarde,*' Guido said as usual, frowning at Zachary's grinning face and handing him a set of bellows. Zachary took them without demur. Working the bellows was considered a punishment, and the hottest place to be in the whole damn workshop. But he needed time to think. It was as if a whirlwind had been set loose in his head.

It was only later that he realized the whole idea of finding Don Rodriguez, the swordmaster, had completely slipped his mind. It struck him; he would be able to pay Rodriguez for any number of lessons now; he would never have to go back to the pigsties of Whitechapel.

The memory of his brothers made him guffaw out loud with a kind of ironic glee. Just you look at me now, you sods, he thought, his mouth set into a grim line. Now we'll see who's master.

Chapter 17

'I am pleased to say we have received written instructions from your cousin.'

At long last. Elspet was standing in Greeting's chambers again. She had walked from West View House and after the fresh air outside, the room was like a bath-house – uncomfortably warm. The windows bloomed moistly with steam.

'And what does he say?'

'Will you not sit, mistress?'

'Just tell me, when is he coming home?'

'I'm afraid he's not. Master Deane has left us to carry out his instructions in his absence.'

'And what are his instructions?'

'Please – won't you sit? Then we can discuss it more comfortably.'

She pulled her skirts to one side, sat down in the leather-backed chair opposite him, and untied the muslin from her hat. He observed her with a careful expression.

'I'm sorry, Mistress Leviston.' She waited while he licked his lips and slid the ink stand across the blotter. He looked up. 'His instructions are to sell.'

He saw her blank expression and repeated, 'He wants his half of his inheritance. You will have to sell, mistress.'

'What? Everything?' Her voice was a whisper.

'Yes. The house is to be sold, and the business will have to go too.

137

I'm afraid he has no plans to return to England at present, and he wishes us to cash his assets and deliver the money in gold to his residence in Spain.'

'You are not – you are not going to act upon his instructions, are you?' She could hardly bring herself to speak.

Greeting had the grace to apologize. 'I beg your pardon, it is not the news you were expecting, I know. But still, I expect you will have an adequate portion from the business when the transaction is completed. But you have to see, my hands are tied. Your father charged me to deliver his wishes and that I must do. You cannot retain half the business if he wants to sell.'

'My father would not have wished this, you know he wouldn't. Father intended to consolidate the business, not divide it. What use is half a business? How could it carry on? As for Zachary Deane – he cares nothing for any of us; not me, not the business nor any of the employees. Are you seriously telling me he can sell everything and there is not a damn thing I can do about it?'

'Calm yourself. I have some smelling salts in this drawer. . .' He bent over and began to fumble under the desk.

'Smelling salts be damned. What happened to your friendship with my father, Mr Greeting? What if he could see you now, taking the roof from over my head, and my livelihood? What would he think then?'

He did not answer, but proffered a bottle with a grubby cork. 'I have asked him to advance you a sum for lodgings until you are wed.'

She leaned towards him. 'Lodgings? Please, Mr Greeting, you know this is not right. You have to help me. At least tell me where Zachary is, so I can write to him and reason with him.'

'His instructions were definite, mistress. To sell as soon as possible. If you yourself have no available funds, perhaps your intended, Mr Bradstone, will be able to purchase shares in the business. Though he must move quickly, as perhaps others will be interested too.'

'And I suppose you are on a percentage of the sales, are you not?' Greeting's eyes shifted away and he slid the ink bottle back towards him. 'I'm right.' She sighed, knowing she had no leverage when it came to coin. 'Please, Mr Greeting, for my father's sake, send word back to Mr Deane and press him to delay, at least until I can try to raise the money to buy the house. I have given my heart and soul for years for Leviston's Lace and I won't see it divided. Just give me time to send—'

He began to bluster, 'I don't see that—'

'You owe us that much.' She stood firm. 'My father lined your pocket all these years, the least you can do is try.'

'I'm afraid—'

'At least give me his address, then. I will write to him myself. I tell you, Mr Greeting, I am not moving from your chambers until I have it.'

She sat back and folded her arms. They would have to drag her from that place before she would give in.

Greeting sighed. 'Very well. You twist my arm. His address, then.'

He reached up to a high shelf where leather boxes were piled in alphabetical order. He took down the box marked 'D–E' and slapped it on to the table. He called to the scrivener in the next room and as the door opened she saw Martha's red tearful face and knew she had been listening. A change in her fortunes meant a change in Martha's and well she knew it.

The scrivener copied down the address, scratching laboriously at the paper with a worn-out goose-nib. When he handed her the paper she read:

Mr Zachary Deane Esq.,
Signe del Naranja,
Calle de Virgenes,
Sevilla

She did not thank him. She simply tucked the paper into her bag and swept out of the chamber. Outside she sucked in great lungfuls of air. Until that moment she had not realized she had been holding her breath.

Elspet handed Martha the letter to post. 'Quick Martha, give this to Broadbank to post. It must go today.'

It was a letter to Hugh to inform him that Zachary wanted to sell; perhaps Hugh might be able to reason with Greeting to stay the sale. Without a shadow of a doubt they would see neither hide nor hair of Zachary Deane once he had the gold in his grasp.

Since the reading of the will she had not been down to the priest cellar; she had been too bitter, unable to find gratitude for prayer. But now she descended, thinking she might find comfort there. One of the servants had left a small taper alight as was the custom, so she pulled one of the horsehair kneelers over the flagstone floor and bowed her head, making the sign of the cross.

She gazed on the small statuette of Mary, who had a half-smile and wide, innocent eyes. Mary held her blue mantle about her as if concealing the mystery. Her halo glowed in the candlelight. She was just an ordinary woman once, thought Elspet, before the angel visited her. Did she have that peaceful expression then, or did she frown and scowl like everyone else and wonder why life treated her so harshly?

Elspet sighed. Would she ever have such a look, or know the secret of her grace? Mary looked so accepting, but Elspet could not accept that she would always be beholden to someone – to Mr Bradstone or, worse, to Zachary Deane – and she did not want to have to beg every day of her life. She stood, frustrated, still unable to pray. Perhaps, after all, even Mary could not help her.

Before she left she lit two small candles, one for Lydia, the child who had died, and one for Joan. Joan would certainly need heavenly assistance when she told her what Father had done. She did not light another for Father, for despite her prayers, her anger still burned hotter than any candle. How could he die like that and leave her with nothing?

This house was hers. Hers. He'd promised her. She banged the door shut on the cellar and drew the drapes so that the metal curtain rings rattled and the fabric swung, releasing a mist of dust.

'Martha,' she called.

She came running at the tone of her voice.

'Have these drapes taken outside to be beaten. And all the curtains at all the doors and windows. And while you're at it, all the rugs.'

'But mistress, it's just started drizzling –'

'Then it will help the dust settle in the yard. Go on now.'

'Yes, mistress.' Martha curtseyed to her and fetched a stool to stand on to take down the curtain.

She wound down the armfuls of cloth and dragged the bundle out of the door. A few moments later the houseboy arrived to take down the drapes at the windows. A fine film of grey settled over the furniture, the pale light streaked through the dirty diamonds of glass. She fetched a ewer with water and vinegar and scrubbed at the windows. The cloth blackened under the vigour of her rubbing.

Martha stopped short in the doorway to see her with her sleeves turned back and a dampened rag in her hands.

'Mistress! Whatever are you doing?' She bustled over. 'Here, let me take that.'

'How long since these were cleaned?'

'Beg pardon, but I don't know, mistress.'

'Well, look.' She held out the cloth.

'I'll see to it straight away, mistress. Straight away. I'll go tell the boy.' Martha snatched the rag from Elspet's hands and ran off.

When the boy came back, he eyed her sideways as if to gauge whether or not she had gone stark mad, but she simply gestured to the windows.

'All of them,' she ordered, pacing up and down before them, 'and the wainscots and banisters.' It was obviously years since they had been done.

After the windows, she gave instructions for a thorough scouring of the whole house, even though today there was not enough sun to dry everything. But the activity and bustle in the house soothed the restlessness in her heart as she waited for Hugh's reply. After a little more than a week his letter finally arrived; she tore off the seal and read his few lines.

Dear Mistress Leviston,

If your cousin wishes to sell, if it means so much to you, then I want to buy. I had half a mind to come to London next week in any case to offer assistance with your preparations. I'll go to Greeting, see what I can do.

Your servant,

Hugh

Thank God. Relief flooded through her. The letter had taken a few days to reach her, so perhaps even now he was at Greeting's. She pressed the letter to her lips and kissed it. 'Oh Hugh!' she exclaimed.

The messenger lad in the doorway smiled, and twisted his cap in embarrassment. No doubt he thought the letter full of terms of endearment. He was waiting for a reply so she sat at her desk and wrote a fervent note of thanks. She folded it carefully, and smiled, for in this mood even the smell of the sealing wax gave her pleasure. She almost skipped down to the kitchen to tell Goody Turner she would take Jakes out.

'A fine idea, mistress,' Turner said, grinning at her obvious good cheer, 'he needs exercise that one, he runs us all ragged if he don't get a walk. But make sure you take your sun-shade. That sun's baking. Nearly fried my ears off on the way here.'

'Come on,' Elspet said to Jakes. 'Walk times! And, Goody Turner, we are going to the drapers to order more cloth for curtains!'

'New curtains? Well, there's something. I was worried. There was rumours your cousin might be closing up the house.'

'Not if I can help it. Mr Bradstone and I won't hear of it.'

'I'm right glad.'

'Here, Jakes!' The dog stopped sniffing the bottom of the door long enough to have his lead put on. 'Shall we stop by the butchers on the Strand, and buy some bones? Bones, Jakes!' Jakes let out a delighted woof. She fetched her hat and fastened it on, calling for Martha, before asking, 'Do we need anything, Turner?'

'I don't think so, mistress, though if you pass the comfit-seller, I wouldn't say no to a twist of pear drops.' She winked.

'Cheeky! Sugared figs for me – but we will see what the man has on his barrow.'

'Pear drops, milk sops, lemon cherry, make we merry!' Martha said, catching the mood and jamming her felted hat on her head.

Elspet picked up Diver and gave him a squeeze. 'You be nice for Goody Turner, now.' He wagged his stubby tail.

She passed him over. Goody Turner ruffled his head and said, 'Don't fret, mistress, he'll be fine and dandy. Just make sure

Martha holds tight to that Jakes, and gets him fixed to the railings in
town. He'd chase a cobble set in the road, that one.'

It was almost six when Martha and Elspet returned, their arms full of
parcels and their mouths full of candied delights. Martha dragged her
feet and complained during the last half-mile. Goody Turner poked
her head up the stairs to see what they'd bought. Now that Father
was gone, Coleman, Broadbank and the lad spent their time in the
stables or below, and they were a house full of women. It made them
giddy.

'Look at those roses in your cheeks!' Goody Turner said to
Martha. She grabbed hold of the muddy and excited Jakes and added,
'Off you go; go on down now.'

Martha and Goody Turner were only halfway down the stairs
when there was a loud knock at the door. As Elspet was so near she
went to open it herself, though Goody Turner appeared again right
behind her. She pulled open the door still in her outdoor clothes.
Below, the dogs set to barking.

Hugh was on the doorstep, and another, shorter, older, man who
was leaning on a stick. 'Hugh!' she said, surprised but pleased to see
him. 'Why, how strange, I've just penned you a letter, not a few hours
ago!'

'This is my father. May we come in?'

'Come in, come in,' she said. 'What a lovely surprise. I didn't
know you were down from Yorkshire, sir. So very pleased to meet
you. Pray take the gentlemen's coats, Turner.'

'No need. We won't be staying,' Hugh said.

She didn't register his words at first for she was busy saying, 'I
have just come in from outdoors myself.' It was only when the men
staunchly retained their hats that she realized something was the
matter.

Hugh was holding himself very upright and stiff, his face was set
and tight. Hugh's father's demeanour was similarly grave. A part of
her went cold and still. She heard herself observe the usual courtesies.

'Have you ridden here?' she asked. 'The stable lad will—'

'No.' His father cut her off. 'Our carriage waits outside. Is there someone from the family who can sit with you whilst we talk?'

'No,' she said, somewhat flummoxed, 'only Martha, my maidservant. I'll call her.'

But Martha had heard the conversation. 'Here, mistress,' she called.

Diver appeared from the stairs, growling, teeth bared.

'Go on down now. Good dog. Goody Turner will get you some supper.'

Diver seemed to sense the odd atmosphere and his hackles were up. He carried on growling, his ears back. Goody Turner had to pull him, whining, down the stairs. When Elspet turned back to the visitors, Hugh's father was raising his bushy eyebrows at his son.

'Mistress Leviston, let us go inside,' he said. His voice was a broader, harsher version of his son's.

'Yes, yes . . . of course.' She led the way and heard the 'click, click' of his cane as the men followed. She pulled an upright chair near to the hearth for Hugh's father, though the fire had not been lit for weeks.

She perched on the edge of her seat and waited silently while they settled themselves. 'He won't sell?' she asked.

Hugh's father gave a slight sideways nod of the head and fixed Hugh with a look. Hugh stood again, and announced, 'I am sorry, Mistress Leviston . . .' he was struggling for words, 'it's this way. I find I no longer wish to be wed.' He sat down again suddenly and looked at his knees.

She leaned towards him. 'Oh Hugh, we can wait a while, if you wish. There is no need for it to be so soon—'

'No.' His father's voice cut in. 'What my son means is that he is breaking his engagement. He does not want to marry, Miss Leviston, not now and not at any future date.'

'Oh.' The word sounded very small.

Her mind raced. Did he mean he did not want to marry her? So the will had made a difference after all. She looked to the father, but he would not meet her eye, and was drumming on his thigh with his fingers.

She stood up again, hearing the rustle of her gown. 'Might I ask you, Hugh, why you have changed your mind?' Her question was too reasonable given that an explosion seemed to be happening in her chest.

'He does not want—' His father started to speak but she interrupted him.

'With all respect, sir, I am asking Hugh. He owes me some explanation at least. Hugh?'

Hugh pulled at his fall-back collar, and stretched his jaw, as if the words were stuck in his throat. Eventually, he said, 'We went to Greeting. I wanted to buy the house and business from your cousin. That's when we found out . . .'

He did not go on, but she waited. Faint barking came from below.

Then he burst out, 'Damn it, that you lied to us. Your father and you both, that Zachary is not your cousin, that he's your—'

'Your bastard brother,' his father interrupted. 'That he is the son of a whore of Cheapside.' His voice was rising now, getting louder. 'That up until a few months ago he was making a living stealing and cheating his betters. That there are records of him and his thieving brothers in every gaol in the city.'

'Is it true, Elspet?' Hugh pleaded.

'I—' She was confused, she sank down in the chair, hand to her forehead, as if to press it there might bring her an answer. 'Truth be told, I don't know. I mean, yes, they tell me Zachary is my half-brother. But I knew nothing of this – this other business, indeed nothing of him at all before he came to this house; my father did not tell me – I mean to say . . .' She struggled to find anything sensible to add.

Old Mr Bradstone cleared his throat and rose to his feet, leaning on his stick, preparing to go. 'The facts are these. We have just found out that Leviston's Lace is not the solid business we thought it to be. There are debts. Debts you did not think to disclose. Add to this your personal history . . .' he wrinkled his nose, 'and what seemed a suitable match is regrettably no longer so. I am sorry, Miss Leviston.' He did not look sorry, just self-righteous. 'Come, Hugh, we have said what we came to say.'

She reached out a hand, a protestation on her lips. 'No, do not get up again,' Hugh said, his face red with heat, 'Martha can show us out.'

Martha jumped up from her seat by the door and opened it. She seemed small and slight next to the two burly men, and her eyes darted in fear first to one gentleman and then to the other.

The full enormity of what it meant took Elspet's breath. She leapt from the chair. 'Wait!' she shouted. 'Hugh!' She put her hand to his shoulder to stay him.

He turned but his eyes avoided hers.

'Will you leave me now, when I need help the most?' She heard the choke in her voice. 'Zachary wants to sell everything I own. And you will let him take my reputation too?'

Hugh made to move away.

She clasped his arm. 'Please, Hugh, think again. I will be a good wife, the best you could wish for – I am skilled in household accounts and with the needle . . .' She knew she was gabbling, clutching at straws. She was humiliating herself but could not prevent the words spilling out.

He shook his head. 'I am sorry, I would not have—'

'Hugh.' His father summoned him briskly. Hugh shook his head wordlessly and strode to the door where it was held open for him.

Elspet cried, 'I am not my brother. I am honest and hardworking and . . .' but her voice trailed away. She had caught sight of his father's face which regarded her with contempt as though she were the lowest worm of the earth.

In haste Hugh ducked away and out of the door. She saw two hats pass the window. A moment later hoof beats rang out, followed by the rattle of wheels as their carriage pulled away. She stood in the darkness of the hall, unable to move into the brighter light of the chamber.

'Martha,' she whispered, 'leave me.'

Martha's shoes clacked away downstairs. Elspet leaned her back against the front door to keep the world out, and the hall fell silent.

Mr Bradstone mentioned debts. What did he mean? She knew of

no debt. Worse, the house would be sold from under her feet. She must face it. There was nowhere else to go, not even a husband and house in Yorkshire.

Part Two

All things which are similar and therefore connected,
are drawn to each other's power.
Heinrich Cornelius Agrippa, De Occulta Philosophia

Chapter 18

August 1608 (a year earlier)
The Royal Court of Felipe III, El Escorial, Madrid

'So what would you suggest?' The young king's voice was irritable; he found the older man's ponderous manner irksome.

'That we should enable all Moriscos to be educated as your father promised. After all, they are citizens of Spain.'

'It has been tried. It achieves nothing, to compel them to undertake instruction, and well you know it. Quiroba is a more astute inquisitor-general than his predecessor. He has proved what we already knew – they pay us lip-service in church, but beneath their nods and smiles lie hearts of treachery. And no sooner have they left our churches, then they band together privately to carry out their heathen customs.'

The king picked up his glass of port and downed it before setting it on the highly polished walnut table, which was set like an island in the vast library. Immediately the glass was removed by one of the courtiers and a fresh glass was clinked down.

Father Fernandez, the Jesuit, who was small and old, was standing by the table sweating slightly. He had dreaded this interview.

When the king asked for advice he did not really want advice, at least not advice that conflicted with his own ideas. And here, looked down on by the painted frescoes of the gods of rhetoric, dialectic and grammar, he felt even more inadequate in his grey homespun.

Despite the support of English Jesuits at court, he feared his opinion was a lost cause but, nevertheless, he had to try. So what if it was the last thing he did? He had already had seventy-two years of good life.

He wiped his forehead and smoothed out a sheaf of unrolled parchments before the king. 'Here are the documents showing the education programme for the Morisco seminaries of Seville, of Madrid, of—'

The king interrupted. 'My father said that he ordered a census of the Moriscos to be taken. Has that been done?' He scooped up one of the documents with a well-manicured hand and scanned it briefly before casting it back on to the table.

'Your father was . . . well-intentioned, but I'm afraid he did not appreciate the difficulties,' replied Fr Fernandez. 'It is too awkward an undertaking. It will provoke bad feeling if we single them out for anything, let alone to be counted. Anyway, the Church simply does not have the manpower; it would be too time-consuming for those in ecclesiastical office.' He picked up the scroll and held it out to the king. 'Why not take a look at these reports, we have had a modicum of success with the re-education measures and—'

'But we need to know how many we are dealing with.' The king paced the floor, his gold-leafed boot heels tapping on the marble tiles. 'How can the Duke of Lerma plan how many mercenaries will be required for their transportation if I don't know the numbers of Moriscos I am dealing with?'

So the king was intent on expulsion. Fernandez sagged. 'Is exile the only course open to us, your majesty? I fear even talk of an expulsion would stir a rebellion, like in the Alpujarras. That was a travesty.' He shook his head sadly. 'So much bloodshed, so little change. Why not allow a little more time? We do not know how successful the Edict of Grace has been yet.'

The king snorted as if to dismiss it. 'The duke informs me the Moriscos are already whispering in the alleyways intent on another uprising, and that this time they will call on the might of the Turks to help them. Can you imagine what that would mean?'

There was no answer he could give to the king's rhetorical question, so Fr Fernandez clasped his hands and looked down at the hem of his robe.

'No, the Crown should act first to purge Spain of this bad seed. I am beginning to think we should not wait until after the results of this Edict of Grace. The edicts are failing anyway, my bishop says. Not enough confessions.'

Fr Fernandez cleared his throat. He felt the words come to the tip of his tongue, but dare not say them. That it was hardly surprising. That since the last *auto da fé* most Moriscos were too terrified to come forward.

He moved away from the table and slowly straightened his aching knees. He made a small bow before taking a deep breath, 'Pardon me for my bluntness,' he said, 'but I feel the trials have become somewhat heavy-handed. Of course it is not the fault of your majesty,' he hastened to add, 'but the Moriscos see their kindred confess and repent, and vow to convert, and yet still they are burnt for heresy.'

The king paused in his pacing and glared at him with his slate-coloured eyes. Fr Fernandez had his attention at last; he waited for the axe to fall.

But the king merely turned away and tapped his foot. The sight of his small beribboned shoe tapping like that in this vast cavern of books made Fernandez angry. It seemed too small a gesture for what was at stake. He did not understand how this king could possibly have earned the title, *'El Santito.'* He prayed, yes – three hours a day. He owned all these books. But was he holy? Fernandez doubted it.

He must drown out that tapping. He threw up his arms in frustration. 'How can we call ourselves compassionate men? In Aragon two women were executed, they tell me, just for wearing the Moorish veil. How can we have come to this? That we burn people in God's name, simply for wearing the wrong clothes?'

The king whipped round. 'You go too far, Father. That's not the point, and you know it.'

Fr Fernandez dropped his eyes as the king turned on his heel and ranged away from him down the length of the room. 'Don't be naïve,' he called. 'Wearing the veil is forbidden precisely because it encourages them to band together and resist integration. Those that were tried and executed were proven traitors to the faith. You know full well their dress was only the outward expression of that.'

'But the trials are a death sentence! How can we bring men to the faith through repentance, if they know that repentance sentences them to the pyre?' The priest's voice echoed against the domes and arches above.

The king tapped back towards him. 'They die because they have not fully renounced their ways. Those who show their contrition by pointing out their Muslim compatriots are left in peace. And surely once they have confessed and repented the Church can instruct them.' He leaned his moustached face towards Fr Fernandez; his breath smelt of cloves and decay. 'Or is it beyond the wit of my bishops to educate a few slaves and servants?'

Fr Fernandez backed away. 'Of course not, but education takes time, your majesty, you have to allow it time,' he pleaded. 'It can be as much as a whole generation before we see the fruits of our instruction.'

'Or perhaps, Father, it is because these are a devious race.' The king went over to the window where light streamed in past the dark columns of the bookshelves. 'Quiroba tells me the courts find no consistency in the Morisco confessions. You know as well as I do, they dissemble, they avoid the truth, they shield their infidel friends. Repentance must be absolute, or it is no use at all. Impenitence is a mortal sin, yes?'

Fr Fernandez nodded wearily. 'Come, your majesty, let's take a look at our successes.' He approached the window alcove with a scroll again, and made to unwrap it, but the king shot out one hand to cover it and flapped him away with the other.

'Enough with your scraps of paper! I'm tired of the whole question.' The king's eyes flicked to the window. Outside, the evening hunting party could be seen gathering in the courtyard. 'I just want the kingdom settled. I am inclined to take the advice of the Duke of Lerma. This came today.' He signalled to a courtier who hurried over and thrust a rolled parchment into Fr Fernandez's hands.

Warily, Fernandez untied the thong and unrolled it. He knew already what it would say. The Duke of Lerma was a notorious bigot. Avaricious but highly intelligent, he was always somewhere behind the king's decisions. He and the queen, who had a hatred of just about everything. Fernandez picked up his eyeglass from the cord around his neck. The king meanwhile had sat again, but was thrumming his fingers impatiently on the table.

'Well, what do you make of it?' the king asked, barely giving Fernandez time to adjust his vision.

'I have only scanned it, so I cannot properly say,' the priest said tactfully, reading on as he spoke. He sighed. It was as he had predicted. 'Pardon me, your majesty, but these are not the enemy. Most of these men have lived here all their lives. They think of themselves as Spanish, your loyal citizens.'

The king let out an unbelieving grunt.

Fernandez knew if he pressed him too far that it would mean the end of his time here in the Royal Monastery. He knew this, yet found himself unable to stop himself. He rolled the paper and placed it carefully on the table. It was now or never. He braced himself.

'As an ordained priest, I could never accept this mass expulsion, no matter what Lerma thinks. Not those who have been baptized Christian. We would be sending them back to a heathen country. In all Christian conscience, that goes against my vocation to bring souls to peace with God. You must wait a while; the Time of Grace may yet show confessions, and more conversions to our cause.'

'Must? You dare to tell me what I must do?'

'I beg pardon, but I thought—'

'I can see you have been tainted by their sweet-talking. You are soft, Fr Fernandez. Lerma says all our troubles stem from this canker in our society. Our Armada was routed by the English, and we will have no peace from God until we prise up the heathen stock here at home. How can we hope for success in taming the infidel abroad, whilst ever Spain offers a home to these heretics?'

The king picked up a bell and rang it. The sound tinkled, like a fairy bell. 'I'm tired of this. My hounds are waiting outside. And I'm afraid we cannot agree, Fr Fernandez.'

He heard the door open behind him. Two guards in plate armour entered.

The king continued, fixing Fernandez with an icy look. 'We are not in my father's reign now, we are in mine. And as of today, there is no place at my court or in my kingdom for supporters of heresy.' He turned to the guards. 'Arrange horses and an escort. Fr Fernandez will take up new lodgings in the Castle of the Manzanares El Real. He can wait there until the Inquisitors can find time to examine his case. Now go.'

'Leave me be, I will walk unaided,' said Fr Fernandez, but the guards held tight. 'May God bless your majesty,' he called, as he was bullied to the door, 'and may he give you what you deserve.'

Chapter 19

London, August 1609

Around them people were already heaving trunks and baskets aboard, but Elspet waited on the quay whilst a white-faced Mr Wilmot said goodbye to his wife Dorothy. She heard him promise her he would return with good news, and telling her not to fret. She averted her eyes as they embraced, but when she turned back it was to see him kiss her tenderly on the lips, stroking a strand of blonde hair away from her forehead.

She repressed a pang of jealousy. Nobody would be missing her, except, perhaps, the dogs. She hoped the hunt kennels would be taking good care of them. She was nervous; the ship looked enormous and the thought of crossing over that vast body of water to France was daunting. A vision of Bainbridge's ships listing at the bottom of the ocean had seized her just as it had seized Mr Wilmot. But what else could she do? She refused to just do nothing until she was thrust out into the cold.

After much pressure, Greeting had agreed to wait before the sale of the property so that she and Mr Wilmot could travel to Spain to discuss the business with Zachary. Mr Wilmot was as angry as she was – after all, he had a whole cohort of men to satisfy, men who would likely be out of work if the business was sold. Like herself, he had assumed that the business would be kept running – the men were used to changes at the helm, it happened all the time in business. But that the warehouses should close? Well, that was quite another thing altogether. Forty men depended on Leviston's lace trade, and who knows how many women crouching in their cottages over their bobbins and pads.

Once on board, Wilmot leaned on the rails, looking over the side and shifting from foot to foot nervously. All around, other travellers were doing the same, anxious to be moving. At the first lurch of the ship he turned back to look for her. Elspet smiled at him. She was glad of his company for she did not know if she would have been brave enough to travel alone on such a journey.

The ship set sail and soberly they watched the land recede. Neither spoke. It was only when they were out of sight of land that Elspet said to him, 'Thank you, Mr Wilmot, for your kindness. I am grateful.'

'No,' he said. 'You give me too much credit. I have another selfish motive besides kindness. I am hoping that a woman may persuade Mr Deane to reconsider his plans. A woman can more easily play on a man's sympathies than a man can. I have a rough tongue and I've been told I am too blunt. I am hoping our alliance will benefit us both.'

'Then I'm afraid you will be disappointed. Mr Deane thinks little of me.' She weighed the words carefully. 'I was hoping your more gentlemanly persuasion might sway him.'

He laughed ruefully. 'So we are both laying our hopes with the other! No matter, perhaps between the two of us we will make him see reason. I don't know how I will face my men if we cannot.'

'He has little understanding of the trade. Perhaps if we can make him see how profitable it could be . . .?'

He looked at her frankly. 'Could be. That's the word, I'm afraid. It has seen better days as I'm sure you're aware.'

'A temporary state of affairs, I'm sure—' She paused. He was shaking his head.

He wrapped his cloak tighter round his shoulders. 'You know he lent to Bainbridge? It was your father who financed the *Flora Rose* and the *Sea Hart*. It left the business in debt.'

'Oh no. I had no idea. Mr Bradstone told me that Leviston's was in ill-repair, but I didn't know why. I thought it was just another excuse for Hugh to break off our engagement.'

'And the shock of it, for a man already in poor health, well . . .'

He had no need to say more. The worry had killed her father. The lurch of the ship made her queasy, but also the thought that she had been so short-sighted. It had not occurred to her that her father had granted Bainbridge a loan. But how foolish, and typical, of her father to help his Catholic friend like that.

'How bad is it?'

'Well, if our Brittany boats come home safe, it will go a long way to putting it back to rights. But I'd say five years. Five years before the sale of it would keep you, mistress.'

His honesty and bluntness took away her breath. No wonder he wanted to persuade Zachary to hold the sale. 'Are you saying that the business is failing?'

'If he sells now, then the debts of the *Flora Rose* and the *Sea Hart* will mean there is little left to come to you. What will you do if he insists on selling?'

She shrugged. She could not even think of it. Already she had sold most of her jewellery to pay her passage. She moved over to the rail where Martha stood, bent over the side, pale and white.

Over by the point, the faint wisp of land was just fading away. The image of her home came to her, the last time she had shut the door. The dust sheets, the shuttered windows, Goody Turner's tears. The scrape as she turned the key in the lock.

She gripped tight to the brass handrail as the rising sun bled a pool of sulphur into the grey morning mist. She would find Zachary Deane and never let him from her sight until he agreed to listen to Mr Wilmot. She would have her proper inheritance. She would find him and she would not fail.

Chapter 20

Zachary watched Gabriel count out his few pesos from his pouch. He had arranged to meet him after the day's work in the grounds of the cathedral where there was a *casa de gula* where they could have a meal and watch life go by. By Gabriel's standards, anyone who could afford a brand new rapier was already a rich man, so he had rapidly realized he could never tell his foundry friend of his good fortune.

A lad in a spotted apron and even filthier cap set down a jug and relit the hog-grease candle at their table.

'That tastes like heaven,' Zachary said, quaffing his ale.

'It surely does.' Gabriel grinned.

The noise forced them to shout to hear each other over the rest of the customers, who conducted their business with expletives and much hand-gesturing.

This casa was the haunt of undesirables, anyone within the cathedral walls being supposedly protected from arrest. It reminded him of St Paul's in London; same unruly atmosphere, same ne'er-do-wells with their eyes on passing purses. What a turning-about, he thought; soon he would be one of those needing to look to his purse.

This is the life, he thought, glancing around at the rickety wooden tables bleached pale by the sun, at the orange trees stripped white up to their branches. Above, the stars were just starting to glimmer through the clouds of wood-smoke from the city pottery kilns, through the pluming columns from distant cooking fires and through the thin wisps from candles.

When the trenchers arrived they wolfed down their food, for the labour in the smithy made gluttons of them both. On the boundary of the walls, and not quite inside the cathedral grounds, lolled three *damas de medio manto*, ladies of the half-mantle, as they were called, each with one hip pushed against the warm honey-coloured stone, faces illuminated by the fixed torchères in the walls.

Their eyes scoured the tables for trade, trying to catch a young man's eye. One of them flashed her blackened eyelashes at them and smiled.

'Don't bother. She's not as young as she looks. I've seen her here every night for the last four years at least. It's all paint and padding,' Gabriel said.

'Do you have a girl?'

He looked down bashfully under his unruly crown of black hair, and his cheeks blotched pink. 'Did have once. Her father didn't like me, so there was no chance. Rigid in the old ways. I'll be more of a prospect once I have a permanent position. I like it at the smithy. A journeyman's life is no life for any woman, and I'm fixing on staying, if Guido will take me. I'm on six-months trial.'

'He'll take you on. You're the muscle in there. He'd be lost without you.'

'Let's hope so.'

Their conversation faltered as a crowd gathered just outside the cathedral gates. They craned their necks to see what was afoot.

'Just another slave auction, by the looks of it,' Gabriel said.

'Do they not have auction blocks here, then?'

'No, they parade them around the markets until they have enough followers, then they just stop and do it, before the crowd loses interest.'

'Let's go take a look.'

'No, I think I'll go on home. My landlady left some things drying outside and I want to check she's brought them all in. If it's not tied down, some cutpurse will have it round here, Sevillians are all ruffians.'

Zachary laughed ruefully with him, though he knew himself to be one of those very cutpurses and cloak-snatchers of whom Gabriel was so wary. Zachary saluted him farewell and watched him wend his way back through the square before he cast some coins on to the table and the waiter swooped on them like a hungry gull.

Outside the gate, he peered over the hats to see what was happening – over the usual dark felts with feathered plumes in shades of ochre and grey, and the more colourful onion-shaped headdresses of the Turkish traders. The slaves were ranked in a row from the tallest to the shortest: two men, three women and a youth. The men were elderly Negroes with downcast eyes. In their ragged and dusty livery they looked tired and well past their prime.

But like most men, his eyes were drawn by the women; of these two were white slaves, Moriscos, with the obligatory brand of an 's' and a line or *clavo* standing for *esclavo* on one side of the face. As was the custom, the owner's own initials were branded on the other cheek. He had been in Seville long enough to understand their brands a little, both on horseflesh and men. The white women pressed together, as though to give each other comfort. They were both bone-thin and one of them had scabs on her arm from a recent graze. The owner was with the auctioneer, showing off the Negro woman to the crowd.

'Only twenty-two years old, look at the brawn on those arms,' cried the auctioneer. 'At least another twenty years good labour from this one, gents. Twenty-five, if you feed it well.'

'What work has she done before?' a man from the crowd called.

'Laundry, kitchen, she'll turn her hand to anything.' The owner, resplendent in a fully embroidered suit of russet and gold velvet, despite the evening's heat, slapped the girl on the shoulder. She remained still as stone, staring out at the crowd as if they did not exist. The other two girls flinched, cowered away from his hand.

'Why are you selling, then?'

'Going abroad. I'll get new in the New World.' He wiped his moustache, then gestured at them. 'Not worth the cost of transport, I need slaves with the local language.'

He turned his attention to the youth, another Morisco, by the shape of him. He was watching the white women in quick darting glances. A look passed between him and one of the women and Zachary understood immediately she was his mother. They had the same features, the small sharp nose and high brow, as if pressed from the same mould. The lad hopped from foot to foot, impatient to know his fate. A barely disguised look of fear flitted across his mother's face.

Zachary crowded in closer. He had taken a fancy to this boy. Now he was rich he would need a runner to do errands and fetch and carry for him. A personal slave, not just a house slave like Ana. He elbowed his way through the crowd until he was right next to the lad. Now he was next to him he could see that the boy was shorter than he thought, his legs thin as rails. Zachary wondered whether he got called 'Spindle-shanks', the way he used to at his age.

Perhaps he was being a little hasty – it might be better to wait and find something a little stronger. At that moment the boy turned to look up at him, and even in the dusky light he could see he had the most unusual blue eyes, blue the colour of the Spanish sky, not the commonplace brown or black. In that moment Zachary's mind was made up.

He watched the bidding with impatience. The two old Negroes, nobody wanted. Eventually they sold for ten reales apiece. The two Morisco women went to the same gentleman when he bid one hundred for the pair.

A dark Jew standing next to Zachary said, 'You buying?'

'I might.'

'He paid over the odds. Moriscos are nothing but trouble. You can't trust them. Slit your throat in the night, given half a chance. Always better with a darkie. They know their place. Ah, here we go.'

Zachary stood on his tiptoes to wave his hand as the bidding started. The Negro woman, described as a devout and baptised Christian, aroused fierce shouts and hand-waving, but finally went for one hundred and eighty, not to the man next to him but to a thick-set man with a nose bent out of joint to one side. He bid with a curt and barely perceptible nod, and was obviously a regular customer. He did not even smile when the girl went to him, but he was slapped on the back by the young and rowdy men who were with him, until he turned and gave them a disapproving glare. They fell back like a pack of dogs.

'Now what are we bid for this one? Forty, shall I say? Good clean young lad, unbranded, ready for you to put your mark on. Worth forty of anybody's money.' The auctioneer started his patter.

The man who bought the Negro woman strode over to inspect the boy – pulled his ears back to look behind them, made him open his mouth, lifted his shirt to reveal a bony ribcage. Zachary did not much like the way he did this, nor the way the lad cowered away, flinching, as if he might be struck at any moment.

Tentatively, Zachary lifted his hand. 'Forty,' he said.

The bent-nosed man stopped his examination, cast him a frosty look and called, 'Fifty.'

The four youths with him surrounded Zachary and the boy. He knew their type; they looked like bodyguards, they had the bound-up torsos of prize-fighters. 'Sixty,' he called out, in a voice cool as he could muster.

'Sixty-five.' At the other man's words a sharp shove came from behind so that Zachary lost balance and stumbled forward. He landed face first into the dirt. Instantly he leapt to his feet, about to turn and protest, but then he realized – it was an old trick, to distract him from the bidding.

'Seventy,' Zachary shouted, brushing dirt from the grazes on his hands.

'Seventy-five.'

A tingle ran up the back of Zachary's neck, the men behind had muscled in, so that he was boxed in on all sides. He placed his hand surreptitiously on his sword. One of them hissed in his ear, '*Vete!* Or we will break your back.'

He ignored them, fingered the paring knife in his sleeve, 'Eighty!'

The crowd let out an 'Ooh', and people turned to stare. A tic moved in his opponent's cheek. 'Eighty-five.'

His men could do nothing now as they had the crowd's full attention. The boy cringed away, sensing trouble. But Zachary pressed on. He would not be deterred. He would have let it go, but the other man's attitude had made him even more determined. Bully him, would he? Not if he could help it. 'One hundred!' It was his last bid. He had only that amount left in cash. The crowd muttered that he was mad, had lost his senses.

'And five,' said the other calmly.

The mother's eyes were on him. There was a hushed pause whilst the auctioneer waited, his clapper held up. It was no good, Zachary was out-bid; he could go no further. Reluctantly, he shook his head.

The auctioneer rapped the clapper. 'Sold!'

He saw the boy droop, and it gave him a sharp pain of recognition.

Zachary turned to walk away. He wished he had never begun. It was one thing to buy goods, but he had felt something for that boy, recognized something of himself. And his mother; the look in her eyes when he failed, had flayed him.

He glanced over his shoulder to see his rival's heavy shoulders push through the crowd, and the auctioneer hold up the deeds of purchase for the crook-nosed man to sign. The boy was still staring at Zachary with an unfathomable gaze. He felt terrible then, that he could not have bought him and given him back to his mother.

He needed to get away. But he hadn't gone ten paces before he felt hands fasten round his throat and a jerk to his neck, 'Hey!' he shouted, but nobody heard him. The four youths bore him off into a shadowed back alley. Flies hung about the ground, telling him it was probably used as a piss-hole.

Before he could say a word one of the men raised his fist and smashed it into his nose. 'My master could have had him for forty,' he said.

The blow brought Zachary to his knees, where he felt the impact of a boot slam into the small of his back. The pain made him nauseous and he bent over to protect his face. There was no time to pull a weapon, nor room. Punches rained down on his head. His hands got the brunt of it; when it eventually stopped, he could hardly bear the pain in them. He looked up to see a pair of soft leather shoes and black hose. The burly man stood there, the Negro woman and the boy-slave shackled at his side.

'Good,' he said.

He ignored Zachary and walked away, his entourage wiping their fists and swaggering behind. As they were about to round the corner, the boy slave turned back, seemed to fix him with his blue eyes. It was not a look of blame, but one of understanding.

Chapter 21

Triana, Seville

Luisa Ortega was waiting for her father to come out of the swordmaster's house, and as usual he was late. She passed the time by helping Daria scrub the vegetables. It was a backbreaking task as they needed so many aubergines to feed all those men with their swashing swords, as well as all the apprentices and servants. Luisa scooped a handful of cold water from the tiled bowl and patted it on her face to cool it.

The water always refreshed her. Papa told her that after she was baptized they rushed her home and scrubbed her face and head with hot water. They did this to all their infants, Papa said, in case the stink of Christianity should cling and turn them into infidels.

She howled so much they had to stop and take her instead to be doused in the Guadalquivir river. But it hadn't made any difference, the Christianity had clung, much to Papa's disappointment.

She liked to think that's what gave her an affinity with water. As a child she was drawn to the jade green of the river and would often submerge herself face down, just floating, her hair drifting about her like weed. She'd lift her chin to breathe in the smell of wet and sand before dipping her head back in to watch the marbled depths for fish and eels. But now she was older there was no time for that, she had to content herself with a few snatched handfuls of water rubbed over her sun-scorched skin.

'*Oye soñadora*, wake up!' Daria passed her another basket of onions, and Luisa began to flake off their papery skins.

'Onions. Oh no. Better cover my eyes.'

Daria smiled at her as she pared the aubergines. Unlike Luisa, she wore the *manto*, the head-covering, so that her face appeared from it like a moon under a drape of cloud. Daria was braver than she was, Luisa thought, because to wear the head-covering was to mark yourself out, and there were few of her age left clinging to that tradition. Mama and Papa approved of Daria, their neighbour's daughter. They said it was women like her who kept their faith alive. They always 'tsk'ed at Luisa, though, at her reckless attitude, at her unconcern for history and their disappearing Arabic tongue, at her devotion to the candle-lit cathedral and the Mass.

Luisa picked up the peelings and tossed them into the bucket for the pigs.

'We'll need more aubergines,' Daria said, shaking her head. 'The men eat enough for two with all their thrashing.'

'There's more in the basket,' Luisa said. 'Amar gave me a full load. Borage and chard too. Nearly broke my neck carrying it all the way from the field on my head.'

Daria pattered over on bare feet and heaved the basket on to the table again, selecting three or four plump, purple fruits.

'Still inside?' Daria asked.

Luisa threw the onions into a bowl and peered through the window again. 'Yes, poor souls. He'll be making them go through the gematria again. Still, at least they are cool in the library.'

After the aubergines were pared, they sliced them and stacked them in salt to draw the bitterness out. Señor Alvarez always had a good supply of salt, unlike at home. Moriscos were not allowed to go down to the salt pans, so Luisa's family never had any. Sometimes she dipped a damp finger into the white crystals when the block had been crushed in the pestle, and sucked her finger to taste the sea, but her conscience pricked her when she did that. It was like stealing, though it was only a few grains.

She heard the murmur of voices outside and rubbed her hands on the sides of her skirts, which were already spattered with glazes from her day at the pottery. She went to the door and looked into the courtyard. Papa was descending the stone steps, his hand feeling for the wall, deep in conversation with the fencing master, Señor Alvarez. Two of the other young men followed close behind – she recognized them as Alexander Souter, the tall Dutch fellow with the pointed beard, and Etienne Galen the narrow-eyed Frenchman.

Señor Alvarez took the two young men off to the corner of the yard where a pile of bucklers lay waiting. Papa glanced in at the doorway and screwed up one eye at her. A moment later he was in the kitchen, lifting the heavy lid of the aubergine pot and bringing his head close to it to see. Papa's vision was not so good.

'Ah, Daria. Expecting the Spanish army, are we?' he said.

'You know what they're like,' she laughed. 'If I don't make enough, they'll be fighting over the last mouthful like dogs – despite all their noble talk.' Luisa giggled along with her.

'How was it at the pottery today?' Papa asked, his arm round Luisa's shoulders as they went to the door. He waved a farewell at Daria, who nodded, used to their routine. Luisa and her father talked as they went, and the men training with swords and bucklers never so much as looked twice at them.

'Good,' Luisa replied to him, 'I'm enjoying pressing the *olambrillas* for the tiles in the new hospital. Unusual octagonal moulds, and the glazes are beautiful. Every time Hammam lifts them from the kiln I think how beautiful they look. Turquoise and green like the river. They're like the ones in the Alcazar, Hammam says. But these are for beggars and the infirm to enjoy. Makes a change.'

'You should have seen the tiles in my old mosque in Granada, they were glorious. You know my nose must have been a hair's breadth from them so often I knew the patterns by heart. That, and the dusty soles of Jamete's feet. He always knelt in front of me.' Papa's laugh was lined with sorrow. 'But they smashed the tiles in the last uprising. They razed the mosque to the ground. I remember seeing the shards in the street, and people stooping, picking them up, unable to believe anyone could have taken a hammer to something so beautiful.'

Luisa said nothing, but squeezed his arm. She was used to him talking this way, as if one of those shards had lodged itself in his mind and, try as he might, he was unable to free himself of the pain of it. Mama could always soothe him. She understood him, understood his strange moods and contradictions.

They walked companionably, taking their time. She had her hand always on his arm to guide him, lest he should trip over some unseen hazard.

'The new student, Girard Thibault, he is not bad. By his voice I thought he would not have the patience for study, but I was wrong. We've been working on Plato's solids, the dodecahedron – looking at the principle of twelve, how the archetype unfolds into everything. The planetary signs, the twelve maidens at the well in the Qu'ran—'

'Yes, yes,' she said, having heard it all before.

'Anyway, when I brought out the Agrippa, he sat with it and I swear he never moved the whole afternoon. I could hear his breath on the pages. He's a good draughtsman, too, by all accounts; he's shown Señor some of his sketches.'

'I know. He asked if he could draw my portrait. Huh. I said no, of course, I don't want—' she paused a moment to bow and greet another of their neighbours returning from the market place.

Papa took the opportunity to interrupt. 'Well, you should have agreed. Thibault is a mild young man, and of gentle blood. He would mean nothing by it except to sharpen his draughtsmanship. Besides, he knows it has always been a tradition in our culture to respect the woman.'

'I can't say I've noticed,' she replied, immediately bristling.

'No, I'm being serious. You are the keepers of the tradition, the long line of blood stretching back to infinity.' He stopped, pulled her into the shade. 'Lalla, Luisa, they want rid of us. There is talk again of us being exiled from Spain, sending the *conversos* back. And when that happens, many will fight – fight for our land and our livelihoods. And as they must, many will die.'

She did not look him in the face, but pulled again on his arm.

He did not come. 'You do not want to believe it, but it is true. Then you will be the torchbearers, you women. Remember the story of Job and Rahma. It has always been so.'

'It is just rumour.'

'But rumour starts somewhere, like a small spring. Soon it gathers more water until it is a river, wide as the Guadalquivir.'

She set off walking again, tugging on his sleeve. She did not want to believe it. It was just tattle as usual, this talk of exile. She had known nothing but Spain since she was scrubbed in the water of the river on the day she was born. She was Spanish to the core. Why did her father insist on calling her Lalla, when he knew everyone else called her Luisa, a good solid Spanish name? What use had she for the name of some half-mad Sufi from centuries ago?

He could not be right. There were too many *conversos* in Seville; the authorities surely would not be able to expel them all. She tugged again at Papa's sleeve in exasperation to make him keep up. Seville was her city, and she loved every last stone of it.

The stories that Papa was so fond of telling, about the expulsion from Granada, that was forty years ago. It was just history. He could only have been a boy then, he probably didn't understand. And he would keep bringing up those old Muslim tales, like the story of Rahma, who carried the ailing Job and his faith to the tribe of Israel. It sounded archaic, all the business of carrying the word of Allah, as if it were somehow a basket on someone's head. Besides, she certainly did not want the sort of responsibility Rahma had.

Anyway, if there was to be an uprising, Papa would be too old and blind to be a part of it. No, they would leave the Sevillians alone, peaceable as they were. They were no threat to anyone, she thought, they had been there too long, they were no raw incomers. She chewed on this as they walked, impatient with Papa, internally rebelling against his hand on her sleeve.

When they reached Triana, she let go and hurried on ahead. Papa knew every turn in the street by feel, and here they were amongst friends. She burst through the door to find Mama had already put out the mat on the floor, the board with the barley bread, and the bowls steaming with fragrant couscous and *cazuela blanca*. She was all smiles to see them as usual.

'Luisa!' her brother Husain leapt up at her and wound his skinny knees round her waist.

'How's my little monkey?' She grinned at him, and tickled him under the arms until he was forced to release his grip from round her neck and wriggle down.

'Will you cut me the crust?' he said, 'I'm starving. Look, I helped Mama make the twist in the bread.'

She squatted and pushed her skirts aside and picked up the knife to cut the loaf. Behind her she heard Papa come in and go through the back to the yard to strip and wash.

Husain jumped up and rushed after him, 'Papa! Papa!'

But Papa sent him away, 'Later, my little chap, give a man a chance to clean up.' Papa made all these ablutions every day, even though she told him it was a waste of time and he would probably not be any holier by doing it. He frowned at her when she said this, and Mama told her to have more respect.

'Are you nearly done?' Luisa shouted, through the opening to the yard. 'We're hungry!'

'Let him have his way,' Mama said. 'If it makes him feel good, let him do it.'

'But we're not supposed to, you know we're not.'

'Where's the harm in being clean?'

'Yes, where's the harm in being clean?' echoed Husain, who was always the grubbiest child in the barrio.

She sighed. Papa insisted on clinging to the old ways like a raft, even though it would bring him nothing but trouble.

Mama went to close the shutters tight, Papa blessed the food, and then they ate. They hunkered down, feet tucked underneath out of view. The oil in the lamps gave a smoky haze to the room, a musky scent that mingled with the smell of cooking. Papa and Mama ate silently, to give the food their full attention. Their silent meals were so different from the busy tables in the market place. But she was used to it; it had been like this every day since she was born.

And it was good to be grateful. Often there was a shortage of bread and meat because Papa wouldn't allow them to have meat unless it had been blessed by someone, and if his friend Patricio the priest could not come, then they went without. Today there was a small portion of dried lamb cooked in olive oil, from the last time he came. Patricio did not understand their Muslim ways but he liked to play chess with Papa, and he was happy to bless their meat.

'A blessing costs nothing,' he always said.

Husain used his bread to scoop the last grains of couscous from his bowl.

'It was good, Ayamena. I think the lamb is better for stewing.' Papa nodded as he chewed.

'Mm, hmm,' grunted Husain, still with his mouth full.

'Nonsense, Nicolao, it was tough and you know it.' Mama pointed to a bit of gristle on the edge of her plate.

'It wasn't so bad,' Papa said.

'Susana's family don't bother with the blessing of the meat. So they have fresh meat every day,' Luisa said.

Mama gave her a warning look, but Papa did not rise to her bait. Mama bustled to put the water to heat on the fire so that they could have their mint tea. Luisa watched her bending over the flames, holding the fabric of her *manto* with one hand to keep it from catching. After a few moments the water bubbled and she poured a hissing steam over the leaves. A shout from outside made her pause midstream. Luisa ran towards the door to see what was going on.

'No!' shouted Papa. Something in his voice stopped her in her tracks.

She hovered in the middle of the room. Mama placed the pot on the trivet very carefully as though it might break.

'What's the—'

'Sssh.' Mama hushed Husain with a hand on the shoulder.

Time stopped. Their listening was so intense it was almost a noise.

Wood splintering and a woman's scream.

'Don't move,' Mama mouthed. Husain questioned Luisa with his wide eyes. She shook her head as Mama tiptoed to the shutter and put her eye to the crack where the two boards met.

'Men from the Inquisitor's,' she whispered, 'they've staved in Alma's door.'

'Come away from that window,' Papa hissed, stumbling to his feet, but she did not come. 'Ayamena!' His voice was harsher.

Alma's voice wailed from outside, 'Leave us alone, we weren't doing anything wrong. We were just eating, that's all.'

There was another noise like a thud, and Mama gasped and recoiled from the window. Husain wrapped his arms over his head and crawled away to the corner of the room.

'What is it?' The piece of bread still in Papa's hand dropped to the floor.

Mama did not answer and Luisa pressed up behind her to try to see through the crack. Mama would not let her near and all she could see was a sliver of bright blue sky like a shining needle above the buildings. Mama's hands were clutching the sill as she balanced on the balls of her feet.

The window went dark for a moment, and there was the sound of a scuffle – and then something hit the ground.

Immediately Alma's voice cried from outside, 'Please, no. Don't hurt him, he's old and sick.'

Papa blundered towards the door, but Mama leapt before him. 'No,' she spat. 'Do you want to risk us all? Sit down and be quiet.'

Papa tried to push past her but she was blazing now, like a cornered tigress.

'You stupid man,' she hissed, beating at him with her fists, 'what do you think you can do? You can't even see to shave your face!'

Father seemed to slump then, and move away from the door. In the silence they heard the clank of metal and chain.

Mama's mouth trembled. She staggered to hold Papa in a clumsy embrace, 'There, there. I didn't mean it.' Over his shoulder Mama caught sight of Husain, watching the whole scene through a gap between his fingers and hurried to envelop him in the folds of her *galedrilla*.

Luisa took her chance and ran to the shutters. Through the crack she saw the black leather breastplates of the king's militia, the Inquisition. Their swords were unsheathed and one of them held the scourge. He slapped the knotted thongs against his boot.

Alma, Daria's mother, had been chained neck to foot. 'This one now,' said the smallest soldier.

They fastened the chains to Alma's ankles. She did not move, her face was grey as chalk, her eyes blank, fixed on something on the ground. Luisa could not tear her eyes away. She could just see part of a tangled heap of blood-spattered clothes, and the torn flesh of a naked back, wizened and wrinkled as a raisin in the sun. Her hand came to her mouth as the man began to moan and move. Tears started in her eyes. It was Merin, Daria's father.

'Lazy dog,' one of the guards said. 'Get up.' And he flicked the whip at Merin's back. 'Your neighbour says he smelt meat cooking on Friday. The smoke came from your chimney.'

'No, no. He's mistaken,' called Alma. 'It was smoked herring. We're good Christians. Ask anybody.'

'The court will decide that. We're to take you all. And anyone else who eats at your table.'

Luisa pulled away. Nausea engulfed her. She cowered back away from the window and spat saliva into the corner.

'Keep quiet,' mouthed Mama, urgently, with one hand dragging the reluctant Husain to her side. She reached with the other to grab Luisa by the arm.

They huddled together, the whole family, pressed to the floor of the sleeping alcove, arms tight around each other, straining to hear what was happening in the street outside.

A sudden hammering on the door jolted Mama to her feet. Papa's heart beat against Luisa's shoulder. Mama's eyes were wide and staring; Luisa felt a hot tear run from Husain's face on to her own but she dare not move.

Outside the door a voice said, 'Nobody in. Shall we burn it?'

'No,' came another voice, 'it's next door to the armourer's. We don't want to risk setting light to that.'

'Why? It won't matter.'

'It will to Don Rodriguez. He told me this man's the best leather beater in town. He makes the armour for all the king's men. You can take responsibility if we do. I don't want Don Rodriguez to find out I had anything to do with it.'

'He won't know it was us.'

'Well, I'm not doing it. He'd soon find out who torched his favourite armourer. Come on, let's take these in. We'll tell Don Rodriguez to warn the leather beater to get out, and come back tomorrow. Then we can clear the whole infested yard.'

A crack from a whip made Luisa shrink closer to Papa. They could hear chains moving away. They lay there quiet for a long while. She saw with horror that Papa's lips were quivering and his eyes leaking tears.

'Don't, Nicolao,' whispered Mama, coming back to them and rubbing at his back.

'What use am I to Allah?' Papa said. 'I can't even help my neighbour. I stay here like a coward whilst they take Merin, Merin who would never lift a finger to a fly.'

'But what else could you do?'

'I could have told them, they are good Christians.'

'You know that's a lie. They pay it lip-service only, like all of us. The more they beat it out of us, the more inward it goes.'

'Mama,' Luisa said, 'they said they'd come back. Tomorrow. What will we do?'

'Pray to Allah,' said Mama. 'And pack our things.'

Chapter 22

Elspet sat side-saddle, and her hip bones ached. Spain was unfathomable to her. So hot and airless, so full of dust and stench. For this last part of the journey they travelled by pack-mule, for Mr Wilmot had insisted on going overland. The grit of the road blew into her eyes and her forehead ached from squinting into the sun. If she walked, every step was filled with yellowing tares and teasels, and even the grass was spiny and sharp, more thistle than weed.

Mr Wilmot's hand leapt to his dagger at every encounter on the road. He even armed himself against beekeepers and washerwomen. It seemed he was afraid of everything. Poor man, she thought as she adjusted her skirts to pad out her uncomfortable posterior, he looks so much smaller away from Father's warehouses and the solid buildings of London.

Wilmot had no Spanish and was forever asking her, 'What did he say?' or 'Tell me the word for . . .' and she must supply the answer. He got frustrated if she could not remember and his face turned sour and taciturn, and he kicked his mule on away from them, sighing, as if the two women were just too much trouble.

Iron grilles barred all the windows, as if everyone in Spain must somehow be behind bars. Martha was slumped in the saddle, her face red with heat, as they passed by cob and brick buildings squatting in red dirt villages. Like Elspet, she was muffled to the neck because of the piercing sun. Elspet tried to ignore Martha's miserable face, filled with guilt that she had brought her here.

Sometimes there were roadside shrines, and in the villages, rough-built churches, a constant reminder that Spain still held fast to the Holy Roman Church. Elspet always begged to look inside.

'Come, Mistress Leviston,' Wilmot called, 'we need to make Toledo by nightfall.'

'Just a few moments. This looks like such a quaint place. Look at the little belfry. And you must be tired. We can rest a moment, take some ale.'

'No,' Wilmot said. 'We must keep moving. We will need to rest soon enough when the sun is overhead. It is unwise to dawdle now.'

'A minute or two, only.' She unhooked her legs from the stirrups, preparing to dismount.

'Get back up, mistress. We are not resting here. If you wish to pray and then fry in the noonday sun, then that is up to you. But I will be riding on.'

She was tense with the heat and with the harsh road they were on. She scrambled down from the mule, tore her skirt away from the tares that had snagged it, and marched towards the church.

He shouted after her. 'Why? Why must you stop at every damn village?'

She retorted over her shoulder, 'I go to church as is my duty. I cannot see what is the matter with that.'

'We need to make Toledo by nightfall, that's what's the matter. While ever we are on the road, we're at the mercy of any cut-throat that chances by.' His angry tone made her hesitate and turn in time to see him throw his hat down on the ground. 'For God's sake, woman, I can't take any more of it, it's tiresome enough without this stopping every few miles whilst you count your stupid beads.'

Up until now they had been cordial and his sudden animosity scared her. Martha watched warily from the back of her mule, her face red and screwed up as if she might cry.

'And whose idea was it to travel this way instead of a comfortable passage around the coast by sea?'

'You agreed to it. You know what happened to Bainbridge's ships. And calculations show one is always safer on land than on the water.'

'Calculations? They're no use to us here. Go on ahead, if you must. I can fend for myself,' Elspet said.

'Don't be foolish. You can't travel alone. I owe it to your Father. You remind me of him. He could be just as stubborn, but he was good to me – he gave me a good livelihood and an education I'll never forget.'

'Then my father. . .' the words threatened to choke her, 'my father obviously cared more for you than he did for me,' she shouted, 'because he has left me at the mercy of a scoundrel like Zachary Deane.'

'He thought you provided for,' he shouted back. 'You should have been married by now. How the hell was he to know what a sorry muddle he would cause? Now come, mount up and let's get out of this infernal heat.'

'No.' She tried to push open the church door, but it was stiff and would not give.

'For the life of me, I can't see what you find so attractive about these churches. They are full of idols. You can pray perfectly well with me when we reach the lodging house, by reading the good book. This outlandish Spanish obsession with saints and sin does nobody any good. I'll swear it does not bring you a whit closer to God.'

'It is not an obsession.' She gathered herself and turned back to face him. 'You don't understand.' She struggled to form the words. 'These churches,' she patted the door, 'they are like home . . . a place I know and understand. I've looked at these same saints since I was tiny. St Christopher, St Anthony, St Francis of Assisi. They comfort me, they are always the same wherever I go.'

'In heaven's name! They are just paint and plaster.'

'But they're all I have. Look at me. I'm filthy and my skirt's rubbed bald with riding. I'm not "Mistress Leviston" of West View House any longer. I'm just another woman on the road, another with no home and no livelihood.'

He looked at her blankly.

She tried again. 'The churches are my compass. Without them, I think I will lose my mind. You have someone waiting who loves you. I've lost everything – my father, my home, my country, but as long as I have the Church, I have a raft. I have something.'

He was wiping his face now with a resigned expression.

She croaked, 'Mr Wilmot, I have to have something.'

'Very well,' he said tightly, 'if it is so important. We will stop a few minutes whilst I water the horses. Though I don't see why you have to make such a fuss about it. Martha, take the mules and the packhorse round the side. Try to find some shade.'

She leaned her shoulder to the door and it scraped open. He did not follow her inside the church, his English habits must die hard. The church was cool and silent. Emotion had made her breathless. In the heat the blood throbbed at her temples.

Three candles were burning, listing at an angle in a trough of sand. Little folded prayers stuck up from the surface, some of which must have been there for years, judging by how faded they were. They were crumbling with age in amongst the wax stubs, leached of their colour by the sun.

She could not kneel for the floor was bare but she sat on one of the rush-seated stools and stared at a painting of the grey-bearded St Martin of Tours sharing his cloak with his enemy, the Roman soldier. It pricked her conscience. She did not want to share her inheritance with Zachary. If she had her way, he would not get so much as a yard of lace.

She remembered him waving at Father from the quay, all smiles. Her stomach churned. Immediately, she retracted her bitter thoughts as unfit for this holy place, small though it was, and prayed fervently to St Christopher instead, for help on the journey.

She was still reciting when she felt the draught of the door behind, and the sudden scent of heat. She had not realized that heat could smell.

Abruptly, she finished, and turned to see Mr Wilmot standing there, hat in hand. 'You have done?'

She nodded.

'Happen you might say a prayer for my Dorothy, and my two little ones next time.' It felt like an apology.

'Gladly,' she said, and her heart went out to him. 'Do you miss them?'

'More than my life,' he said, and turned to walk away.

She went after him and put her hand on his arm. 'I'm sorry,' she said.

'No, the heat makes me short-tempered,' he said, 'and I worry about letting my men down. I couldn't bear it, to go back to them empty-handed.'

'We won't go back empty-handed, I promise you. I'll make that scoundrel—'

'Let me talk to him first. I'm in a better position to explain the profits and losses and the trading timetable, and I fear—'

'I know – you fear I will be too hot-headed and jeopardize our cause. I understand you, Mr Wilmot, well enough.' She sighed. 'We will do it your way.'

He looked down at her and gave a conciliatory smile. Then he took her arm and escorted her back to her mount like a gentleman.

Chapter 23

18 August 1609
Mr Zachary Deane, Esq
Sir,

My condolences on your bereavement. I write to you from Toledo. I am on my way to Seville with the express purpose of meeting with you with a view to discussing the lace business of your father, the late Nathaniel Leviston. If it is managed properly, I am sure your father's business can yield even greater profit.

If you will let me go through the figures with you, you will see how great an investment it is, and that it would be worthy of your consideration to keep it trading rather than proceeding at this less-than-fortunate time with the sale. I would be grateful to meet with you at the earliest available opportunity.

I will be residing at the lodgings of Señor Cisbón close to the new Alameda de Hercules, under the sign of the ball and claw. I await your instruction.

Your humble servant,
David Wilmot (Overseer, Leviston's Lace)

Zachary threw the letter down and shouted for Ana. 'If a man calling himself Wilmot should call, an Englishman, tell him I have moved. To Madrid. On no account are you to admit him. Do you understand?'

Ana stared at his black eye and cut lip. And then at his hands. 'English man. Wilmot.' She repeated the name, and Zachary nodded his approval.

'And you are gone to Madrid.' Her eyes looked doubtful.

'Yes. That's right. He's not to come in.'

'Will that be all?'

She retreated, still gazing at his beaten face. When she was gone, he paced the room. Curses. As if he had not trouble enough, but now he must be dodging all the time in case he should have occasion to bump into Wilmot. The man must have lost his senses, to come all the way over here to press him to keep the lace trade running.

Wilmot feared for his employment, no doubt. Elspet Leviston and her tomfool husband probably sent him, to try to dissuade him from selling. But it was too late, he'd already sent the order to Greeting weeks ago and by now he should be executing it to the letter. Zachary had no wish to speak with that pedant Wilmot. He would sell, as was his right, and if any of them wanted a share, then they would have to bid for it, like everyone else.

He read the letter again, and then opened the lid of the writing slope. But maybe he'd pen a letter to Greeting, suggesting that Bradstone might like to offer for the business, as Wilmot seemed so mightily keen. A little competition might raise the price.

He pictured Elspet Leviston's reaction, asking her husband to bid for what should have been hers by right. A queasy feeling lurked in the back of Zachary's mind. He recognized it as guilt. The same tainted feeling that came every time he picked a pocket or snatched a cloak. But he was on his way out of that life, with the help of Leviston's money. So he quashed it, like drowning something that gasped for breath.

Zachary was sure Guido was about to say '*Tarde*' again, but he was too stunned to say a word when he caught sight of Zachary's bruised face.

'Tsk. Been fighting?' Guido said.

'No. I was set upon by some thugs near the Corral de los Naranjos.'

Gabriel and the rest gathered round.

'Why?' asked Guido.

'I bid against a man at an auction, and he took exception to it.'

'What were you buying?'

'A slave. A Morisco lad.'

'Then you're more of an ass than I thought. Let's see your hands.'

He held them out. 'Sorry, Guido. They won't be much good for a few days. They served as my armour.'

Guido felt the swollen fingers with a practised touch, whilst Zachary winced. 'Nothing broken. You fool. You're lucky they did not fix them for life. Have you had ice on them?'

'No.'

'Gabriel, fetch ice from the casa at the end of the road, and aloe vera.'

Zachary leaned against the pillar that supported the roof, aware of Guido's disapproval hanging in the air.

'That looks sore,' Gabriel said, on his return, holding out a wooden bucket with a layer of crushed ice at the bottom.

'Quick, put them in before it melts,' Guido said.

'It's all right,' Zachary said with a bravado he did not feel, 'They don't grieve me nearly as much as they did at the end of my first day here.'

Guido frowned at his attempt at levity.

'I had blisters on my blisters,' Zachary insisted. He laughed, but drew a sharp breath as he lowered his hands into the burning ice, and did not tell them how much it hurt his face to smile at all. 'Anyway, I've had worse.'

Guido's disapproval seemed to be melting with the ice and was replaced with an expression of concern. 'Rest,' he said. 'Today you will watch.' He must have read Zachary's relief, for he wagged his finger and said, 'You will watch as if your life depends on it. And one day, I tell you, it will. Take note of everything, how the metal is worked, how the grinding is done. You will watch and remember. Then your sword will be *precioso*.'

'Yes, Guido. And thank you.'

'Do not thank me with words. Thank me with your attention, yes?'

Years later, Zachary would remember that time as the happiest he had ever spent in his life. He loved the whole business of the smelting, the beating, the chiselling and polishing. The making of something beautiful from base metal. He loved the taste of iron dust in his mouth, the men with their sleeves rolled under leather cuffs, their hands encased in gauntlets. He even grew to love the leather aprons that protected the wearer's linens from flying splinters of molten metal.

Guido's deft touch crafted the steel into blades as strong and flexible as sinew. Zachary forgot his bruised back, his swollen lip, his hands stiffening and aching in the ice bucket – he was completely engrossed. From the outside it might look like the labour of hell, but he had found his own heaven here in Seville.

It was almost three weeks later that he was recovered enough to go to the fencing school at the Arenal. He was up early to get there before his day's labour at the smithy. The previous night he had oiled his old sword so it would slip easily from the scabbard, and had spent an hour patiently grinding his daggers on the whetstone.

He hoped the scars on his face would make him appear more serious as a potential student. In the glass he had seen the remains of bruises and scabs, and he worried that these made him look less the gentleman. To counter this effect he dressed in his best doublet with the slashed breeches. Ana shone his shoes so that they gleamed.

He was still awaiting the coin from the sale of Uncle Leviston's estate, and he knew these things took time. But Greeting's copy of the will was in his satchel and hopefully Greeting's letter would convince the master Don Rodriguez that he could pay.

He found his salon easily. It had a smart newly painted sign outside, with Rodriguez's name and a pair of crossed swords over the horns of a bull. A studded and black-tarred door was beneath, which obviously led into an inner courtyard. He took hold of the iron ring and twisted and pushed, but it did not open. He banged it hard against the metal knocker. A few moments later a surly faced youth peered out.

His first glimpse inside the yard showed a line of about thirty men in leather armour practising sword drill in the shade of the walls. A staccato pattern and rhythm marked their practice as they moved in unison, and he was already itching to join them.

'I am here to see Don Rodriguez,' he said, pushing past the youth into the yard.

'You a student? He's not taking any more students.'

'Perhaps he has room for one more,' he said cheerfully. 'My name is Deane, I'm from England. Tell him I'm here.'

'He's not here yet. And he doesn't like strangers in his yard.'

'When will he—?'

'Don't waste your time.' The boy tried to shepherd him back to the gate. 'I've told you, he's not here.'

'What's this?' A deep voice sounded behind him.

'Sorry, señor. He just pushed his way in. Another foreigner who wants to learn to fence.'

Zachary swivelled round and his first impression was of a black wall of men. He backed away. He was face to face with the crook-nosed man from the auction. Behind him stood the Morisco lad, laden with water gourds. His mouth dropped open in astonishment. He had bruises and a black eye to rival Zachary's own.

'Back for more?' the man said.

'Are you Don Rodriguez?'

The men behind sniggered to each other.

Zachary moved towards the door. It must be a mistake. 'It doesn't matter,' he said, 'I thought you were someone else.'

One of the men stopped him dead, with a hand on the shoulder. He tried to shrug it off but the man's big paw kept him there.

'Going somewhere?' Rodriguez said, smiling. 'The lad said you wanted to learn to fence.'

'Not with you,' Zachary said lightly. 'Now, excuse me gentlemen.'

The man nearest the gate banged it shut and stood in front of it, barring his way. No other way out was in view.

Rodriguez glanced sideways at his men with amusement. 'Seems to me you should be given a lesson, if that's why you came. Though

I would have thought one was enough.' He smiled and strolled over.

He leaned in until his face was a hand-width away and said, 'You cost me dear. I could have had the slave-boy for forty and you drove up the price on purpose.'

Zachary stood his ground despite the growing fear that he was out of his depth.

'I bid as much as I could afford. Like everyone else. It's what happens at an auction.'

'Not in Seville,' said a student from behind him. 'Everyone knows not to bid against Don Rodriguez, if they know what's good for them.'

'Quiet, Fabian.' Rodriguez stepped away and ordered the training men in the yard to stand easy.

They stopped and lined up in ranks of twelve. Zachary pushed down the fear that threatened to make his hands shake.

Rodriguez drew his sword, with an almost silent rasp of metal on wood. He smiled and tested its edge on his thumb, before saying quietly, 'You want to fence? Well, let's begin.'

Zachary's hand shot to his scabbard, but Rodriguez handed his blade lazily to the man behind him, the big-shouldered man with the jutting jaw.

'You can take on Fabian.'

Zachary sized up the other man as he performed a quick business-like bow to his master, Rodriguez, took up a back stance and twirled the blade with his wrist as if to feel its weight and calibre.

Zachary reached for his sword, but without any warning, Fabian had already leapt forward and was advancing with well-trained precision. His weapon hissed through the air.

Zachary floundered, off guard, retreating, parrying the blade of the bigger man. His breath came in short, sharp bursts, he felt like a windmill, all flapping sails. Thank God for his nimble feet, he let Fabian come in a little, waited for his thrust and at the last minute dodged with all his power to one side.

Fabian's over-reach gave Zachary just enough time to order his thoughts and make a quick assessment. He was surrounded, so it made no real sense to try to fight on. His best bet would be to try to get to the door – to make a run for it.

He held his blade out before him and drew Fabian over to the gateway with a series of quick, small jabs to the stomach and chest. At the last minute he hurled himself backwards out of the door, but he mis-timed. Three of Rodriguez's men jumped him and grabbed his arms.

Even as he struggled, he knew it was hopeless. He stumbled backwards and his sword clattered to the ground. The men would not let him put down his feet but kept him hanging humiliatingly, like a puppet between them.

'Too lily-livered to fight?' Rodriguez loomed over him. 'There's a lesson for cowards like you. Hold him, boys.' His hands fumbled for the flap of his breeches and moments later a stream of hot yellow piss hit Zachary directly in the forehead.

He twisted his head away, closed his nose and mouth and screwed up his eyes but still the stinking liquid trickled over his face. He gasped for air and the stench hit him at the back of the throat.

Rodriguez fastened himself and laughed before signalling to his ranks to follow suit.

His men had Zachary's arms in a grip like metal tongs and, struggle as he might, he could not free himself. In the end he just quietened and endured it. When all the men had emptied their bladders his captors thrust him down into the pool round his feet.

He almost retched, but instead struggled to his feet. His eyes stung, he did not dare swallow. Some madness made him shout at Rodriguez who was laughing with one of his soldiers.

'One day, you will be sorry you did this to me. I'll return and you will fight for your life.'

'A challenge, is it? Oh, very well.' Fabian sniggered and cast down his glove into the urine-spattered dirt. Rodriguez guffawed with laughter, and as if on cue, the rest of the students laughed too, a proper circle of rooks.

Zachary stooped to pick up the glove. He knew he looked ridiculous. His hand trembled with humiliation. 'I accept the challenge.' More laughter.

'Fool. You will lose your life,' Fabian said, looking at him with an incredulous expression.

The blood rushed to Zachary's face, he shouted through the stench, knowing he had lost his senses. 'I do not jest. You set the challenge, now name the date.'

Rodriguez sneered, 'Get out of here, pisspants. We've wasted enough time on you.'

'Why not let him try?' one of the other men said. 'It will be entertaining.'

'A chicken fighting a bull,' one of his men whispered.

'No,' Rodriguez said to Fabian. 'Kick him out. He stinks, like the yellow coward he is. The rest of you – get back in line.'

'At least I don't jump men from behind. At least I have my honour.'

Rodriguez sighed. 'And what's honour? Just a milksop's fantasy. Get out. And you'll leave Seville, if you know what's good for you. If I see you anywhere on these streets, you won't see the light of another day.'

Just before he was thrust outside Zachary passed the Morisco lad, cowering by the door. He looked up at Zachary with his sky-blue eyes and whispered, 'Please, sir, I beg you – don't come back.'

Chapter 24

At Toledo, Elspet secured the services of Gomez, a Spanish guide, to help them find Zachary Deane. It had been a relief to find a tavern at last with good rooms and a bath-house nearby. They rested a few days and bought necessities for the remaining journey, and three weeks later they approached Seville. The landscape became dotted with houses, the roads more populous, and the taverns full of herders and cloth-searers, farmers and tanners.

The prospect of arriving at their destination was both a relief and a worry. She was not sure she trusted Mr Wilmot to negotiate for her – he wasn't the one losing his home. And she did not like the idea of men's talk going on behind closed doors, not when it concerned her so directly.

As the bleached landscape shimmered in the heat, Elspet thought of all the ways she might ask, beg or argue. The sweat trickled between her breasts. For she feared that whatever Mr Wilmot said, however fine or well-thought-out the reasoning, his words would not persuade Zachary to part with one bean.

They pushed on into the night, as their destination was so close. Gomez was driving, with Mr Wilmot deep in thought beside him. Mr Wilmot's brows were permanently furrowed now, he had lost his paunch and his nose was red and peeling from the sun. She felt sudden empathy for him – for he had travelled with her all this way with the weight of her father's business on his shoulders.

Across the wagon Martha's flaccid form shook with the jolting of the carriage. She was wrapped in a bundle of shawls, her arms folded on top of the bags, her head resting there like a pillow. She slept – something Elspet could not do. Instead, Elspet looked up at the stars and picked out the constellations. How odd it was, that they should be the same stars as she saw from the windows at home, still shining here in this unforgiving landscape.

A movement in the corner of her eye, and then she saw it – a shooting star.

It slashed a diagonal white trail in the black. So bright she could almost fancy to hear its noise, its brief fizz like gunpowder, but then, just as suddenly, it was gone; the sky kept no trace of it. She sat up, trying to penetrate the distance.

It meant something, of that she was sure. A sign. A sensation of longing filled her chest, so strong that it made her want to stretch out to claw back that brief light. It was a longing for home, but not a country to travel to, no, not that. Rather, some country deep inside herself.

Chapter 25

October 2nd 1609 (two weeks earlier) Denia, Valencia

'Are your men ready?' called the commander José Velez Garbali, reigning in his horse.

'Yes, sir.' Rodriguez stepped forward from the group of about twenty mercenaries gathered on the crest of the hill outside Denia. 'I don't think many will try to run, though. Word has spread that we are up here,' he said, sweating in the heat haze that in a few hours would deliver another flawless blue sky.

Below them the ships gentled at anchor, three long rows of dark masts and a flotilla of small dots that signified the ferry boats. On the quay a *tercio* battalion of men from the Netherlands stood ranked in strict formation, their pikes resting upright against their leather-armoured shoulders as they awaited the first batch of Moriscos from the point of embarkation at the market square.

Scanning the scene below, Rodriguez saw that the narrow track to the quay was lined with more mercenaries like themselves, arquebusiers and swordsmen. From up here their dark ranks against the yellow dirt looked like the inked lines on a map. Around them milled dots of people who had come as spectators to see the Moriscos go, and cheer or jeer them on their way.

Garbali held his horse still by sawing at the reins. He shouted down, 'There will be many thousands. I've passed herds of them on the way here in the last few days. Some of them are trying to smuggle goods out in their clothes, but they won't get far. Idiots. Don't they realize our men on the ships will divest them of anything illegal? And a few stupid Moors will try to make for the mountains. You can deal with them, yes?'

'Yes, sir,' said Rodriguez.

'You have enough arms?'

Rodriguez nodded, pointed to a pile of muskets under a scrubby olive bush.

'No prisoners, you understand. If they run, they're not worth the trouble. Like deserters.' Garbali laughed at his own joke, and Rodriguez forced a smile. Garbali dragged at the horse's mouth to turn it. The horse tossed its head, the bit jangling between its teeth. 'Get on, you lazy brute.' He clapped its ribs with his spurs so the horse rolled its eyes and shied, before he wheeled around and galloped off towards the next rise. 'Keep good watch,' he shouted back over his shoulder.

Rodriguez fixed his eyes below; he was taking no chances. The previous night there had been a skirmish with a group of four families who had somehow managed to gather arms and dismember the parish priest. There was no part of the priest in the same place when they'd finished with him. Rodriguez was under no illusions about the capability of desperate men. His best swordsmen were with him, though; big men, skilled and ruthless, trained to obey orders with no question. He had picked out four Sevillians for their aim with a musket to accompany him. He'd use them first, but if anyone penetrated the lines of shot, then his swordsmen would finish them.

There was a palpable air of tension as there always is before any battle. Even the sparrows were silent. It was as if the whole town held its breath.

'Did he say how many?' Fabian, his right-hand man approached. The question disturbed Rodriguez. It was unlike Fabian to be rattled.

'We don't know. Maybe they'll go like sheep. Maybe they'll try to break away. Nobody knows how it will go. But I don't think we'll have much trouble. They're not organized, and they have their women with them. You know a man can't fight properly with women in the way. They bring in the tender heart, and then their intent is lost.'

Fabian stamped his feet, though it was not cold, and glanced again at the mountain path winding down to the town. 'I thought we were only coming to Valencia to watch,' he said accusingly.

'We are. Or we'd be down there in the thick of it, with that *tercio* under our command. Don Garbali's put us here because this is the best vantage point, and Denia's layout is similar to Seville.'

'I didn't know we were going to fight. I thought it was just a recce.'

'We might not have to. But we can see how the thing unfolds from up here, then when it's Seville's turn, we'll be down there with four *tercios* under our command.'

'All Sevillians?'

'Some, yes. But one of the units will be convicted men from the Catalan prison, trained up. There are other ports enforcing the expulsion order at the same time and the Crown couldn't raise enough men. My men will be on the quayside – like those.' Rodriguez pointed. 'We'll put the prison mercenaries behind, bringing up the rear, and in the warehouses where they must leave their children. You'll have charge of those. I need someone reliable.'

'In the warehouses? With the children?' Fabian swallowed. Rodriguez watched his face. He knew this was not what Fabian wanted to hear, so he tried to explain.

'That is where the most delays will happen. We'll need to keep everyone moving. I need someone who has the necessary detachment, or it will turn into a fiasco. You will have the *tercio* of Catalans, who have a vested interest in obeying orders. They know if they do not, they will go for galley slaves, or back into the vault in Catalonia.'

It had started. A slow tide of people was moving down towards the shore. They were kept tightly together by armoured guards, whose steel breastplates caught the sun and reflected shafts of white light towards the waiting galleons. Odd sounds drifted up to them, the shout of 'Moros, Moros!' from the spectators, the sound of crying, the sound of people singing, a song with unfamiliar words in a strange, haunting tongue. From here they could watch the people herded on to the ships.

'They seem quiet,' observed Rodriguez, more to himself than to Fabian.

When a consignment was on board, that ship inched away and set sail, and another was rowed into its place.

'Where are this lot bound?' Fabian asked.

'Oran. Back to Araby, where they belong. They don't want them there either; who would? They're the dregs of society. Ours from Seville are going mostly to Rabat, but there's resistance there too. They know most of them are just vagrants, with no skill or trade. Old slaves, some of them, or women past child-bearing age. No use to anyone.'

The whole road below was now a moving river of flesh. At the quay, it fanned out and broke up into smaller pockets of people. A sudden retort of gunfire and a plume of smoke rose into the air. A small contingent had broken free and was running, scattering in different directions.

'Trouble,' Rodriguez said, and his men jumped to attention, ran for their weapons, tamped them with powder and shot. Fabian put on his helmet and buckled the strap. When they looked back there were more dark twists of bodies lying on the quay.

This prompted a commotion at the quayside, with some Moriscos trying to turn back to run the way they had come. Rodriguez caught a glint of steel from within the crowd, but those behind were oblivious to the disturbance and kept marching forth, pushing the crowds down into the narrow funnel of guards before the quay. Those at the front must have managed to smuggle in arms. A sharp retort and clouds of smoke caused the pikeman to fall away, as others hit the ground wounded.

More gunfire. A swathe of Moriscos writhed and fell, and those behind tripped over them, and still they were being pushed forward.

'Why don't they stop!' Rodriguez said. 'Are they deaf? Surely they heard the musket fire? They should halt them until order's restored—'

'Too late!' shouted Fabian. 'Look at that!'

The line of pikes disintegrated, and people poured out through the ranks. Some scrambled to board the boats that would take them out to the waiting convoy, some ran towards the town, some scattered into the fields. Those who ran out to the sides produced muskets from somewhere and blasted at the soldiers from behind. The wall of soldiers wavered and then collapsed under the weight of the pressure from behind. Still the battalion behind pressed them forward.

'My God. It's chaos. Get ready.'

They positioned themselves behind the brush and the bushes, the musketeers flat on their bellies before them, squinting down the barrels towards the path.

They heard them before they saw them – the panting breath, the noise of their feet. Three men sprinted towards them, clothes flapping, eyes wild. One of them dragged a heavily pregnant woman by the hand. Rodriguez waited until they crested the brow of the hill before giving the command. 'Now!'

The man at the front crumpled over his exploded chest, blood spattering over the bushes and path. Behind him, the second man jerked with the impact of the shot to his head and was thrown backwards at the feet of the man coming up behind. Rodriguez caught a glimpse of the other's shocked face and his sudden move to place himself in front of his wife, but the musketeer sought him out with the muzzle of his gun. The musketeer took aim precisely, and the shot took off the top of the Morisco's head.

The woman screamed and collapsed to her knees over her husband, her eyes wide with terror.

'Cease your fire!' Rodriguez gave the order. The musketeers reloaded, ignoring the woman keening now over her dead husband, and aimed the muskets down the track ahead. Rodriguez looked to Fabian, 'She's not worth a bullet. Fabian, despatch her.'

Fabian unsheathed his sword and approached the woman. She clasped her hands, brought them up before him, wringing them in the gesture of asking for mercy that transcends all languages, her eyes blank with dread, entreating. Rodriguez saw Fabian hesitate, and mentally willed him on. The woman whimpered something and looked down to her belly. Fabian sucked in his breath in a rasp before he made a practised lunge to skewer her through the heart. Her mouth bubbled blood before she toppled over and he could put his boot on her to extricate the sword from between her ribs.

Fabian turned away, white-faced, and cleaned his sword on a rag from his pocket. Rodriguez noticed his hand was shaking.

'That's two more who won't be going home!' laughed one of the other foot-soldiers.

'One less Moorish brat for Spain to feed,' agreed Fabian, panting.

He had recovered himself well. Rodriguez exhaled with relief. He would be up to the task in Seville after all.

The musketeers took down four more runaways, all young men, before no more ventured their way. The smoke from their muskets must have alerted any other rebels to their presence.

They picked through the clothes of the Morisco men, where they were not too mutilated to do so. They found coinage sewn into the clothes, small valuables and tokens. All of the Moriscos were wearing many layers of clothing so that Rodriguez' men had to peel them apart layer by layer with their knives, like skinning rabbits.

With a look to Rodriguez for his approval, Fabian slit the woman's blood-soaked djellaba and folded it open until she was down to her skin. In the last layer he bared her breasts to find a small bag sewn there with clumsy hurried stitching. He ripped it open and a few small items spilled out. A child's plaything – a small bone rattle, a hank of dark hair tied together with a leather thong. Two or three pearls rolled away, and he snapped his hand out to retrieve them. It was only when he opened his palm that he saw they were a child's baby teeth. He grunted and flung them away from him into the scrub, then spat into the dust.

'What was that?' Don Rodriguez asked him.

'Nothing. Just stones.'

'Look, they've got the formation back together now. But we've seen what can happen. There'll be no mistakes like that when we're in charge.'

Below them calm had been restored and the procession of people was still moving. They watched for several minutes before Fabian said, 'There must be thousands of them.'

'There'll be thousands more in Seville,' Don Rodriguez said.

Chapter 26

Luisa liked living at the fencing school, even though it was on the other side of Triana and further away from the pottery where she worked. At least here there were a few young men. Much better than their old yard full of toothless old women, and the pot-bellied grandfathers who congregated at the *bodega* at the end of the street with their thick black coffee and their endless chess.

There had been no news of Alma and Merin. And poor Daria had gone to live with her aunt – too grief-stricken and distracted to carry on working. It wasn't until they were gone that she realized how much their lives had been intertwined. Papa missed Merin, and Mama had nobody to go to the market with. The kitchens at Señor Alvarez's school were empty without Daria constantly scrubbing vegetables. Luisa missed her, and the next *auto da fé* wasn't for three more weeks. Now there was the Time of Grace, if you could ever call it such a thing.

Mama and Papa chewed over it in low voices, squeezing each other's hands, bending their heads close together so that Husain should not hear about how they wring confessions out of innocent men with water torture and the rack. They were snappish and on edge, for they knew it could have been them the *familiares* came for.

Luisa was so angry at Mama and Papa for their stupid Muslim practices that she could barely speak to them. If they would only stop, everyone could breathe safely in their beds. She was tired of watching

Husain leap to hide under the table at every little noise. A loving parent would surely keep their children safe first? It exasperated her. Why did they hold on to it all? Mama said it was tradition, but who for, when their children were standing right there in front of them in bare feet begging them to stop?

But with Daria and Alma gone, the kitchen empty and bread mouldering in the crock, Señor Alvarez needed someone to step into Daria's shoes.

Mama was happy to help Señor Alvarez as long as the family could stay there. 'Cooking is physic,' she said, 'and physic is cooking. And it is better to be busy.' It was safer there, too, she said, in a yard full of men with swords and bucklers.

And Señor Alvarez – well, Papa loved to talk with him. They sat long into the night, with their dry-dust arguments about long-dead philosophers. She was sure Papa should have been a Greek himself, he spent so much time talking about them.

They were deep in one of their conversations again – a discussion about Heraclitus and the logos, and whether the world was rationally organized, can you believe it, when Uncle Najid arrived. A rapping on the courtyard door, and when nobody from the house went to answer it, Señor Alvarez rose from his cushion to go out himself. Husain leapt up too from where he had been playing catch-stones at their feet.

'No, Husain. You stay here,' Mama said. 'We don't know who it is.'

'Aw, let me go with Señor Alvarez, it might be the fig-seller, or the man with the canaries.'

'Or the Inquisition,' Luisa muttered.

Mama threw her a look of knives.

'Then they have a very polite knock today,' Señor Alvarez said, catching her eye, but he buckled on his sword just the same. The knock sounded again. And he was right, it was a gentle knock.

'Come on, then, Husain. You can carry the lantern,' Alvarez said, and Husain picked up the nearest light and hop-skipped in front of him to the door.

They waited, straining to hear, but shortly Husain's excited voice called out: 'Papa, Mama, it's Uncle Najid!' Husain looked proud to have remembered him, holding him by the sleeve and pulling him into the room.

Mama stood up and hurried to the door to greet him. '*As salaikum*,' she said, full of smiles, embracing him. He made the traditional reply, '*Wa alaikum salaam.*'

'This is my brother Najid.' Mama then introduced Señor Alvarez and bade them both sit, and went to make more tea.

'My, how you've grown. Look at you now with your butter-and-milk face, so pretty.' Uncle Najid smiled at Luisa, but his cheeks were thin and haggard and there were cuts and scratches all over his hands. Something had come in with him, some sour atmosphere: the odour of fear.

Luisa looked down in embarrassment, conscious she was staring.

'How old are you now, my little hen?' Uncle Najid smiled in an effort at jollity.

'Old enough to help her mother,' Papa said pointedly, gesturing with his head to the back room where the smoke of the fire clouded through the open door. Of course she understood this meant that just the men were to talk without them. Even the boy Husain, who was not old enough to understand anything.

She stood up and pulled aside the curtain to go and help Mama who was rolling vine leaves around morsels of rice and peppers. As she went out through the door she heard Papa say, 'We are all brothers here. Señor Alvarez can hear what you have to tell, for there is something, is there not?'

She closed her ears, determined not to listen, and concentrated on folding the leaves, slippery with olive oil, and piercing them with the twigs of rosemary to hold them together. Mama's attention was not on the task, Luisa thought, she had been rolling the same parcel for too long, and she must be curious to know what her brother was doing here. It must be four, no, maybe five years since they had seen him. The last time he came he was fatter and sleeker, and full of hopes of setting up his loom and making his fortune from the rich merchants of Seville. But he was not expecting so much competition here, so Mama said. Seville was full of weavers and embroiderers.

Here he was a speck of dust in a lentil pan, and in the end he had returned to Valencia where his skill was better known.

Husain's face peeked round the curtain. He was scowling. 'They say I've to come and help,' he wailed, his mouth turned downwards in a mutinous scowl. 'Papa won't let me stay.'

Luisa pulled him to her and planted a kiss on his head. 'Here,' she said and gave him a vine leaf to fold. The men talked in whispers and in snatches of Arabic that she could not catch. Neither she nor Mama spoke, but placed the food on the beaten copper tray, and added the crock of olives and the last of the goat's cheese, along with the hot honeyed tea.

Mama looked at her disapprovingly and Luisa knew what she meant. She smoothed down her hair and lowered her eyes before going back through the curtain.

Already she sensed something different in the room.

'We have to tell them,' Papa said.

Uncle Najid said nothing, and an awkward silence ensued.

'Why's nobody talking?' Husain whispered.

Señor Alvarez broke the silence. 'They have expelled anyone they suspect of being Muslim from Valencia. Even *conversos.*'

Mama did not react but put the tray down softly, and said to Husain, 'Go watch the men practising in the yard for a while.'

'Really? You'll really let me watch?'

Señor Alvarez smiled at him and nodded, and he scampered away.

'Tell us, Najid,' Papa said.

'Forty thousand men and women have gone to Oran.' Najid opened his hands in a gesture of defeat. 'My city is lost. There is no one left, the streets are empty of traders. Looters fill the shops. We had three days' notice, to board ship or to suffer the penalty. They left us no choice. Any converso or Muslim left after three days was to be put to death.'

'We heard rumours,' Mama said, 'but we never thought . . .' She moved towards him, her hand outstretched, but he shook his head. His eyes were glassy with unshed tears. Mama pulled her hand away again, for fear her affection would make him lose control of himself and weep.

'You must stay here,' Papa was decided.

'Have you no one with you?' Mama asked. 'How did you get here?'

'A few of us disguised ourselves as women, with draperies and head shawls. We sat by the side of the street to ambush a Christian party of soldiers on horseback. We wanted the horses, to go into the mountains, raise a rebel army. But it went wrong, they recognized one of us, and in the fray only two of us managed to break free. We escaped up the mountain pass, but my friend was badly wounded from a sabre cut, and I had to leave him.'

'Oh Najid,' Mama whispered.

'Well, you are welcome here,' Papa said. They would never be able to do that in Seville. The whole city would collapse without our labour, and well they know it.' His words were bracing, but Uncle Najid's eyes looked hollow just the same.

'It was my friend Ali, remember? Who you met. We've been friends since I was . . .' He paused then, his hands twisting over and over. 'When I got to the caves where we were to meet, there was no one there. They must have caught up with the rest. I was the only one. I waited a few days. I stayed in the darkness and prayed, but nobody came.' He laughed, but it was bitter as green olives. 'You are looking at the only rebel left alive from my whole city.'

Chapter 27

Elspet flapped the flies away from her face with her kidskin gloves, the only purpose they were fit for in this heat, and searched the crowd restlessly for a glimpse of Zachary. She had been in Seville a whole week and still no meeting. Mr Wilmot had written to him from Toledo and had also left a letter with the slave girl at his lodgings.

Mr Wilmot had persuaded her to go down to the harbour in the hope of spotting Zachary 'by chance' there. The fleet of ships bearing gold and silver from the Indies was on its way, and the whole city had turned out to see the entertainment.

Mr Wilmot hurried right into the sun to get a closer look, but she and Martha hung back impatiently in the shade. She had bought a cheap lace mantilla to protect her face from the sun, and now she cracked open her parasol which used to be a glorious shade of blue but had turned faded and yellowish-green under the glare.

Like wasps around a crust of bread, a frenzy of activity buzzed around each vessel. No wind for sail today, so the progress was slow as the galleons were rowed in, inch by inch, past the sandbank at the mouth of the greenish river. Once docked, turbaned slaves lugged the coffers of bullion from the holds onto pack mules or waiting carts; gold destined straight for the king, where it would be melted into coin. To protect this mighty treasure, ranks of musketeers and pikemen in gleaming helmets fidgeted in rows along the quay.

Women rushed by, baskets teetering on their heads, filled with patatas, pineapples, vanilla and chilli-pods. A man with a mule loaded with a consignment of skins and furs pushed his way into their shade. It brought an unwelcome image of Hugh Bradstone to mind. She cringed; the humiliation still stung.

Had she not problems enough, without dwelling on him?

She moved out of the shelter and waved, to catch Mr Wilmot's eye. He was engrossed in watching a knot of merchants haggling over brightly coloured bales of cloth. He stood a little to the outside of the group, a sombre figure in his dark English doublet.

When he returned to her side he said excitedly, 'If I was your brother, I would want to invest in some of that cloth. I've never seen designs like it. And they sold it so cheap. I've just worked it out – less than two pence a yard! No wonder the Flemish and the French are flocking here.'

'Yes,' she said drily, 'but we won't be investing in anything unless we can persuade Zachary to keep the business.' She moved towards one of the tall palms where some other traders had just vacated the shade. 'Sorry, Mr Wilmot, but your way isn't working. I simply can't bear to wait any longer. Letters be damned. I don't care what you think, we will call at his house and be done with it.'

'Politeness costs nothing,' Wilmot said, 'and I was only trying to ensure us a more reasonable reception.'

She snapped her sunshade closed and reached for the fan at her waist instead. 'Reasonable? Mr Wilmot, they tell me my so-called brother was brought up by a whore on Cheapside, and made his living thieving and fighting. You are wasting your proprieties on him. I have made up my mind. I shall go this evening, whether you will accompany me or no.'

Mr Wilmot opened and closed his mouth at her forthrightness, and flapped his hat ineffectively in front of his face. The white gnats that swarmed in the sun were bothering him. The cloud of insects cleared, but immediately re-formed. 'As you wish, Mistress Leviston,' he said tersely. 'But I hope you know what you're doing.'

Chapter 28

'More vigour!' Guido called over Zachary's shoulder. 'Do you want a blade with no energy?'

Zachary rubbed harder at the blade resting on the leather on his lap. But when Guido moved away, Zachary slowed again. What was the point if he could not get more training? What use was a splendid sword when he had nowhere to practise its use?

'What ails you, friend?' Gabriel had noticed his lacklustre mood.

'Nothing.'

'Something does. You have a face as long as a mule. Did you go to Rodriguez?'

He nodded. He was not going to tell anyone of his humiliation. Of how he walked home drenched through, steaming in the heat, the flies buzzing round his shoulders, and how he had to plunge himself and his best clothes into the Guadalquivir before he dared come out again. And that his heart beat fast with fear that one of Rodriguez's men might be round the corner.

'He didn't take you, did he?' Gabriel sucked in his cheeks. 'Shame. I didn't tell you before, but I know he favours the big men. And he doesn't like foreigners.'

'It was nothing to do with my size,' he snapped. 'He's no room, that's all.'

Gabriel gave him a hurt look and moved away.

Zachary tipped the powder on to the glass-cloth and rubbed at the metal half-heartedly.

Guido was over in a trice. Zachary swore there was nothing that man did not see. He had eyes in his backside. He stood right in front of him with his big belly, feet planted, and said, 'Whatever ails you, you must leave it outside my door. There is no place for it here. Your sword is your life, and whenever you have need to use it, then there will be strife enough. What point to make more enemies?'

Zachary was suitably chastised. He thought he could walk free here in Spain, but this morning he had to keep checking that Rodriguez or his spies were not somewhere on the street. He had touched wood so many times, his fingers were almost sore with it. Yet he seemed to have had enemies all his life, had always walked with one hand on his sword, and ears and eyes taut as bowstrings. Why, even his own family were his enemies.

He polished away at his blade, distracted by his inner vision of Kit and Saul lying in wait for him round the corner of the street. He remembered how they'd jump him and then Saul would sit astride him crowing while Kit tore out clumps of his hair and waved it before his face. It hurt like hell, and made his eyes water, but his brothers knew damn well it wasn't a wound you could easily see.

They had lots of tricks like that, stamping 'accidentally' on fingers or toes, frisking him for the day's pickings. He learned to avoid them, to be wily and cunning, for he could never have told his mother they were bullying him, it would hurt her too much. And it was a matter of pride. At least he'd never been a tattle-tale.

But Rodriguez had turned him into that small whimpering boy again. With it came a feeling of impotence, and an anger he didn't know what to do with. The only thing that had ever helped him had been to practise and practise with his rapier, fantasizing all the while that one day he'd get back at his tormentors. One day they'd see that he was a master of the sword and he was the one wielding the power.

He put down the cloth and stretched his fingers that were still a little stiff in the joints. It seemed he was just as feeble as he'd always been. How stupid was he, to challenge one of Rodriguez's men? He'd probably die if they saw him again.

He sighed and glanced over at Gabriel, who was bent low over the furnace turning a metal bar in the heat. Gabriel had only been trying to help. Zachary wished he had not spoken to him in such an offhand way. Guido was right; he needed all the friends he could muster.

Next time Gabriel passed, Zachary touched him on the arm and said, 'If I offended you earlier, beg pardon. I'm like a baited bull this morning.'

Gabriel sat down at the bench next to him, and said, 'You were disappointed that Rodriguez did not take you on, it's only natural. Never mind. I know how to bring the smile back to your face – you can come with me to the tavern tonight – there will be dancing and music and . . .' he winked, 'beautiful women.' He mimed blowing on his fingers as if they were red-hot.

'Only if you let me pay.'

'You paid last time. My turn.'

'No. I pay, or I don't come.'

'Come into money, have you?'

'I had some news from England – a small legacy.'

Gabriel's face broke into a grin. 'Then what in hell are you looking so glum for! Anyone would think you'd lost a fortune, not gained one! Let's go out and celebrate.'

It was impossible not to be taken with Gabriel's enthusiasm. 'It sounds good. Tell me how to get to the place then, from the Calle de Virgenes.'

'I'll call by and fetch you.'

'No – no, don't do that, I'll meet you there.' Gabriel might find his lodgings too lofty and it would drive a wedge between them.

'The Corral del Toro, then, ten of the clock. It's in the *gitaneria* in Triana. You will have to get there by crossing the river.'

'Fine, I'll be there.'

That evening Ana fetched boiled water and Zachary scrubbed himself down with a sponge and a linen cloth. He was still shirtless when there was a hammering on the door. Ana went to answer it and he heard her say, '*Bien. Momento por favor.*' But then there was the low voice of a woman in the lobby below. He walked over to the balcony, still towelling himself, and peered over. But he saw nothing, no horses, no gig or carriage.

A few moments later, footsteps sounded on the stairs outside, and the door burst open. He did not recognize the man at first but the woman he knew straight away. His mouth fell open.

He snatched up his shirt and bundled it on over his head, to buy a few moments to regain composure.

'Cousin Elspet,' he said. She could not be here in Spain.

'You are not my cousin, you are my half-brother, or so they tell me. We tired of waiting for you to deign to give us a moment of your precious time. We have travelled all the way here at some considerable inconvenience and—'

'You want to talk money,' Zachary said, cutting her off before she could get wind in her sails.

The man stepped forward, and only then did he realize he knew him – it was Wilmot, the overseer, except that he had grown thin and his face was peeling from the sun. Why had Ana not sent him packing to Madrid? He stared at him, saw how the Spanish heat would torment blond men such as he.

'Mr Deane,' he began, 'we would like to come to an arrangement—'

'Arrangement be damned. We are not in England now.' English words already sounded strange on his tongue, thick like soup. Zachary pulled back his shoulders and stood tall. 'You are not in my house by invitation, so please leave.'

They held their ground, as he thought they would, so he fastened the strings on his shirt and reached for his tunic. He wished he did not still look as though he had already lost a fight.

'Mr Deane, be reasonable. We have travelled all the way from England. Surely as a fellow countryman, you would at least do us the courtesy of hearing us out.'

'As you can see, I am hardly dressed for company. Mistress Leviston has just told me why you are here, Mr Wilmot, and I am not a simpleton. Greeting has my instructions and there is nothing—'

Elspet had perched herself on the only chair by the open

casement, and glared at Wilmot who interrupted: 'But we understood from Mr Leviston that it would be Mistress Leviston who would inherit the business, and that it would carry on as usual. Won't you reconsider? If you do not want to look to the warehouses yourself, then you could put in an overseer—'

'Like yourself, I suppose?'

'No, no. I didn't mean that – it's just there are many men and their wives depending on the income from Leviston's Lace. I am here for them.'

'Well, that sounds very noble. But I do not want to run a lace business, Mr Wilmot. Why should I? Leviston left half of it to me, and I will do with my portion as I please.'

Elspet got up and stepped forward. Her eyes were glittering. He wondered if she was about to cry. 'What did you say to him? How did you persuade my father to leave you the house?'

Wilmot put a hand on the back of Elspet's chair, as if his legs would not hold him. 'Don't, Elspet. Let me negotiate.'

'No. I want him to hear what it means.'

Zachary braced himself. She approached him until her eyes were level with his own. 'I took care of Father these last seven years since Mother died. I mended his hose, starched his collars, sat with him when he was ill with the plague. Where were you then? If you are his son, where have you been all this time? Answer me!'

Zachary turned away, he felt his stomach contract. She had hit on a truth and it made him wince.

She followed him. She was blazing. Her white knuckles gripped tight to the folds of her skirt, her cheeks were fired with red. 'Who wrote the letters to the lace makers?' she cried. 'Who told him what was fashionable, what would sell?' She paused, before balling her fists in frustration, 'He had no idea. He was a man. Men have no idea . . .' She struggled to spit out the words. 'But for me my father would have had no damned business. And now you crawl your way into our lives and expect me just to stand aside whilst you reap all the profit by it. Well—'

Wilmot seemed to have regained his strength and grasped her by the shoulders. 'Elspet – Mistress Leviston, enough. Shouting will do no good.' He pushed her down on to the chair. Her chest rose and fell in her bodice as she tried to regain control.

'I beg your pardon,' Wilmot said wearily. 'Mr Deane, we have had a long, arduous journey, and the heat makes fools of us. Mistress Leviston did not mean to be rude.' He smiled in a placatory manner. 'Let us sit and talk this through like reasonable men.'

Zachary did not want discussion, he just wanted them to go. Out of this house and out of his life. 'I have already said, Mr Wilmot, I am not negotiating. I instructed Greeting to sell. The matter is closed. And as for Mistress Leviston . . . well, I assume she is married now, let her husband look to her. I am no charity to hand out alms.'

'How dare you!' Elspet leapt to her feet, her hand raised as if she would strike him.

'She is not to be married,' Wilmot said.

Elspet turned away.

Zachary seized on his words and lashed out at her back, 'So your furrier changed his mind?' She turned back to say something, but he blundered on, 'Can't say I blame him. Has he found a better match elsewhere?' The words were out before he could prevent them, and too late he caught the wounded look in her eyes.

Her silence and discomfiture showed him he was right. Immediately, he felt a sliver of remorse. He had not truly meant to belittle her in this way. She had provoked him, cornered him. He always struck out when he was cornered. Now he felt like a dog. Why did they have to come? Hang it all, he had done nothing wrong. If her father was fool enough to leave him half his estate, there was not a damned thing he could do about it. But he hadn't predicted this; that the furrier would pull out.

Wilmot offered Elspet a kerchief and persuaded her to sit. 'Look,' he said, 'it has been a shock for us all. There are some things you need to know about the business, Mr Deane, and I make no bones about it, it would be to your advantage to wait a while before selling.' He approached Zachary and held out his hand. 'Why don't we two meet tomorrow at the Tavern by the cathedral; you know it?'

'I know it.'

'Shall we say six o'clock?'

'You will meet without me?' Elspet asked.

'Best that way,' Wilmot announced, and he was rewarded by a look of pure venom.

'But why not now? It is surely a simple thing to—'

'I have a prior engagement,' Zachary said. 'As you can see, I am dressing to go out. It must wait until tomorrow.'

'Nevertheless, you will be there?' Wilmot said.

Zachary sighed and nodded, having no intention of it. 'Ana!' He called for her though he knew she would only be on the stairs, listening as usual. Ana held the door open and Wilmot gestured for Elspet to go first. 'Till tomorrow then,' he said.

Elspet swept by, her chin held high. She clearly could not bring herself to look at him, but her voice protested at Wilmot all the way down the stairs. Poor man, thought Zachary, he must have suffered that all the way from England.

When they had gone he sat on the balcony in the gathering dusk and pondered what to do. He leaned his arms on the warm metal railings and scanned the passing heads with unseeing eyes. He had never expected Elspet Leviston to have the courage to come here to Spain. That hadn't been in the plan at all. It was awkward. And if she was not married, well, she would need to live somewhere, he could see that.

She would manage somehow – women like her could always find some gentleman to give them house room – if she would let go of her pride. Poverty leeched the pride out of everyone, as well he knew. And he wagered that his lily-white cousin had never had hardship the way he had suffered it. Did she ever scrape a rind of bread from the gutter and keep it from the hands of two bullying brothers? No, from the look of it, her childhood had been soft quilts and feather mattresses, silver cutlery and leather books.

Below him a family passed by. The man had his arm hooked into his wife's elbow. Two young girls clung to her hooped skirt and scampered to keep up. The wife looked up at Zachary briefly and smiled a greeting before sauntering on.

It gave him a pang of jealousy to see a family like that, bonded together as if nothing could ever divide them. He had never belonged anywhere. When he was in London, Elspet had seemed like an unwelcome distraction and he had never thought of her as anything to do with him; she had not figured in his view of Leviston as family. Now Wilmot was acting as if Elspet was somehow Zachary's responsibility, but he had never in truth been her kin, he knew. All that was a lie. He sighed. Obviously he could not have it cut both ways.

As he fastened on his doublet, he thought of his mother; what she had to do with men like Leviston, and hardened his resolve. The wheel of fortune had come round; that was all. Time for his chance at a fat life at last. And Wilmot, well, he would be able to find another position. He was not too old and a man of his experience should be well-placed to pick up something else. After all, his mother had waited long enough for Leviston to open his purse.

He pictured his uncle's face smiling in satisfaction as Zachary pretended interest in his bobbins and bales, saw again the age-spots and the characteristic mole on his chin just above where his beard started, remembered how he used to fold the bread into a square before popping it in his mouth. He wanted to hate him, but he couldn't.

Once you had sat at a man's table, broken bread with him, then lies were so much harder. There was something holy about breaking bread with someone, even though you might never acknowledge the fact. Damn Elspet, why did she have to come after him?

Chapter 29

Zachary walked quickly, his hand on his sword, looking over his shoulder in case Rodriguez or his men should appear from a side street, but Gabriel's sketchy directions were enough to lead him straight to the Corral del Toro. He stood a moment outside, listening to the melancholy twang of a lute or cittern and a guttural wailing voice. The sound wavered, hung on the night air.

The must be the *gitaneria*, the gypsy area. He'd heard tell in Toledo of the flowing-haired gypsy girls, with their peacock dress and loose morals, and ability to rend the heart with song. He had not thought about women for so long that, despite Elspet Leviston, the thought of meeting a gypsy girl sent a frisson of excitement up his back.

The tavern itself was a dilapidated squat brick building backing on to a courtyard. Grass grew out of the tiles on the roof, and the central square was overhung with twisted vines casting strands of shadow from the moon overhead. Pulling in his sword and buckler, he went through the arch into a square courtyard where sconces smoked against the walls. Rickety tables and disintegrating rush stools filled the central area. The tables were illuminated by spouted earthenware lamps; each wick flickered with a thumb-sized flame.

Clearly this was not the sort of place Rodriguez would frequent, so he exhaled and made his way over to where he could see Gabriel's broad back. He was leaning back against one of the wooden pillars that supported the wispy canopy of foliage. Zachary dragged out a stool next to him and Gabriel grinned, pushing the jug of ale and a cup towards him.

'You came!'

'I need a drink,' Zachary said, pouring the ale. He could not get over it – Elspet Leviston was actually here in Spain, the thought of it unsettled him.

Gabriel opened his mouth to speak, but before their conversation even had a chance to get started a jangle of strings cut through the chatter, and an old man in a ragged waistcoat started to play. Poor old man, he was almost toothless; a shock of greying hair stood vertically from his forehead making his lined face appear even more swarthy.

'What's that he's playing?' Zachary asked.

' *"Cuando yo me muera",*' Gabriel whispered.

'No, not the song, the instrument.'

'Oh, *guitarra morisca*. They're quite common among the gitanes in the taverns.'

Zachary had never seen anything like it, so small, yet the sound so penetrating. Nothing like the English lutes or citterns he was used to.

The old man dragged his fingernails over the strings in a series of crescendo-ing arcs, then sang, his instrument silent on his lap. He started with a long-drawn-out lamentation, followed by words that seemed to rake across the room, his face screwed up in anguish. Zachary's stomach lurched and from then on he was mesmerized by this man's voice as he sang of the irresistible attraction of love, its passion and terror, of the fear that you might lose your lover, or yourself into love's madness:

. . . te pío un encargo,
que con las trenzas
de tu pelo negro
me marren las manos . . .

'That with the braids of your black hair they tie up my hands.' The words startled him. It was so naked, his ardour. In England such a ballad could never be sung – it would be all birds and trees and courtly euphemisms. Whilst the old man's voice held sway, no one picked up a cup to drink, or moved to fill their pipe. His voice was a river, with rapids and whirlpools, rough water and slow curves. Zachary was absolutely in his thrall. The old man's claw-like hands gestured to the open sky above as he sang his last crooning note, eyes closed.

He spat noisily into the spittoon and cackled, showing his toothless smile. The spell was broken. Loud applause and movement returned to the tavern, girls bustled over with more ale, tankards lifted once more. An itinerant seller in a gold-cloth turban and embroidered waistcoat appeared at their side and plied them with dried meat and fish. They bought meat which was tasty but salty and caused Zachary to down another cup of ale. Seville was so warm, his thirst was never-ending.

He scanned the women at the tables, the way the other men did. He nudged Gabriel as his curious glance was returned by two dark-haired women leaning on the bar. He looked over and the two women turned away and whispered to each other. One of them was shaking her head and frowning. The other, the taller one in vivid green, kept looking over and smiling.

'Those two?' Gabriel said.

'Do you know them?'

'I've seen the one in the green before. She's nice, she works in the *fruiteria*. The other one's a dancer, I've seen her dance, but never spoken to her. Shall we offer them a drink?'

'Go on, then.'

Gabriel waved them over. Behind them an eagle-faced man fixed Gabriel with his eyes.

'Their father, I'll bet,' Zachary whispered as the girl in green approached, reluctantly followed by the other.

'I know,' Gabriel said. 'Don't worry, we will be careful.' As they reached the table he smiled and stood, 'We would like to buy you a drink.'

'We like to know the names of those we drink with,' said the girl in the yellow shawl.

'Gabriel Lopez and Zachary Deane at your service,' Gabriel said.

Zachary stood too, to offer his seat.

'Maria Nuñez,' said the girl in green, sitting, 'and this is my friend—'

'Luisa Ortega,' said the other girl, pulling up another seat.

'He's English.' Gabriel wagged his head in his direction. It sounded as if he was apologizing.

They fetched sweet Madeira for the ladies, but had barely begun a conversation when the thrum of the guitar started up again. Zachary was torn between wanting to listen and wanting to talk.

But Luisa had already put her cup down.

'My time,' she announced, and pulled her shawl from her shoulders to tie it tightly around her hips. 'Save my seat, Maria.' She hoisted her flounced skirts out of the way of the tables and chairs as she made her way to the front.

In the lamplight her face was serious and gaunt. Her hair was wound in a heavy knot at the nape of her neck and fixed with a horn comb. She reminded Zachary of a bird, there was something light-boned and insubstantial about her. She waited a moment before beginning a few tentative steps, her arms stretched above her head, white fingers forming pointed beaks. She stamped her sandalled feet in small staccato movements. Bells at her ankles gave a shimmering sound. Her back was long and straight, her skirts falling in a cascade of ruffles to reveal neat ankle bones and sun-browned feet. She was beautiful. Zachary let out his breath; he had been holding it without knowing.

She swayed, eyes closed, to the rhythm of the guitar, hands curling down to her waist and back to above her head. Tack, tack. Her feet stamped. The guitar continued its rhythmic pulse.

Mid-movement she sighed and dropped her arms. She turned crossly to the guitarist and gesticulated, he paused in his play as she bent to talk with him. She walked back to our table, untying the shawl from her waist and flinging it back around her shoulders.

'Aren't you going to dance after all?' Gabriel asked.

'No.' She looked distressed. 'No, I can't dance tonight. I have no spirit for dancing.'

Maria reached over and pressed Luisa's hand where it lay on the table. Luisa turned to Zachary, an accusing look in her eyes. 'You are English?'

He started to say, 'No, half-Spanish, but—'

She interrupted him. Her sloe eyes searched his. 'A good Catholic, yes?'

He looked to Gabriel, who shook his head as if to warn him to keep quiet.

Luisa still looked at Zachary with an odd intensity. It frightened him, that look. Maria filled the awkward silence. 'Luisa had bad news. Last week she had to move out of her house, and now she's just heard from her uncle that some of her friends in Valencia have been deported.'

'I'm sorry to hear that.' Gabriel spoke politely.

'Don't, Maria.' Luisa frowned at her. 'It's none of their business. I just don't feel like dancing, that's all.'

'What's wrong? They should know. It's no secret, is it?' Maria said. 'The authorities have always treated us like dung. And now a man at the bar has just told me what they are spending our fines and taxes on.' Her voice was bitter. 'Guess what? A new gaol in the Castle of San Jorge so they can keep more of us *conversos* under lock and key.' She laughed mirthlessly. 'Not only that, but the prison is to have a special chapel where we will receive instruction in the Catholic faith. They will force us to their God with torture.'

Luisa gave her a warning glance. 'Leave it, Maria. It's not his fault.'

Maria ignored her friend. She thrust out her chin as if to dare them to react. 'If we comply and take instruction meekly then they might deign to let us out of their stinking gaol a little earlier. If not, there will be more taxes or more torture. More galley service.'

Zachary looked to Gabriel. He didn't know what to say, he was unused to such outspokenness in women.

Behind Maria, her father was approaching; he must have sensed something was the matter. 'Maria?'

She stood up. 'You – Englishman, you want to know what life is like for us? Here, Papa.' She took her father's hand and pushed his claw-like hands before Zachary's eyes. 'See these – see these broken fingers? Galley service. Three years of it, where they beat your knuckles with an iron rod if you do not row quickly enough. What a waste.'

'Maria, enough.' Her father pulled his hands away but she did not stop. Her sallow cheeks were tinged with pink as she leaned forward, palms planted on the table, eyes blazing. 'Too many good men have hands like these. My father was a calligrapher. And he must spend three years inside the belly of a stinking ship. Now he can hardly lift a pen. And you – you are all the same. You expect Luisa to dance for your entertainment. To dance for nothing. Well, she won't dance to please you or anyone else. Come on, Luisa.'

Maria untied her shawl and swathed it tightly over her nose and mouth in the Morisco way and pushed through the throng to the door. A man near the bar let out a whistle. She turned long enough to send him a barbed look, her dark eyes framed by her scarf. Her father granted them a small bow, a laconic smile on his lips.

'She means no harm. Good evening, gentlemen,' he said.

Maria paused at the door for her father, and then swept out.

'What a firebrand,' Zachary said to Gabriel behind his hand.

'She's that.'

Luisa jumped to defend her friend. 'It's true though. To the authorities we are nothing but one big open purse.' She pressed her lips together in disgust. 'Señor, how long have you been in Spain?'

Zachary confessed, 'Just six weeks.'

She shook her head, and her gilded earrings tinkled. 'Ha. Then you don't know the half of it. In Valencia they have sent everyone of Moorish descent back to the Barbery Coast, but they dare not do it here. Trade would collapse without our fines. Besides, if they did that, who would make their sandals?' She glanced scathingly down at Gabriel's hempen footwear. Gabriel retracted his feet out of view under the stool. 'Sandal makers and farm labourers. That's all they think us fit for.'

Gabriel looked abashed. 'Here,' he said, 'let me pour you some more wine.'

Luisa folded her slim arms across her chest but she did not leave. Zachary was reminded of a wild animal. It felt like a privilege that she had appeared at their table. But he was on tenterhooks lest she should decide to run off. Finally, she took a few sips of wine and seemed to relax. By now the guitarist was playing a softer melody of rippling strings.

'I didn't mean to offend Maria. Shall I go after her?' Gabriel asked.

'No. She'll soon calm down. And she's with her father. She's always been hot-tempered. She'll get over it. It isn't your fault.'

'Zachary didn't mean to rattle her like that, I'm sure. It's just, I expect they know little of our country in England,' Gabriel said as if apologizing for him, 'and he's not been here long, after all.'

'I can see that.' She smiled fleetingly at last. 'He looks like a foreigner.'

Zachary was affronted, but did not react. He had been dazzled by her smile. 'I thought she seemed nice, your friend Maria,' he said to her, aware that this sounded a little stupid.

'She needs to watch her tongue.'

There was a silence then before Luisa asked, 'What are you doing here in Spain? Englishmen do not get much of a welcome unless they have money to spend.'

'He has money to spend, right enough,' Gabriel replied. 'His uncle left him a legacy—' Zachary frowned at him. He was not anxious that everyone should know his business. Gabriel fumbled to change the subject. 'He is making a sword. I work at Guido de Vega's swordsmith's and Zachary is making a sword. A fine thing,' he gabbled. 'It's almost finished already. That's how we met each other. At first I thought he was a mad fool, a gentleman like him. I thought he'd never do it.'

'A sword, you say? I'm sick of swords.' She grimaced. 'My father has just made us move to a fencing master's house. Papa's employed by the school of the sword. He teaches them geometry and rhetoric. Heaven only knows why that's any use for fighting.'

'And you say you live there now? That must be interesting.'

'Papa used to go down to the rapier school a few evenings a week. Actually, they don't pay him. It's a scandal. I keep telling Maria, they should be paying, gentlemen like that. Heaven knows, they get enough out of us Moriscos already, with all the fines and taxes. But Papa won't have it – he says he does it for the love of it. He gets on well with the fencing master. He's the only one he can discuss philosophy with, he says.' She shrugged and raised her eyes to the sky. 'We had to leave our other place, so now he's there all the time. Still, at least he's happy.'

'And you say it's a school of fence?'

'Yes. Near the Church of San Jacinto. But it's only a few students. I don't think Señor Alvarez's method is very popular. They call it *La Verdadera Destreza*.'

The name took a moment to register. He leaned forward. 'Here? In Triana?' He could hardly contain his excitement.

'Yes. But it's not a big place, not like the government one run by Don Rodriguez in the Arenal. Why, do you know of it?'

'I've been looking for it. Is there a man there, a man with white hair, but young, not an old man?' He could not contain his excitement.

'Señor Alvarez, yes.'

'You'll never believe this. I really have been searching for it. Here—' he raked in his satchel and brought out a corked bottle of ink and pen, and a scrap of paper. 'Write down the address for me, won't you?'

'I can make you a map if you like.'

She scratched out the curving inky lines of the riverbank, the narrow passageways and fortress walls, and pointed with the goose nib where to go. Her fingers were long and slender, there was a fine down of dark hairs on her forearms. She pushed the paper towards him. The map was oddly familiar. A crack opened in time. Déjà vu, the French called it. A quirk of the moment that made him shake his head to rattle it free of a history that had not yet happened.

'The sign of a spread-eagled man,' Luisa said, pulling back the paper and drawing quickly. 'You know it?' Gabriel shook his head.

She had drawn a man spread out like a five-pointed star. Like in Vitruvius. Uncle Leviston had talked of him. It was an omen, it must be.

'Will I need an introduction?' he asked, folding the precious piece of paper and putting it in his bag. 'I mean, would your father vouch for me? I can pay.'

She was waving her hand and laughing. 'For that place? No. But be careful. Don't waste your good money. If you are after proper training, the men say Don Rodriguez is the best.'

He did not answer; he knew enough of Rodriguez to know his methods were not for him.

Part Three

The Spirit that is principal in the Man
is the fundamental basis of all the Exercise of the Arms.
Carranza – Dialogues

Chapter 30

Luisa paused behind the sheet, her mouth full of split-wood pegs. She was hanging clothes on the line to dry before going to work, when a noise made her stand on tiptoes to look.

There he was, that pipsqueak Englishman, standing in the yard looking lost. He had found his way there, so her map must have been good enough for him to follow. She had never expected to see him though; thought it was all talk. And she wasn't so sure she wanted to be associated with someone who had so clearly been in a fight. She took the pegs from her mouth and smoothed her hair. But Maria was very keen on his friend, the journeyman smith, though of course she pretended not to be. Maybe the English man wasn't so bad after all.

She hurried over, the empty basket at her hip. '*Buenos días,*' she said.

He replied in Spanish and smiled. His English accent was strong, but not unpleasant. He had arresting brown eyes which made her drop her gaze.

She told him the others were indoors, that they had quiet study for portions of the day, and other times they trained here in the yard – she pointed to the straw targets nailed up to the walls. He looked with polite interest, but the targets looked pathetic, most of them tattered through use and homes to mice. As she talked, she noticed that his fingernails were bitten to the quick, and that he had very shapely calves. When she showed him the targets she did not tell him she dreaded the mice would not move quick enough, when the men started their target practice.

He listened, watching her closely, his head cocked to one side.

After that she ran out of things to show him, and stood feeling a little stupid. Her face grew hot. She looked up and caught his eye, and a spark ran between them, quick as lightning. She turned to hurry indoors, her face flaming.

'Where might I find Señor Alvarez?' he called.

'Here.' Señor Alvarez appeared at the top of the flight of stairs at the corner of the courtyard. Sometimes it was uncanny how the señor sensed when a stranger was in the yard. When Uncle Najid came, the señor was already alert and listening, before he even knocked, she could tell by the way his attention was outside and not inside the room. Luisa went into the kitchen and watched from the window.

As he approached, the Englishman bowed low, and introduced himself. 'Zachary Deane,' he said, and she remembered this time to note his name.

Don Alvarez appeared to know him. 'Haven't I seen you before? He thought a moment. 'Ah. The man who is unpopular with the farmers. They seem to want to box your ears. I met you in London, did I not?' he asked.

'Yes, sir. You did. And I've looked for you all over. I want to learn everything you can teach me. I went to France, but they can teach me nothing. I want to learn to wield a weapon the way you do.'

'If you think you have nothing to learn from the French, what makes you think you can learn anything from me?'

'I've seen you fence. And I know you are the best.'

'You flatter me. Where do you stay?'

'In lodgings, close to the cathedral.'

'You will come every day?'

'As many hours as you have, to teach me all you know.'

Señor Alvarez smiled. 'Or to pull from you what you know already, but have lost sight of.' He sighed, shaking his head. 'I don't know, first a Dutchman, then someone from France, now an Englishman. What's wrong with my own country? Do they not need to know how to fence?' He sighed again. 'Still, I suppose I'll take you.

After all, you're here, which clearly my own countrymen aren't.'

'You mean you'll teach me?' His voice was so delighted, Luisa suppressed a smile.

'You'll find a place to leave your things in the passageway by the kitchen. I'll get Luisa to show you—'

She called, 'I'll take him,' through the open window, realizing as she did so that she had just given herself away.

He came to the door and she motioned him to follow. She pointed to the row of wooden pegs where the others had hung their cloaks. He swung his off, and she hooked it up. It was a fine velvet one, soft to the touch, and warm where it had been close to his neck.

'They're all in the library with my father,' she said. 'Every day – an hour or so by the glass, they talk about geometry before they come out in the yard.' Now she could not keep the note of pride from her voice – it was pleasant to be able to show the place to someone else. And the library had more than fifty books. Fifty! Papa thought he had died and reached the Rose Garden already, to live here and be able to handle all those books, even if he could barely read them anymore.

'Thank you,' he said, 'Señorita Ortega.'

Was he serious? She was unused to being called Señorita anything, and was surprised he had remembered her name. She glanced sideways at him, for he looked so taken with the fact that Señor Alvarez was to train him, like a small boy who had been given his favourite toy. He asked about the others who studied there, and again he listened carefully to her reply and watched. This was very strange. Perhaps this was the English way, certainly no Spanish man had ever let her talk like this without wanting to tell her his opinion.

And he thanked her again when she left him at the library door. His eyes widened at the sight of all the books, and at all the other young men earnestly engaged in their studies with callipers and straight-edge.

'A new recruit,' she said. 'Señor asked me to bring him up.'

'Oh not another,' grumbled Papa. 'Now I'll have to start at the beginning again. I keep telling him it's no use, all this coming and going. We need consistency.' She looked to see how the Englishman was taking it, and exchanged a shy look with him. He slipped into the vacant place next to Alexander, the tall Dutchman. Papa flapped his hands at her and she ran down the stairs, faster than she should because they were worn slippery with use, so anxious was she to share the news with Mama before she had to leave for the pottery – all about the new Englishman who was to study with Señor.

In the afternoon when she returned from work, she saw that the others had drifted away, keen on a few hours respite before the evening training, but Mr Deane was still in the yard on his own, practising his moves, a fierce expression on his face.

She watched him through the window as she helped Mama prepare the vegetables. Of course she didn't want to look, but he drew her eye. He moved like a dancer, she thought. His body moved with ease and grace, but it was as if he was angry at something; he lunged at the targets over and over until the sweat slid down his face. She heard the clang of metal on stone as the blade pierced through the targets. Clouds of dust rose from the ground where he skidded and stomped. When he was finished, he slumped against the wall, panting. She stood to the edge of the window, holding a red bell-pepper in her hand that she had intended to core and peel.

He did not look her way, but dabbed at his sword hand with the corner of his shirt. It was probably blistered by now from wielding the corded grip all those hours in the afternoon heat. The English were crazy, she thought. He blew out air on to his upper lip to cool himself. A nice-shaped mouth, she thought and she blushed. It was a sensation that made her withdraw, as if it were too intimate, watching him unseen from this window.

The next day, after her work was finished at the pottery, Luisa hurried back to the fencing school to see if the Englishman was still there, and what Papa had to say about him.

'Hey there, little pumpkin.' Luisa ruffled Husain's hair as she ducked under the lines of laundry, and crossed over the yard at the back of the house.

Husain stood up from where he was rolling his toy wooden cart in the dirt and hurried after her, tugging at her skirt.

'We're going to France, Papa says. He says we're going on a boat. I like boats.'

'What barrel of nonsense have you picked up now?' she said, as she went to the water jar and scooped out some water to rinse her hands. Though she'd tried to wash them at the pottery the grey river clay still lodged in her fingernails.

Husain fiddled with the hem of her skirt; he loved to crack off the dried daubs that always seemed to get there somehow, no matter how careful she was. 'He says Señor Alvarez is going to get us some horses and we'll run away. I don't know why we're running away, though. Is it priests, Luisa, or bandits?'

'I don't know what you're talking about. Come here and give me a hug.' She hoisted him up and he wrapped his legs around her waist. She rubbed noses with him and then said, 'It's all right. There's no need to be frightened. We're quite safe here. There are all those men with swords in the yard.'

'No. We're going next week. On a boat. Papa said I'd to pay respects to my friends this week because after that we might not see them for a very long time.'

A shadow fell across her heart; she put him down and went inside to where Mama was unloading a batch of fruit from a wicker pannier. Outside she could hear Husain clucking happily, making the noises of horse's hooves as he played with his cart.

Mama looked up as she stormed, 'What's this that Husain is saying about boats, and leaving? Am I the only one kept in the dark in this family?'

Mama put down the lemon in her hand, 'Your father thought it best. There's rumours that they might try to send the Moriscos back to Barbery, and if they do, then there'll be no choosing where we go. We have distant cousins in Bordeaux who might shelter us awhile until we can get to Fez. At least there we will be amongst friends.'

'But—'

'No. Listen to me. When I went down to the river with the laundry they were saying that there'll be no welcome for us in North Africa. The Africans think we're Spanish cheats and liars. There'll be no work for us there because they won't trust us.'

Luisa opened her mouth to protest, but her mother carried on, 'Don't look at me like that. What do you expect us to do? We've

Husain to think of. We're doing the best we can. We didn't say anything to you because we knew you wouldn't like it.'

'But France? We can't speak the language. How will we manage? I don't want to be some French woman's lackey. And sure as I stand, if we're not welcome in Africa, we won't be welcome there either. Anyway, who said this?'

Mama went back to sorting the fruit and vegetables. 'It was Aliya who told me.'

'Her. Huh. What does she know?'

'News is always first from her lips, you know that.'

'She's a blabbermouth. We never hear anything good from her big mouth. I don't know why you even listen to her.'

'Enough. I never thought I'd hear my own daughter malign our neighbours so. You know yourself, you never know when you might have need of them. These are dark times. Think of Daria and Merin. Do you want to end up like them, locked up in the Castle of San Jorge? Well, do you?' She threw down the knife, a look of frustration etched on her face.

'You're stupid if you believe anything Aliya says.'

'Do not speak to me that way. Do you think I have only you to consider? Your father is half-blind. What do you think it will be like on those boats? A pleasure outing? Wake up, Luisa. You can pretend you are Spanish all you like, but they can see it even if you can't – the Morisco blood flowing in your veins. If you don't come with us to France, they'll send you to Africa. Or put you in the cells at San Jorge. Which would you rather, heh?'

She blazed back, 'I'm not a Morisco. I'm a Christian. I don't understand Islam. It's your fault. Why won't you just do as they ask? Attend to what they say in church. It's not so bad. In fact, it makes more sense than anything in the Qur'an. Other people do it. Why not you? Then we could all stay here and be safe.'

Mama stared at her with her mouth set in a line, said nothing though her eyes had turned glassy. She unpacked more lemons from the basket.

Luisa pleaded with her, 'It might not happen. Nobody's said anything about it at the pottery. How would you feel if you uprooted our whole family again and it was all just gossip and scaremongering?'

'I am out of patience!' Mama hurled a lemon at Luisa, but it missed and hit the wall behind her.

The air in the room seemed to grow thick.

Mama had never in all her life thrown anything at her. She saw her mother stoop to pick up the lemon from the floor. She swallowed before she spoke to Luisa in the measured tone of voice she sometimes used for Husain. 'However much you protest, you know we will do as you father says as usual. And his mind is made up. Señor Alvarez has agreed to help us.'

'I'm not going.' The words were almost a whisper.

'Suit yourself. We will go without you.' She pushed the bowl of lemons to one side, tipped the *patatas* into a bowl and began paring them with grim concentration.

Luisa could not answer. She took up the bowl of lemons and the knife, turned her back on her mother and walked away, out into the yard. There the new Englishman, Mr Deane, was practising again in the late afternoon heat. She had hoped to be private, so the sight of him made her angry. She ignored him and went to the shady bench under the vines. Her heart beat fast under her bodice from the argument with Mama.

If they went to France then she would be left alone. She had never been without her family before. But heaven help her, nothing would make her go with them, she'd rather die on Spanish soil than go to France. She'd miss the pottery, the tavern where she danced, everything familiar. Why would she want to go to a place where she had no history, no past? But then, she thought bitterly, what would it be like to stay behind, when her whole history had gone to France without her?

She picked up one of the fruits and dug the knife into the peel.

She suddenly resented having to make the lemon drink that the men consumed so much of. She peeled off the rind, cursing as the juice stung in the small cuts in her fingers.

Mr Deane was practising a backward-stepping pattern with the sword jutting forwards from under his elbow, like a boar's tusk. She did not mean to watch him, but he was right there in front of her.

When he saw her looking, he thrust his weapon forward, with enough attack that the end of his rapier quivered from the force. She looked back down at her peeling. The rind dropped by her feet and one of the hens from the back yard had somehow found her way in and pecked and scratched at it.

'Shoo.' She hustled the hen angrily back through the small door that was set into the back gates and shut it after her. When she got back to the bench Mr Deane was sitting there. 'I could not resist the smell of those lemons,' he said.

She sat down on the other side, with the bowl between them. She made an effort to talk normally, as if nothing was the matter. 'It takes ten lemons to make the drink you are all so fond of,' she said. It came out as an accusation, but he did not flinch.

'It's very good, that stuff. We need it in this heat. I called in to the smithy this morning, to pass the time of day with Guido and Gabriel. Gabriel was still talking about Maria. Have you seen her today?'

'Yes, I see her most days. That's where we get the lemons. She works at the *fruiteria*.'

'Oh yes. I remember now. I'm sorry if we upset her.'

'No. It's not your fault.' She paused, then said, 'It's hard for all Moriscos right now.' He raised his eyebrows so she went on. 'Seville is full of rumours again. It's nothing new. But my parents believe them all, every time. And they took away our neighbours for cooking meat on a Friday. It was horrible. They beat them, and dragged them away. We haven't seen them since. Mama's scared they'll come for us next. Now my father wants us to move to France.' She grimaced. 'And Señor Alvarez has agreed to help us,' she said miserably.

'Will you go?' He watched as she plopped the peeled lemon into the bowl.

'No. I don't know anything about France.'

'I've just come from there.'

'I thought you came from England?'

'I was in France for a while before I came here. But I couldn't stand it, that's why I'm here.'

'Why?' Curiosity had got the better of her.

'I was looking for a fencing master. Everyone I met in France was an "expert" who wanted to add you to their list of successful conquests. But most of them could barely hold a rapier point side out, so I gave up in the end, it was an insult to fight such men.'

'But what was it like, France?'

'Cold. And people close their shutters on you if you cannot speak their language. I had a hard time finding a place to stay when I was travelling. Mind, they certainly know how to eat. Best beef stew I've ever tasted.'

Luisa frowned. The beef stew worried her immediately. Father refused to eat meat until it had been blessed. 'Are there many Moriscos there, do you know?'

He looked apologetic. 'I'm sorry but I don't know. I didn't take much notice.'

'Did you see any mosques, or hear a muezzin calling folk to prayer?'

'No, not that I can recall. But then, I wasn't looking for them. I'm sure there must be. Your father must think it's safer there, or he wouldn't have suggested it.' She frowned. It was not what she wanted to hear. He paused a moment and looked away into the distance. 'I'd listen to your father. Like most parents, he is probably only trying to keep you safe. And if Señor Alvarez thinks it's a good idea . . .'

She twisted a piece of lemon peel in her fingers. He was trying to be pleasant, she knew, but he didn't understand. 'I can't speak French,' she said stubbornly.

'Neither could I. But I got by with sign language.' He mimed rubbing his stomach and pointing to his mouth. The effect was comical and in other circumstances would have made her smile.

'I might have guessed. All you men can think of is your stomach.' An awkward silence was broken by the sound of talking, as at that moment two of the other men appeared at the front gate with their arms cases.

'Looks like it's time for the evening session.' He stood and bowed. 'I shall look forward to tasting your lemon water, Señorita Ortega.' His bowing made her blush, but she dropped her head quickly to hide it. She was sorry she had been so rude, but she felt like an impostor; she was unused to young men treating her this way, like a queen.

She watched him cross the yard and saw the others smile and greet him. He looked back once and caught her eye. Inadvertently she found herself lifting her hand in a wave.

Chapter 31

The next day Zachary unwrapped his new blade from the oilcloth and laid it on the bench. The hilt-smith looked up from where he was grinding an amalgam in a mortar, put down the pestle and wiped his hands on a rag. He turned the blade over, and pursed his lips in approval.

'It is like a woman's weapon, this, so light and fine. But a good edge on it too, I see. Let me show you some designs,' he said, fetching some vellum sheets. 'Something small like this can take a swept hilt rather than the usual basket.'

Zachary looked over the patterns and chose an elegantly curved confection, all flowing vine-like curves, with a cherry-wood handle. When he had negotiated a price, he left the blade with the smith, feeling for all the world as if he had abandoned his only child.

As he came out of the hilt-smith's door he breathed in the smell of the wind. It was the first time he had felt some respite from the heat. It was good to be alive, he thought, as he walked jauntily down the Calle de las Armas towards the Guadalquivir river and the tied pontoon bridge to Triana, where the fleet was anchored off the sandbank, masts bristling up against the sky.

As he made his way across the bridge, the tied planks shifted slightly over the boats that supported them. The first time he had crossed he had found it disconcerting and had been tempted to grab at the stake and rope handrail to steady himself. But Sevillians had used it as a common thoroughfare for generations, and even carts and horses trundled over it. The bridge was busy at this time with packhorses and he had to queue. A few more folk pressed up behind him, all anxious to get to their day's labours.

He was about a third of the way across when he saw them. A familiar knot of marching men. He looked again to make sure. Don Rodriguez and a group of his men were approaching from the other side; they had a man between them in chains. They must have come from the Castle of San Jorge which loomed large and forbidding on the opposite bank of the river.

Zachary licked his lips. His mouth was dry. He turned to go back the way he had come, but the route behind him was blocked. Those in front were clearing the way for the group, who were in armour and had the air of officialdom that uniform gives men.

'Excuse me,' Zachary tried to squeeze past the woman behind him to go back.

'Hey!' she cried, 'What are you doing? You want to push us off the bridge?'

He muttered an apology, and tried to force his way back through the crowd. By now everyone else in front of him was retreating or moving aside to give the approaching men room.

Fear made his voice high-pitched, 'Soldiers are coming, we've got to let them pass,' he said to a man with two donkeys, but the man shook his head and refused to move. He could see their helmets above the crowd now. They were almost upon him and his heart was hammering in his chest. Somehow he elbowed his way through the crowd and ran to the shelter of one of the stalls set up by the river.

From here he saw Don Rodriguez, Fabian and his men march their unfortunate victim towards the city. He cursed himself. Why had he not stood his ground? He had fought any number of men in duels and had never been afraid. But Don Rodriguez was something else. A fair fight was one thing, but humiliation at the hands of these men, well, he feared it.

He went to the fencing school feeling out of sorts. Señor Alvarez took one look at him and set him repetitive drilling up and down the yard until he was almost on his knees, and then to sweeping the yard.

Sweeping was not something he had ever thought he would be doing as part of his sword training. But then Señor Alvarez was an unusual master.

Zachary was unsure what to think of him, but some authority about him commanded respect. Though they had not practised many techniques yet; Alvarez was intent on teaching them what he called 'the principles', which seemed to be mostly angles and geometry. And he'd certainly need more than mathematics to stand a chance against hard types like Rodriguez and his men. With a jolt, Zachary realized that Rodriguez had somehow replaced his bullying brothers in his thoughts. The same humiliation burned in his chest; the same desire to get even.

He swept the small pile of leaves from the corner of the yard out into the street and wondered if the others were enjoying their cleaning tasks as little as he was, and how they had come to study at Señor Alvarez's. What a ramshackle collection of individuals. For a start, there were only five of them, and none of them looked remotely like fighters, nothing like the ranks of leather-armoured men at Don Rodriguez' salon.

One of them – Alexander, a tall, rangy man with a lugubrious face and deep-set eyes – revealed that he had won several tournaments in his own country, so he must be better than he looked despite his drooping appearance. Zachary was keen to test his mettle in a bout or two. But no, they both had to start from the beginning, like children.

As he swept, the bristles of the broom scratched rhythmically. Zachary thought back to the day before when Señor Alvarez had made them each draw out a circular training diagram in the empty chamber upstairs, with a nail, string and chalk.

When Zachary's was done Alvarez instructed him to stand in it. He lifted up Zachary's sword until the tip was outstretched to the circumference.

'Perfect stillness,' was all he said.

Zachary was expecting to stay a few moments, but as he stood, the moments stretched into minutes. Señor Alvarez sat watching the whole time. Zachary struggled to maintain the position. A fly landed on his cheek followed by another on the trickle of sweat at his hairline. He felt their tiny legs prickling his brow, tried to blow them away, but from the corner of his eye saw Señor Alvarez frown.

The minutes stretched on until he understood it was some kind of test. He refused to give up. The bell sounded the half, then the third quarter, until his shoulder throbbed and his arm trembled. When more than one hour had passed and his eyes were closed in searing pain, Alvarez's voice made him start.

'Good,' Alvarez said. 'Now you know your range to the North. Turn to face the South.'

Zachary raised his stiff arm, suddenly understanding. He would have to do the same to the other directions. He clenched his teeth, so that was to be it – no fencing, no glimpse of a bit of duelling action, but he stuck with it. He knew every inch of those walls now – the cracks in the plasterwork, the knot in the floorboard where the ants crept in and out passing through the shafts of sunlight as they marched by.

When he got home, his arm throbbed like the devil, but it was strange, as soon as he held out his arm he could sense that circle.

He paused now, outstretched broom in hand, to see if he could still feel it. Yes, the sensation was still there. Zachary finished the sweeping and set aside the broom with relief. No sooner had he done so than Alvarez appeared and handed it back to him, instructing him to join Alexander inside, where the Dutchman was polishing the tables and chairs with beeswax.

'Are there no servants to do this?' Zachary grumbled.

Señor Alvarez was waiting in the doorway and must have overheard. 'You want a clean mind? One fit for fighting? Then sweep. *Metáfora*, you understand?'

A metaphor. Yes, but a metaphor would not help him keep his body ready for action, thought Zachary, irritated with the whole thing. He'd come to learn to fight. Any fool could sweep the floor. After they had done, he let his besom clatter to the floor and turned to Alexander, 'Carry on like this and I'll be worthless for a duel but I'll be the best house slave in Seville.'

'Do you want to train with Señor Alvarez, or not?' Alexander said, looking up from his polishing.

'Of course I do, it's just—'

'Then stop complaining. It wastes your energy. And you'll need it if you stick with him. He's the best fighter I've ever seen.'

Whilst Zachary was sweeping, across the river Elspet fanned herself and shifted impatiently on her balcony, behind the hemp awning which had been pulled down to afford her some shade.

As soon as Mr Wilmot rounded the corner she sagged. It was not good news, she could tell. His head was bowed and his shoulders drooped. He was carrying his hat, flapping it ineffectively before his face, and his sparse blond hair was stuck to his forehead. She hurried back into the room and down the stairs.

'What?' she asked, before he had so much as a chance to get himself through the door.

'I waited two hours, but there was no sign of him.' He tore off his coat and threw it on to the floor. 'Bloody heat. Your brother did not come.'

'Don't call him that. Are you sure you did not miss him?'

'I'm sure. No, you were right. The man is deliberately avoiding us.' He ascended, dragging his feet and wiped the perspiration from his brow with the back of his already damp shirt sleeve.

'Then we'll go back to his lodgings again,' she said, following on his heels, 'Make him see us again.'

'He won't admit us. The girl told me he had gone away. Madrid she said.'

He was ready to give up, she could sense it. 'I am not leaving Spain until I have a settlement from him in writing,' she said.

Wilmot laughed. 'Then what will you do? Force him against his will? He was clear enough he is not going to change his mind. I think we should go home and see if we can somehow band together to buy a part of the business back.'

'The business, the business! Is that all you can think of? What about the house? How shall I live?'

'Mistress Leviston, Elspet, I—'

'I am not leaving. It is up to you what you do, but I am staying.

I will hang at Zachary Deane's elbow like a mosquito if need be. He'll be so weary of the sight of me, he will agree simply to rid himself of my presence.'

'I cannot leave you here alone, Mistress Elspet. It is out of the question. How would you get home?'

'The same way as I came, I suppose. It is not beyond a woman's wit to book a passage, you know, Mr Wilmot.'

'No. Impossible. You must travel with me, Mistress Elspet. It is not safe for women to travel alone. I insist.'

She suppressed a laugh at the idea that he was any form of protection. 'Insist? Well, in that case you will have to pick me up and carry me, for I have not come all this way to give up at the first difficulty. He has not left Seville, of that I am sure. He is a liar, but he does not fool me.'

Wilmot sat down. He loosened his collar and flapped it back and forth. 'For heaven's sake, be reasonable. I cannot argue in this heat.' When she continued to stare at him, arms folded, he blew out through his mouth and said, 'You're right, the girl was lying. I got talking to a fellow in a tavern – I asked after him there. They pointed me to a smith and his apprentice. The apprentice told me he's signed on with a master of fence across the river.'

'Now that sounds more like the truth. A master of fence. That will be my cousin. He was ever obsessed with fighting. Where?'

'In the gypsy quarter of Triana. You would be better advised to look for him there.'

'Then I shall go there tomorrow. You will accompany me, Mr Wilmot?'

Wilmot pressed both his hands over his eyes and smoothed his fingers over his eyebrows and cheeks with a long exhalation, before looking at her mournfully and shaking his head. That, she took to be his agreement.

They paused under the sign of The Spreadeagled Man and looked at each other. Mr Wilmot pushed open the door under the drooping bougainvillea, and Elspet saw a deserted courtyard and a yard swept so clean that even the dust bore the marks of a broom. Elspet blinked in the dazzle of the sun. The only sound was the chirruping of a bold cricket, which had not yet succumbed to the heat of the day.

'There's nobody here. Where do they train?' Something about the place made her whisper.

'I don't know,' Wilmot said, 'but look.' He pointed at the targets nailed to the wall. 'This is definitely the place.'

She turned around, scanning the windows of the house, and caught sight of a movement inside. Through the window on the first floor the dim form of a man dressed in a black doublet could be seen. Mr Wilmot had seen him too so they climbed the stone steps towards an upper door. She signalled Martha to follow them, but before they could lift a hand to knock, the door opened.

'Yes?' the man asked in a low voice, his eyebrows raised. He had a sun-weathered face but the most surprising thing about him was his hair – it was pure white. He was not an old man, though, she judged him to be in his thirtieth year or thereabouts.

Wilmot nudged her to speak in Spanish, 'Are you Señor Alvarez, and do you have a student called Zachary Deane?' she said.

'Yes to both,' he answered.

'We would like to speak with Mr Deane.'

'Is there a difficulty of some sort?'

'What does he say?' Wilmot asked her. She shook her head at him; it required all her concentration to understand.

She could not think how to explain, but instead said, 'I am his . . . his cousin.'

He looked at her appraisingly. She found herself quailing under such a frank gaze.

'Well, you may speak with him at the end of the morning session. Not before. Wait on the bench in the shade, if you wish.'

Just before he shut the door she caught a peek inside the room. The floor was whitewashed, with a circle and a cross inscribed upon it, and over that a sundial of intersecting lines like a pagan symbol. She would not be at all surprised to find Zachary was involved with the black arts. It made her wary. Best not mention the symbol to Wilmot, he was afraid of his own shadow. He might want them to leave straight away.

'Well, what was all that?'

'He said we've to wait.'

'How long?'

'Until the end of the morning.'

'What?'

'We've come all the way from England, Mr Wilmot. A few more hours is nothing. We might just as well wait.'

As if she had not tarried long enough. Zachary Deane was somewhere behind that door and she could have cried with frustration.

Unaware of his visitors, Zachary watched Señor Alvarez's apprentice get out the paper and quills. The book creaked as Señor Alvarez prised it open. He had obviously opened it at the same place many times before because he smoothed out the page and it stayed perfectly flat. It was a facsimile of the *Book of Human Proportions* by Albrecht Dürer, and they were to measure each other, something Zachary did not want to do. He worried he would seem laughably small in comparison with Alexander's broad shoulders and barrel-like chest. Zachary began to fidget with the buckle of his scabbard.

Señor Alvarez turned to him. 'Pay attention, Mr Deane. You must know your own measure inside and out. The circle and the cross – a map for the good ordering of your mind. The general must have control of his army, yes? And not let it be subject to the will of a multitude of barbarians. So it is with your thoughts. Besides, you will need to be able to get the measure of your opponent.'

Zachary was sceptical, but Alvarez said gently, 'Mr Deane, you may not see the point of it now. But I tell you, without knowledge of the principles, nothing can be achieved.'

How the señor could see inside him to know what he was thinking, he had no idea. It disturbed him. From the training room the noise of clashing rapiers filled the air as the other three men put each other through their paces. Zachary sighed. He would much rather be in there with them.

In the end, the task was not as bad as he feared. He enjoyed measuring Alexander, who stood like a mammoth as he stretched to wrap the tape around him. Alexander's drawing of him was strangely pleasing. Though not an artist like Girard Thibault, Alexander had a neat hand and Zachary liked to see himself labelled, ordered so.

Whilst they were both admiring their work, the bell tolled midday. He was astonished that the time had flown by so fast.

'Come on,' he said to Alexander with relief, 'I could kill for a glass of ale.'

They stumbled out of the dry air of the house into the cool of the courtyard, shaded by lime trees. He barely had time to inhale the breeze when he heard someone call his name.

'Mr Deane.'

Wilmot, the Englishman, stood there, looking bedraggled as usual.

So he was to have no peace. 'Who let you in?' he snapped, 'Go away and leave me alone.'

'Did you forget our meeting?' Wilmot persisted.

'Yes,' he said, tired of him. 'On purpose.'

Wilmot looked visibly shaken that he had decided to forgo the pretence at pleasantry. 'I cannot persuade you—'

'We will not leave until you agree to talk with us.' Elspet Leviston emerged from the shadows of the foliage in her ridiculous dark English gown, all bones and bows and stiff as a post.

'Fine,' Zachary said, 'if you wish to sit here for ever.'

He saw the dark circles under her eyes, and that her hands clenched and unclenched, but he did not want her to tickle his conscience. He wanted her out of his sight.

'I make no jest,' she said tightly. 'I will simply wait here every day, until you agree to discuss it.'

Over in the dark shade of the vines their English maid loitered, pale and scared, eyes darting from one to the other. As he glanced over to her, he spied Señor Alvarez's dark figure watching them from an upstairs window.

Damn. That was all he needed. The señor might not like female hangers-on in his yard. Curse Elspet Leviston. And his new friend Alexander was staring at the three of them, with a puzzled expression.

He ignored Elspet and Wilmot and sauntered over to Alexander and took him by the arm, whispering in Spanish, 'Come, let us take our refreshment.' He was anxious to divorce himself from his visitors. He felt Alvarez's eyes upon him. Distractions to the training were frowned upon.

He steered Alexander across the yard, deliberately ignoring Wilmot's bleat of 'Mr Deane!'

On the other side of the courtyard was a small cool room where refreshments were laid out at midday. There was lemon-water today, and it reminded him of Luisa Ortega of the dark doe eyes. Zachary and Alexander joined the other three men, all of them silent. Señor Alvarez did not encourage talking whilst on the premises. They should conserve their strength, he said.

So he filled his tankard from the jug quietly, and stood with the small group supping tangy lemon-water and tugging on the chewy local bread with his teeth. From the corner of his eye he saw Elspet Leviston sit down stone-faced under the vine, on the only bench in the yard.

Zachary dropped his backside down on to the ground, to lean on the lime-washed wall under the shade of the jasmine creeper. A lizard scuttled away in quick, flicking movements. He did his best to ignore the huddled group on the other side of the yard, tried to pay them the same unattached attention as he did the lizard.

A moment later, Señor Alvarez emerged from the training hall as upright as a sapling. He swung a small wooden tray as he walked, and even his walk was graceful, spacious. He placed the jug and three cups on the tray, and added a platter of bread.

Next time Zachary looked up, he was offering the tray to Martha the maid. Zachary paused, his bread halfway to his mouth at the sight. Martha bobbed a hasty embarrassed curtsey and set the tray on the ground, then stooped to pour the liquid as Alvarez went over to Elspet and, with a small bow, offered her a twist of bread. She smiled and accepted it, thanking him in Spanish.

Zachary could not believe it. Alvarez offered it in turn to Wilmot, who accepted a portion but then stood shifting from foot to foot in decided discomfort. He looked as if he did not know whether to eat it or not. Señor Alvarez glanced over at Zachary. Ashamed, Zachary dropped his head. He did not look at them again, even when it was time to go inside.

Elspet shifted on the bench to move out of the filtering sun. Mr Wilmot was angry, he slapped a broadsheet from his satchel at the buzzing flies, and huffed and puffed, and it made her even more uneasy.

'Your cousin is not going to change his mind. You must face it, Mistress Leviston. I see no point in us waiting here. We should go home.'

'I have told him I will wait and I meant it.'

'But he is as stubborn as you are yourself!'

She flushed. 'You can go if you wish.'

Wilmot stood uncertainly, sighed, and then leaned back against the wall.

She could not give up, not now. Not after all she'd been through on the journey. It was to be a battle of wills, that much was clear. She pressed her lips together and folded her arms. Well, so be it, he would see that she was not for moving.

In the afternoon, the yard remained quiet, the only noise the sound of chopping on a wooden board from the kitchen window behind. The smell of rosemary drifted on the warm air.

Mr Wilmot would not keep still despite the piercing heat, and paced up and down by the wall, peering out into the street and then looking up at the windows. When the sun crept lower and Zachary and the others still did not appear, he started to get agitated, but she ignored it. At the sound of the clash of rapiers and feet scuffing on the wooden floor from the balcony above, he caught her eye as if to say would she not give up waiting, but she set her mouth and looked away.

What if Wilmot was right, and Zachary were to stick to his word? She would be waiting for nothing. Time passed. She drew out her rosary beads and threaded them between her fingers for comfort, they rattled on her lap, pale against her dark skirts.

'Mistress Leviston.' Mr Wilmot interrupted her thoughts. She turned to look at him again. He was the colour of whey, unlike his usual florid complexion. He swayed before her. 'I must get indoors. It's the heat, I think it's making me ill.'

She immediately stood so that he could sit, but he shook his head.

'No, I must go and lie down. I am reluctant to leave you but I must go to our lodgings. You must give up this nonsensical vigil, and . . .' he swallowed, staggered to the bench and collapsed on to it, head in hands.

The back of his coat was dark with wet. Martha, with the sixth sense that servants have, was at his side in a moment. 'I'll find a pump,' she said, 'fetch water, and something cool to drink.'

As she was about to go, Mr Wilmot leaned forward and retched over his shoes.

Elspet and Martha hurried to the kitchen door and thumped loudly. An older woman in a Moorish veil opened the door and Elspet managed to explain with much gesticulating, and Martha anxiously peering from behind. The woman took one look across to Mr Wilmot and bustled over on her bare feet, calling behind her, 'Luisa!'

A girl came running out, wiping her hands on her apron, full of advice and concern when she saw Mr Wilmot slumped forward over his knees.

Elspet helped him out of his coat, which was wringing with sweat. The old woman flapped her arms at the mess in the yard and ran away to fetch a pail and a broom to clean up. Luisa pulled open the door to the street and yelled something unintelligible, but Mr Wilmot let it all happen round him, as if he was barely there. Before they knew it, a donkey and cart had appeared to take him home and Martha and Luisa helped Mr Wilmot up. They asked if Elspet would go with him.

There was a long moment's pause, but she shook her head.

'I'll wait,' she said, 'for Mr Deane. He is a student, with Señor Alvarez.' They stared at her in disbelief.

'You go,' Luisa said.

'No,' she said, feeling guilt like a needle in her stomach, 'I'll wait.' She looked away from their accusing eyes.

A servant was fetched to go with Mr Wilmot and Martha, and the clatter of the donkey and trap faded into the sounds of the hawkers' cries, the church bells and the rattle of other more distant wheels. The old woman whispered to Luisa and shook her head, disapproving. Luisa eyed Elspet with suspicion before going back indoors. Elspet sat back miserably to wait.

Shortly after, Luisa – now minus her apron and with her long hair let loose from its knot – hurried past. She nodded briefly at her as she left. 'I hope your poor friend feels better soon,' she said pointedly in Spanish.

'Thank you,' Elspet said, feeling conscience-stricken.

Luisa ignored her and opened the door to the street and slipped through. She moved like a cat on her bare feet.

If only I had her grace, Elspet thought. She felt staid and plain in her English boots, the sleeves of her taffeta gown pressed against her arms; the lace on the sleeves was a nuisance, it kept catching on hanging foliage wherever she walked.

Luisa's clothes were light and her skirts seemed to flow round her in vivid hues of yellow and red. She wondered how old Luisa was, and realized that they might be the same age, though she felt somehow aged enough be her dowager aunt. The thought made her sad. After a half-hour Luisa returned with bundles of provisions, but did not speak, just let herself back into the house. Dusk was falling and inside someone had lit candles in the upper rooms. Elspet was alone in the courtyard.

She had grown stiff from sitting so long, when there was a sudden commotion and a group of men descended the outside steps in a flurry of cloaks. The jangle of metal made her sit up straight. Zachary was bringing up the rear with a tall, moustachioed man. His face was alight with energy, he smiled at his companion and waved his arms in a demonstration of swordplay.

She leapt up and planted herself at the door to the street. The men cast curious looks her way but passed through. As Zachary went by he dodged past, but she grasped his cloak to stay him. He ripped it from her grasp and pushed in front of his friend.

'Zachary,' she cried, 'wait!' But he had gone into the street.

She looked out of the door and he was hurrying down the road into the gloom.

'Zachary Deane!' she shouted, 'Zachary Deane! You will talk to me! You will talk to me or . . .' One of the taller men turned back to look, but they all carried on like bulls, jostling each other down the street. She heard their laughter as they went.

It was a moment before she could bring herself to move. She was panting as if she had been running. She let out a low moan. She had thought he would listen, if she wanted it enough. Things had always fallen into her lap if she wanted them enough, her father had seen to that. But her impotence was a shock. That she could not control the world, had no influence over her own destiny, that she held no sway over others, least of all Zachary Deane.

She would have to accept it. That she would lose her home and control of the business. That she must rely on her bastard brother for everything. Mr Wilmot was right, she would have to go back to England.

England. Homesickness hit her like a fist. She had a longing to be back in the cool chambers at home, with Jakes nosing his big brown head into her lap. She wanted to lift Diver up to her cheek and feel his squirming weight in her arms. The longing was so intense she had to lean against the wall, clutching her arms around her chest.

'Señorita?'

She looked up to see the white hair of the fencing master. She wiped her eyes, and started to apologize. 'I'm sorry, I—'

'Here.' He offered a small flask. She shook her head. He uncorked it anyway and handed it to her with a gesture of encouragement. She put it to her lips. Brandy. The sting of it made her cough.

'Ah, better,' he said. 'Come, sit a moment.'

He took her arm and led her back to the bench in the courtyard. His grip was gentle but firm. She allowed herself to be led. In the shadow of the vines the bench was in a deep cavern of black, but she could still make out the white of his hair and the whites of his eyes, though not his expression.

'We will talk a few moments, then I will ask Luisa to accompany you home.'

'You must wonder—' she began.

'Tell me about Zachary Deane,' he interrupted.

'I don't know how to begin.'

'At the beginning,' he said.

So she told him in halting Spanish about how Zachary came to them, how Father's interest in him turned to obsession, about how she came to find out he was her half-brother. Señor Alvarez said nothing, just let her pour it all out. The fact that her Spanish was simple made it easier. The explanations were halting and spare, and it was easy to talk in the darkness to a stranger. It reminded her of confession, having the listening presence beside her in the dark. She even told him about her father's mistress. When this evoked no reaction, she confessed her disappointment about her engagement to Hugh Bradstone.

'So you see,' she finished, 'I came to try to persuade Zachary not to sell the roof over my head. Please, señor, will you speak with him for me? Persuade him to listen?'

A pause. 'I regret, but I cannot do that. I cannot interfere between you. Besides, I have only heard your truth. His might be something else entirely.'

'But I've told you the truth!'

'Ah, but truth has a habit of moving about, depending on who owns it. But I was interested to hear what you had to say. I am particularly interested in the parts of their lives my students disown. And Mr Deane is a man of many contradictions, is he not?'

'I hardly know him. He spent more time with Father.' She heard her voice crack.

'You see him only as an obstacle to your inheritance. For me, well, he is probably one of the ablest students I have ever had. It is exciting for me to teach him. He could be a great swordsman.' He paused a moment. 'Yes, he has a feeling for it and the determination. But he does not take instruction well. He resists.'

'He was like that with my father. But don't ask me about his background because I simply don't know. He won't even speak to me about his past.'

'You don't know anything about him?'

'Only rumours. The servants gossiped when he came to us, as you'd expect.'

Señor Alvarez surprised her then by saying, 'I met him in London once, he was asking me about training then, but we were interrupted. I remembered his face, the way his eyes lit up. He must want it badly to come all this way.'

'In London? Oh. I did not know you had been to London.'

'I had some business there, with a wine importer. I have a small vineyard. But the trade routes are too difficult at the moment, so in the end it all came to nought. But I remembered the little English firebrand. He needs discipline, that's all.'

Elspet could not have agreed more, though she was too polite to say so.

Señor Alvarez was still speaking. 'What will you do now?'

'I don't know. Zachary will not listen so I might as well go back to England, I suppose. Though heaven only knows what I shall do, with no home to go to . . .' She swallowed.

'Don't rush. From the look of it, your companion is not fit to travel. I would wait a few days until he is feeling better. It could be heat-sickness, or worse – the flux, and these maladies can take a few days to come out. If you remain in Seville a few more days you are welcome to come back and try to speak to Mr Deane again. But I'm afraid I cannot help you – it is up to the pair of you to resolve your differences.'

'Thank you. Thank you for listening. It felt good to talk to someone.'

'I'll fetch Luisa, she'll accompany you to a sedan.'

He stood then and went in through the kitchen door, emerging a few moments later with the Morisco girl carrying a lantern.

'Where do you live?' Luisa asked.

'Near the new Alameda de Hercules? Across the river.'

'Goodnight, then,' Alvarez said. 'Luisa will see you safely to a sedan.' He lifted his hand in salute and she lifted hers in reply before following the glow of the lantern out into the twisting labyrinth that was Triana.

Chapter 32

After Elspet dismissed the bearers and went upstairs, Martha's anxious face appeared over the banister.

'He's bad, mistress. Been vomiting, and he can't keep anything down – not even herb tea. I've put a house slave to fanning him, but he looks hot enough to set the sheets afire.'

She followed Martha to his chamber. Mr Wilmot was shockingly thin, pale as a wraith, now that she saw him lying there in just his shirt. His hair was damp with perspiration. When they had set off from England, he had seemed so solid and present somehow. Now he looked like he was melting to bones. He tossed and turned in a tangle of sheets and called piteously for Dorothy, his wife.

'If he's no better by the morning, we'll have to find a doctor,' Elspet said. Compassion for him washed over her. He had lost his livelihood because of her cousin. And how must it feel to be ill in a place where you cannot understand even the simplest conversation?

She told the slave to fetch a damp cloth and Elspet sponged his face with a gentle touch over the skin still peeling from the sun. He groaned and pushed her away. After an hour or so she was so tired that her eyelids kept closing and her chin nodded to her chest. Mr Wilmot, too, finally slept.

The following day, he was no better and, what was worse, Martha had succumbed to the same sickness. Both of them were abed, chamberpots on the sheets beside them.

She asked at the apothecary's for the physician, Señor Morcillo, and he called and bled them, and told her they should rest now and drink plenty of warm, weak ale.

'Be assured, señorita. They will soon regain strength now,' he said. 'All they need is rest. But the quicksilver and antimony – is not cheap, so . . .' And he held out a bill for his fee.

Elspet fetched her purse. It was worrying how little was left inside.

'Please,' she said, 'I have little coin today. Can you come back tomorrow?'

'Very well. I'll call and see how the señor does. They may need another draught, we'll see.' He bowed formally and left.

When she went to visit Mr Wilmot and Martha in their chambers they groaned and begged to be left in peace.

She needed money for the physician, and the week's rent was due. Perhaps Señor Alvarez would have tried to persuade Zachary to see reason after all. A small bird of hope fluttered in her chest. She could do nothing further here; Morcillo seemed to think rest was the best remedy, so she would go to the fencing school again. Besides, Señor Alvarez had been kind, he would not turn her away. The thought of him produced a faint shiver of anticipation.

Her feet were roasting in the black leather bootees she had been wearing all the way from England, and the undersides were holed now from use. On impulse, on the way to the fencing school she bought a pair of hempen sandals and, hoping her skirts would cover her naked feet, rid herself of the stiff boots.

Nobody seemed to notice her feet, or that she travelled alone, with no retinue. Everyone was too intent on their own business. She walked with a spring in her step. The sensation of the breeze against her toes was cooling, and it felt a little wanton, even exciting.

At Señor Alvarez's she positioned herself in the same spot in the courtyard, just as she had the day before. A silhouette moving at the window informed her that the hawk-eyed swordmaster missed nothing. Luisa arrived with a basket of vegetables and bread balanced on her head and stopped to ask, 'How is the señor?'

'He is still poorly. My maid Martha too.'

'Oh. They have seen a physician?'

'Yes.'

'Huh.' She pursed her lips and shook her head dismissively, as though this had answered all her questions. With a smooth movement she hitched the basket on to her hip, pressed the latch on the kitchen door, and disappeared into the gloomy interior.

The yard went quiet, the only sound the scratch of a broom being wielded somewhere in the house. A few moments later, Luisa passed again, minus the basket, waved her arm airily and was gone out of the gate.

Elspet sat to wait, feeling strangely liberated in her bare feet. From habit she passed her rosary beads through her fingers but she had lost the will to pray. She was nervous, and the fact that she had a few hours uninterrupted peace simply made her more restless. Her shoulders stiffened, she rubbed her temples and the back of her neck. But gradually the heat and silence soothed her. Small things took her attention, the curl of a vine leaf, the lace of shadows swaying over her skirts. Finally, to make up for her lost sleep, she dozed a little.

A noise startled her awake.

'Your companion is still ill?' Señor Alvarez stood before her.

She gathered herself hurriedly. 'I'm afraid so. As is my maid. And I need Zachary to advance me something for the physician,' she said.

'Yes.' Señor Alvarez merely stated the fact. 'If you are set on waiting still, you could use the library where you will be out of harm's way. The men will be out here soon with their rapiers. Mr Deane will be busy until six o'clock. You may wait to speak with him, but you understand, I do not want the work interrupted.' He said the word 'work' as if it had a capital letter. 'Only at the midday siesta, or after we are finished in the evening. My apologies – we train long hours, it is necessary to build stamina.'

'Of course,' she said, embarrassed that she was causing a nuisance, 'Thank you for letting me wait here.'

He smiled. 'You are welcome. But come, we will go up. It will be cooler there, and you will find something to occupy you. This way – I'll show you.'

He set off up the stone steps and she followed. At the top of the stairs they passed through the upper chamber with its strange circle and cross pattern painted on the floor. She would have averted her eyes, but two young men were fencing there, nimbly stepping from one point to the next, their swords just touching and then moving apart. The cardinal points of the circle were inscribed with Roman letters and the young men repeated the same exercise over and over. She could not help but slow, to stare at what they were doing.

Señor Alvarez stopped too, and the two men's movements became more precise, more concentrated. His very presence seemed to intensify what was happening in the room.

'Better,' he said to them, before beckoning to her. One of the men flushed furiously red.

What kind of a man was this Señor Alvarez, she wondered, who could discomfort a grown man so?

He moved her through into a corridor with two doors off it. One of the doors stood ajar and with his gentle push it opened silently and they were plunged into cool darkness. As her eyes became accustomed to it, she took in that it was full of books. Many, many volumes – open on the polished wood tables and others in trunks below. Spread out on the table were old maps, and a book open at a page with the same circle as was drawn on the floor below, but with the addition of a spreadeagled man drawn over it.

'Ah,' she said, understanding, 'the Vitruvian, like on your sign. My father described this to me.' She moved in for a closer look.

'Ah, yes. You know of Vitruvius. But this is the circle of Heinrich Cornelius Agrippa. Not just the circle, but how to square the circle, that is the secret. The circle is the foundation of our training, we use it as the map of our science of arms.' Seeing her lack of comprehension he added, 'Just as sailors use a compass to avoid the reefs and banks of the sea, so we use our circle to order our movements, protect ourselves against attack.'

She let out another 'ah' of understanding. So the diagram was not a pagan symbol, but more like lines on an archery court where the men could train direction. She pointed to the illustration before her, 'It is beautiful, this engraving,' she said.

'Harmonious order is beautiful,' he said. It was an awkward moment, as if he had forgotten she was not one of his students to lecture and instruct. He softened his tone. 'You can sit here. No one will interrupt you, morning study is finished. When you hear the men lay down arms in the yard you will know it is time, and you can speak to Mr Deane.'

He bowed formally and left her alone in the room. He was an attractive man, she thought, yet she had seen no sign of wife or family, just the servant women, and an old nearly blind man who tap-tapped with his stick across the yard.

The light filtered in, yellow as butter through the grill of the small window. A curved iron balcony threw black shadows across her feet. The room was larger than Father's study but had the same familiar aroma of paper and leather, except here the tables were buffed to a high sheen and there was no patina of dust, no reek of stale tobacco.

She turned a few more pages of the Agrippa. Numerous pen drawings of the human form were captured there, annotated with faintly engraved captions and numerals. Next to the open book stood two other matching volumes upholstered in vellum; they were closed. She gently lifted the covers to read the title pages and realized that it was a set of three volumes, *'De Occulta Philosophia.'*

Occult philosophy. Oh my saints. Father would turn in his grave. It was his own fault, she thought. But for his obsession with Zachary Deane, she would still be safe at home in West View House.

Father's voice came back to her, 'Devil worshippers, heretics, most of them.' If anyone ever mentioned Agrippa he'd snort and dismiss it scornfully as 'a lot of old horsefeathers, mystification for mystification's sake'.

But here it was, and the lure of it was like forbidden fruit. Soon she was drinking in the words, amazed at the new ideas held between the pages.

Agrippa, this man from Germany who lived a mere century ago, this learned man who could quote Ovid and Virgil, who was so well-read, was no grizzled old sage – he was only twenty-three years old when he wrote this. Her own age! His dates of birth and death were engraved on the fly leaf. His voice spoke to her over the years, she sensed his enthusiasm for the task, his feverish writing to fill these books with everything he thought he knew or understood in his short lifetime.

She read of the four elements – earth, air, fire and water, and a fifth that joined all that existed in heaven and earth. She paused, raised her eyes from the pages, puzzling over this mysterious fifth element.

As she pondered this, her heart jumped, a wave of heat suffused her face. The strange thought came to her, but I know this diagram already. She pressed the back of her hands to her burning cheeks to cool them, unsure what had occurred. The diagram looked exactly as it had a few moments ago, except that now she realized it was familiar to her. Was this magic? She shivered. This Cornelius Agrippa – he was reaching out to touch her, even though long dead. The thought persisted, would not let her go.

She looked over her shoulder, as if to catch his presence in the room, but there was nothing. Intensely alert, she kept on reading, possessed by his words.

By the end of the afternoon, she had devoured most of Book One. She was so engrossed that it was a little while before she realized that the yard had filled with young men sparring under Señor Alvarez's tutelage. The tang of their clashing blades called her to the window.

She hurried to the window. Six men arranged in two lines. Zachary was at the far side of the yard. He was clad only in his shirt and breeches, and looked smaller still from up here, but fierce, like a terrier. His tall friend fought opposite, perspiring in the heat, a stiff ruff round his neck. His movements were sharp and staccato, well-controlled. In comparison, Zachary's leaping looked wild and erratic.

Señor Alvarez's black hat moved down the row of students, taking each in turn as a partner, his rapier balanced easily in his hand, and every now and then he intercepted with a light cat-like touch to halt their moves and show them how it should be done.

He glanced up at the window, and she shrank back.

His voice called out, 'Stop!'

Peering from the side of the window she saw the men had stopped instantly, exactly where they were, like a tableau. She found she, too, was holding her breath. A horsefly buzzed past, she heard a cry from the street. Zachary's friend's muscles twitched in his calves as he struggled to retain his pose.

Señor Alvarez walked up to one of the men, a dark Spaniard, whose sword was trembling with the effort of maintaining the position. 'If your arms are aching, it is because you have not gained the relaxation necessary to use the rapier with no effort. Your body maintains too much tension.' The man did not so much as blink. Señor Alvarez strolled round as Zachary stood like stone, eyebrows furrowed, an expression of grim determination round his lips. The master had absolute control.

'Lay down your arms.'

The tableau suddenly burst to life and the men rambled to the edge of the yard, stretching out their arms and shaking their legs, sheathing their weapons to free their hands to rub their shoulders. Señor Alvarez gestured up at her, and she hastened from the room, hitching her skirts as she half ran down the stone stairs and into the yard, to stand opposite Zachary who was turned away, picking up his satchel from the ground. When he stood back up, he took a startled step away.

'You will hear me out,' she blundered, in the heat of the moment. 'If you are my brother, then you will behave as a proper brother should, and make provision for me. In all Christian charity, you owe me that much.'

Zachary was backed up against the side of the house, and could not easily move. His eyes swivelled from side to side, searching for a way to escape her gaze.

His companion took himself politely away, to where the rest of the group were untying their scabbards. He whispered a few words to the others and they looked over with curiosity.

Zachary frowned, aware of the fact that this woman in the yard was drawing all their glances. Over in the corner, Señor Alvarez leaned against the rough-cast kitchen wall, his arms folded, watching openly from under the brim of his hat.

'Very well,' Zachary said, in a forced tone of pleasantry. 'If you insist on tormenting me with your presence, I suppose I shall have to discuss the matter. Five minutes I'll give you.'

He sauntered over to the bench, and she followed, feeling somewhat stupid, as though she had fallen by mistake on stage in a courtyard drama.

She noticed the other men begin to disassemble, to pick up their arms and make their way out of the door in the wall, but Señor Alvarez did not budge, he watched like a puppet-master might watch his puppets.

She was already talking to Zachary's back. 'Mr Wilmot is ill, and I need to pay the physician, and for our bed and board. If you could see your way to advance me a loan, just until—'

'I can't.'

'But just a—'

'I'm telling you, I can't. I have no money. Not until Greeting proceeds with the damn sale.'

'But my father gave you a good purse, and a trunk of coin, and another of plate.'

'It's gone. A man has to live, and pay his passage. I have used it to pay for my lodgings here and in France, and my training – six months in advance. Now, if you in your wisdom had not instructed Greeting to hold the sale—'

She lowered her voice, aware that they were attracting attention. 'Have you nothing at all?'

'Nothing but a few pesos. I was not expecting a delay. But I'll write to Greeting again and tell him to proceed with the sale no matter what your opinion. So until then, no.'

'Oh no, please don't. Not yet—' She was taken aback. 'Wilmot tells me that the business is not in such good shape as it was. He advises you to wait, at least until the fleet from Britanny docks safely and its cargo has been sold.'

'What are you saying?'

'The business is in debt. That's what Wilmot's being trying to tell you. There is no money. Not until the Brittany fleet comes home.'

'Is this some sort of ruse?'

'On my life, no. Father had money in Bainbridge's ships.'

He stood and paced up and down. She heard him thump one fist into his other palm and spit out, 'Damn, damn, damn.' He came back to the bench. 'How long before the fleet comes in?'

'Just a month more, God willing. Lace has to come from all over the region. But it might be many more months before the goods yield profit.'

'Months?' He was taken aback.

She capitalized on the moment. 'We would have time to look at the household goods. If you could just . . . I mean, there are items from the house . . . some personal things I would like to keep. Won't you come home to England, assess the business too, make a proper inventory? Mr Wilmot would be glad to assist you.'

'No. I can't come back to England now. I will stay here at least six months to finish my training with the señor.'

'Why so long? Can you not come earlier?' She pressed this slight movement in her direction.

'Once you leave this salon, you cannot return. Señor Alvarez insists the training has to be done with no break.'

'But why?'

'Ask Señor Alvarez. It is his rule. Once you begin training you must carry on for at least six months, so the body becomes obedient, he says. So I could not come until April. Then, perhaps, if the weather—'

'You mean you will hold on the sale until then?'

'No, I mean – I didn't say that—'

'But you just said you will come back to England in April and look into it properly.'

'I said I'd consider it. As long as you leave me in peace.'

This was just a platitude, she knew. If she was to leave, there would be no guarantee he would keep his word. She dare not trust him. As far as she was concerned, blood was not thicker than water but like oil to it – ever destined for separation.

'Wilmot and I are sworn not to go back to England until you come with us, to make proper arrangements.'

'That is folly. I have no desire for your company, or that of your tiresome steward. Go home. You will do nothing here except make me angry.'

She walked away from him and sat down deliberately on the

bench. She would sit, then, and not move from this place.

He watched her, his hand combing through his hair, a frown of frustration etched into his features.

Suddenly, he walked towards her. 'All right,' he snapped. 'I did not know about Bainbridge, about the losses. I will be generous. I will hold on the sale until April, by then the ships should be in and the state of the business should be better. But only if you keep out of my sight. I never want to see you here again, hear me? I will come to England in the spring when my training is done, God and the weather willing. Go home now and wait for me there. I will write to Greeting. Tell Mr Wilmot to inventory the business ready for sale.'

He turned on his heel and marched away from her. As he passed Señor Alvarez, she watched him speed his step and bow his head as if embarrassed.

Elspet took out a kerchief and dabbed her forehead, before screwing it into her fist. She did not know whether to be relieved or dismayed. Certainly she did not relish the thought of telling Mr Wilmot of this conversation. Had he not enough to deal with, without knowing that he was going home to no future employment or livelihood?

Chapter 33

By the end of the week, Zachary was exhausted, not in the body but in the mind. He slid his sword into its scabbard. Perhaps Luisa Ortega had been right, and the regime at Señor Alvarez's school was no sort of training for a man. It was frustrating, this exactitude, this point and thrust along a fixed line.

Señor Alvarez was a hard taskmaster – one finger width off the line of attack and he made you repeat and repeat. But Zachary was determined to come up to the mark now that finally he had found him, though it galled him not to be duelling straight away; after all, folk always said he could handle a weapon. But this geometry, it was hard. And the tiny adjustments to posture. What was worse, now he had to contend with Elspet Leviston and the tiresome Wilmot.

He cursed under his breath. That the lace business was not the gold mine he had anticipated was a body blow, as if a purse had been snatched from his grasp. Had he gone through all this soul-searching and deception for a few measly coppers?

Deep in his own morose thoughts, he threw on his cloak and set off down the street. Of course he had only agreed to go back to England to get rid of her. April was a long time off; maybe something else would have occurred by then; the Brittany lace fleet would be in and he'd sell at a profit. Then, praise the Lord, he wouldn't have to go back to England.

Alexander ran up behind him. 'Hoy, Zachary! Wait. Will you take some ale at the tavern?'

'All right. But let's go to the one on the other side of the town, not the one we usually go to.' He feared bumping into Rodriguez or his men.

'Whatever you prefer.' Alexander's long strides easily kept up with Zachary's breathless pace. 'That Englishwoman who waits for you every day, is she your wife?'

Zachary suppressed an indignant laugh, but did not slow. 'No, not my wife—' He hesitated for a moment as he jostled past some folk coming in the other direction, 'my half-sister. When my father died she and I fell to blows – she wants to lay claim to my inheritance. Now she pursues me, even to Spain, to make me relinquish my English house to her.' The words sounded more reasonable than they deserved. He wished he could tell Alexander the truth, but it was all so complicated.

Alexander dodged a mule and cart, and persisted, 'She must be strong-minded to sit alone in the yard, with no maidservant there to accompany her. And Señor Alvarez noticed her – I saw him talking to her this morning.'

'I wish he wouldn't. After all, it's none of his business.' Zachary looked at Alexander sideways as he walked.

'It is, if she's in the training yard every day. He's particular about who comes in and out. He doesn't like the work disturbed, and quite right. It's distracting, having her sitting there. It makes the men act differently.'

'What do you mean?' Zachary stopped. He could feel Alexander's disapproval.

Alexander nearly cannoned into him. 'Well, she's an attractive woman. It brings out the competitive streak. It's not good for the training.'

'I didn't ask her to come.' Zachary was indignant. 'It's nothing to do with me – I can't shake her off. She's like a horsefly, she won't leave me alone.'

'What does she want of you?'

'Look,' Zachary said, 'I can't tell you here. Let's get out of the sun.' He dragged Alexander sideways into the shade of an olive tree where a small handcart displayed fruit juices. They ordered two lime juices from the turbaned man behind the cart and he handed back the change with a wizened, leathery hand.

They propped themselves on the falling-down wall that surrounded a patch of unwanted bare shrub and thistle.

'I think she wants me to give her a settlement. I'm not sure I will. After all, it's my house and I don't owe her anything. It was left to me by my father. But I've agreed to go back to England, provided she keeps out of my sight,' he said. 'I don't want her hanging around the school either.' As he said it his conscience prickled, but he ignored it.

The turbaned man set down a tray with two blackened pewter cups with wooden stirrers sticking out. Alexander thanked him and swirled the lump sugar round in his cup.

'When?' he asked him.

'Not for a while. At least six months.'

'Good. The señor doesn't like you to break your training.'

'I know. And I feel like I've hardly learned anything yet. Why do we have to do all these diagrams? And the gematria with Señor Ortega? It's so slow. I feel like I am treading water.'

'It's part of his training. To have the patience, I mean. And anyway, where's the hurry?'

'I want to challenge someone to a duel. I don't know anyone else so I've been meaning to ask you – will you be my second?'

Alexander did not answer for a moment but tipped his head back to drain the sugary dregs from his cup. 'You ask me only because you know no one else? Flattered, I'm sure. What does that say for my skill at arms?' He laughed. 'No; I said I would not do it again. I have watched three men die in duels – all friends to me. I would not witness the same again.'

'You won't. I don't intend to die.'

Alexander raised his eyebrows to the heavens as if to say, that is what they all say.

'I'll wait a while, maybe six months,' Zachary pressed him, 'so we will have had time to prepare, to take in all that Señor Alvarez can teach us—'

'You would hold a grudge that long?'

'I want to win.' An image of Fabian's scornful face jumped into his mind.

'Pah.' Alexander let out a scathing laugh. 'And you think you can learn everything in six months?' He looked him over with a frown. 'You are more crazy than I thought. Listen, friend, Señor Alvarez is not some back-alley charlatan with a few tips and tricks, he's the real thing. There's no doing it overnight. If you want his skill, you'll have to be prepared to change and give up what you know. To jettison all your fighting habits and start again, building up from the beginning. It could take years. Have you seen him fight?'

'Once, in London. That's why I came.'

The sun had moved behind them, low in the sky. Alexander squinted into his face. 'If you've seen him, then you know. *La Verdadera Destreza*, the true skill. It's not just a name, it's worth the long training. Many come, but not many stay – they have not enough faith. They are like you, my friend, and they cannot spot the true art when it is under their noses.'

Zachary was surprised by the vehemence of Alexander's words.

He had not thought Alexander a passionate man. His Dutch stiffness and his formal way of speaking made him appear a little like a respectable town clerk.

Alexander carried on, 'What does this duel hang on? I thought you had only been in Spain a few weeks. Is it someone at the smith's?'

'No, not there. Guido de Vega is sharp as his swords, but a gem. And the forge apprentice and I drink together sometimes of an evening. But Gabriel would be no good in a fight – he hasn't the training.'

Alexander waited, rolled a pebble under the sole of his boot.

Zachary weighed his words carefully, 'I went to train with Don Rodriguez before I came here. It was not a happy experience. I have sworn to myself to fight his student, Fabian, when I'm ready.'

Alexander sucked in his breath. 'So you know all about Rodriguez and Señor Alvarez, then?'

'No. What about them?'

'They used to train together. They both trained with the legendary Carranza. But then maybe you didn't know – news of

Carranza's death has only just reached us here in Seville. He died in Honduras, where he'd gone to be governor. And since his death, inevitably, there's dissent amongst his students.'

'Why should his death cause trouble?'

'Very few men were lucky enough to receive instruction with him. He was a scholar and a friend of the Duke of Medina Sidonia, and a busy man, so he took very few students. And all of them nobles, high-ranking intellectuals. But Señor Alvarez and Pacheco de Narváez were both lucky enough to train with him. Now Carranza is dead, anyone who had the slightest contact with him is claiming his reputation for their own and wanting to take over his legacy. The one shouting the loudest right now is Pacheco. They call his students "Pachequistas". You've heard of him?'

Zachary hadn't. 'What's this got to do with Rodriguez?'

'Don Rodriguez is one of Pacheco's men. And Rodriguez is telling everyone that Alvarez's methods are not the ones passed down from Carranza and that Señor's teaching is worthless. Of course Pacheco claims that his own method is exactly what Carranza taught.' He snorted derisively.

'What do you think? Is he right?'

Alexander rubbed at his beard before fixing Zachary with a look. 'I don't know. Carranza himself was a complex man. On the one hand, there's no doubt he was a consummate swordsman, but volatile – not easy to work with. But everyone says that to watch his swordplay was like watching a snake – fluid but deadly.'

'And has Pacheco his skill?'

'I've never seen him fight. And I have had little contact with Rodriguez. But the rumour is that Rodriguez's methods are brutal beyond necessity. From what I've heard, the Inquisition uses him when it wants to make sure there's no one left to tell tales.'

Zachary nodded. He could vouch for Rodriguez's methods.

'And what about Alvarez? You say he learned with Carranza?'

'I don't know about his teaching, how much of it is Carranza's. But I have an instinct about him, that he is a good man, a man of honour. Señor Alvarez claims he is a true Carrancista. He told me he embodies the spirit of Carranza's school. His methods may vary from

Carranza's, but the principles are the same.'

'Principles. Don't say that word again, I'm sick to the gut with it.'

'But Alvarez says true knowledge is a living tradition that has to be adapted for each new generation.'

'I'm not sure I agree with that, or what's the point of tradition? That sounds like an excuse to me by someone who doesn't really know Carranza's methods –'

'You saw Señor Alvarez fight. What are you? A clouthead?'

'No, I'm just—'

'You've done nothing but criticize Alvarez since we sat down. If you don't want to train with us, then go on back to England.' Alexander sprang up and walked off down the street without a word.

Zachary thrust the tray and cups back to the juice-seller and ran after him. 'Hey!'

Alexander did not slow but shouted back over his shoulder, 'Go back to Rodriguez, then. If all you want is to defeat his student in some sort of vengeance match, then go back to Rodriguez and his mercenaries.' He rounded on Zachary, his hands in fists. 'It's what you deserve if you don't want to work. Rodriguez will give you his so-called *bottes secrètes* that are nothing but deceptions. Then you can make a fine show. Everyone will say, "Look at him, the Englishman is the best swordsman in Seville." ' He spat out the words, 'But it will all be brute strength and fakery, not skill. His is a left-hand path. You want the true skill, you say. But for what? To make you a bigger man?'

Zachary blanched. He was rooted to the spot. Alexander trembled with rage. Zachary did not know what he had done to make him so vexed or to cause this outburst. And he had no time to reply, for the Dutchman hiked off towards the centre of Seville with never a backward glance, his shoulders pulled back, his hand guarding his sword as he weaved his way through the throng of other pedestrians.

A passing cloud threw the street into shadow. Zachary took a deep breath. It was as if he had been punched. He strained to watch Alexander's retreating back, but all he saw was the top of his plum-coloured hat before it bobbed sideways into the narrow wynds of the town.

Chapter 34

Mr Wilmot had grown weaker, he had barely the strength to eat or drink now. When Elspet went in to ask Martha how she fared, Martha wept at her out of terrified eyes.

'Help me, mistress, I don't want to die. Take me home, I beg you, don't make me—' She leaned over to retch piteously, her body racked with the force of it.

The house slave brought some Spanish port mixed with watered ale, and Elspet made Martha down a good measure of it in a drench, though Martha pleaded with her to leave her be; she did not want it all to come back up again. Thanks be to God, it worked and Martha fell to sleeping at last.

Elspet was desperate to rest herself, for she was near dropping with tiredness. It was all she could do to kneel and make her prayers. When she climbed into the creaking bed she tossed and turned, her thoughts jumbled together.

She recalled the strange effect of Agrippa's diagram, the snatched phrases of Zachary's dismissive words, both caught in the memory of the uneasy rattle of Mr Wilmot's breath. The three things chased each other, hunted each other down the mazed corridors of her thoughts, making her restless and full of agitation.

Although for the last few days there had been a breeze, the walls seemed to retain the heat so she threw open the window and lay only in her shift. The incessant buzz of insects filled her with distraction and she swatted at them to keep them from nipping her bare arms and neck – with little effect, and in the end she wrapped her long hair round her neck like a scarf, though it stifled her, but still she could not sleep.

The next morning, her head throbbed. Pray God she was not getting the same illness as Martha and Mr Wilmot. Her heart filled with dread. She lay in the pale early light, damp with perspiration, and dozed a little. A noise at the foot of the bed roused her.

'The physician, he needs paying, señorita.' The Negro house slave stared down at her with eyes that took in everything.

'Oh, oh yes,' she said and swung her long legs out, reached for her skirts and bodice. The slave continued to stand there as she dressed, openly staring at her white calves. 'Go tell him I'll be there shortly,' Elspet said.

The slave was back again in the time it took for Elspet to lace her sleeves, staring at her from the door.

'How is Mr Wilmot?' Elspet asked.

'Bled them both. No good, see. His medicine is no good. You better ask Señora Ortega, the Morisca.'

Elspet did not answer, not sure a slave girl's recommendation would do either of them much good. Elspet looked in her purse for some coinage. 'How much?' she asked.

'Eighteen reales.'

Elspet swallowed. She knew already there was not that much in her purse, and the slave's flickering eyes told her that she knew it too.

'Mr Wilmot's purse is in drawer,' the slave said, 'by bed.'

Elspet rifled through it for the coin she needed, uncomfortable that her penury was so transparent, even to a servant. She paid Morcillo, who was attired in immaculate black velvet doublet and silken hose. He looked askance at her unkempt hair, and her face still creased from sleep. His demeanour suggested a man who had never been hot in his life.

'Señorita, I will return tomorrow,' he said, 'to bleed the gentleman again,' and she could not gainsay it, no matter that she did not like him – not when poor Mr Wilmot still languished there so ill. Of Martha, he made no mention. She supposed he thought her of little account.

As Morcillo went out, the slave girl threw the door closed after him and wiped her hands as if she had just hurled out the pigswill.

'Señora Ortega – is cheaper,' she said firmly, and walked down the stairs. A few moments later Elspet caught sight of her from the back balcony, marching off in the direction of the river with the foul and overflowing laundry basket under her arm.

With a sense of foreboding, not knowing what she might find, Elspet looked in on the two patients. Thank God. She was relieved to see them both sleeping, pale as dough. She put her ear near Martha's chest to hear the thump of her heart, then stood back and rubbed her hand over her forehead wearily. She longed to go back to bed too, but she dare not.

She did not trust Zachary. No, she must get him to sign something before they set sail for England, something to prevent him from going back on his word. Her father had always pressed on her that a signature was binding in law.

She tussled to draft a document she hoped he would sign, a document instructing Greeting to stay the sale and bestowing upon her a small settlement. She pushed her hair out of her eyes, and wrote deliberately in her most legible hand, the ink drying almost as she wrote. That she had come to this. Forty pounds only, less than the cost of a new gown. The minimum she might need to start some sort of life for herself. She rolled it up tight and tied it in a workman-like ribband.

If only Zachary would sign.

It was quiet without Martha to fuss around her. She had to tie her thick unruly hair in the manner of the Spanish, with a winding cloth to secure it away from her face. She eyed her English boots which were sturdy for walking, but already she had grown fond of the new hempen sandals, so she tied them on instead and brushed her skirts down to hide her feet. She chided herself for being so short-sighted earlier as to spend her money on sandals.

And then she realized – Martha.

She would have to tell Martha the stark truth – that she had no money to afford a lady's maid, and neither would she be the sort of lady who could afford a maid in England. But even worse, she had no way on earth of paying Martha's passage home.

There was no alternative but to venture out alone, into the streets of bustling Seville. No one paid her any mind, for there were stalls along the streets with vivid canvas awnings, and hawkers yodelling with all manner of goods – figs, pearl buttons, bright yellow songbirds, ripe persimmons. She was carried along towards the river in the throng of tinkers and Turks, maids and madams, slaves and freedmen – all vying for walking space on the narrow dusty streets.

She crossed the pontoon bridge into the ramshackle barrio of Triana, grateful for the shade of the labyrinthine streets. She pressed herself against a wall to allow a donkey laden with fodder to pass. Overhead the crumbling stone dwellings leaned towards each other to almost touch above her head.

She pushed open the door from the street and crept into the yard, the rolled agreement tight in her grasp. Within, the young men were already gathered in a knot around Señor Alvarez, who was explaining about the blade, holding his own rapier out on its balance point on his palm.

'Twelve divisions,' he was saying, but she did not stop to hear him.

The men had their backs to her. She easily spotted Zachary in the middle of the group. She tiptoed past. Though Señor Alvarez did not acknowledge her, she sensed his attention sharp as a thorn, and knew he was aware of her presence.

Feeling a little bold, she padded up the stone stairs and into the library. The books had been stacked under the table in wooden coffers. If only she could just spend the day reading. She wished she didn't have to talk to Zachary, did not need to steel herself for another confrontation. But it was essential to have something in writing. Reluctantly, she closed the open volume on the table and moved over to the window instead.

She could not decide what was best, to wait until the morning session was over, or to interrupt the men's business to speak with Zachary. She stood looking down on them in an agony of indecision. A bead of sweat ran down her forehead and into her eye and she blinked it away. Señor Alvarez was still explaining, pointing at the blade of his rapier and reciting the names of the divisions like a litany, '*Uncia, Sextans, Quadrans, Triens, Quincunx, Semis* – that's half a pound – *Septunx, Bes, Dodrans, Dextrans, Deunx*, and so to the whole length.'

The names of the divisions caught her attention; the Latin half familiar to her ears. The tall Dutchman asked him to clarify their names.

'Ah, Alexander, good question,' Alvarez said. 'They are named in Latin after the twelve divisions of a Roman pound, which concords with the proportion of the sword arm.'

'But why not three divisions? Three always served the Italians well enough,' Zachary grumbled.

'Three is not sufficient; it does not give enough sensitivity, what the French call *sentiment*.' He sheathed the blade. 'Get ready, we will try at point six, *semis*.'

Zachary swished his rapier through the air, impatient to start, and strolled over to Alexander who was ready with his sword outstretched. Alexander abruptly dropped his sword down and walked stiffly away to face another student who nodded, and they took up position. Zachary was left standing alone in the morning sun, his face dark as thunder.

It was an obvious snub. What could have estranged the two men, Elspet wondered?

Zachary sheathed and unsheathed his blade, unable to be still.

'Mr Deane,' Alvarez said, giving him a sharp look, and as he had no partner, Alvarez lined himself up opposite Zachary to demonstrate. In Alvarez's hands the rapier seemed to bend as if by magic. When Zachary made a thrust, Alvarez's rapier was already there sticking to it. There was no possible way Zachary could penetrate his guard.

Alexander smiled a smug smile across at Zachary who scowled and made a sudden lurch towards Alvarez. Alvarez twisted his blade with a flick of his wrist and Zachary smacked on to his back on the ground, his face clearly unable to take in what had just happened.

Alvarez stood calmly before him. 'Get up, Mr Deane.'

Zachary scrambled up, brushed himself down.

'That was coarse – gross. You were so intent on piercing through, that there was no chance you could change direction. Your mind was fixed. It made you an easy target. What you need is to develop *sentiment*.'

He looked up then to where Elspet was watching, half hidden by the shutters at the window.

'Mistress Leviston!' He shouted her name, addressing her the English way. It sounded strange in his accent. She was too astonished to answer. 'Come down, if you please.' The men trained curious eyes on the window, but it was Zachary's face that she saw, his mouth pressed together in an angry line.

She stepped back inside, hand to her chest. Señor Alvarez must have changed his mind about her using the library, or perhaps Zachary had convinced him after all to send her away. She almost tripped and fell down the stairs in her hurry, steeling herself for one last attempt to persuade him. By the time she reached the yard, she was agitated. She waved the agreement at Señor Alvarez.

'I beg pardon if I have offended, but I must—' she began.

'Stand there, if you would.' Alvarez pointed at a spot to his left.

'But I—'

'There.' He pointed again. It was an order, and she found she obeyed. Something in his voice commanded her. Even when he went to a leather arms case and handed her an old rusty rapier she took it from his hand without demur, tucking the paper into the hanging pocket in her skirts.

'A moment's favour.' He smiled at her. 'Hold the weapon out thus.' He stood with one foot forward, his sword arm extended. She placed her feet exactly where his had been.

'Mr Deane,' he said, 'you there.' He indicated a spot opposite her. 'You need to learn the gentle touch. Who better to learn it from than a woman?'

'But I know nothing—' She began to protest again.

At the same time, Zachary said, 'No,' and made to move away.

'Stop.' The sudden command fixed them all to the spot like a spell. Nobody moved. Like the men, Elspet stayed immobile until, after a long pause, Alvarez's voice said quietly, 'Mr Deane, it is your choice. Either you take my instruction, and learn the art of swordsmanship, or you leave and do not return. Your choice. Which is it to be?'

A small muscle worked in Zachary's neck. He looked over Elspet's shoulder; he would not look her in the face. His humiliation moved her, and she felt for him. She lowered her sword.

'He need not, I will leave him alone,' she said.

'Stay where you are please, Mistress Leviston. Raise the rapier.' Reluctantly she raised the sword again. 'Choose, Mr Deane.'

'I stay.' His voice was a croak.

'Very well. And Mistress Leviston, as you are so intent on sojourning here, you might as well be of some use. Begin.'

She held the sword out in front as he had shown her, and Zachary advanced to each side of it in turn, touching exactly at point six to move it away in a parry. At first, Elspet felt like a wooden signpost with its arm stuck out in front, but it made her shoulder ache so she had to relax a little. She hoped nobody noticed it had dropped.

Zachary's eyes were fixed on his own blade, but it hardly touched hers. It was as if he was miming the exercise, she did not understand why, unless it was that his sword was new. It looked it, an expensive-looking thing with an elaborate silver-gilt guard. His breath hissed as he moved forward, a sheen of damp on his forehead.

'No, Mr Deane,' shouted Señor Alvarez, approaching, 'you must blend your sword with theirs, become one blade first, then your opponent will mistake your movement for their own . . .' Señor Alvarez guided Zachary's wrist – 'here, subtle, like this.' He pushed the sword against hers.

When he left, Zachary ignored the instruction and went back to pretending to make the move, never actually contacting her sword. But after half an hour he was tiring. His was the more strenuous role, and the tension of not touching showed in his raised shoulders, the clench of his other hand.

'Change,' Alvarez's voice rang out. Zachary stomped away from her towards the other men without so much as a nod.

Alvarez called out from the other side of the yard, 'No, Mr Deane, you will keep your partner. And Señorita Leviston, your turn to advance.'

Zachary kicked a foot hard against the wall, before turning and coming back to face her. She dared not look him in the face. He stood rigidly and a palpable mist of anger almost shimmered in the heat. She ignored his glowering expression, felt the weight of the hilt in her hand and lifted the sword.

'Don't you dare touch my new sword with that rusty blade,' he hissed.

'Advance!' Alvarez had come to stand next to them. Zachary turned his face away as if to divorce himself from what was happening. She advanced tentatively, feeling a little foolish, and mimicked what Alvarez did with his sword.

She shifted forward with her sword held aloft until the weight of it rested against Zachary's weapon. In that instant his angry eyes met hers. It disconcerted her, her hand jumped like a fish. She averted her gaze, tried to blend with his blade.

'Good. Again.' Alvarez watched them. Zachary's lips trembled, whether from humiliation at being paired with her, or from exhaustion, she did not know.

All morning they drilled. One exercise after another in the growing heat. Zachary was forced to contact her blade at last and perspiration ran down her legs under her heavy skirt. But the feeling of moving, of doing something, was a release. She had spent so long waiting, with nothing to occupy her, and she could think of nothing else when she was engaged thus. Not the future, nor about what would become of Mr Wilmot and Martha. She could only concentrate on the shaft of metal at the end of her arm.

When it was clear that she was to remain his partner, Zachary treated her with disdain, as if she were no more than a tilt-horse. It made her more determined. When the call finally came to lay down arms Zachary made a vicious swipe and the rapier flew out of her hand to clatter on the ground behind. Angry, she stooped to pick it up, and by the time she had retrieved it he was sitting with a few of the other fellows and shaking his head, examining the edge of his blade. She put the rapier back in the arms case and went to sit on the bench, as far away as possible from Zachary and the staring gaggle of men.

The Dutchman Alexander walked over, bowed and raised his eyebrows in question. He held out a cup of ale, and mouthed, 'Drink, mistress?'

His courtesy touched her, so she smiled, and mouthed back 'Thank you,' embarrassed, because her hair had worked loose from its binding and was hanging unkempt round her face.

She was thirsty enough to drink it all at once in one long draught. She would have never have contemplated such a thing at home, nor would she have sat alone in a courtyard full of men. But somehow this was a place apart. She had the sense that different rules applied here, that once you were through that gate you were in a whole different order of things. It was Señor Alvarez. How he did it, she did not know, but it was as if she could taste Agrippa's quintessence.

Perhaps it was to do with the silence. When the men were not engaged in the training they did not talk. Where else were people dumb for so long, except at Mass? She was glad of it, though; it meant she need not try to converse, need not put on any airs or explain anything.

She let thoughts of the future, the sea passage and England, drift away. Her legs shook after the morning's exertion, her heart was only just beginning to quieten in her chest. She was glad to rest, let the quiet and the gentle breeze soothe her.

Alexander sat a little apart, not with the other men, but closer to Elspet. She saw him glance at Zachary, and Zachary's eyes stray to him and then back to her. Suddenly she remembered the agreement – she had been sitting on it. She brought it out, distressed to see it was damp with perspiration. She baulked at handing Zachary such a rag of a thing to sign, but another chance might not come. She steeled herself.

As she walked towards him, he turned to his companions and whispered something with a smirk, provoking a muffled explosion of laughter from the men. She knew they were talking about her and her cheeks burned, but she kept on walking.

'Who spoke?'

It was Señor Alvarez. Nobody said a word. Zachary looked down at his lap where the remains of his bread rested half-eaten.

'Who has read Agrippa's *Declamatio*? Nobody? I don't see why not. It is in the library for all to see. *Declamatio de nobilitate et praecellentia foeminei sexus.*'

She caught the Latin words, and immediately understood it to concern her, as the only woman in the yard. 'Whilst you train here,' he said quietly, 'women are to be treated with every respect. If you are to fight, you need their qualities. Perhaps you thought fighting with a woman was a punishment, Mr Deane.' He smiled. 'On the contrary, it is a privilege. Women have something to teach us. If Señorita Leviston is willing, she will partner you again this afternoon.'

Elspet felt her cheeks grow hot. The idea terrified her, but she remained where she stood only because she might yet have the chance to reason with her cousin, to find the right moment to petition him to sign.

'You agree, yes?' Alvarez looked to her.

She dipped her head in an almost imperceptible nod.

'Now silence. Finish your refreshments and rest.'

Zachary pressed his lips together in a scowl, did not look up, just began to rip the bread into smaller and smaller pieces and scatter them on the ground. She returned stiffly to the bench, the eyes of the men upon her. She ignored their attention and turned her back to them.

In the afternoon after more drills, they were sent into the cool of the library for silent study. She stretched her aching legs under her skirts despite feeling awkward, as though she should not be there. That was until she overheard Zachary take the señor to one side and ask him why he allowed her to stay.

'She stays by my invitation,' he said.

After that she relaxed a little, since she seemed to have Señor Alvarez's blessing, and she set herself to study along with the men under the señor's hawk-like gaze. Zachary deliberately positioned himself away from her at the far end of the room. Fortunately, the Agrippa was free, so she was able to re-make its acquaintance after all.

A passing thought about what on earth Mr Wilmot would make of her activities was quashed by her interest in the book. Soon she was engrossed in Agrippa's ideas, and the room settled into quietude, broken only by the slight creak and hiss of the turning pages.

In the late afternoon they were made to drill more. When she stood, her legs had stiffened so much that she had to limp downstairs, and her wrist was already aching from the morning drill.

When she gathered with the others around Señor Alvarez, she was acutely aware of the way her skirts brushed the ground; the only woman amongst all these men.

It was a lesson on how to hold the sword. In the morning, she had just held the sword as if shaking someone's hand and that was difficult enough. Now she was expected to apply leverage and control – the index finger round the heel of the blade, the fingers tightly round the grip, so that the pommel sat in the hollow of the wrist and the quillons lay horizontal.

The leather grip was soon damp in her hand, her fingers not quite long enough to lie straight where they should. The proper way was painful; it gave her blisters and made her wrist ache.

Elspet and Zachary advanced and retreated up and down the yard, fighting the new technique and each other with wordless concentration. At one point she caught a glimpse of the Morisco girl Luisa, passing by with a chicken squawking under her arm. She paused to stare at them as if she could not quite believe her eyes before calling through the kitchen window, 'Mama!'

Moments later the old woman was peering out of the door to look at this new spectacle of a woman fencing. Zachary had noticed the audience too and put on a nonchalant, easy air, adding extra cuts and thrusts as if Elspet was completely beneath his notice. Elspet struggled to keep away from his blade, ignoring the watching women. It took all her concentration simply to wield the rapier.

When the word came to lay down arms, she seized her chance.

'Please,' she said, grasping Zachary by the arm, 'I wanted to ask you to sign this.' She drew out the rolled paper, in its sad, damp state.

'What is it?' he said, narrowing his eyes, and attempting to free himself.

'It is a paper asking Greeting to stay the sale of the house and business. You said you would reconsider.'

'Only if you kept out of my sight. That was what I said.'

'But I have to have something in writing, you know I must. It is not my fault we are tied together through my father's will. The half of the business won't be enough to house me, not if you sell now, so it is an agreement to stay the sale, and I've written in a modest settlement.'

'Damnable woman! I don't see why I should agree to give you anything more.'

'Because I did not expect to find myself in this situation. Will you sell now, and leave me with nothing?' His stubborn face drove her to raise her voice, so frustrated was she that he refused to understand. 'Because it's unfair, because I was to be married, and now . . .' She was out of words, she had tried them all. It was hopeless. She threw the paper down on the ground, let her knees buckle and sank into the dirt, pummelling the ground.

Zachary wrested his arm away, looked around to see who was watching. 'Get up. Get up, I say! You humiliate yourself.'

'And so would you, in my place,' she cried. 'I have to live, cousin. And poverty makes beggars of us all.'

He looked at her then, a long, hard penetrating look. His face softened, as if recalling with regret someone he once knew. He picked up the paper from the dirt and untied it, sitting to read it twice. She stood, feeling foolish and hardly daring to draw breath, thinking he might lose patience, and refuse again.

'Very well,' he said, 'I'll sign it. And then perhaps you will stop hounding me.'

She nodded, hardly daring to breathe.

'Have you ink?' he asked.

'I'll ask someone.' Quickly, in case he should change his mind, she hurried to approach Alexander, who bent to hear her, and then produced a box with quill and ink block from his carry-all. She knocked on the kitchen door and asked Luisa for water. Luisa brought a pail and a cup, then hung around outside the kitchen pretending to water the pots by the door, but glancing at Zachary with sidelong darts of her eyes.

Zachary plucked the cup from her hand, poured a few drops of water on the ink block and scribbled his signature with a flourish, looking up to see if Luisa was still watching.

His name dried instantly in the warm air and he rolled it up and tied up the ribbon before holding it out.

'There. Now for God's sake go back home. Leave me in peace.' Now the tears came. She gulped them back. It was the relief.

'Thank you. You've no idea how much this means—'

He shook his head and said, 'On the contrary, I think I have.'

After practice, Zachary threw on his sword and buckler and dived out of the door and away into the welcome darkness of the narrow street. He did not want company. The men would mock him, having to fence with a woman. But now perhaps he'd be rid of Elspet Leviston and the tiresome Wilmot.

Alexander was avoiding him; that much was clear. He obviously didn't like Zachary questioning Alvarez's methods. But to Zachary's mind it was better that way than to follow blindly like some damned goose.

He strode along the street dodging the wheel-ruts and cracks in the ground. Some houses had lamps lit and hanging outside their doors, and so he aimed for the pools of light in-between them before being plunged back into the darkness. Many an unwary stranger had broken their ankle just walking in Seville at night, or so Ana had told him with relish.

His cheeks burned as he remembered being watched by all the servants, and worse, by Luisa Ortega, the mathematician's daughter. Though she was not smiling, her lips pressed together, he had not missed the hint of merriment in her eyes. She was beautiful. It was all he could do to keep his mind on the training, and whenever the kitchen door opened his eyes drifted there, hoping for a glimpse of her.

He did not stop at the tavern as he usually would have but went straight home to his chambers. The catches on the arms case slid open easily and he lifted out his sword. How could Señor Alvarez let Elspet Leviston touch his fine new sword with that rusty old blade? Why, he had only collected it from the hilt-smith that morning.

He drew it from its scabbard and examined it for nicks and marks, but to his relief it was just dusty. The watermarking gave him a glow of satisfaction; that this beautiful pattern was made by his own hand, and the sight of it cheered him. He had never had anything specially made before; his possessions were all second-hand, stolen mostly from those more stupid and careless.

He stroked the edge of his sword feeling for rough edges, brought out the buffing leather and the soft lint cloth for polishing and then went out to the balcony where he rubbed at the blade with a passion.

What if he had made a mistake in agreeing to postpone the sale of the business? God help him if he was developing some sort of conscience; that would never do. Scruples served men no purpose, except perhaps to make them sentimental fools – his childhood of coney-catching on the streets had taught him that.

Poverty creates beggars of us all, Elspet Leviston had said, and didn't he know that to be true. Just the thought of it had caught him off-guard. Now he'd signed the blasted paper, and he supposed he must honour it. Alvarez laid great store by honour. A gentleman's honour. He worried that they were all too good for him, all these worthy well-to-do gentlemen, for one look from Alvarez and he felt himself tumbling, as though the pit of his former life yawned beneath him waiting to reclaim him. He feared that the old Zachary, the nip and foister, the petty thief, the gambler and cozener, must be visible to the rest of the men.

Sometimes the temptation of their purses, left so carelessly lying by the wall, was almost too much. His fingers still itched to pocket them. And now he had spent Leviston's coin, well, he struggled to resist the lure of their satchels yawning temptingly open. Just the other day one of the other students, Girard Thibault, had caught him eyeing his jewelled cloak pin; he couldn't help himself, it was a habit.

'What are you looking at?' he asked, and Zachary thought quickly and said that his brother had a pin just like it. Of course Thibault replied that he couldn't have, as it had been commissioned by his father from a goldsmith in Antwerp.

Zachary set down his sword and polishing cloth, and the pot of rank-smelling potash he used to clean off the dirt. He washed his hands in the ewer and dried them. Thibault was an odd fellow, he thought, obsessed with his stubs of lead and his draughting. And yet so were they all, Alvarez's students – men who did not quite fit into society, men who seemed awkward, as if they could not bear the world as it was, like everyone else did.

'Hoy, Zachary!'

He sheathed his sword, put it down on the tiled floor and leaned over the railing.

'Gabriel!' His apprentice friend craned his neck up at him from below.

'Thought it was you.' Gabriel moved himself back into the middle of the road and shielded his eyes to see better. 'Is this where you live?'

'Yes,' Zachary shouted back.

Gabriel whistled softly, and shook his head, his eyes catching twinkles of light.

'Wait there, I'll come down.' He feared Gabriel would ask to come in and see how well-appointed it was in comparison with his baked-brick room in Triana. He would think Zachary far too grand. And yet only a few moments ago Zachary was wondering if he was good enough for the elevated company at Señor Alvarez's. He sighed. He did not seem to fit in anywhere. But he girded on his sword belt and pulled on his boots.

'Ana, I'm going out. Won't be long.' He turned the key in the lock and shouted to the kitchen as he passed.

'Hey, it's good to see you.' He clapped Gabriel on the back. 'What brings you to this part of town?'

'I had to deliver a dagger that Guido made for one of your neighbours. A fine-looking thing, sharp as a buzzard's beak. And a twisted steel handle wrapped in padded velvet, like the one he made a few weeks back.'

'Come on, let's have a jug or two and you can tell me how things are at Guido's.' They walked in the direction of the cathedral which rose like a cliff above the other buildings. 'This dagger, was it the one he started while I was there last week?'

'No, he finished that. This was another, with a longer blade. I tell you, I wouldn't like to be on the end of that thing. The customer, Don Calveros, is convinced he will be set-upon at night by gangs of Moriscos.'

'He sounds like a fearful man.'

'No, he told Guido that the Moriscos are getting restless with all the rumours of their deportation, and are planning an uprising. He seems to think members of the Inquisition are not safe in their beds.'

'He's an inquisitor?'

'Aren't all cowardly men? Seems to me they turn *familiares* because otherwise they must take a stand against them.'

They walked up the winding alleys until they came to the edge of the cathedral square, the tower of the Girandola looming above, but then Gabriel said, 'It will have to be a small jug, I said I'd meet Maria at the Corral del Toro in Triana.'

'Maria?' Zachary nudged him in the ribs and Gabriel rewarded him with an embarrassed grin. 'Why didn't you say? We'll go straight there. Maybe this time I'll get to see some dancing.'

'If you're sure?'

'Let's not keep the lady waiting. Maybe she'll be able to introduce me to a pretty friend.' In his head he was already picturing Luisa.

They strode quickly down the street for the breeze had got up and they had to keep a hand on their hats to keep them on. The bridge swayed alarmingly as the river mouth acted as a funnel and the wind was gusting there. They teetered across with the water sloshing over their boots and the noise of flapping sail in their ears.

The wind made it hard to talk, so they waited until they were seated in the shelter of the vine-shaded courtyard. There was no sign of Maria, so Gabriel asked about the training, whether it was all he'd hoped.

'Yes,' he said, 'it's going very well.' He was not going to tell Gabriel anything about Elspet Leviston, or about his doubts about Alvarez's methods. It was easier that way.

He seemed genuinely pleased, and asked what they did. Zachary bent the truth, told him how they were learning more subtle techniques than the Italians, and told him that some of Alvarez's methods were so secret he could not divulge them.

'Oh,' he said, and an awkward moment passed between them, as if Gabriel could sense his evasion. He covered it by pouring the ale, noticing how Gabriel's eyes kept sliding to the door every time it opened.

It was Luisa who came in first, this time in a vibrant blue skirt and bodice over her cotton blouse, a blue like the sky just before dark. She did not see them and went straight over to the counter, but Maria spotted them, and tugged at Luisa's arm. Luisa glanced towards him, uncertainty written all over her face. She shook her head at Maria and gestured to the guitarist at the side who was just plucking the strings, to tune them.

Maria came over to join them. 'I don't know what's the matter with her. She seems taken with sudden moods these days. But her friend was arrested by the Inquisition, so I guess she has good reason.'

'She told me. It sounds terrible—' Zachary began, but the sound turned into a whine as the musician tightened the pegs, then he played a small arpeggio and began to strum.

'Our fathers would kill us if they knew we were here,' Maria shouted over the music.'

Luisa made a show of ignoring them, and put her foot up on to a chair to remove her shoes. She kept her back towards them as she swayed over to the empty space in the corner and strapped on a belt made of silvery discs which tinkled and caught the light. The guitarist slapped a palm on the body of his instrument in a *zapateado* and Luisa grasped her skirts and swirled them in a flurry of blue as the first chords strummed out. A boy came round to light the candles.

The bar man called '*Olé!*' and Zachary saw the flash of Luisa's skirts, and felt the draught of their swing. The boy moved on and now Zachary caught Luisa's rapt almost angry expression. A power from her feet seemed to climb up inside her so that it erupted in fluid, graceful movements that spread to the tips of her fingers. Her feet stamped into the ground as if to pull up some force from the earth with their hammering. And all the time her fingers snapped out the rhythm at the end of arms raised in an elegant curve.

He was transfixed. She was strong but graceful. The fabric of her dress flowed around her knees as if she stood in a stormy sea. By now the bar man and three or four more slapped their hands together in staccato *palmas*, the handclap.

'More ale?' asked Gabriel.

But Zachary shook his head impatiently, eyes fixed on Luisa.

She arched backwards from the waist as the guitar strummed into a crescendo, her heavy hair fell from its comb, the belt rattled as the vibration moved upwards through her hips and exploded in an almost Dionysian ferment of stamps and snaps. The final posture was with her arms flung outwards. Her eyes sought his in a look of defiance and disdain.

He was gripping so tight to the chair that his fingers were rigid. He exhaled, and she swept away, back to the bar where a number of men crowded around her with expressions of appreciation.

'She's something, isn't she?' Maria said.

He could do nothing but nod.

'She has caught what we would call *duende* – the spirit. She was made to dance. There is something about the Arabic blood, it sings of the stars and the desert, and the men, well, they feel it. They all do – look at them.'

He allowed himself to glance over. Luisa sat unperturbed amid a crowd of three or four men.

'It transforms her somehow,' Maria said. 'Shall I get her to come over?'

Zachary looked to Gabriel. He feared that she would come and join them, and he feared that she would not. His discomfiture was absolute, and he knew Gabriel had seen it. Maria did not wait for an answer but hurried over to talk to Luisa.

'Have a drink, my friend,' Gabriel said, to distract him from the women.

Zachary supped the warm yeasty liquid gratefully, bringing himself to calm. Never had a woman affected him so. He had gone with a few women in his time, but all of them on his terms. One look at this woman dancing was enough to show him that she would make her own conditions. He saw now that his view of her as just a servant was mistaken. But he had hardly ever seen her smile, her gravity was part of her mysterious attraction.

He pretended to be engaged in conversation as they approached, by asking Gabriel about Guido, and whether he was making any more weapons for the men of the Inquisition. But Gabriel hadn't time to answer before the women were upon them.

'Good evening,' Zachary said, rather too formally.

They ignored him and sat down. Maria leaned over towards Gabriel, whispered something, and took hold of his hand. He squeezed her fingers and traced the back of her hand with his thumb. Zachary knew Luisa had seen it too, but Luisa looked icily over Zachary's shoulder.

'That was beautiful. I mean, you dance wonderfully,' he said, attempting to open the conversation.

'Thank you.' She looked away.

'Will you dance again? I mean . . . I would like to see you dance again.'

'And I suppose you will offer to pay me?' She spat out the words.

Zachary saw Maria watching, and felt as if a knot was tying itself in his guts. 'No, no. I didn't mean that. I just thought it was the most intoxicating thing I've ever seen. I've never seen anything like it.'

'Does no one dance where you come from?'

'No. I mean yes, they do, but not like that.' She frowned and opened her mouth but he leapt in to rescue himself before she had time to speak, 'I mean the dancing is not so . . .' He searched for the word – 'so impassioned.'

'Perhaps tomorrow it will not be. It is different every time. That's the beauty of it. It is never the same.'

'Ah,' he said, latching on to something he could tell her, 'in England the dances are fixed, and everyone knows where to step and where to move. The patterns are all thought out beforehand.' He blundered on, unthinking, 'and no woman would think of dancing without a partner.'

'It sounds dull.'

'Have you ever danced with a partner?' He could not stop himself, although his words hung between them as if they hovered on the edge of an abyss.

She did not answer. The words waited as if cut from the air. Then she stood abruptly, and gestured to one of the young men over at the bar. His mouth split into a smile. He swaggered over to the tiny space where the guitarist waited, who at his approach burst into a torrent of song. Luisa stalked towards them and stamped her feet.

Zachary could barely watch. It was both humiliating and exciting. The man had a roughness to his movements and an attitude that was both coarse and sensual. Luisa seemed to taunt him with her swaying hips and twirling wrists. They played out a drama of passion, their eyes locked together as they circled each other, he beating out the rhythm with percussive steps and flicks of his heels, she inciting him with lowered brows, her lips pressed together in a scowl.

'Eh, asi se baila! Agua!' called someone. The fire between them was unmistakeable. Zachary could not drag his eyes away.

The thrum of the guitar built in intensity until Luisa's bare feet hammered the ground in a kind of frenzy, the gitano lifted his chin and pushed out his chest, staring down on her as she paraded before him. He took hold of her shoulders as if he would kiss her. Zachary saw her glance momentarily his way. A feeling rose up in him, the urge to break the table before him to pieces, to take a chair and smash it into that ugly gitano's face.

He leapt to his feet and blundered out of the courtyard, down the road towards the river, blood beating at his temples. After he had walked for a quarter hour or so, he slowed to look out over the water at the lights of the city, and then up at the winking stars above his head. He was panting, not from exertion, but from emotion.

He leaned up against a fence by the shore, put one foot on the rail. He could not go back to the city yet, it felt as though his chest had been cut open. He wondered fleetingly what on earth Gabriel would be thinking of him.

'Bloody woman,' he cursed, but he knew it was more than that. It was the old feeling of powerlessness he could not stomach. He was afraid. That was why he liked to fight. He was not afraid of death, but he was afraid of love.

Chapter 35

All Elspet wanted when she returned home after the long day at the fencing school was to bathe and rest. She slept well for the first time in months, but awoke groggy and listless. She knocked gently on Mr Wilmot's door, but he did not answer. She creaked it open and eyed the miserable heap of bedding with horror. He lay still and white, his breath hoarse in his throat; his cheekbones protruded through his flesh. Martha too was not up, but lay in bed moaning.

She did not dare go out whilst they were both so ill. She must do something. Could she afford the physician? She took her purse and fingered again the paltry amount of money before pulling the cords tight and tucking it away. Not enough.

All day she watched them, like a mother hen. The following evening they seemed no better and she knew she would not sleep for worrying. She found her way down to the kitchen by the smell of burnt rice. Several hostile pairs of eyes swivelled towards the door as she entered. The kitchen workers were all dressed in Moorish dress.

She paused awkwardly on the threshold before addressing them, 'I am looking for . . .' But then she realized she had never even asked the house slave's name.

Fortunately, at the sound of Elspet's voice, the girl stood up from where she had been wiping something from the floor.

'They're worse. I'd like to know where I can find – where I can find the woman you spoke of.' Elspet addressed her directly.

The girl nodded and said, 'Come. I'll show you.' She dumped the cloth back in the pail and rubbed her hands dry.

'Tell me your name.'

'Gaxa,' she said.

What a strange name, she thought, but then she pointed to herself and said, 'Mistress Leviston.'

'Yes. I know.' She did not blink.

'Elspet,' she said. Gaxa nodded.

Elspet followed her and was surprised to find that they were heading back towards Triana. 'In Triana?' she said, breathless, trying to keep up with her.

'Yes,' Gaxa said.

'Oh, I wish I'd known,' Elspet mumbled, but then gave up the conversation to concentrate on weaving through the narrow streets. Her legs had stiffened from the previous day's wrestling with the sword, and her feet were sore. It was all she could do to keep up.

They passed down narrow alleys where the houses were simply built of local stone or clay, plastered with a mud render. Some of them had glowing ovens built on the outside; from others smoke came from inside the house through a hole in the roof. She stepped around a pool of vegetable peelings and a dark patch of what could have been blood on the pale earth.

It was close to nightfall, it was as if a dark cloth had been thrown over the streets, and she began to fear she might never find her way home again. Finally, they arrived at the back of a row of larger houses. They had yards with pots of herbs growing and she could hear goats bleating in the fields behind. Gaxa hammered at the shutters of one of the windows. A yelp of surprise came from within, but no one came to open up. Gaxa knocked again, but the house stayed silent.

'Wait,' she said. She went around to the side of the house and called softly, 'Ayamena! It's Gaxa. Only me.' A pause, and then, 'Look and see, just Gaxa.'

She came back to where Elspet stood. 'They won't open the door.' She pointed. 'Looks bad. Blood on the ground up there. That's why. We'd better leave.'

But just then the wooden door in the bleached double gates

opened a hand-width and the frightened eyes of a woman looked out.

'Gaxa,' the woman whispered, 'it's late. What is it? What's the matter?'

'There's a woman very sick. Needs your help.'

She looked past Gaxa to where Elspet stood. 'This woman?'

'No,' Gaxa said scornfully, 'her servant. But she can't pay.' She said this accusingly, indicating Elspet with a wag of her head.

'I know her.'

Elspet took a better look at the woman on the threshold. At first she wondered if her Spanish had let her down and she must be mistaken, but she came out further into the light, and recognized the woman from the fencing school.

'Oh, yes,' Elspet said. 'You work for Señor Alvarez. Señora Ortega, is it? I am sorry to disturb you, but my friend Mr Wilmot and my maid are very sick.'

She looked around, and realized with embarrassment that they were outside the fencing school, just that this was the back door. The servants' entrance, where goods and pack-mules came and went. She was chastened by her own stupidity.

Ayamena was speaking. 'I'm not sure, Gaxa, there's trouble enough. I don't want to treat any white woman. If she dies, they'll accuse me of sorcery.'

'She'll die if you don't.' Gaxa stated it as a fact, and planted her brown-toed feet firm in the dirt.

Elspet could think of nothing to say, so she waited.

Ayamena looked from one of them to the other, then beckoned them in. 'Quick, quick. Before someone sees. In this world gone mad, the least I can do is offer tea.'

She followed Gaxa over the threshold and through a wooden door into the gloom of a chamber. Immediately, a man was there in front of her, asking, 'Who is it?' but before he even finished his question Ayamena said, 'Only Gaxa, and the Englishwoman, the friend of Señor Alvarez, who needs some help.'

By the light of the smoking candles Elspet took in that all their possessions were in a pile in the middle of the room. Cooking pots, rolled-up rugs, a stick cage with a squawking bantam inside. The man in front of her looked familiar, and she realized she'd seen him coming and going in the yard with his stick. He always had his head forward, looking at the ground as if he could not see properly, and carrying a bundle of books wedged under his arm.

'Who is it, Ayamena?'

'Good evening, señor. It is Mistress Leviston. Elspet Leviston, Mr Deane's cousin. I am sorry to disturb you. But Gaxa thought you might be able to help my . . .' She paused. She could not think of a way to describe Mr Wilmot and his relationship to her.

Gaxa finished the words for her. 'The Englishman who was here. He's worse. And the maidservant. I think it's the sweating sickness. Will you come?'

The man turned to his wife who hovered at his arm, her eyes wary. 'It's not safe to treat them. Not wealthy foreigners. If it fails, it will draw attention to us. We need to stay hidden, if we can, from rich men.'

'You should both go,' he said to her. 'Do not let them change us, my love. That's what they want. We should still have compassion, do as we would have before all this.'

She looked at him doubtfully. 'I don't want to leave you. What if something happens while we're away?'

'Nothing will happen. I'll carry on sorting the rest of our things.'

Just then Luisa appeared from the curtain to the back yard, carrying a basket of clothing on her hip. She stopped as soon as she saw them. She recognized Elspet straight away, and set the basket down.

'Mistress Leviston,' she said. Her eyes shied away.

'Luisa!' Elspet said. 'I didn't know . . . we have come to seek your mother's help.'

'You know each other?' the father asked.

'Papa,' Luisa sighed impatiently. 'It is the woman I told you about, who fights with Mr Deane.'

Everyone in the room stared at Elspet then, as if she were an oddity in a sideshow.

'Well, then, if she is a friend of Señor Alvarez, no reason now not to go.'

Ayamena pursed her lips in disapproval, made a kind of snort and, thrusting the curtain aside, disappeared into the back chamber.

'It's all right,' Luisa said. 'She's gone for her things. You'll see.'

Elspet waited. To make conversation she asked, 'You are moving?'

Gaxa and Luisa exchanged a look.

'We have just moved,' Luisa said. 'We are always moving on. They do not want my family anywhere.' She sighed and spoke as though explaining it to a child. 'They dragged off our neighbours for cooking meat on a Friday and they have burned our houses. No matter that we have done nothing at all. They are false Christians, these men. They beat us with one hand and raise the other to confess it all to their priests and ask forgiveness. No matter that we are baptized Christians just like them.' She shook her head in disgust.

Elspet squirmed. The words were aimed directly at her.

'So now we must leave Seville. We cannot stay here for ever with Señor Alvarez. And we don't know yet where we will go.' Luisa said this like a challenge, and Elspet felt her venom, knew it was her Roman ways she spoke of. Ashamed, she looked at the floor.

There was an uncomfortable silence and she was unable to think of anything more to say, until the father broke the atmosphere by saying, 'We are lucky, we have friends everywhere. They will make room for us.'

Luisa sniffed as though she did not believe it. 'I'm tired of moving.' Just then Ayamena returned, carrying a lidded basket and a bundle. 'Told you,' Luisa said.

'Well, I suppose you could pack up your books whilst I'm gone,' said Ayamena. A small boy appeared from the back room. 'Husain, you're to help your father with his books. You can take down the herbs hanging in the yard, too, and pack them. And bring the goats round the front, ready. We can't take them to France, but we can sell tomorrow.'

'Sell them? No, Mama, we can't—' The boy's face crumpled.

'You will do as I say.' Ayamena wrapped her shawl around her head and fastened it. 'See what I must contend with? Now be good, Husain. We'll talk about it later.'

Husain pouted at these instructions, but Ayamena plopped a kiss on the top of his head before pulling open the wooden door. She pushed her head out then turned back to them. 'Come, quick now, whilst there's no one to see.'

'Go safe,' called her husband.

Gaxa ran on ahead with Ayamena tight-lipped and silent, following after. Luisa walked in front of her with long, loping strides. Elspet stumbled at the rear, feeling a mixture of trepidation and relief.

Thank God Ayamena had agreed to come. She fixed her eyes on the older woman's flapping manto so she would not lose her in the dark, as they weaved their way down the narrow passages to the river. The Morisco woman's pantaloons seemed eminently practical, as did Luisa's frameless skirt. Her own skirts were bulky and heavy with whalebone and swung against her legs as she trotted to keep up. When Gaxa reached the front door she stopped. 'Front or back?' she asked.

'Front,' Elspet said, abashed. They went inside, and up the smooth tiled steps.

She took them to Mr Wilmot's room first. After the fresh night air the room stank of bile and faeces, and the shutters were tight closed. She was about to throw them open when she saw there was someone else in the room. It was Morcillo.

'Mistress Leviston,' he said, bowing low. 'You are too late. I did what I could.'

She stared at him, and from him to the bed, where the body there was motionless, the face covered over with a white sheet.

'The kitchen girl let me in. I bled him again,' Don Morcillo said, 'but it was no good.' She followed his eyes to where an earthenware basin on the table gleamed with red congealing liquid.

'Martha?' Her words were a whisper.

'There is no change in her condition. I did not know if you wanted me to treat her, as you are . . .'

She knew what he meant. He meant as she probably could not afford to pay. She was speechless. She was about to protest when she saw Gaxa and Ayamena turn and slip out of the door.

Morcillo continued in the same self-righteous tone. 'I'm afraid there was nothing more to be done. And no time for the rites, so you might want to send for the padre. Padre Sanchez. He is used to foreigners. A simple burial, I suppose. Quicker the better this time of year.'

She licked her lips. No, it could not be true, that Mr Wilmot, who had accompanied her all this way, was now lying lifeless under that white sheet. She had a sudden image of him bending to kiss his wife on the quay.

'Oh my Lord in heaven, his wife,' she whispered. And his youngest was only four. She stared again at the white silhouette on the bed.

'If that's all, then I will take my leave of you,' Morcillo said, but continued to stand there.

'Oh, of course,' she said, numb with shock. She fumbled in her purse.

'Fifteen reales?' he said.

That much. It was as if a bucket of cold water had been thrown over her; such was the shock she could barely count the coins, but there was not quite enough. She went to her trunk and took out the gold and pearl drop earrings that had belonged to her mother. She held them out to him and he scooped them up, his cold palm brushing against hers.

He bowed again, unnecessarily low. 'I hope to see you in the morning at matins,' he said.

'Yes,' she said, in a kind of desperate politeness, willing him to leave.

He turned slowly, counting his coins. His shoes squeaked as he walked away. She was alone in the room with Mr Wilmot. The room was still dark and silent, so she took a taper from the hall and lit a candle on a branched stand. The candlelight flickered over the bare floor. It hardly filtered to the bed which was marooned in the ocean of terracotta floor tiles. So she lit another wick for his soul, one set in a hand-holder, because she needed to see his body for herself.

She traversed the floor on tiptoe, afraid to break the silence. When she pulled back the hem of the sheet, she saw that someone, Morcillo probably, had placed two iron discs on Mr Wilmot's eyelids. Not coins, she noticed. He would not waste his coin, even for this. Mr

Wilmot's hands were folded one over the other over his heart, in the gesture of death. His fingernails had grown long and pale. His hands no longer looked as though they had ever done a day's work and the face that rested there had ceased to resemble her disgruntled friend; it was smooth and dull as the wax of a candle. Even the eyebrows looked sculpted, as if painted with gesso on to the skin. She put down the light.

'David,' she said. She used his first name, though she had never done so in life. Somehow being with him in death was an intimacy, and it humbled her. She made the sign of the cross and placed her fingertips on his cold forehead as if to bestow some blessing there.

Her heart contracted. If only his life at the end could have held some crescendo. But no, a ragged journey through the heat and dust – to what? To a stinking room and an ignominious death with no loved one nearby. She got on to her knees on the hard tiles and begged forgiveness for bringing him to Spain. She prayed to the Lord out loud, to deliver his soul from evil. She said it as if spoken words would be heard more clearly – the Pater Noster over and over, her voice rising with panic.

She must find the padre, to intercede for his soul; her own prayers were not enough. It was her fault he was dead. She leapt up and snatched her shawl from where she left it on the hall chair. A slight smell of burning and the sound of coughing filled her with dread. Martha. What had happened to Gaxa and Ayamena? She hardly dared peep round the door into Martha's room.

When she did, her eyes widened, and she brought her hand over her nose. Ayamena had her basket open beside her and the room was full of choking fumes. In a small earthen dish several items of clothing were alight, as if in a brazier. The smoke coiled upwards in a thick column, and the upper part of the ceiling was swathed in it. The dish contained herbs, too, she guessed, for it smelled sweet.

Martha was coughing, her hair plastered to her head with sweat.

Luisa turned as she entered. 'She will be better soon,' she said. 'How you can know that?' Elspet said. 'Mr Wilmot is dead.'

'Morcillo. He kills as many as he cures. Everyone says.' Luisa was scathing.

Ayamena glanced over her shoulder. 'I am sorry,' she said. Elspet made out the words from behind her veil. 'Sorry I was too late.' Then she turned back to wipe Martha's forehead. Martha was wan, her eyelashes spider-dark against her white face, her mouth almost bloodless.

'I must find the padre,' Elspet said dully, but the others paid her no mind.

Ayamena left the damp cloth on Martha's brow and unfolded some packets. She crumbled herbs into a basin, and began to crush some small bulbs against a knife. Elspet recognized the odour of garlic. 'Fetch me boiling water,' she said to Gaxa, and Gaxa hurried off, her hand over her nose.

'Is that . . . her nightdress?' Elspet could not keep the incredulity from her voice. Elspet recognized the still-smouldering cloth as Martha's crumpled cotton shift.

Ayamena ignored the question. She seemed perfectly comfortable squatting on her haunches next to the bed pulverizing her herbal medicine. When Gaxa came with the heated water she poured it over the mess of herbs, and a cloud of steam drove the fumes to the edges of the room.

'Señora – Ayamena,' Elspet tried again. 'I must go find the padre, arrange for Mr Wilmot to receive blessing and burial.'

'No,' Gaxa said. 'Better to wait. Wait until Señora Ayamena is finished. Martha will sleep soon. Then you go.'

'She means it will be dangerous for us if you bring him here whilst my mother is still working,' Luisa said. Her fierce expression cowed Elspet.

So she waited. She sat on a carved wooden chair and watched. Ayamena sang to Martha in a soft croon, words she could not understand. But it calmed her, and then Ayamena administered the herbal drink, and Martha sipped at it. It took perhaps a quarter hour before it was all gone and Ayamena put down the bowl.

'She will hold that down,' Ayamena said, 'then she will be better.'

'Thank you,' Elspet said.

Ayamena moved to extinguish the still-smoking garment in the bowl.

'What does it do?' Elspet asked.

'I burn her clothes. The demons hate the burning, hate it when I give back to them what they have given her.'

Elspet shivered. The talk of demons made her uneasy. Ayamena passed her a green bundle. 'It's parsley,' she said, 'strew the bed with it in the morning. She'll sleep now, by the will of Allah.'

'I'm sorry,' Elspet said, 'I can't pay you. Morcillo had the last of my purse.'

'Nobody mentioned payment,' said Luisa, in an offended tone. 'You are a friend of Señor Alvarez.'

Ayamena stood up away from the truckle bed and began to pack away her things. 'Luisa, go find more hot water. Make tea.'

Luisa opened her mouth to protest but her mother snapped back, 'Now.' Luisa and Gaxa went.

Ayamena looked up from where she knelt over her bundles and bags. 'You need tea for the shock,' she said.

'Do not trouble yourself, I really have no need of it,' Elspet said. But she had no will to move. She slumped down again, her legs leaden, exhausted.

'You were close to him?' Ayamena asked.

'No, I mean yes. It's complicated. He came with me to Spain, to help me reclaim my inheritance. My father, when he died – there was some business with the will . . .' She stopped to see if the older woman had understood her Spanish.

Ayamena was looking up at her with such sympathy in her eyes. 'You lost your father too?'

A lump rose in Elspet's throat. She turned her head away.

'When?'

Unable to get out a word, she was seized with a wrack of weeping. Her whole body shook with grief. Not for Mr Wilmot, but for her father, whom, she only just realized at that moment, was lost to her. Or perhaps had been lost to her even as a child. Ayamena said nothing, but when Luisa arrived noisily with the tea she gestured at her with a shake of her head and Luisa retreated wide-eyed downstairs. Elspet heard her own groans and wails as if they were someone else's.

On the bed Martha stirred, and Ayamena went to settle her before handing Elspet a cloth. It smelled of cloves, and she buried her face in it to stem the weeping.

When she was done weeping, her eyes felt thick and swollen and her hand trembled as she took the cup Ayamena offered. The tea was strong and minty. The taste of it brought her back from her painful childhood memories and into the room. The only sound was of Martha's breathing. It was comforting to hear the sound, the hush of the breath, the sound of life.

'It's good.' She gave Ayamena a watery smile.

'Drink, then. Time enough for the padre tomorrow. Sleep tonight.'

Elspet sipped for a while. It did not matter when she went for the padre, she realized. Mr Wilmot would probably have been aghast at the thought of it anyway, a popish burial, but in this country, how could she do anything else? But today, tomorrow – a few hours – would make no difference.

This woman, still kneeling, stirring the pot of tea, she had been so kind. The thought of it brought fresh tears to her eyes. She remembered then that Ayamena and her family would soon be gone.

'You are leaving. Where will you go?'

'Nicolao will have thought of someone, never fear.'

'You could come here. There is room, and I would be glad to have you, and Martha would—'

'No.' She slapped away her suggestion. 'You have not understood. All the Moriscos are leaving. They will make us leave or they will kill us. So we must leave Spain, go to our own kind.' Seeing Elspet's face, she softened her expression. 'But thank you. It is not often a woman like you would offer help to someone like us.'

A slight noise alerted them to Luisa silhouetted in the doorway from the sconces in the hall. 'I'm ready,' Ayamena said.

Luisa helped to gather her things and Elspet accompanied mother and daughter to the door. Gaxa opened it for them and the wave of warm air swept in from outside.

'Thank you,' Elspet said. 'God be with you.'

Ayamena lifted her hand and Elspet watched the two women's

backs go down the road and around the corner into the black huddle of the city.

'Go to bed, Gaxa,' Elspet said. 'It has been a long day, and tomorrow I must make arrangements for Mr Wilmot's internment.'

'As you wish, mistress,' she said. Then, shyly, 'Will you sleep?'

Elspet was touched by her concern, 'Who knows?' she said. 'But let's try.'

Chapter 36

'Bravo!' The call made Zachary stop his training to look. It was Girard Thibault, just arrived. 'That's a beautiful sword you have,' he said.

Zachary could not resist telling him, 'I forged it myself – see, it is narrower and longer than the average blade. I went to Guido de Vega's on the Calle de las Armas.' He held it out for Girard's inspection.

Girard blew out through his teeth. 'You're a craftsman, Deane.'

Zachary feigned nonchalance. He wiped the blade on his sleeve again and smiled, admiring the grain of the metal.

Girard and Zachary began the basic walking of the circle, practising angles of offence, in the chill early morning light. Although Girard had been there the longest, and his training was supposedly nearly done, Zachary was a good match for him. After they had been going a while the sky turned from the colour of a pale cheese to a vivid blue, and reflected sun leapt from their blades. Thibault's sudden concentration told Zachary that Señor Alvarez had appeared to watch and check their paces.

'Stop,' Alvarez said. 'Come here.' They went over to him.

'Swap swords.'

'What?' Zachary was sure he could not have heard him right. But Alvarez took Girard's sword by the grip and handed it to Zachary, holding his hand out for Zachary's blade. There was no option but to give it to him. Zachary watched as his beautiful sword was placed in Girard's eager hands. That buffoon, who had a grin on his face like he had found a treasure chest in a dung heap.

As they drilled, Zachary was intent on Girard's handling of his sword, fearing that he would nick its blade, and as for Girard's sword, it hung too large in his hands, it tipped forward, the balance of it all wrong. They circled each other warily.

'Deane, you must put aside your feelings about the sword,' said Alvarez. 'You are too attached to it. In a fight you would save your sword and forget to save yourself. Señor Thibault will have it this morning and the other men and then Mistress Leviston. Everyone will try it, and you will work with their weapons too. It is not good to identify too much with your own creation.'

Zachary kicked against the dirt and said, 'Guido de Vega said you have to know your own weapon like your lover. An extension of yourself.'

'That's true of course. But first you have to know yourself, heh?' Alvarez raised his eyebrows at him. 'Now, begin.'

They walked the circle again. All morning he worked with that useless lump of metal Girard called a sword. The weather was cooler, but they still worked up a sweat. The training was relentless. His arm ached; he began to wish it was time for more book study, or more geometry. But Alvarez pushed them all on.

'Quicker!' Alvarez called out. 'Footwork!'

From the corner of his eye Zachary saw Luisa come out from the kitchen and unload some sacks of grain from a handcart near the back gates to the stables. He could not help himself, she drew his attention like a jewel. Next thing he knew, Girard had slipped easily under his guard and knocked his sword to the ground.

Girard whispered, 'She is pretty, hey?'

'It's distracting having them unloading in the corner of the yard,' Zachary grumbled, picking up the weapon and testing its edge.

Girard smiled, and did not look convinced.

'Thibault, Deane! Repeat!' called Alvarez. Zachary redoubled his efforts at the feint and strike and tried to ignore Luisa and the goings-on in the yard. When they were allowed a pause for a break midmorning the handcart had been spirited away and there was no sign of her.

Zachary sighed and lounged back against the wall, felt the freshness of the breeze dry his sweat. Thibault took out paper and lead as usual. He was working on a book to sketch all the techniques. *A Manual of Fence*, he called it, making it sound very grand. Zachary ignored the scratching lead and tipped his hat over his eyes to feel the warmth of the sun penetrate his tired muscles.

A hand touched him on the sleeve and he shot to upright. When he pushed his hat back, Nicolao's wrinkled face was squinting before him. 'I have a message for you,' he said, 'from the English señorita, your friend. It is about Señor Wilmot. He died yesterday. His requiem is this afternoon.'

'What?' Zachary shook his head, trying to take it in, but couldn't think of anything to say. 'Oh God, the poor dog,' he managed. He remembered Wilmot in his apartment, trying to get him to change his mind about selling the business. Surely that sweaty man with the determined face couldn't be dead?

'What happened?'

'The sweating sickness, Ayamena says. The doctor bled him. Too much, too late, she says. He couldn't be saved.'

Thoughts raced through Zachary's mind – was it his fault? Had he somehow brought it on him? And how on earth would Elspet travel home now, without his protection? 'I am sorry to hear it.' Zachary rubbed his hand over his mouth. This would drag him further into involvement with Elspet, he knew. He did not want any further entanglement with her, even the sight of her reminded him he was a liar and a cheat.

'Señor Alvarez says you may go to the service.' Nicolao's words reined in his thoughts.

'Today? I'm not sure . . . I'll miss my training.'

'If Señor Alvarez says you may go, then you should.' He pursed his lips. 'It is a mark of respect for your countryman. The poor Englishman can have few to honour him being so far from his home. And there is Mistress Leviston also – Señor Alvarez says she will need your support.'

Oh no. Would he never be free of her? He did not want to go to the funeral, but at the same time he wanted to make a good impression on Alvarez, make him think he was worth his time. Perhaps he could pretend to go, but go somewhere else instead. But then Alvarez would be sure to ask him about it. He tussled it in his thoughts, then shook his head. 'What time?'

'Four o'clock at the Church of Santa Maria La Blanca.'

He saw Elspet waiting red-eyed and quiet as they brought out the body, and a shiver of guilt went through him. A few nuns were there, from the convent of the church, gathered like grey jackdaws round the padre who was to lead the procession. Surprisingly, quite a few other mourners had gathered too – all seemed to be Spanish; there because of some religious conviction of their own. Elspet beckoned to him to fall in next to her behind the bier. He noticed that she was wearing black gloves. Black gloves in this heat.

The worm of guilt reared its head again. He stepped in next to her. This was no time for their argument, for this sombre procession reminded him of his mother's death. No fine funeral for her. He swallowed, pushed away the memory.

The coffin was draped in a white cloth and the padre led the slow gathering down the narrow streets, the silver-gilt cross held before him. Behind came the shuffling nuns, with paper cones containing lighted candles. Then the pair of them, unlikely mourners, followed by the Spanish rabble.

He knew that walking so close to Elspet gave people a false impression, signified an intimacy they would never share. He wondered if she was remembering her father, and an unexpected wave of regret washed over him. Leviston had tried to do his best, he knew. Old fool that he was, he had a good heart.

He glanced to the side, and a lump came to his throat. What a scoundrel Leviston would have thought him, to gull Elspet this way. But how could he tell her he was not her brother now? When those ships came in, he would be a made man.

Folk stopped to remove their hats and make the sign of the cross as the cortege passed. Cobblers ceased their hammering, young children ran over to stare, fingers in their mouths before scampering off on bare feet to fetch their friends, to gawp as they wended their way past. The doleful air of the nuns chanting the *Miserere* washed over him as they walked. The coffin moved maddeningly slowly. He just wanted it to be over.

Outside the church they paused yet again for more sprinkling of holy water over the coffin, before entering thorough the big arched doorway, carved along its edge with what appeared to be giant teeth. It put Zachary in mind of a huge jaw.

Inside the church it was gloomy after the outside sun. He shivered. He had not been in a church since leaving London. New plasterwork was in progress, a dust in the air with a slight tang of lime-wash in the back of the nostrils. Even here, more building, as if Seville was remaking herself, putting off the dark of the plagues and failed harvests of the past for a gilded future. '*Exultabunt Domino,*' chanted the padre.

Zachary slid into the pew and sat dry-eyed through the requiem Mass. Who would attend his funeral when it came? he wondered. Would he be like poor pathetic Wilmot, with only Mistress Leviston and Zachary, who cared not a whit for him, as his mourners?

But if Zachary were to die tomorrow, maybe there would not be a single soul at his funeral. Not Elspet. Señor Alvarez? Could he call him a friend? Gabriel? Alexander? He thought of Rodriguez. As usual he seemed to have made as many enemies in Seville as friends. The thought was sobering.

The padre swung the censer and the pungent whiff of frankincense transported him back to Mass with his mother, to waiting in the darkness whilst she made her confessions. The remembrance of her face, as she emerged cool and serene to squeeze his hand, as if all her troubles had been rinsed away, made him wince.

He had not made confession for many months. He feared it. He dare not look inside his soul for he knew he would see the black stain of deceit pooling there.

A man stood to let him pass to the front, but he shook his head. To take communion was unthinkable, and he gripped the pew as the other attendees went to kneel at the altar. Elspet tilted her head back to receive the host as if it were the most natural thing in the world. He swallowed back salt water. He was moved, that she should open her throat to the priest like that, as if exposing her life and soul to him in that very gesture.

When she returned to the pew he could not meet her gaze. He listened miserably to the absolution:

Liberi mi, Domine, de morte aeterni, in dii illa tremenda:
Quandi coeli movendi sunt et terra.
Dum veneris iudicire saeculum per ignem.

He knew he had turned away from God somehow. But could he bring himself to confess he was not Leviston's son? The devout and blameless Wilmot was no doubt on his way to heaven. The words of the absolution sent an involuntary shiver up Zachary's spine. A judgement of fire. That was what awaited him, he was certain.

Chapter 37

The third day after Mr Wilmot was buried Elspet turned over and hugged the feather bolster to her chest, unwilling to rise and greet the day. She thought of home, and the remembrance was faint, a mirage wavering in the heat. At the same time her heart filled with such a sharp pain of longing.

'Mistress?'

She sat up. Martha was holding out her petticoat. Her hands were thin and blotched pink, her hair scraped back under her cap above hollow cheeks. She looked as if she might fall over if Elspet should so much as blow on her.

'Martha. Are you feeling—?'

'Quite well today, thank you, mistress. Gaxa told me about Mr Wilmot. I'm sorry I was not at the burial. Such a kind gentleman. Will we be going back to England now?' Her face was hopeful.

Elspet swung her legs out from the bed. 'Are you sure you should be up?'

'Sure, mistress. You'll be needing someone, now Mr Wilmot is . . .'

'Yes. Thank you, Martha.' Elspet dare not say she had no means to pay her, nor a way of leaving Spain. The last few days had passed in a whirlwind of letter-writing and parcelling Wilmot's effects. She could not bring herself to sell his belongings, though she had need of the money. Dorothy would want them.

She took the petticoat and began to dress. Martha picked up the farthingale and held it out, but she shook her head. 'No, not today. It is too much of an encumbrance.'

Martha made a disapproving face, but patiently handed her each item of clothing. Elspet waved away the embroidered forepart which she made to pin to her petticoat, but agreed to the overskirt, the V-pointed bodice with its row of tiny hooks, the slashed sleeves.

'I have no mourning costume,' she said, 'save this. It seemed dark enough. And we will need to pin up my skirts. They are too long without the hoops, and I want to hide my petticoats.'

'The Spanish ladies have very large hoops still,' Martha said.

'I know. But they are far too much to manage, and I want to be able to move about the city without making too much of a show of myself.'

'I would love to wear hoops like these,' Martha said, stroking the chair where Elspet's were dangling. Elspet felt her envy sharp as a bodkin. It had never occurred to her that her maid might covet her clothes.

Martha finished by dressing Elspet's hair in a caul behind, by which time Martha looked exhausted. Her hands trembled and were moist with a sheen of perspiration.

'Martha,' Elspet said gently. 'It is no use dissembling. You know you are not really well enough to attend me today. Now go back to bed and rest. I can manage without you. I will ask Gaxa to bring you some strong broth to build up your strength. Now shoo.'

Martha smiled thinly. 'As you wish, mistress.' Her face registered relief and she seemed glad to totter out of the room. She grasped the door jamb for support as she left.

When she had gone Elspet tied on her hempen sandals and picked up a basket. Mr Wilmot was dead and it was as if a void had opened in her life. She thought of Joan, safe in her convent, but the idea of convent life held no appeal. On the one hand her stomach lurched with nerves, but on the other she felt an unexpected lightness, a freedom, as if more possibilities had suddenly opened to her.

She would go to the fencing school. Señor Alvarez had been so kind. She guessed it was he who had sent money for the funeral and had persuaded Zachary to attend. Zachary had barely said two words to her, let alone offered his condolences. But Zachary Deane held the key to her future and she would not let him out of her sight.

The door to the yard creaked open at her touch and she made her way to her familiar stone bench seat. A sparrow pecked at a late fig that had fallen from one of the trees next door. She watched its fluster of feathers as it tried to lift its prize and carry it off.

'Good morning!' The Spanish words caused her to turn and look. It was Ayamena, throwing back the shutters of the kitchen.

'You startled me,' Elspet said, jumping to her feet to go over to her. 'Martha is so much better. She was up out of bed this morning already.'

'She will be weak for a few days. She will need metals and minerals to help her regain her strength.' Ayamena dried her hands on a muslin cloth. 'If you come later I will give you something.'

'I cannot thank you enough. I thought I would lose her too. And she is my only friend in Spain.' As she said this Elspet realized with a jolt that it might be true. 'Where should I come? Where will you be living?'

'We are still here. In the servants' quarter above the kitchen. Our plans . . . well, they changed. Look,' she angled her head and looked up – 'that window just up there. With the hanging passiflora.' Elspet tilted her head to look. Ayamena continued, 'Señor Alvarez insists we stay. But it is a risk he takes. So we try to be quiet and little trouble, and help him out with the cooking and the chores.'

Elspet looked over her shoulder. The men had arrived for the day's training and were disrobing and preparing themselves. They swung their arms, shook out their legs, circled their shoulders. In the corner, Alexander stepped on the spot, lifting his knees high. Ayamena flapped her hand and laughed as if to dismiss them, and pulled her head back behind the window.

Zachary swaggered in from the street with his cloak thrown back, his leather arms case over his shoulder. He was soon doing a set of vigorous exercises with the rest until they lined up and began the drill. Señor Alvarez appeared from the upper door and perched on the stone steps at the side of the yard, observing.

'Mistress Leviston,' he called out. 'Here again, heh? Partner Alexander, if you please.' She blushed and jumped to her feet. Zachary turned in annoyance and their eyes met briefly across the distance before she gave him a haughty look and hurried to Alexander.

Alexander picked up a second sword and held it out for her, waiting. He bowed and smiled, his brown eyes creased at the edges from the sun. She grabbed the sword in what she hoped was a manly way and tried to copy the rest of the men on her row. Señor Alvarez was watching and she was desperate to perform it correctly.

Soon she had grasped the nature of the movement, but her body would not respond quickly enough. Having a blade pass so close to her face made her gasp, even if it was only what they called a 'blunt' with a pad on the end of it. She could feel her heart pumping under her stomacher. Pray God Señor Alvarez could not see her fear.

Alexander struck towards her with his edge and she stepped aside, angling her blade so he clashed up against her guard. From there she was supposed to turn to push him away. The first few times she forgot to turn and their blades locked. They did the move over and over until it was smooth. She was panting with exertion. But as she worked, the crushing tension that had lodged in her chest had seeped away.

By the time the sun was high in the sky she had forgotten about anything else except the practice and the sharp-eyed presence of Señor Alvarez. The November sun beat down on her head, and her hair blew in her face so she tied her muslin neckerchief over it to keep it back and to keep the sun away. The piercing light made her squint to try to catch Alexander off guard. But he parried her neatly every time.

'Stop!' Alvarez called. Their bodies lurched to a halt. She was hot with effort. A slight breeze caught at the laces on her chemise and it tickled her neck, but she did not move. Señor Alvarez inspected their stances, and adjusted each one into a more balanced position. She held her breath as he placed his hand above her shoulder but he did not touch her. She let the shoulder soften and relax. 'Good,' he whispered.

She glowed with his praise.

The rest of the morning they spent indoors. Señor Alvarez brought them all to the circle. Now she understood it for what it was – a device, like a compass, for training direction and angle – she was itching to work on it. With luck, Señor Alvarez might let her try.

Elspet could not help but admire Alvarez's physique. Even the way he moved around the circle, pointing with his long cane, had an ease and dexterity.

'Forget the Italian way,' Alvarez said, 'Morezzo, and the complexity of all those separate moves. Look at the circle – it is one line.' He pointed. 'We are used to dividing the world. We want to polarize everything into two opposites. Agrippa teaches that there is no point in making two moves – one for offense and one for defense. The one move can be both an effective guard and an attack. Think how the bullfighter moves, around the circle to come in at an angle with his *banderilla*. But if we want to do this, we have to have accuracy. Accuracy depends on the application of your will as a force.'

The men nodded, taking it in. But Zachary looked disgruntled. 'Do you mean willpower?' he asked.

'Be careful. It is not just willpower. Too many students think they already have willpower because they come through that gate and practise every day, but it is a different quality I am after. It is something absolutely unbendable.'

Zachary persisted. 'But you said that when a man is rigid, he is open to attack. I thought the idea was to blend with our opponent's intention.'

Elspet winced at Zachary's lack of respect, but Alvarez did not react. He merely shook his head. 'We want our will to be strong but fine, exactly like a sword. A sword is the expression of it. Here, pass me your blade.'

Zachary unsheathed his sword and passed it to Señor Alvarez, who meanwhile had drawn on his gloves. 'Look closely. The blade keeps its shape and direction, yet it is flexible too.' He bent the blade into a gentle curve then let it go.

It sprang back to its original form.

'That is what we want, see? You all know how a sword is forged, but Mr Deane has seen it first-hand, is that not so? So where is its strength, Mr Deane?'

They all looked to Zachary for an answer.

Zachary floundered, and folded his arms. 'I don't know. I suppose it is tempered by heat, and by beating and folding the metal over and over.'

'So you know about this, yes? We apply heat – this is the training,' Alvarez said. 'No, I do not suggest I should beat you.' Gentle laughter from the men, but Elspet did not like to join in, lest it draw his attention to her.

Alvarez continued, 'But you need to endure, and you need to repeat. And you need to be awake.' He handed Zachary back his sword. 'This is as important as technique. This is what will enable you to see a gap in the other's defences and press past it.'

Alvarez walked purposefully around the edge of the circle, his heels clacking on the wooden floor. He tapped his cane on a painted notch on the circumference. 'The first element marked on the circle – fire. You should recognize its quality. This week we will work with fire. Air of fire, water of fire, earth of fire, even fire of fire, and –' he paused, 'fire's quintessence. But first, we need to know what fire is.'

He called for his apprentice who waited by the door. 'Bring candles please, and tinderboxes.' The boy grinned and scurried away. When he returned he had a basket clinking with iron tinderboxes and beeswax candles which he set up on a long side-table.

Elspet hung back until the men had taken their places, fearing she might be excluded from the exercise. But there was a place set for her after all, and Señor Alvarez nodded at her to take it. She felt a blush creep up her neck.

For a moment all that could be heard was the scrape of metal on flint. Elspet made several futile attempts to strike the flint with the D-shaped firesteel before a spark appeared. In her desperation to prove herself as good as the men, she blew too hard on the shredded cloth, so the spark died and the charred cloth scattered on the floor. From the corner of her eye she saw Zachary suppress a smile. She scrabbled to pick up the shreds of cloth.

She repeated the strike until she managed to land a spark on the cloth and it glowed red under her coaxing breath, and a tiny transparent yellow flame sprang up, almost invisible in the light of the day. She teased a splinter of wood over it until it caught, and finally she was able to light the wick of the candle.

She exhaled. She had done this very rarely. At home in England the servants always lit the fires or trimmed the wicks, once a flame was in the house. This creating fire from nothing was new to her. She marvelled at how quick the flame snapped into to life. One moment it did not exist, then suddenly it was there leaping in front of her.

The candle burned with a steady heat. A small smile of triumph came to her lips. She turned to see how the men were faring. All held lit candles before them, even Zachary. Zachary glanced over to her, but quickly snapped his eyes back to his candle. Alvarez stood at the end of the row. He was watching her face. She dropped her gaze and paid attention to the flame. It never wavered.

How is it that Alvarez discomfits me so? she wondered; it was as if he saw right through them all. Whenever he was in the room it was as if they all sat on a knife edge.

Chapter 38

Zachary did not see the boy at first, for he was intent on his exercise with Alexander. They'd been at it for an hour or so that evening and were tiring. Both of them had suffered blows to the trunk, and though they were using blunts, they still bruised. Thank goodness, his long-boned friend had softened over the last few months, now that he had seen Zachary was serious about the training. Mind, Alexander was slow as a bear, never quite sprightly enough to catch up with Zachary's nimble feet.

They were both running with sweat even in the cool of the evening, so Zachary went over to his satchel to fetch a kerchief. As he picked it up out of the bag, there he was, Luisa's brother, a small boy with enormous brown eyes peeking out from under the shadows of the trellis. Zachary gave him a wink and he did not move, but his body tensed as if he might run away.

He reminded Zachary of that slave boy, the one he got into trouble about, when he had first come to Seville. The thought of that boy made him sad. Where was he now, he wondered. Was he still with Rodriguez? He hoped not. He remembered his bruised eye and the way the boy told him not to come back.

Zachary plucked his leather water bottle from the bag and tipped a draught into his mouth. Funny, but he didn't seem to want a slave now. He'd like an apprentice, though, like Señor Alvarez had, someone to look up to him; Señor Alvarez's apprentices worshipped him.

'Come on,' shouted Alexander, 'Alvarez might be watching. What's taking you so long?'

'Coming,' he called, and they set to again. This time he was facing the buildings and Alexander faced the gate to the street. From here he could see the boy watching them still. He had a short stick in his hand and he was copying their movements. Zachary had one eye on Alexander and the other on the boy. He was giving a marvellous mimicry of Alexander's stance, right down to the slightly stooped shoulders and jutting chin.

Eventually Alexander stopped, and held up his hands. 'Go on, tell, what's so interesting behind me?'

'Hey, you!' Zachary shouted to the boy. The boy stopped what he was doing and his face filled with apprehension. 'It's all right,' Zachary said in a soothing voice. 'You fight well. Muy bien,' he repeated. The boy still stared as if he might turn tail and run.

'Do you want a lesson?'

The boy nodded and approached warily.

'Watch out for Alvarez.' Alexander looked dubious.

'Oh, come on. It's just a bit of play. Señor's gone inside. Look, stand like this, with one foot forward and the other behind it, in line.' Zachary demonstrated. The boy followed behind him, placing his thin legs one behind the other with serious concentration.

Alexander grinned despite himself and said, 'Ah good, someone your own size!'

Zachary wagged his head and put up a thumb at him. Alexander put up a thumb back and took the chance to rest. He slumped against the wall and swigged from his bottle. He watched Zachary and his new friend with amusement.

'So now,' Zachary said to the boy, 'you hold the sword out in front like this.' He held his sword out in the *en garde* position. The boy did the same, but the swords did not touch – his stick was too short. Wordlessly, Zachary stooped to pick up Alexander's sword where it had been discarded on the ground.

'Hey!' Alexander shouted, but too late; Zachary had put it in the hands of the boy, whose scrawny arm held on to it with a determined grip. Alexander shrugged, and said, 'Don't kill him, Deane.'

Zachary grinned at the boy, 'He's joking. Now, as you thrust towards me, I step aside, like this, see?' He leapt sideways. 'Now thrust.' The boy tentatively poked the tip in his direction. 'No! Harder than that!' The boy tried again.

'No. Look, you must put your whole body weight behind it. Watch me.' Zachary made a fearsome yell and mimed skewering somebody and withdrawing the blade to wipe it on his boot. The boy gurgled a laugh, and the sound made Alexander and Zachary laugh too.

'I'm ready,' Zachary said, taking up an obvious defensive position, 'Now give it all you've got.'

The boy opened his mouth to roar and, with a sudden plunge, drove the point of the sword at Zachary's chest; he was only just out of the way in time, and it whistled past his ribs almost overbalancing him. Alexander's eyebrows shot up in surprise.

'Husain!' The voice was sharp and he turned to see Luisa bearing down on them. One look was enough to tell him she was as angry as a hornet. She grabbed the boy by one scrawny arm and said, 'What in God's name do you think you're doing? Is there not enough bloodshed in the world, but you must go add to it?' The boy struggled and tried to pull away, but she kept tight grip of his upper arm and almost hoisted him off the ground.

'I'm sorry,' Zachary said, 'it was my fault. I invited him to try.'

She looked at him coldly. 'You want to teach him to kill, do you? Men. You are all the same.' She let Husain off his tiptoes, wrestled the sword from his grasp and flung it down before him into the dust.

Alexander stood up in his defence, 'Zachary was only entertaining him. He meant no harm by it. The boy was laughing.'

'You don't understand, do you? There'll be time enough for all that when he's older. Can't you let him have at least a few years? Teach him those skills and what will he do? Look for a fight to test them. And who's to say who will come off worst? Let him enjoy a few more years before every day is a war.' She looked at them both in contempt. 'Bloodshed looks for places where it's welcome, doesn't it? Why send it an invitation?'

'Sorry, Luisa,' the boy said, his eyes welling up. 'I was only—'

She scooped him up and he twined his legs around her waist, buried his head in her shoulder. She cradled his head with her hand, rubbed his black hair and clasped him tight as if she would crush him to her. 'It's alright, little hen,' Zachary heard her say, as if to convince herself, but her voice cracked. 'Everything is alright.'

She turned on her heel then, without a backward glance, and carried the boy with her into the house. As she went, he felt as though a chasm had opened in his chest. He should be angry, but he was not. He was chastened. She fascinated him, just the way she moved and carried herself, and he had wanted to impress her. Not one day passed where he didn't look out for her, and he fancied he'd caught her watching him, too. But now she had made him feel as if all his training was for nothing. Whatever the small flower was that was growing between them, he had just trampled it.

In another part of the city Don Rodriguez was receiving his orders from Garbali. The men were relaxing over a glass of port in Garbali's opulent chambers. Although the stuccoed rooms and carved, gilded furniture did not really belong to Garbali. Formerly they had belonged to a rich textile merchant who had just been found guilty of heresy and executed.

Garbali looked quite at home in his borrowed domain. 'We were worried we could not transport them all, but I've just heard the fleet has been secured. Despite the fact we all know the Duke of Medina Sidonia has little enthusiasm for this expulsion. Too many Morisco servants, I suspect. But he's agreed at last – I believe he was leaned on a little,' Garbali said.

So the 'Invincible Armada' has some use after all.' They laughed companionably, sharing the joke.

'Now, Lerma recommends that we tell the Moriscos of Seville that the expulsion only applies to those who live within twenty leagues of the sea. We must do as he requests – a security measure.

That way, the inland Moors will believe themselves exempt.'

'And are they?'

'Of course not. The King wants a total purge. But we need to

316

keep it peaceable if possible. Quash any rebellion before it has a chance to catch fire. Your district will be in the next wave – Murcia, Andalusia and Granada. Oh, and the troublesome enclave at Hornachos. But that need not concern us. Seville is an embarkation point so it will need proper managing. I want you to seal off the roads, and put troops into the surrounding hills.'

'I've planned to make another base in the Roman ruins of the old city,' Rodriguez said. 'No one goes there, it will provide shelter for horses, and a place to despatch troops to the coast with efficiency and speed. Quicker than trying to get in or out of the town.'

'Lerma wants no more prisoners. If they run, they are to be strung up as examples. There is not enough space in San Jorge or the prisons of Seville, and we cannot afford to feed those who won't go peaceably.'

'I saw what happened in Denia. We are well-prepared. Not a single Morisco will be left in Seville, you have my word.'

Chapter 39

Luisa stepped outside from the warmth of the pottery and untied her scarf to shake out her hair. She unwrapped her bread and fruit from the cloth and sat on one of the tattered rush stools at the front to watch the world go by, even though the weather was cooler now and winter skies had begun to appear more and more often.

This time of the day was full of people hurrying home for their noonday rest, but she often preferred to work more hours and bring home a few more *maradinos*. Besides, she enjoyed her work, the way the mud turned into something so beautiful and durable. She loved painting the dull glazes on to the leathery clay and seeing them transform to something that shone like water and gold when they emerged from the kiln. Papa called it alchemy.

She took out a fruit knife from her pocket and wiped it on her skirt.

'Luisa?' The sound of her name made her look up from stoning the peach.

It was Maria. And she wasn't alone. The Englishman was with her, Mr Deane, a cloth bag held in his arms. Luisa hurriedly wrapped up her meal again and stood up, flustered.

'Mr Deane was asking where the pottery was,' said Maria. He said he wanted to speak with you, so I insisted he come right away.'

Mr Deane looked hot, there were two patches of red flaring on his cheeks.

'Forgive me interrupting,' he said, 'but Maria told me you wouldn't mind. And I wanted to apologize. About yesterday – your brother.'

Maria was reluctant to go. Luisa raised her eyebrows at her, and she said, 'Oh well, then. I'll leave you now. Be sure to call in on the way home,' she said. Luisa knew this meant so she could tell her all about it. They watched her departing back in awkward silence.

'I'm sorry, please carry on eating. I only wanted to apologize. I should have asked you or your mother if it was all right to teach him. It was thoughtless. And you were right, I shouldn't encourage him to get into trouble.'

Luisa was unused to apologies. In her family when people had a disagreement, they just ignored it until it faded away. She could think of nothing to say, and he was looking at her so earnestly.

She pointed to the other stool. 'Since you've come, won't you sit a moment?'

He sat, and together they watched the people pass up and down the street. She felt a little stupid, with him, the gentleman, apologizing. Usually it was the other way around.

'Here,' he said, 'I brought you some fruit.' He opened the bag.

She smiled to herself. Crafty Maria had persuaded him to buy enough oranges and late pears to make preserves for the whole winter. 'I've had some,' she said. 'I always call at the *fruiteria* on the way.'

'Oh. Well, do you mind if I do?'

She shook her head. So polite, not like the Spanish men. She watched him from the side of her eyes as he took out three oranges and tossed them up into practised arcs.

Despite herself, she smiled. He was skilful, and juggling was something she did not see every day. 'Husain would love that.'

'If I show him this instead of sword skills, am I forgiven?'

'Maybe.'

He caught them deftly in one hand, then peeled an orange and scooped out the pips, flicking them into the gutter one by one.

'Do you want to go somewhere with a better view?' The words tumbled out before she could stop them.

His eyes looked back steadily at her. 'The view from here is fine.'

She brushed her hair from her face. Was he complimenting her? It made her heart flutter. 'No, I meant if you don't know Seville very well, I can show you somewhere with a magnificent view of the city. I have another hour before I need to be back at my bench. Shall I show you?' She was suddenly shy again.

'Me too. I have an hour.' He smiled and put the bag of fruit in his haversack.

'Come, then.' She led him through the narrow wynds to the road that ran along the edge of the Guadalquivir. Here houses were being renovated, piles of stone stood in the road, and wooden scaffolds rose up from the ground, supporting rickety platforms.

Every now and then she would turn to see if he was still following, and he would smile at her. Her heart was racing. What would Mama say if she knew where she was and who she was with? The thought of her disapproval made Luisa feel even bolder.

She stopped outside one of the grandest most ornate houses, a tall stone building with curled balconies and a heavy baronial front door.

'My, what a place!' he said.

'Yes, it must have been so grand once. But look at it now.' She tilted her head at the broken railings, the disintegrating rush blinds, the paint curling away in patches from the shutters. 'They started to renovate it about eighteen months ago, but nobody's been near it for months. They must have run out of money. Fortunes are lost just as quickly as they are made in Seville. But we can go in, there's a grand view from the top floor.'

He was staring at her mouth as she talked. It gave her a bubbling feeling inside.

'In here,' she said, pushing on a rusting wrought-iron gate. It opened into a yard overgrown with grass and littered with debris of stone and ship's timbers. A back door was broken up into planks. She pointed.

'Señorita Ortega! Who do you think I am? A cat? I can't crawl through that gap. I need to eat less, I think.'

'It's not so bad – it opens.' She dragged on the door which, to his surprise, creaked outwards on bent hinges. 'It's the servants' stairs. Come up.'

She led him up narrow winding stairs, heard his shoes crunching on the layer of grit before they came to the big chamber, high-ceilinged, with a wooden-beamed roof. From there she bounded up the wider staircase to the top.

She was panting a little, exhilarated from the climb and her own daring.

'How on earth did you find this place?' He was not out of breath at all.

'Husain. One of his friends found it, the way children do. But Mama banned them from coming here – too dangerous with all the building going on. But when I saw it, I just kept on coming, for the view.'

She pointed to the open shutters, and watched as he walked towards the balcony. She clasped her hands in expectation.

He stared out a moment, and she heard him let out an exclamation. When he turned to look over his shoulder she was almost as excited as he was. She smiled and went to join him at the open window. The green ribbon of river could be seen winding its way towards the sea. On either side the city was like a map spread out on a table, the sky a huge blue dome dotted with cloud.

'I come here when I need quiet. Or to think,' she said.

'It's beautiful. Thank you for bringing me.' He accidentally brushed her hand with his fingers. She held her breath, the air seemed to grow silent but she did not move her hand away.

'It must be one the finest views in Seville,' he said. She was still enough to hear her own heart beating as his hand curled into hers.

'I think so,' she said, carrying on the conversation as if nothing at all was happening between them. 'I keep thinking I'll come one day and it will be full of workmen.'

'One day I'd like a house like this. If I had it, I couldn't bear to see it lying empty.'

Now his hand held hers tight, and his thumb circled on her wrist. She stared unseeing at the view; all her senses were afire. She knew she should move away. He was everything she should avoid. Her mother would be horrified. Not only was he not of her family's faith, he wasn't even Spanish. She swallowed. But then she might not be in

Spain much longer, the world was changing so fast. She had the sense of stepping off the edge of something, allowing herself to fall.

He turned her, to look into her face. 'I meant it,' he said quietly. 'Did you know, you are more beautiful than any view.'

She shook her head, but the protest had no heart behind it. 'Mr Deane, I am just a girl from the pottery. You are a gentleman . . .'

He laughed. 'I am not a gentleman. At least I wasn't until six months ago. I was a . . . well, never mind. But you are a dancer, and I am a fencer. There is something in common there, I think.' He rested his other hand on her shoulder.

'You fight well,' she said, desperately looking for conversation, knowing that they were both gripped by something they could not control. 'I heard Señor tell Papa you are one of his best students.'

'Really? He really said that?'

She nodded. 'True, as God is my witness.'

'Then I could kiss you,' He brought his lips down towards hers, and very slowly, inevitably, she turned her face towards his in an invitation.

His lips rested on hers lightly, she felt his arms close around her back. She moved into him, tingling all over. She wanted to draw him close, for the moment never to stop. His hand wound itself into her hair, she opened her throat to press her mouth to his with more fervour. When he withdrew, his hand came out to stroke her forehead, but she broke away, disorientated. The world had changed in a moment. What had she done?

'I must be getting back to the pottery.' She had a sudden urge to turn back time, for everything to be as it was, safe and familiar.

'But I thought you said you had an hour?' His hand kept hold of hers.

She was panicking now, it was all too much. Her thoughts were in confusion. 'I'm sorry, I shouldn't have come, I shouldn't have brought you here, I must go.' She broke away and turned, hurried down the stairs.

'Then I'll come with you, escort you back to the pottery,' he said from behind. She heard his boots clatter down the stairs after her. When she got to the door at the bottom of the servants' stairs, it was jammed. She jerked at it until it swung open but he caught up with her in the passage.

'Luisa, I was too forward,' he said. 'Forgive me. I should have been less—'

'Please don't say anything else. We will forget about it, yes?' She tried to be calm and reasonable, but her body was alive to his presence. She paused and looked up at him standing away, the brim of his hat screwed up in one hand, at his dark questioning eyes. 'It's just I –' She could not move. She heard her own voice come out of the darkness, 'No, kiss me again.'

Chapter 40

For a month, Elspet and the men trained in the art of fire. They learned to draw the sword like the sudden shooting up of a flame. Over and over they slipped it from the scabbard so that the movement became seamless and sudden.

Elspet dreaded that she would fall behind, that she would become a liability in the training, and that the señor must secretly think her a burden. She knew her arm looked weak and ineffective next to the men, especially Zachary, who was becoming fast as a whirlwind. She redoubled her efforts. They practised the quick leaping quality of the blade with point-strikes and thrusts, and in the evenings Alvarez made them study all types of flame.

They even watched the flame trickle along a fuse to a heap of firepowder – such a small pile like a sprinkle of salt – until she had to clap her hands to her ears at the crack of the explosion and shield her eyes from its brief flaring light. The whole time she watched Alvarez with a fierce attention, both to learn from him and because he held for her a fascination she could not fathom.

Zachary had been forced to accept her presence. Since the death of Wilmot he seemed less intimidating. Señor Alvarez treated her with exactly the same respect as he did the other students so Zachary had been coerced into doing the same, simply because Alvarez expected it. Her cousin kept his face blank when she was asked to partner him. And even he had to concede that no more students had come to the señor's door for training, and with there being five men it was better to have her as a partner than no partner at all.

Lately, Elspet noticed that Zachary was distracted, always looking out of the window. Alvarez was tough with him and made him stand an extra hour in the *en garde* position. As for Elspet, she relished it all. She tied her skirts further into her waistband and left off her sleeves. She had never worked so hard in her life; her muscles ached, her chemise was soaked, her right hand blistered from gripping the sword. She worked with them all now, with Girard Thibault the artist, with the courteous Dutchman Alexander Souter, with the young devout Spaniard Pedro Gutierrez, with the watchful Frenchman Etienne Galen.

By the time they had moved on to training with the element of air, the weather was cooler. One of the days she partnered Etienne to practise speed, timing and distance. When they had finished their drills, he saluted her with a mock bow. 'You do well for a woman,' he said.

She reacted automatically, 'No, I feel like a cack-handed fool next to you men.'

'You take on the stance better than we, and you have a natural grasp of distance. We men, well – we have so much already in our bodies from other teachers. It is hard to let it go, yes? But you have no need to un-learn someone else's methods.'

'Perhaps.'

'Come, let's go sit,' he said. She went over to the bench. Etienne made to perch next to her, so that she had to move tight up to one end. He wedged himself in beside her.

'Will you fight?' he asked.

Fight? The idea had not occurred to her. She had not thought beyond the training. 'I don't know. I don't think so. I'd be no match for a man.'

'Then why do you do it?'

He was looking at her, an intent look in his pale eyes.

'I suppose I just fell into it somehow. I was here in Spain to see my cousin – Zachary. And I cannot go back home without him. So I will train with him until he is ready to leave.' It sounded reasonable, as she said it.

'But why? You could go back to England without him, surely?'

His questions were making her uncomfortable. She decided to be honest. 'My father left his business to us jointly and no funds can be released until Zachary signs for it. I am dependent on his charity for now, and he will not return with me to England until his training is done, in the spring. I stay to keep him to his word.'

'So Zachary Deane is a rich man? I would not have guessed it from his bearing.'

'I . . . my father was in trade, and—' She stopped herself. Etienne was sitting far too near to her. His breath rasped close to her ear.

'What trade is that?' Etienne asked.

'Oh, nothing. Lace. The haberdasher's trade,' she said, standing. 'Excuse me, I must get a drink.' She walked away and as she glanced back over her shoulder she saw his eyes were still fixed on her.

In the patchy shade of the vine, Zachary was pouring a drink. 'Etienne seems to have taken a liking to you,' he said. It was the first time he had opened an exchange with her in a pleasant tone of voice.

'We were just talking, that's all.'

'Well, he was watching you all morning when you were working with Girard. I know because Etienne was my partner, and he couldn't keep his eyes on the game. At first I thought he was watching Girard, but then I realized it must be you he was looking at. You have an admirer.'

Discomfited, she poured herself some watered ale from the jug, and ignored him. She did not like Zachary making such personal comments. She remembered how keen he was for her to be wed. She found herself wishing it was Señor Alvarez who was her admirer, and not the over-familiar Frenchman.

As if her thoughts had summoned him, Señor Alvarez appeared. Elspet tried to act with a nonchalance she did not feel. They stood aside to let him near the table. Señor Alvarez turned to her, 'Mistress Leviston, if you are to continue, we need to discuss when you will make payment. I'll be in the library this afternoon. We can discuss it then.'

'Of course,' she said, but he had caught her off-guard. She had never thought about how she would pay. She looked around to catch

Zachary's eye but, curse him, he was gone, like a wily fox into the forest. 'Yes, I'll come this afternoon,' she said.

After he left, she stood a moment, crestfallen. This would be the end of her training.

The library was dim after the brightness of the yard. Señor Alvarez was waiting, his black hat on the table before him, so she was surprised all over again by his white hair. 'Please sit,' he said, but she stayed standing.

She blurted out, 'I'm sorry, but I cannot pay. There is no money left. I cannot even feed myself or my maid. I'm sorry. I'm grateful to you for paying the burial expenses, as I said. And I am thankful for what I have learned so far, and I'll send money as soon as I am able, but I cannot train with the men any more.' She was almost in tears as she turned to leave.

'Wait.' His voice was commanding.

She hesitated. 'I can't pay, so it is no use my wasting your time.'

The apprentice was getting the books out for afternoon study, and quietly placing them out on the tables. The thought of the books and the study she would miss made her catch her breath.

'Please – do take a seat.' Señor Alvarez gestured at the chair.

She sat. He tapped his fingers on the table, and then rubbed his hand over his upper lip. His face was tanned from the sun, slight creases lodged around his eyes.

'Mistress Leviston,' he said, 'I do not yet understand why you are here, but you are here nonetheless. And as you are here, there must be some purpose behind it. So you will be trained. And payment will be exacted.' He paused a moment and then smiled. 'I have never had a female pupil, so you must pardon me if I occasionally forget your sex.'

'But how will I pay?' she protested. 'I have no funds at all until I can persuade Zachary to come to England, and he says you will not let him relinquish the training, even for a short while.'

'Once someone has begun, I must keep up the pressure. If the momentum I have built up is lost, then the training must begin again.

I am not a young man, and times are . . . uncertain.' He sighed. 'Zachary and his companions are my hope for the future of *La Destreza*. Who knows, perhaps you will be my last students.'

'But could you not make an exception?'

'No. No exceptions. I am sorry.'

'Then I cannot pay.'

'You will pay with your effort and with your dedication to the art. That is the law under heaven; nothing will be given without a proper exchange. And in the meantime, how are you paying your maid?'

She looked down guiltily. 'I have not been able to pay her these last two weeks. And I cannot tell her to leave my employ, she has been ill with the sweating sickness, and besides, where would she go?'

'You must pay Martha. That is her name, is it not? As a condition of the training. The payment to me will wait, but you must not keep your maid without giving her fair recompense. What do you own?'

'Nothing. A few travelling trunks, my clothing, a few silk shawls, mementoes of home, that is all.'

'Can you sell any of it?'

'Well, I'm not sure I could . . . I mean, I don't really want to part with them . . .'

'You are mourning Mr Wilmot, are you not?' She nodded. 'So you are wearing only this dark gown. Can you wear the silk shawls for the training?' His eyes were arresting and slightly amused. She squirmed under his gaze.

'No, I suppose not.' She thought of the tawny silk with the ecru lace trim, and the French navy damask with the seed-pearl fringe, both packed with camphor to keep off the moths. All her gowns had farthingales and stiff busks. And it was true, she had been in the same sleeveless gown all week.

'Come with me.' He stood abruptly. 'Alfonso – call in the gentlemen for afternoon study. We are going out.' The apprentice bowed, picked up a bell and rattled it.

Alvarez put on his hat and led the way downstairs with Elspet following. They passed the men clattering up the stone steps, Zachary's eyes questioned her, but she ignored him. Alvarez's stride was long and loping, and yet he did not seem hurried in the slightest.

To her surprise he headed out of the yard and down the street.

Elspet jogged at his heels.

'Do you feel the need for a chaperone?' he asked over his shoulder. 'No,' she called.

After a fifteen-minute walk he led her through the Gate of Macarena and outside of the city walls. Before her was a vast sand-coloured building in the classical style. Señor Alvarez halted. '*La Sangre*,' he said. She had no trouble understanding the word – it meant blood.

Work was still going on there; the paths were unfinished, and labourers could be seen lugging barrows of masonry. She stared at its tile-covered towers rearing into the sky at each corner. Flanking the main entrance were two impressive family escutcheons and some sculptured stone figures which appeared to be Faith, Hope and Charity. The figure of Faith showed a young winged woman with a sun radiating from her chest, and a spear in her hand. She was entranced by it.

'Is this what you wanted me to see?' she said, 'It's beautiful.'

'No. Though you're right. The carving is very fine. But come, we will go inside,' he said.

She followed him into the shadowed cool of a long entrance hall, galleried with columns and colonnades. Ahead of her was the entrance to a church. So it was not a palace, after all, but a place of worship. Nobody stopped them, the long gallery was empty. A woman in a nun's habit crossed hastily from one side to the other, her sandals slapping on the tiled floor. It made Elspet think of her sister, Joan.

The nun paid Señor Alvarez no attention at all. From somewhere in the chambers beyond the columns came the sound of someone moaning as if in pain. The lofty ceilings echoed and magnified it. Down the long paved walkway they walked until a waft of frankincense tickled her nostrils.

The church. He was taking her into the church. She puzzled over what this had to do with her payment for fencing lessons. Above soared a vaulted nave and dome, and before her an alabaster altar lit by flickering candles. She made the traditional genuflection, and stood off to one side as Señor Alvarez did the same.

'Ah,' he said. Ahead of them a woman turned to see who had come in. At the sight of Señor Alvarez, her passive face split into a smile. She bustled over. A sister wearing a hempen habit in faded grey.

Elspet had thought her to be an older woman, but on closer inspection saw she was not much older than Elspet herself. The misshapen clothes gave her that appearance, and the fact that her hair was invisible under the nun's veil.

'Good to see you, Ramon.' She leaned forward and embraced Señor Alvarez on both cheeks. Elspet noticed her feet were bare. Long bony toes protruded from under her skirts.

'Sister Josefa, this is Mistress Leviston. I've come to give her a little tour.'

'Good, good. Follow me, then. Sister Paulina is admitting a few more whilst I am away. A woman just passed away, hence my prayers.' She talked as she walked. Señor Alvarez listened intently, stooping to hear her words.

They returned the way they had come and turned sharp left into a corridor from where Elspet heard more moans. As they turned into the room, the first thing that hit her was the stench and the flies. Instantly she bent to cover her mouth and nose. When she looked up again she took in the rows of trestle beds, and palliasses laid on the floor, and the curious eyes of all the occupants.

'Is this . . . a hospital?' She could barely utter the words. Señor Alvarez was already approaching the first bed where a woman in a malodorous brown garment churned in the bed.

Josefa whispered to her, 'Her fever is acute. Its progress is quick, and the symptoms violent. See these livid spots? They show a putrid state of the humours, so we call this fever malignant. She will not be with us much longer, I fear, but then she is only one of many.'

She gestured around. It was a scene from hell. Some of the women, and they were all women, were ill with the pox. Their faces were unrecognizable because of the disease. Others were wounded, and the blood was vivid red or dark brown on their bandages. Now she understood why this place was called the *Sangre*.

Why had he brought her here? She dared not breathe, for fear of catching some pestilence. She kept her mouth firmly shut. Her hands clutched her chemise at her neck.

'Without the beneficence of men like Señor Alvarez, *La Sangre* would not exist,' Josefa said, ignoring her discomfort. 'The rich men of the city give us alms to carry out our work here.'

'No.' He had overheard and called out, 'Without the sisters' charity nothing at all would be possible.'

He kept Elspet there for about a half-hour, but it passed by in a blur. She followed Sister Josefa and Señor Alvarez round the vast wards of patients. Everywhere hung the stench of blood, urine and the opium poppy, so much so that she longed for a bag of lavender to press to her nose. But she could not fail to be impressed by the sheer vigour of Sister Josefa's tireless ministrations – the bloodletting, the wiping of face and body, the ability to sit next to a woman who no longer resembled a woman, with her hair and teeth all gone, and still to smile and jest with her, pressing her hand in hers.

When they finally came out into the light of the courtyard and she looked back at the grand façade of the building, she was reeling so much she had to sit on a wall at the edge of the road. The scale of the suffering behind those walls awed her.

'She is a saint,' she managed.

Señor Alvarez passed her a flagon. 'She is. A woman becomes like her only because she wishes to be closer to God. The men of Seville respect her, and uphold her.'

'Do all the sisters at her convent do this?' She drank a draught and felt the clean liquid swill her mouth.

'No, she has no convent. She is a *beata*. She has vowed chastity and to keep herself only for God's service. She can come and go in the world as you can, but she owns nothing. She survives on alms and on God's grace.'

Elspet comprehended immediately and was humbled. Here she was, wondering whether she could bear to part with her gowns, idling in camphor in their trunks, whereas this woman had nothing – not even a pair of shoes.

'They call her the Barefoot Beata,' he said quietly, as if he had read her thoughts.

'I have understood well,' she said to him, standing up. 'It was a good lesson. I will sell my clothes and make sure Martha is paid, as she deserves to be.'

'Good.' He smiled at her, and his eyes danced with light. 'You have a fine heart, mistress,' he said, 'one that will serve like Josefa's given the right moment.'

She did not know what to say to this, but a warmth spread inside her. She looked down and saw the yellow dust under her feet, and a small green weed struggling to push its way up through the cracked ground. His presence heightened her senses somehow, as if he had woken her up from a deep sleep.

As they walked back towards the training yard side by side, she pondered about the sister, Josefa. A woman like herself, yet unencumbered by social rules or by her status as a woman. Elspet admired her, yet she was not sure she had the courage to be someone like her.

Señor Alvarez halted abruptly at the city gate and hailed a sedan. She was surprised, as she expected to walk, particularly as the sedan was expensive.

He handed the bearers some coins. 'Go now,' he said to her, 'without delay – whilst it is fresh in your mind. Go and seek out what you can sell, and pay Martha. Then you may come back to the school. If you wait, the fire will go from your action.'

'Yes, señor. And thank you.'

'It is nothing. Instruct the bearers, then. There is no time to lose.'

In the cool dark of her room she rang the bell, and Gaxa came. 'I want to sell these things,' she said, pointing at the trunks under the bed. Gaxa's eyes narrowed, but she said nothing. Can you arrange for someone to call and view?' Gaxa nodded.

'Today?'

'Don't know about today.'

'Well, just see. I'd like to do it today, if I can. I'll wait.'

Gaxa padded away on bare feet. How was it she had only just noticed them? Elspet looked down at her sandals, and pulled out her boots from under the bed and put them to one side. Her dark blue dress was almost white at the hem with dust. She untied it and stepped out of it, then shrugged out of the sleeveless embroidered doublet too, until she stood in her shift. She had mourned enough. The hospital had made her grateful for life, for the health and strength of her body.

She scraped the first travelling trunk out from under the bed and fingered the contents. She would keep these – the flannel petticoats and lawn shifts, and the yellow carsey skirt which was plain as oatmeal, with its square-necked bodice. She kept only one other serviceable gown of walnut brown, smoothing it out on to the bed. Were two gowns too many? She could not decide. She put aside all the underpinnings – the rowles and the buckram stomacher.

Then she put on the ugly carsey skirt and laced up the bodice.

She held the other gowns in her arms a long while, reluctant to part with her silks and her Norwich satins, worn and faded though they were. She ran her fingers along the fine lace trim on the front panel of her old favourite, the rose-pink that used to belong to her mother, which she had sewn for her outing to the theatre with Hugh Bradstone. How far away that life seemed now. She had thought she was heartbroken, but no, she thought, she felt no affection for Hugh any more. It had simply been her pride that was injured.

She folded the gown, marvelled at the lace that had travelled so far just to be a decoration for her vanity. Her thoughts ran to Señor Alvarez. She recognized the shiver of anticipation at the thought of him, and realized she was more than a little attracted to him. She dismissed it with a shake of the head. It was only natural to feel a degree of attraction for such a consummate swordsman. It did not mean anything.

But if she sold her gowns, then how would she look fetching when she went to the fencing school? She wanted to look attractive for Señor Alvarez, she realized. The thought made her laugh. Unless she sold her gowns, she could not go back there.

She could not rid herself of the image of the Barefoot Beata, and the palatial surroundings that masked the grim stench of the hospital. Señor Alvarez was right, she was weakening. She must strike now, whilst there was still some heat left in the iron. She stuffed the fine silks hurriedly back into the trunk and banged down the lid as if closing the lid on temptation itself.

It was not long before Gaxa returned and informed her a merchant had arrived in the lobby below, and that Martha was waiting on him. Elspet went down to greet him, and saw a short, square, pig-eyed man with what was obviously his son hanging behind him. Martha and Gaxa carried the trunk down between them and dropped it down at his feet.

She asked Martha to show him the gowns and the shoes, fearful she might change her mind. 'Is she going to buy new gowns?' Martha whispered to Gaxa, frowning, obviously thinking of her owed wages. Gaxa shook her head, indicating she did not understand.

'Perhaps,' Elspet said loudly, to show her she had heard. Martha bowed her head and bit her lip.

Martha threw out the tawny Norwich silk for the merchant's inspection. He felt the hem, turned the bodice, pulled at the trim.

'Five reales.'

The stooping boy behind him concealed a slight smile, so she knew this was a low offer.

She bargained with him until he shook his head and then, tired of it, she said, 'How much for them all?'

He dragged out her fine-tailored doublets and gowns and held them up to his nose as if to inspect their cleanliness, an act she found deeply offensive. Then he named a ridiculously low figure, but it would be enough to pay Martha's wages.

'Fine,' she said.

'Beg pardon, mistress, but are you sure?' Martha obviously thought she had lost her wits. 'You can't even buy a pair of fustian bodyes for that.'

'On second thoughts,' Elspet said, 'I will keep these.' She gathered up the rose-coloured silk bodice and tie-on sleeves, the lace trimmed overskirt, and the hooped farthingale.

'The same price, but one gown less.' Martha looked relieved.

The merchant was more reluctant, but finally, when she offered him the trunk that contained them too, he prised open his purse and counted out the money. The son watched the whole transaction with greedy eyes.

Elspet waited as they lifted up the trunk, but she could not bear to watch them lug it out of the door. When they'd gone, she called Martha, the money still in her hand. 'Your wages,' she said, holding it out on her palm.

Martha glanced at Gaxa, and then back to Elspet, her expression doubtful.

'Go on, take it,' Elspet said, 'it is only what you are owed.'

'But mistress . . .?'

Elspet thrust the money into Martha's hand and closed the maid's fingers around it.

'Thank you kindly, mistress . . .' Martha began to back away.

'And these.' Elspet scooped up the rose silk and the farthingale in one swift movement and bundled them into Martha's arms. 'They are for you. I have no need of them any more.'

Martha's pale face stared back blankly from above the heap of silk; the farthingale dangled limply from one arm.

'You admired them, didn't you?' Elspet said.

'Yes . . . yes, mistress, of course I did, but—'

'Then they're yours. They will suit your colouring very well.' She turned and walked to the door, and as she took the handle to close it, she saw Martha and Gaxa staring incredulously at each other before Martha let the gown slide out from her grasp to drop into a heap before her.

Chapter 41

Zachary stood on the balcony of the old empty house and gazed up into the night sky. A thin sickle moon like a thumbnail rested above the black rooftops. There was a smell of damp vegetation drifting from the river, which glittered with the lights of night-time craft. Downriver towards the sea there was a larger cluster of lights from the fleet gathered there. His palms were sweating, although the nights were cooler now. He hoped Luisa would come again, he had thought of nothing else all day. The silky feel of her long plait, the soft warmth of her lips. But she had said the last time that it was awkward for her to come out alone, her father worried.

The creak of the door alerted him, and he smoothed down his doublet. He was nervous, he realized. He heard the light pat of her feet on the stairs, and suddenly she was in the room.

'Papa thinks I'm with Maria,' she said breathlessly.

He held out his arms, all nervousness gone. A sweet smell of frangipani oil came from her hair. She tilted her face so he could kiss her. He wrapped his arms around her and felt the lightness of her ribcage through her thin cotton blouse; such a small cage to hold her beating heart. He felt protective of her, as if he should shield her from the world.

'You smell good,' he whispered.

She sniffed his hair, and then brushed his lips with a kiss. 'So do you, Mr Deane.'

'Luisa, you can't keep calling me Mr Deane. Not now, when we're . . . I said before, you can call me Zachary.'

'But I like it. It sounds so, so English. Zachary is hard to say. I like Mr Deane. You will always be Mr Deane to me.'

He laughed. 'But it sounds like you're my servant. And it's not even my real name. My mother was Spanish. She was called Magdalena Medina. When she came to England, she found it too cumbersome, and when we went to war with Spain she shortened it to Deane.'

She swayed back to look at him.

'It's not your father's name?'

'No.' He did not say more. She looked at him closely, and almost spoke, but then changed her mind. He squeezed her hand.

'Medina,' she said. 'I have heard my father talk of it. His family came from there. It is one of the largest cities in Araby. Perhaps your mother had some family there, too.'

'But wouldn't that be a marvellous thing, to find, after all, we are related.'

'No, it would not. Do you think I would do this with my relation?' she said indignantly, kissing him again. 'No, you are Mr Deane, the fine Englishman, and that's all I know.'

He walked her over to the balcony. He had found an old wooden chair on one of the lower floors and brought it up.

'Look, I brought you a throne, to survey your kingdom.' He sat on it and pulled her on to his knee, twined his hands round her waist.

'What a night,' she said, gazing out over the city. 'Seville looks enchanted on nights like these.'

'Is your father still intent on France?'

'Yes.' She pulled away. 'He believes every bit of gossip. He has never been the same, Mama says, since they were forced out of Granada. He thinks it will happen again here, and is making plans with Señor Alvarez to move us all again.' She sighed. 'I thought he had agreed to stay. I just want to feel the ground under my feet a little longer. And since Najid came and told us about the expulsion in Denia, Papa's even worse.'

'What's happened to your uncle? Is he still with you?'

'No, thank heaven.' She wound her hand into his. 'But he's as bad as Papa. After the shock wore off, he went crazy. He was all fired up with vengeance and now he's gone to join some other rebels in Cordoba. He'd heard a tale that some of the Morisco people from Denia never got to Oran, but were robbed by the crew and pushed overboard. Mama fears for him, he hardly knows what he is doing. But she couldn't stop him, he was like a raging bull.'

Zachary sighed. 'The rumours worry me. I keep thinking that one day I'll wake and find you gone.'

She leaned her head against his chest. 'Not you too.'

'Aren't you worried?'

'Only that I keep thinking I must be dreaming you,' she whispered.

'Does your father know we've been meeting?'

'No. I'm not sure he would understand. You are . . . well, my parents would think I do it to hurt them, on purpose. And they have enough problems. But they guess something. Mama looks at me, like she is searching for an answer.'

'Come here,' he said, turning her head to kiss her again, 'let's give her something to look for.'

'Ten o'clock already,' said Fabian.

Etienne Galen looked around. At Don Rodriguez's yard the great clock in the corner chimed its final bell, and as if on cue, Don Rodriguez appeared to join them, removing his mail gloves and casting them with a thud on to the table. Fabian poured his master a drink.

'Tired?' Don Rodriguez asked Fabian, indicating one of the other men slumped onto his forearms on the table.

'It's those leaded shoes,' Fabian said. 'My legs were light as a feather when I took them off, I felt I could jump over mountains.'

'So – I rest my case.' Rodriguez grinned and swigged from his tankard, then wiped the froth from his moustache.

'They do not use those at the school of Alvarez, I can tell you,' Etienne said.

'Yes, tell me more about what goes on there, I'm curious. Here's your purse.' Rodriguez passed Etienne a leather bag rattling with silver.

'Thank you, sir. Like I say, it is no match for your training. They have not much equipment, little armour. The men read geometry and philosophy. Their minds, well, they may be learned, but their bodies – they are weak.'

'But what do they do?'

'There are not enough men to make proper formation, so they drill on what Alvarez calls the swordsman's seal – the circle and cross. But he has all foreign students, none from Spain. Oh, except one. And a woman is there too.'

Rodriguez paused, his pewter tankard halfway to his mouth. He put the tankard down. 'Alvarez must really be on hard times if he has sunk to training a woman. Are you sure? Carranza would never have agreed to that.'

'Yes, a woman is there every day. An Englishwoman, cousin of a student. Pretty.'

'The Frenchman only has eyes for a pretty face,' Fabian said.

'Can she fight?'

'*Pas un seul petit morceau*,' Etienne said, shaking his head and laughing. 'What do you think!'

Rodriguez snorted. 'So you don't think Alvarez will be an obstacle for what we have to do?'

'No, sir. They are too few, and they have no discipline, and no focus. I am sure they are not in training for anything, except perhaps a duel or two. But Alvarez, he is something.' Etienne let out a low whistling breath. 'That man moves like water, impossible to scratch him.'

Don Rodriguez frowned. 'To the untrained eye he has a modicum of skill, perhaps.'

Etienne swallowed, realizing he had made a gaffe.

'But his are false methods,' said Rodriguez. 'The real *Destreza* is with Pacheco, and through him to me. There are two aspects to a fighting art; the fighting and the art. Here we concentrate on the meat of it, the fighting, but Alvarez,' he sneered, 'he concentrates only on the art.' He stood up. 'A rumour reached my ears that Alvarez took in some Moriscos from the barrio near the leather beaters, this is why I ask whether he will be an obstruction to our cause.'

'It's true. He hides the family of the mathematician, Nicolao Ortega,' Etienne said.

'Then it would be better to be certain his men will cause us no trouble. Foreign students, you say? Well, perhaps we can persuade Alvarez's students to go back home. Besides, we do not need two fencing schools in Seville.'

'Surely we can just close the school down, if it is a threat to the expulsion?' Fabian said, leaning in over the planked table.

'No, not yet. There are no legal grounds until the proclamation for Seville is made. Harbouring these Morisco rebels and foreigners is not an offence unless they are proved to be rejecting the faith. At least it is not an offence yet. But that will change once the order is given for their expulsion. Then we will act quickly to disarm them. Until that time, we will have to be more circumspect, disrupt their training, make sure they cannot be organized enough to offer resistance. Etienne, can you get us into the school at night?'

'Certainly I can. Alvarez puts a bar on the front gate to the street, but the back, no one takes much notice of that. Two bolts only. The yard is left wholly unguarded. Why, what were you thinking, sir?'

'Best you don't know. That way you will not be tempted to let anything slip.' Etienne was about to protest, but Don Rodriguez waved him away with a gesture. 'I know you think you would not, but I know Frenchmen and their big mouths.' He cast a few more coins on to the table, which glinted in the light from the torches as if they were red-hot. 'An extra five reales for you if you leave the bolts open, understood?'

Etienne scraped the discs from the table and they chinked as he added them to his bulging purse.

Chapter 42

The day after her visit to *La Sangre*, Elspet was back in the yard at the training, wearing the carsey gown. By this she hoped to signal to Señor Alvarez that she had followed his wishes. He was right; selling her things had felt like making a commitment, and now she was dedicated to the art of *La Destreza* just as much as the others.

The men looked and nudged each other, sensing something different about her when she arrived, but their faces were kind. She had tied her hair away from her face, like the Barefoot Beata, Josefa. She attracted no attention now on her way to the fencing school as people assumed her to be a nun or a *beata* in her homespun and sandals. She soon discovered the new clothing was much less of a hindrance and enabled her much more freedom of movement.

For the next few weeks, as the weather had grown colder and wetter, they continued to study the books of Agrippa, Plato and the masters of geometry. They copied Dürer's diagrams and stepped through their measures on the painted circle and cross in the upstairs chamber under Señor Alvarez's watchful eye. The circle was fading a little under their scuffing feet, the letters and lines worn faint through use.

She always enjoyed partnering Alexander and Girard, and the stocky Pedro Gutierrez. She avoided Etienne if possible, for he kept seeking out her eye, and was forever making an excuse to stop and hold her too closely by the arm to show her a technique.

Zachary seemed softer, less angry somehow, though there was still tension in her relationship with him. We are unhappy bedfellows, she thought. But she was beginning to understand him a little. Like him, she relished the feeling of learning this skill, of feeling her whole body move behind the sword. The early mornings were for drills and repetitive exercises of thrust and parry, pierce and feint. And in the evenings they studied the elements. They had moved on from fire and air now, and were working with water.

She had hoped the training might become easier or gentler, but no. She had to train to flow round an obstacle like water, and it was a skill she struggled to master. Her evasions were stilted or jagged. She could not find the correct footwork. If her sword arm was in the right position, then her feet were making the wrong move. Señor Alvarez showed them again and again, his movements fluid as honey.

They were working with sharps now, and the training yard had become a serious place. She saw Luisa walk close up to the wall to get safely to the front gate, and already Alexander had a nick to his thigh and a blood-spotted bandage tied around it. Today she was partnered with Zachary. They had only made a few lunges up and down the yard when Zachary suddenly cried out, 'My fault!' He dropped his sword on to the ground and rushed towards her. For a moment she was unsure what was happening, but then she put her left hand up to her cheek. When her hand came away it was smeared red with blood.

Everything seemed to be happening at once. The men gathered around, and Alexander thrust a kerchief towards her. Zachary was leading her to the bench, apologizing all the while. 'Press it hard on the wound,' called Pedro from behind the throng.

She had not even felt the cut, but now the thought of it made her legs weak.

'What's this?' cried Señor Alvarez from behind. The men moved aside to let him through.

'It's my fault, I wasn't quick enough,' Elspet said, ruefully.

'Let me see.'

She lifted away the kerchief which was blotched with blood, and tilted her face up to him.

'It's deep,' he said. 'It will leave a scar. Who were you working with?'

'Me,' said Zachary.

'What were you doing? Have you no sense to keep your blade away from a woman's face?' Señor Alvarez said.

'I'm sorry,' said Zachary, 'I lost concentration, and it moved off target.'

'Here,' Alvarez pressed the kerchief back to her cheek, and covered her hand with his. 'Someone fetch Señora Ortega. Quickly now.'

Elspet was aware of the touch of the señor's warm dry hand, and his solicitous concern. She hoped he could not see how her heart was beating.

'Don't fret,' Elspet said to him, taking back the kerchief herself. 'I've said, it was not Zachary's fault, none but my own lack of skill. It's to be expected, if you train with blades. And I don't want different rules from the men.'

'That is admirable, but it does not excuse Mr Deane. He should not aim for a lady's face. Not in training.'

Zachary came running back then with Ayamena, who pushed the señor to one side. 'It is not so bad,' she pronounced. 'Just a flesh wound. Now leave me to dress it.'

The men drifted back to their drills, all except the señor, who loomed over Elspet as Ayamena did her work. Señor Alvarez took Elspet's hand as Ayamena put four stitches into the wound, and she clung on, as now the piercing pain of the needle made her want to twitch and move away. 'Try not to smile or move your face,' Ayamena said.

'Close your eyes and hold tight; it will help,' said the señor. She found she was more aware of gripping the señor's hand than she was of the pain.

When she opened her eyes afterwards it was to see his dark eyes looking straight into hers. 'Are you all right?' His tone of voice was so tender, tears started in her eyes and she could not answer him, but a look ran between them, swift and bright as quicksilver.

'Still now!' snapped Ayamena. 'I need to dress it. Señor, move out of the way, so I can put my bowl on the bench.'

His hand slipped from hers and she had the urge to pull it back.

'I think, rest today,' he said quietly, still hovering nearby. 'I will plan some observation work for this afternoon. Or do you need to lie down? You may use my quarters if—'

'No, no,' she said, ashamed of the thought that had arisen, of how much she would like to see where he slept. 'I would like to join the men. Alexander just carried on again when he was cut. I shall do the same.'

'I admire your determination, Mistress Leviston. But I beg you, stay here in the shade a while. And take some liquor, for the shock.'

'I'll look to her,' Ayamena said firmly. 'You can away now, to your men.'

Señor Alvarez hesitated a moment, shuffling from foot to foot, but Ayamena fixed him with a frown, and he walked away towards the other side of the yard where the men had gathered in a small knot. Within a few minutes they were back to their drills, and he was back to his usual decisive manner.

'What are you putting on it?' Elspet asked Ayamena when he had gone, screwing up her eyes as Ayamena dabbed at the wound with her fingers.

'Plantago, polygonato, aloe vera, so many. Allah is merciful. All good herbs for cuts and swelling. Though I think now I should need some medicine for wounds of the heart, heh?'

Elspet said nothing, but Ayamena shook her head at her, raising her eyebrows in question. They exchanged a smile.

Later that afternoon as they walked down the path to the river, Zachary stopped her by a hand on the arm. 'Elspet,' he said, 'Does it hurt much?'

'No. Ayamena has dressed it and it feels a little tight, that is all.'

'It does not look too bad. I expect there will be a scar, and for that I apologize. Scars are different for women, I know. We men do not set such store by our appearance.'

'You could have fooled me. You always seem to sport the latest fashion in doublets and hose.'

'*Touché!*' He laughed.

They hurried along the edge of the water to catch up with the rest. Señor Alvarez set them to observe the currents, and how the ships floated on them. They sat on a rocky headland just outside the city walls, watching the wide snake of river on its way to the sea. Elspet found herself contemplating the way Señor Alvarez's white hair curled from beneath his hat rather than observing the water as she had been instructed.

Señor Alvarez turned to look over his shoulder at her, and she was flustered by his gaze so she turned to look towards the city where a group of colourful Morisco women slapped their laundry against a rock. Something caught her eye on the horizon and she held her hand over her eyes to shield them from the setting sun.

'What are all those ships doing, gathering out there just beyond the point?' she asked.

'I don't know,' Girard said. 'Perhaps they are awaiting a delivery of oil or of grain.'

'But we don't export anything much these days,' said Pedro.

'Silk,' said Girard, 'You export silk.'

'Never mind the ships, watch the water,' Señor Alvarez said, but she saw he himself had his eyes trained downriver on the flotilla moored further downstream. Something in his watchful demeanour gave her a sense of foreboding. She followed his direction, trying to bring the darkening blur of masts into focus. He was motionless, his hand halfway to his face in a gesture he had not finished making. She averted her gaze, blinked, and tried to return her eyes to the water, but the feeling of unease persisted. She shivered; Dusk had brought a sudden drop in temperature, and for the first time in Spain she was cold.

They watched the river for a good while, though the surface of the water reflected the fading sun, and she could not fathom what lay beneath. It was quiet here away from the city, and she should have been relaxed. But her cheek stung and throbbed now, and her head ached from the effort of concentration.

Even as she watched, the current carried a lump of wood spinning and twirling, heading with the current towards the sea before it was sucked under water by a hidden drag. More ships had heeled into view now, and Señor Alvarez studied the nearest one intently as it slid into position with the others. A galleon, like a slave galley. The mass of ships were still, almost like a picture on a tapestry.

'Time to leave.' Señor Alvarez set off abruptly towards the town. He did not even look at her as he passed. She felt unaccountably hurt, but gathered her sword belt and arms quickly with the rest who trailed in his wake.

'Perhaps it is the fleet waiting to bring in gold from the Indies,' Girard said.

'No, that cannot be true,' Alexander argued, 'they would sail right in, not lurk out there, out of sight of the harbour.'

'But they're not enemy ships, are they?' Zachary said, 'Some have the Spanish colours flying.'

'Who cares?' Etienne slapped Zachary on the shoulders and jostled him away. 'I tell you, it's just a fishing fleet.'

It took a few days for the wound on her cheek to feel more comfortable, but as Ayamena had divined, Elspet's feelings for the señor seemed to have grown, to the point where she was jumpy as a hare. He was in her thoughts all the time, and no matter where she was she felt his presence as a yearning she could not shake away.

Over the next few weeks the rain made the yard slippery so they trained more indoors. Martha had become awkward. She refused to sit and watch the training any more, and Elspet could not force her, there was nothing for it but to leave her at home.

Late one evening after training was done for the day, it was time to redraw the circle. The previous night they had repainted the floor with lime and size and now the room was lit by tall-standing candelabra at each corner. The breeze made the light sway a little, giving an underwater feel to the whole room.

Girard seemed to think it his prerogative as an artist to be in control of the procedure, and his bluff voice issued the instructions.

'Come on, fellows. I have to leave for Antwerp soon so I want to leave a little drawing behind. Something for you all to remember me by, eh?'

'It won't be the same without you. Someone will be lacking a partner,' Zachary said.

'I was never intending to stay at all. But that's the señor – he hooks you somehow. Anyway, maybe he can persuade another woman. Maybe Ayamena would like to try?'

They all laughed at the thought of the stout Ayamena with a sword and buckler. Elspet laughed with them, happy to have gained some sort of acceptance.

'Now,' said Girard, 'pass me that tape.'

Elspet meanwhile had a pouch of charcoal dust slung on her belt, and fed a string into it to coat it with the powder.

Alexander and Zachary pulled the string taut between them and snapped the string down on to the floor to make the mark. The charcoaled string produced a long cloud of black dust, which made Alexander cough and laugh, but a perfect straight line.

'Look at that!' he said proudly.

They continued to mark all the mid-points of the square and then join them with snap-lines into the circle and the cross, what Señor Alvarez called 'the swordsman's seal'. Elspet stood in the centre to hold the nail as Girard walked the circle with the stretched string and stick of charcoal.

'Keep it taut,' said Zachary when the line sagged.

Elspet watched as Alexander labelled the lines on the diagram with the basic Latin inscriptions, *diameter perpendicularis, transversa interioris, linea pedalis.*

'Mistress Leviston, fetch the gall, would you, from the kitchen,' Girard said.

She carried a single candle with her. A sudden clatter, and the impression of a moving shadow. Someone was in the kitchen and had knocked a pot to the ground.

Her voice rang out sharp into the dark. 'Who goes there?'

She held her candle aloft and it fluttered in the breeze from the open door. She ran to the opening, shielding the flame with her palm, but could see nobody. The yard was empty.

'Zachary?' she called, thinking this was some kind of practical joke.

No answer.

She shivered, and swung her candle round the room, but the table was scrubbed clean, everything neatly stacked as Ayamena always left it. Perhaps it was a rat, or one of the cats.

The pot of gall was where they said it would be, on the shelf next to the door. On the ground lay a fallen pot, cracked into two pieces. She picked it up and put it on the kitchen table.

Someone must have left the door open, and it was blowing in the wind, that was all. She shut and bolted it before taking the paint pot and climbing back up to the upstairs chamber. There, the men propped themselves up against the wall, conversing in low voices, sharing a flagon of ale.

She did not mention the broken pot, but thought she must tell Ayamena in the morning. The men put down their flagon and they set to work, inking the outline. It was painstaking work, using a wooden straight-edge, a hog's bristle brush and a steady hand. Their shadows continually got in the way of the candles which were burning low.

'Ah.' A voice from the doorway.

The brush jerked in her hand as she started and looked around. It was Señor Alvarez. How did he know, she wondered, that they had nearly finished?

She raised her brows to Alexander and he smiled and nodded, as if to say, I told you so.

'Don't let me disturb you, mistress,' Señor Alvarez said. 'Finish your last few letters.'

She knelt back down, embarrassed, dragging her skirts to the side. She picked a stray hair from the edge of the brush, and concentrated where the 'L' had gone awry to try to neaten the edge.

'Very fine. Put the brushes down now, and bring more candles,' Señor Alvarez said, when she was finished.

They replaced the guttering stubs and stared down at the newly repainted diagram with pride.

'Neatly done,' he said. 'And while it is fresh in your mind, we'll do a little exercise.'

They put down their things and waited expectantly.

'Imagine,' he said, 'that the lines are light. Take your time to construct it upright in front of you. The circle and the square. Every line. Make it bright.'

Elspet swayed slightly as she tried to draw the image inside herself. The room sounded like the sea, full of their breathing. She was intent on the señor's voice, she felt as if her whole body buzzed with it. The glow of the swordsman's seal took shape behind her eyes.

'Now, bring it inside yourself. Bring the centre to your heart and down to your navel, the circumference to the top of your head and the edge running under your feet.'

At his words it entered her like a fire.

He snapped his fingers and she blinked, as if suddenly brought back from a long dream. Around her the men looked dazed.

'Dawn tomorrow, as usual,' the señor said, and Elspet put her hands to her hot cheeks, took up her cape and stumbled away into the dark.

Zachary looked up at the stars peppering the sky, the formation of the cross of Cygnus in the vast black above reminding him somehow of the design he had just painted.

'Better get a good night's rest,' Etienne said. 'We'll be put through it again tomorrow.' He peered back through the gate.

'Come on, then,' said Girard, slapping Etienne on the back, 'What are you hanging about for?'

'Just checking the señor is coming to bar the gate.' He dragged it closed behind him.

Outside the gate, they heard the scrape and clunk of the bar before parting to go their separate ways, except for Alexander and Zachary, who were walking the same route home. They waved to Girard, Pedro and Etienne as they crossed the road to go in the other direction. Zachary was about halfway down the street when he realized he had left his bag behind.

'Hey, Alexander, I've left something. I'll have to go back for it.'

'Can't it wait until tomorrow? We'll be back there in a few hours.'

'It's got my whetstone and peening iron, and my leather polishing cloth in it. I'll need them to grind my sword-edge ready for tomorrow.'

'Can't you do it in the morning?'

'I'll only be a few minutes. Just hang fire whilst I nip back for it.'

Alexander sighed, and leaned himself up against the wall with a resigned expression. Zachary dumped his arms case at his feet, and sprinted back up the street. He was going to knock at the back gate and hope the señor would let him in, but as he pushed he realized it was open, Alvarez couldn't have locked it yet. He loped up the stairs in the yard two at a time. The Ortega's quarters were in darkness, and he hoped Ayamena and Nicolao were fast asleep. It was then he saw a light from the training hall. A light passing the window and briefly shining into the yard. The señor must still be in there.

He hesitated, wondering whether to disturb him. But then there were more noises, sounds like paper tearing, the thud of something being dropped, and low muffled voices, people talking. He crept up to the door and peeped through the crack. There were men in the room, but none of them Señor Alvarez, he would recognize his rangy form anywhere. It was dark, though, and there was only one lantern lit and he could just make out legs and boots silhouetted by the whiteness of the painted floor.

At first he could not grasp what was going on, a pool of black reached like a black glove across the white paint. One of the men scuffed his boot in it, dragging it all over the floor. Someone stifled a laugh.

'Oy!' Zachary shouted, thrusting open the door.

The men turned. All of them had bandanas tied round their faces and their eyes were shadowed by their broad-brimmed hats. One of them dangled the pot of gall upside down. Liquid dribbled out on to his boot, but he flung the pot insolently down on to the floor where it span in a spatter of ink and then rolled slowly away.

'It's all right. He's on his own.'

The words spurred Zachary into action. His sword flew out of its scabbard like lightning. It disconcerted the biggest man who stepped back out of range.

'It's that Englishman,' he said, 'the one we pissed on.'

'Bastards!' he yelled. He shouted over his shoulder, 'Señor Alvarez! Quick!'

Zachary wielded his rapier just inside the doorway, so none of the intruders could pass, but still Alvarez did not come. Where was he? Zachary would be no match for three of Rodriguez's men. He drew his blade side to side, threatening, to keep them at a distance, but one blundered at him, his cloak flapping. The tip of his sword shot out towards Zachary's face.

Breathless, Zachary stepped to the side and his attacker's thrust met empty air – enough to unbalance him. He toppled past, his hat bowling away into the corner of the yard. A second man cannoned at him with his metal buckler as Zachary turned to watch him fall. The force of the buckler thudding into his solar plexus sent Zachary flying down the stairs after him.

His head cracked against the stone step but he leapt up, too afire to heed it. Besides, the boots of the third man were running down the steps towards him, and he knew he was in trouble. Zachary backed off, his sword at arm's length. He was panting. All his swordplay lessons streamed through his head in a succession of images – angles, techniques, footwork, the criss-cross of lines of the swordsman's seal, but none of them stuck. Fear gripped his heart as he was corralled to the wall by all three men.

'Finish him,' growled the biggest man.

A man with a dark bandana, who smelt of sweat, moved in before him. Zachary read the intent behind his eyes and saw that his opponent was a much heavier man than he. The fear rose up in him and the world began to move very slowly. The man curled his arm from the shoulder and raised it up, the tip of the sword struck a light from the rising moon. He smelt the stench of the man's armpit as he leaned away before putting his weight and both hands behind the blade. Zachary heard himself gasp.

A sound, the clash of metal on metal. His attacker's sword whirled out of his hand and skittered across the yard. The man's eyes registered complete astonishment over his bandana.

Señor Alvarez had appeared from the darkness, his sword pressed to the man's throat, his shock of white hair bright in the dark. The third man was flat on his back in the dirt, his sword lying useless on the ground.

One of them yelled and made a run for the back gates, clutching a wrist dripping blood. The man on the ground leapt up and fled after his friends.

'Stop them!' shouted Señor Alvarez, but Zachary was too late. He could barely see. His head throbbed and the gates were a blur as he stumbled through the door after them. They ran out into the dark, but although he could hear their running boots, the men had soon disappeared into the shadows beyond.

'Leave them be,' Señor Alvarez said, sheathing his sword.

Just then Alexander arrived. 'Hey! I was coming to find you. Some men just ran out of here. They nearly knocked me down.

What's going on?'

'Just thugs . . . They've been in the hall. The seal – they've ruined it.' Zachary said.

'No – you jest.'

'Would that he did,' Señor Alvarez sighed. 'They've made a proper mess. We'll get a better idea of the damage in the morning. Did you see who they were?'

'No, they pelted past with their cloaks flapping, and nearly knocked me down. I thought they might be opportunists, thieves.'

'Zachary, did you recognize anyone?'

'No. Of course not.' He was on the defensive straight away, but then realized that Señor Alvarez knew nothing of his history, and tempered it; 'I've never seen any of them before. I just came back for my bag. Alexander will tell you. But look, one of them's left his weapon behind.' He retrieved it from the ground and held it up before him.

Alvarez handled it. 'It's as I thought. Don Rodriguez's men. Of course I cannot be certain, but they train with heavy two-hand swords like these.'

'But why?' Alexander asked. 'Why would they want to do this?'

'Who knows?' said Señor Alvarez. 'Perhaps Don Rodriguez perceives me as a threat. Though I don't understand why – he has many more students than I do, after all.'

'It is because you are the better swordsman and he cannot bear it, that someone is better than he is.' Alexander spoke with passion. 'And he knows Carranza favoured you more than he did him.'

'Is that so?' said Señor Alvarez. 'And how would you know that? Were you there?'

'No.' Alexander was sheepish. 'But everyone says so.'

Alvarez sighed. 'Remember your training, never just accept what people say. Test it for yourself.'

Alexander looked chastened, and Zachary tried to catch his eye in sympathy. 'Now,' Señor Alvarez said, 'get on home to your beds. Zachary, go and get some attention for your head.' He paused. 'You know, I can't understand it, I could have sworn I'd bolted that door. Still, what's done is done. It's too dark to see much now, we'll deal with it in the morning.'

They heard the bolts shunt behind them as they stepped outside. Zachary paused there; the back of his head throbbed and his backside and hip were stiff from his tumble down the steps. It was as if there was gunpowder running in his veins. He wondered if the intruders came because of him, because they had heard he was still in Seville.

'Are you all right?' Alexander asked.

'Bastards,' he said. 'Do you think we should go after them?'

Alexander gave him a look that plainly said he had no intention of doing any such thing. 'Come on.' Alexander set off, and he had to half-run to keep up. He was striding towards the town.

'Wait,' Zachary said shouldering his bag. 'I don't want to go home yet, I need to walk a while. I'll see you tomorrow.'

'Shall I walk with you?'

'No, I'd rather go on my own.' He could not tell Alexander he'd promised to meet Luisa again at the old house, and she would already be waiting. 'Sorry, my friend, but I'll just take a brief stroll. I'm too tired to talk.'

'Well, if you go out past the city gates, make sure you're armed.' Zachary patted his sword hanger.

'See you tomorrow, then.' Alexander strode off towards the bridge.

Chapter 43

When Elspet arrived at her lodgings after marking up the seal, Gaxa was waiting for her in the hall.

'Martha's gone,' she said, looking her up and down disdainfully with her large eyes. Elspet saw how her attention stuck on her cheek where the scar made a long dark line.

'Gone where?'

'Back to England. She say to tell you.'

'What? What did she say? Where is she? How can she have gone back to England?'

Gaxa planted her bare feet more firmly apart. 'She sold them fancy clothes, to pay for her passage. She can't stand no more of Spain, she say. She missed home so bad. A carrier took her to the port. She took Arif from the kitchen to be her serving boy. She say to tell you, sorry.'

The thought flashed through her mind that she had given Martha the gown because she coveted it so much. She should have been grateful, not thrown her gift back in her face.

Gaxa's eyes gave her a sideways look, and she went on, 'She say it's not right, it looks like you the maid now, and she the mistress.'

'What do you mean?'

'You don't act like a lady. She only want to work for a lady, she say.'

She was not sure now if it was Gaxa talking, or Martha. 'Did she say that?'

Gaxa pressed her mouth together in a stubborn line.

'Did she say that I wasn't a lady?' She put her hand on to Gaxa's shoulder but Gaxa flinched and backed away.

Elspet pushed past her and went into Martha's room. Empty. Nothing on the hooks in the closet, no dusty shoes standing under the bed. The wicker shopping basket was gone from its usual place behind the door. She had even taken the candle stub from the candlestick on the chair by the bed.

Gaxa had followed and was standing by the door.

'Gaxa, just tell me when she went.'

'Soon as you left at sun up. She's long gone now. The sailing was noon – I asked yesternight at the harbour front.'

Elspet sighed in frustration. And she was hurt that Gaxa had been a part of this whole plan, conspiring with Martha to ask the sailing times. She thought they had become friends after that night when she helped her fetch Ayamena. But she could see that perhaps a maid and a slave might have more allegiance to each other than they would to her. And now Martha even had a serving boy.

There was nothing more to be done. Martha was gone, and no amount of complaining would bring her back.

'Where was she going in England?' she asked, fearful in case she was going home to her closed-up house in London.

'Her mother's place.'

'All right, Gaxa,' Elspet said, in a tone that reasserted her authority. 'You may go.'

Gaxa's expression showed she knew it to be an order, and was glad.

That night Elspet slept alone in the huge apartment. She remembered Martha's sickness on the ship from England and imagined her now, keeling over the side, seeing the ocean flash past in the darkness with the smell of brine catching the back of her throat. And she remembered Mr Wilmot's wife, Dorothy, standing on the quay to wish them well, the ribbons of her bonnet blowing round her face, and the way she had stood on her toes to kiss her husband's cheek as he left.

Tears formed in her eyes but she held them at bay. Señor Alvarez set great store by the power of determination and steady thinking, and she would heed his training. Weeping would do no good. What she needed now was strength and willpower.

When she left the house it was early, the sun barely a tinge of pink behind the façades of the buildings and the crenellated city walls. But she woke with the chill of the dawn and could not stay abed a moment longer. It was as if the fencing school was the centre of her world now.

She wanted to get there before the men, to practise some feints that Señor Alvarez had shown her on the new diagram in the upstairs room. It was better to try them alone – far too embarrassing to attempt them in front of the men. So she did not even wake Gaxa, but washed hurriedly in the Sevillian soap she was so fond of and, shivering, dressed herself.

Her step was springy as she bounced down the Calle San Pablo towards the bridge. The aroma of yeast drifted by, as the Morisco bakers began to open their shutters behind her, she noticed the clink of hammer on the cobbler's iron last as she passed by his shop.

At the yard she pushed on the gate, but it rattled against the bar. Someone must have heard her for a few moments later it swung open and Ayamena was there.

'Ey, ey!' she said, in surprise, from behind her manto. 'Here already?'

'It's a lovely morning,' Elspet said. 'Look, no rain!' She told her about how Martha had gone home to England, for she knew she would ask after her, she always did. It was the only thing they had to bind them together.

Ayamena dipped her head and shook it slowly back and forth. 'You will miss her,' she said.

Elspet swallowed, looked at her shyly and admitted that she would. 'It was nice sometimes,' she said, 'to talk in English.'

'Yes. The mother tongue. Is important.'

'You miss your own language? Do you have a chance to speak it much?'

Ayamena's expression suddenly became wary. 'Excuse me, mistress,' she said, 'I have something cooking.' And she hurried away. Elspet could smell nothing cooking though, and no smoke came from the oven chimney.

She could not wait to go and admire her handiwork from the night before, so she hoisted her skirts and hurried up the stone steps to the training chamber for a quick peep. The door was already ajar, perhaps Señor Alvarez would be there.

At first she could not take it in, the black pool of ink, a red spatter that could be blood, the prints of men's muddy boots. Shreds of torn and crumpled paper lifting slightly in the breeze. She stared, one hand clamped over her mouth.

The door to the library was open. She skirted round the edge of the room, avoiding the mess, hardly daring to look in.

A whirlwind might have been there in the night. Books were littered everywhere, divorced from their covers, the pages tossed about the room. The leather bindings gutted from their pages, the leaves ripped apart. One of the volumes of Agrippa lay on the ground, its pages blurred with wet. It was only then she smelt the stink of piss. She bolted from the room.

'Señor Alvarez!' she cried, beside herself. 'Señor Alvarez!'

He appeared in the yard in a moment, pulling on his doublet, and mounting the steps. 'Yes, yes,' he called, as he came, 'I know. It was last night. Someone came in the dark and did this.' He must have seen her horrified face, for he gestured at the floor. 'It is only a bit of paint. It can be done again.'

'Again?' she was aghast. 'What's happened to it? Who did this? And the library?'

His face fell. He passed his hand over his brow wearily. 'The library too? I haven't been in the library.'

She nodded. He groaned, and walked with her to the door. He stood at the door and she saw him press his lips together. 'We must see what we can salvage.'

'But who did this?'

'Someone who bears us a grudge, by the look of it,' he said, moving away.

How could he be so calm? 'It's ruined. When we left it was exact, just like Agrippa's diagram. You saw it.' She was speechless a moment with anger. 'The Agrippa, it's on the floor . . . I can't believe anyone would do this. And Martha's gone.' Her voice threatened tears.

'Sit down a moment,' Alvarez said. He took her by the arm but before she could reach the chair she was holding tight to him, and his arms closed around her in an embrace. They were still for a long moment. She felt his hand pressing her to his chest, heard the thud of his heart. Finally, he moved away to look down at her, holding her by the arms.

'Things change.' He swallowed, as if to take control of his voice. 'The perfect seal is inside you now, is it not? The essence of what it is?' He spoke urgently. 'Think now. The four elements, and a fifth, the quintessence.'

She could not answer him, for her mind was racing, blood beat at her temples. She took a deep breath.

'Try to understand me,' he said. 'What matters is that the knowledge is inside you. No one can take that away. It is more real than any painted glyph. You have made it real yourself by your own work.'

He was looking at her with that peculiarly intense stare that he had. She nodded. It calmed her. He was right, last night they had absorbed something, as if the circle and the cross had been burnt somehow into their bones. She searched inside herself for the sensation of the pattern, and surprisingly, felt it hum there, like a vibration, subtle but insistent.

He moved away further until her hands lingered in his. 'Understand me, the training comes first. Before everything else.' She felt the cool air as his fingertips slid away.

She swallowed. It was a rebuff, and she felt its keen edge.

He gathered up a few papers and looked at them as if unsure what to do with them. Eventually he said, 'Perhaps my students do not really need the training floor. We will clean up, and put things in order. But it could be that this is timely. We do not need the diagram as much as we might suppose. Perhaps you do not need a maid. We will try today without, heh?'

She looked up at him. His eyes locked with hers. Heat spread up her chest to her neck. He was about to speak, but then seemed to think better of it. Instead, he signalled her to the door. She followed him out. As he went he banged his shoulder into the door frame, and let out a muffled curse.

Zachary looked over to the kitchen door to catch sight of Luisa. Last night she had brought blankets and cushions and they had spent long, wakeful hours in each other's arms. He could not tear the vision of her nakedness from his mind. She had been concerned at his cut head, but her tender solicitations had led to more than he dared hope for. Now he was in an agony of expectation, looking for her to appear.

But Etienne, Girard and Pedro demanded to hear his story once they had set eyes on the seal. Zachary described his assailants, parted his oiled hair to show where he had hit his head, and praised Señor Alvarez's swordsmanship in routing the three men. The little group were subdued, it gathered them all together against this common enemy. They sat on the steps, eyeing the weak morning sun and the scudding clouds, before buckling on their sword belts and taking off their sleeves.

'Don't you think it odd that the señor asked us to take the pattern into ourselves, and now this?' Alexander said. 'He knew, don't you think, that something like this would happen?'

'How?' Zachary asked. 'He can't have known those men would come here and do that.'

Etienne said, 'You're not suggesting someone let them in?'

'No, of course not. Just that he knows things – I think sometimes he has powers that we do not have – that somehow he knew something like this would happen.'

'Pah,' Etienne said, rolling his eyes.

'You think he can tell the future? Like M'sieur Nostradame?' Zachary was amused.

'No, maybe not that, exactly.' Alexander backed down, uncomfortable. 'But don't you think it's odd?'

'It's all part of the training, that idea of putting the symbol into memory,' Girard said.

Etienne spat into the dirt and wiped his lips. 'A coincidence, c'est tout.'

'Perhaps Alexander is right, I was reading the Agrippa. He has the opinion that everything is linked together in a chain of causal effect,' Elspet said, venturing an opinion for the first time.

Alexander caught her eye and smiled, but Zachary said, 'As far as I can see, if Señor Alvarez knew it was going to happen he should have locked the gate.'

Etienne protested, 'It was locked when I left, I heard him do it, bolted from the inside.'

'Then I think someone must have been inside the yard already, maybe hiding in the kitchen to let the others in,' Elspet said. She told them about the noise in the kitchen and the broken jar.

'Why the hell did you not say anything?' Zachary spluttered. 'We could have stopped them. Those three thugs nearly killed me. If it hadn't have been for Alvarez, I would have been nailed to the ground by now with a rapier through the chest.'

She tried to explain but he shook his head in derision. 'So much for being alert and watchful,' he muttered. Then he leaned in towards the others, conspiratorially. 'But I'll tell you this: last night I passed by Don Rodriguez's sword school.'

'What?' Etienne said.

'You blazing fool. You went there after we left?' Alexander was incredulous. But then his curiosity got the better of him. 'Did you find out anything?'

'No. Not a sign of those men. Maybe they weren't from there after all. But there's something going on. A whole army seems to be training there. In the middle of the night.'

'How so?' Girard asked.

'There's a long tent set up in the yard – alongside, like a barracks. I sneaked round the side and looked through a gap in the wall. There are piles of muskets and shot, and soldiers that looked like they were drafted in from all over Spain. They were parading and drilling in the yard in full plate armour.'

'But Rodriguez's men – they are swordsmen, not musketeers, are they not?' asked Alexander.

'No. You must have made a mistake. Spain is not at war. Unless the English plan once more an attack,' Etienne said pointedly, looking at Zachary.

'Hey! Don't go blaming the English. Anyway, they'd come from the sea. This looked like a land force – foot soldiers, musketeers, pikes.'

'Sounds like Don Rodriguez planning a rebellion to me.' Girard shook his head.

Etienne flapped his hand dismissively. 'What for? Who he rebel against? I think Zachary makes a mistake. Rodriguez always has many men training. It signify nothing.'

'I'm telling you all, this was no ordinary training. And then I walked over to the bend in the river. There are more ships gathered there now. There are sixty or more gathered on the Guadalquivir. Slave ships and mercantiles, and a host of other smaller craft.'

'See, I tell you,' Etienne said. 'The English, they send a fleet.'

'It's not the English,' Zachary said. 'I can tell. These aren't war ships – that's what I'm telling you. They look like trading craft. It's sinister, them all waiting out there like that.' 'Have you told anyone?' Elspet asked.

'Told anyone what?' asked Señor Alvarez appearing from the house.

They all looked to Zachary to see if he was going to say anything.

'Nothing.' He clammed up, and his face flushed bright red.

Señor Alvarez gave him an irritated look. 'Idle talk wastes time and energy. Go arm yourselves.'

Elspet hitched up her skirts and tucked them into her apron. Zachary was already heading towards the pile of swords and bucklers.

'No,' Señor Alvarez shouted, 'not with those,' and he pointed to the corner of the yard where a motley collection of besoms and pails had been gathered. 'The upstairs training hall – I want it spotless.' They smiled regretfully to each other and got to work.

Zachary and Elspet worked in the library side by side. They washed the floor as best they could, wringing out the cloths in the bucket. What would Father have said to see them both scrubbing in the stench like servants? When she looked out of the window she saw Alexander and Pedro rinsing pages from the books in the trough and weighting them down with stones to dry in the breeze.

Zachary seemed not to notice her, his eyes were far away, as if he only had half his attention on what he was doing. This was unusual, for it was often Girard the draughtsman, not Zachary, who daydreamed out of the window.

Zachary suddenly sat back on his haunches. 'Why do you stay?' he asked her in a low voice. 'It has been many weeks now.'

For the first time she saw it was a genuine question.

She answered him frankly. 'I don't know. I wish I did. At first it was because I did not trust you, but now I suppose it is because I want to have my future settled – for you to come home to England with me, so we can sign the papers. I need to know how I will live now my father is gone. And it is all the more urgent now that Wilmot is no longer in charge of the warehouse—' She paused, but then more words seemed to tumble out without her bidding – 'and partly it is because I like the training . . . I mean Señor Alvarez, there's something about him . . .'

He put down his cloth and met her eye. 'Do they know about Wilmot's death? Greeting and the men at the chambers, I mean?'

'Greeting. Oh – oh yes. I wrote. I had to. I asked him to put the head warehouseman in charge until I could return.' She tried to keep her tone flat, without accusation. 'And I had to write to Dorothy – David's wife – of course, to tell her. I told her if I could, I would make a donation – for the children.' She looked to gauge his reaction but he just nodded. 'Wilmot was good to me, and I think it only fair. He might still be alive if it wasn't for me.' She stopped, aware that talking was not permitted. She heard the dribble of water as he wrung out the cloth.

He scrubbed the cloth over the patch of floor in front of him, then sat up again. 'It's a good idea.'

She was amazed. He was actually agreeing with her about

something. She galloped on in a whisper, whilst he was listening. 'There will be a lot to do, to get the business straight, and I'm not sure the deputy overseer has much head for figures, and I'm sure he'll be ruling the roost with David gone. And the house has been locked up too long. All the drapes will need airing and . . .' She flushed, realizing she had been carried away. The unspoken question hung there between them, though she did not push him to answer it.

'After last night, I thought I had a duel to fight,' he said. 'I wanted to get even, seek revenge on whoever did this. And I hate to be beaten. But I am beginning to see that it serves no one if I go after them. No one but myself, I mean. It is only my pride it satisfies. They will think us cowards if we do nothing, but I do not care if men like that think ill of me.'

'Who?'

'Rodriguez. From the sword school in the city. I think it's his men who did this.'

She put down her cloth. 'Why? Is it something you did? Is that why they came?'

'No, I had nothing to do with this. But I did fall foul of Don Rodriguez once, in an argument over a slave boy . . . never mind, it matters little now. I need to think. To think why I am fighting, who this is all for . . . and about making a life in Spain . . .' He paused. 'Because I think I might never come back to England at all if I don't come soon.' His gaze strayed out to the window, before it snapped back. 'Alvarez is right. You have waited patiently. I will come back to England as you wish. For one week. I will talk to the Señor, see what can be done. Find out when the next sailing is.'

He picked up the pail and walked off with it. She was so stunned, she could have been felled with a feather. Was he really prepared to break off his training? She could not believe it was possible. Yet had he not said to ask about a passage? She went to the pump to wash out her cloth and scrubbed her hands in a ferment of excitement. She was going to go home, home to her lovely house, home to London, to plain English food and secret Mass and lit fires in the hearth! She clasped her hands in a private prayer of gratitude. Perhaps Father was right, and she and Zachary would be able to make something of his inheritance together after all.

She must tell Señor Alvarez their plans. She hurried up the steps. By telling him, she hoped this would somehow solidify them; that once Señor Alvarez knew it would make it more real, for she still could not quite believe it. But Ayamena told her Señor Alvarez had ridden out with the artist Girard Thibault, to do some business and then to say farewell to him, and that the señor would not be back until later in the afternoon.

After the first flush of enthusiasm she was strangely deflated. It would look ungrateful, she thought, not to finish the training. As if she had not valued it – him – at all.

They studied in the newly scoured library as usual. The ruined books were drying still, and were awaiting the bookbinder, so Pedro said. But there were others that had been overlooked by their night-time visitors, so it was those that they were to study. Elspet pounced upon a copy of Hugues Wittenwiller, a manuscript which looked to be of some age, and which some previous student had helpfully annotated by placing sheets of diagrams between the pages.

'These aren't bad, but not as good as Girard's sketches,' whispered Etienne, appearing late, but peering over her shoulder.

'I'll miss Girard,' Elspet said. 'It is a shame his training is done. And I'd like to see his great book when it is finished.'

In the afternoon she trained with the half-sword, an earth technique, where the blade has to be grasped firmly by the fingers. At first they had worn their leather gloves, but now they learned to work without them. Alexander took hold of Elspet's palm and pressed it to the blade, to show her that it was actually safer, the tighter the grip.

'It is designed to cut as it slices,' he said. 'If it does not slip, it will not cut.'

As he held her hand it did not make her heart race, though he was pleasant enough. It was Señor Alvarez who had that honour.

When she saw him pass through the yard at last, she excused herself and took a moment to settle her breath and compose herself before ascending the stone steps. Her hemp sandals made little noise as she passed through the indoor training hall – clean and tidy now that lime had been painted over the mess to make a simple white square. She walked around it in case it was still wet. The library door was open a little. She paused a moment at the door, looking through the crack where it joined the jamb.

Señor Alvarez was sitting, hunched over one of the tables. Beside him lay a volume of the Agrippa and some of the torn-out pages. His head sagged into his hands. He slowly rubbed his palms over his face, pinched his eyebrows as if he had a headache, and let out a long sigh. When he looked up again his eyes were listless, his face grey. He picked up a torn page and slumped back on his chair, his face a picture of defeat.

Was this the invincible man who taught them to spar every day?

She knew she should knock, but could not bring herself to, so arresting was this new vision of Señor Alvarez. An urge arose in her to go and comfort him, but she stayed still. She saw him stare blankly out of the window into the distance.

A slight movement must have caught his eye because he looked up, suddenly alert. Almost immediately she saw him put on his formal teaching face. It was a strange experience to watch him construct the mask before her. She knocked then, and he called out, 'Come!'

She went in. 'Señor Alvarez,' she said, 'Have you a moment?'

'Of course,' he said, the picture of joviality. 'Please sit.'

She sat carefully, taking her time so that they might both regain their composure, and draping her skirts so they hid her bare toes. She looked him straight in the eye and said, 'I've come to say that Zachary and I are leaving.'

The shock registered in a slight backward movement of his body, but then his calm returned. 'Back to England?'

'Yes. I have persuaded Zachary to come with me at last to go through the legalities of my father's will.'

'That is good news for you, is it not?'

'As you know, I've been waiting months for him to agree, and after that I am afraid I will be very busy with the business in England and . . .' She paused, choked, an upsurge of emotion threatened to overwhelm her.

'And you will have no more time for Spain and the study of the sword,' he finished for her. 'I quite understand.'

His matter-of-fact response unnerved her. She retorted, 'You make it sound as though I have not valued it. But I have. I will miss it a great deal. I have never felt so . . .' she searched for the word, 'so unfettered. Partly it is just Spain. In England, my behaviour would be unacceptable in the society in which I live. Partly it is you – your teaching here.' She fumbled for words, but they escaped her. She found herself becoming more and more agitated, but still could not find words for what she wanted to say.

He waited.

' . . . There is some magic here that I will never find in England.'

He was shaking his head. 'I am just a fencing master. But I hope you have learned something. It has been a privilege to teach you. I have never taught a woman before – it has given me much, the experience of it. Tell me, when will you leave?'

She dropped her gaze, before the words came out, more bald than she intended. 'As soon as I can. Tomorrow, perhaps. I dare not delay in case Zachary changes his mind.'

'So soon?' Something unreadable passed across his eyes. 'I thought . . .' He paused, thought better of it, and said, 'Well, I wish you well on your journey. You will come to say goodbye to the others before you go? They will expect it.'

She began to speak, but only a croak came out. Her shoulders started to shake and to her horror hot tears began to trickle down her cheeks. She covered her face with her hand. From between her fingers she saw him produce a white kerchief, which he pressed into her hand, and heard his even voice.

'Mistress Leviston, it is good to cry. In Spain, tears are like the rains, they make the world a more fertile place. Do not be ashamed of your tears.'

'I'm sorry,' she stuttered. 'I don't know why I am crying.'

'Your heart knows perhaps.'

Her eyes met his and she saw his pupils darken. His hand moved as if it would take hers, but it stopped just a little short, and he withdrew it and looked away out of the window.

She blew her nose and gestured to him that she would keep the kerchief. She tucked it into her waistband.

'What about Mr Deane?' he asked.

'I think Zachary intends to carry on his training, if you will let him. He is doing this for me, señor, so please do not punish him. Let him return here, if he wants to. I know it means everything to him, as it does to me . . .' She brought out the kerchief again.

'I am sure your cousin will come and talk it over with me.' He sighed. 'Girard Thibault too, he has gone. But I know he will not be back. His training is finished and he is going home to Antwerp. And now another.' He shook his head. 'A few weeks ago I sensed my training was needed, but now something in the air has changed; it seems most of my students seem to have other ideas.'

She could do nothing to reassure him. There did not seem to be anything else to say, so she stood up. Her knees trembled a little, and she was still blinking back tears. 'I will come again tomorrow to say my farewells,' she said, and floundered to the door.

Señor Alvarez did not move, but called out to her, so she turned to catch his words: 'You will be missed, Mistress Leviston. The men will lack your company.' And something in his tone told her it was the man speaking, not the mask, and it was he who would miss her, not the men.

Elspet asked Gaxa if she would go down to the harbour and find out about the sailings. Gaxa did not ask questions, for which Elspet was relieved, but just accepted the instructions. She used to think how pleasant it must be, to simply follow orders. But now she saw that it was different when you had been forced to hand over your personal power to someone else.

Whilst Gaxa was gone she packed what was left of her personal belongings. She left out her other gown, and a travelling cloak. The rest of her things would now fit in one large handbasket, with a bit of persuasion, so she packed them that way.

Running footsteps alerted her before Gaxa burst into the room.

'Nobody leaves,' Gaxa said. 'Not for three weeks.' She held up three fingers, gasping for breath. 'They sending the Moors back. The port is full of ships and soldiers.'

'Why?' Elspet felt her heart jerk in her chest. 'What have they done?'

'Nothing.' Gaxa looked at her scathingly. 'Just be alive, that's all. But there's trouble. They say they'll get guns and fight.'

'What about trade ships?' Elspet said.

'I tell you. Nothing's going out. Not till they gone.'

Part Four

May the rain sprinkle you as it showers,
Oh, my time of love in Andalusia:
Our time together was just a sleeper's dream,
Or a secretly grasped moment.
Traditional seventeenth-century Morisco song

Chapter 44

January 10th 1610

'Fetch your father.' Mama swung the basket down from her head but did not even unload it on to the kitchen table. Luisa could see by her face there was something the matter.

'What is it?'

'Don't just stand there, go and find him.'

Luisa was about to go to work at the pottery, so she considered arguing back, but Mama was distracted, her eyes shifting around the room as if they could find no place to rest.

Luisa made to comfort her, but she ignored her. She went straight out the back door to their sleeping chamber, and Luisa followed.

'Go, can't you!' she shouted.

Luisa ran. As she hurried out of the door she glanced back to see Mama had sunk on to a cushion; she was swaying back and forth making little panting noises like a woman grieving.

She ran shouting into the small backyard where Papa usually taught Husain his Greek and Latin. Sure enough, there was Papa, sitting on a wooden stool with Husain chanting a catechism back to him.

He looked up at the intrusion and frowned. 'Mama says you've to come,' Luisa said. 'Quick! Something's the matter.'

Mama never interrupted Husain's lessons, for the time for his study was precious. Few hours remained when they were not all engaged in eking out a living with work or chores. So Papa frowned and came straight away, Husain holding his arm to guide him, still carrying his scratching-board and point with him.

Papa went to her. She poured out a rapid discourse in Arabic.

Luisa could only catch a few words, she was so upset.

'What? What is it?' Luisa cried.

Mama's fingers clawed at Papa's back as she tried to get out broken words between gulping sobs. When she paused for breath her father pulled her to him and they held each other tight.

Husain looked frightened and began to cry.

'Papa, what's the matter?' she asked, bending to scoop up Husain. 'What's so terrible?'

Mama spoke in Spanish at last. 'They are deporting us. All of us. All of Moorish descent.' She stifled another sob. 'We have twenty days to sell everything, gather what we can carry and report to the authorities.' Papa did not look at her. Mama pulled back her manto to reveal her stricken face. She signalled for Luisa to pass over Husain, and she gathered him into the folds of her djellaba where he buried his head in the fabric.

'I don't believe you. It's a mistake. That can't be right. You've got it wrong, you must have misunderstood them. She must have, mustn't she, Papa?'

Luisa's question seemed to have brought Mama back to her usual self. She was angry now. 'No. When I came out of the market into the square I had just missed the reading of the expulsion decree. There was uproar. I had to throw down my basket and run. Men were throwing stones and grabbing anything to serve as a weapon, but the King's mercenaries were there. Hundreds of men in full plate armour. The city's surrounded. They've cut off all the passes out of Seville.'

'It's not possible. There are too many people, we can fight them. We'll fight back, or we will hide you somewhere.'

'You don't understand. It's not just us they are sending,' she said, 'you too, though you were born here. Because you have not Christian parents. All of us. Even baptized Christians. They have a harbour full of ships waiting to carry us to North Africa. If we remain there is a law to say they can kill us. They've started building gibbets at the roadsides.' Husain began to howl.

'Be quiet,' Luisa snapped at him. 'They can't send us to Africa. I'm Spanish. I don't know anything about Africa.'

'Then you must learn,' Papa said sadly.

She did not answer. She ran blindly out of the room. She knew one thing. She was not going.

Mama's voice echoed after her, 'Lalla! Lalla!' but she did not stop. She had to think. She fled down the street to the Church of Santa Dominica and hurled herself in through the open side door. But the quiet solitude she craved was not to be. She was not the only woman with this idea – twenty or so other Morisco women were gathered just inside the door. Nobody had ventured into the stalls or near to the front of the church, as if already the church had ceased to belong to them. Christ's head was bowed on the cross as if even he did not want to look at them, his eyes turned aside to salute the light from the east window. One of the women turned and made a grim smile of greeting.

'So you've heard,' said Maymona, one of the other workers from the pottery.

'Is it true?' Luisa begged.

'Well, I for one will be singing my way to the ships,' announced an older woman. 'Baptised my children right here, I did.' She spat at the font. Her spittle dribbled down the coarse pale stone in a dark line. 'Bastards. Doesn't matter how much we *salaam* to them, or dance attendance to their ways, we've never been welcome here, just couldn't afford to go home. I'll be glad. They say they'll provide us with food for the journey.'

'That's what they say,' Maymona said. 'But never believe anything they say. My husband says it's a plot and they'll kill us all once we're on the ships. Loot our gold and throw us overboard. He's organizing a resistance. They're meeting by the Saladin Gate.'

'They won't kill us, don't be stupid.' Another girl, even younger than Luisa, holding her small sister by the hand, looked terrified. 'They wouldn't do that.'

'My mother says they won't let us stay, so where's the choice?' Luisa said.

'We're going to try and get out of Seville, the whole family – go to Toledo. We have Christian friends there who will vouch for us.' Another young woman spoke calmly.

'Don't you believe it. No one will hide us,' said the older woman with finality. 'Your Christian friends will change their minds when they find out the penalty is six years' galley service.'

No one spoke for a moment as they took this in.

The silence was short-lived. The door swung open again and more worried women crushed in off the street. 'Is it true?' Some did not even bother to kneel and cross themselves, but launched straight into the conversation. Luisa felt faint. She was trapped in the middle of the crowd. It went round again, people repeating the news, talking of the rumours, of the decree, of past atrocities, like vultures picking over a corpse. No one had an answer. The air crackled with the babble of women talking, shouting over one another for their point to be heard. Just when she thought she would suffocate with all their talk, the priest appeared, flanked by two armed mercenaries.

'What are you doing? Leave this building at once.'

They looked to each other before a spokeswoman appeared; the older woman. 'We are good Christians, we have only come to pray. We worship here every day, Father, you know we do.' The priest looked uncomfortable. 'We came to pray, to ask God why this is happening to us.'

There was a general murmur of assent. The women were meek now, a meekness of habit, cowed not only by the authority of the Church, but by the two men with muskets at his side.

'This is not the place for this sort of gathering,' the priest said, 'only for individual contemplation and confession. Now go on home.'

'Or wait till you get to your own country,' said one of the mercenaries under his breath. The other laughed.

'This is my country!' Luisa flashed back at him, and several women behind cheered.

The priest held up his arms as if to herd them out of the church.

'Time to move on now, ladies. There will be no noon office today.'

But the mercenaries had already moved round behind the group, prodding at their backs with their muskets as if they were cattle in a pen. One of them aimed his musket at the back of the older woman and shoved her in the back. She turned by instinct and her hand shot out to push the musket to one side, as if she did not quite realize what it was. Luisa saw her mouth open as the man crashed the musket hard down on her head. She dropped like a stone. She caught a glimpse of the priest's horrified face.

A frozen moment of inaction before mayhem broke loose.

The women leapt upon the mercenaries like Furies, and the soldiers flailed and swiped out wildly with their weapons, before one had the presence of mind to pull back a trigger and let loose a deafening blast.

Luisa dived for cover under a bench, as the sharp crack of shot hitting a window showered glass needles over the crowd. The commotion brought men in off the street. She did not dare move. From her low viewpoint she recognized the legs and feet of Abdul the cobbler, saw his hand drag his leather-cutting knife from its hanging sheath and swing it past his hip.

She knew the fish-seller by his blood-stained apron and hatchet as he passed, and the feet of many more men scrambled to get into the action. The mercenaries were outnumbered and the second one fell next to her. His helmet clanged against the flag floor, his hands clawed to find a support to lift himself up but too late, he was bludgeoned by the rampaging mob until she could see no more glint of his breastplate, just the backs of men.

When they left him he had no face, the only thing she could recognize was his armour, greasy with blood. She covered her head with her hands, rocked back and forth.

She had to get out. She searched the legs of the crowd vainly. There was no sign of the robes and sandals of the priest. If he was not dead he would have gone for the authorities. She crawled out just in time to see two women run for the altar table and heave it over. Another two tore at the altar cloth, shouting 'For Allah!'

She staggered from behind the pile of armour and towards the door. The other mercenary lay in her path. Some fool had left his dagger embedded in the man's neck. His armour was split open like a chestnut showing pale bones beneath the oozing flesh.

As she stumbled panting towards the side door, her feet skidded in a slick of blood. At the threshold she fell outside into the fresh air to see a large force of black-clad men approaching from the other end of the street.

'Get out!' she yelled back through the door, in a panic for her friends inside, 'They're coming!' she shouted again in Arabic, her mouth spitting out the half-remembered words.

But no one paused in what they were doing. Her heart seemed to jump in her chest like a small creature trying to get out. The splinters flew from the altar, the men intent on destruction, unable to hear anything beyond the thud of metal and the splitting of wood. The church reeked with the smoke of votive candles overturned, flaring in pools of wax.

'Run! The King's army!' she tried again.

The wax crept towards the motionless figures on the floor. Abdul the cobbler smashed at the windows in a frenzy with a large gilt candlestick. And above it, just before she ran, she saw the figure of Christ, his head still turned away to the side as if he was ashamed.

Zachary had an instinct something was afoot, before he knew exactly what. An unruly crowd had tumbled past his door in the middle of the night shouting, 'Moros!' Bells started ringing raucously from the minarets but suddenly died mid-clang. Several times he heard unearthly, tuneless wailing. It was a while before his sleep-befuddled brain identified the sound as a muezzin's call to prayer in Arabic, and it was answered by many more ghostly voices until a volley of shot put an end to it. He went out on to the balcony but could see nothing. Only a few plumes of smoke from over by the harbour. Nevertheless, he slept with his sword within reach.

Next morning, when he set off for the school, he soon saw that the streets were in ferment, the main thoroughfares clogged with armed men and handcarts of terrified Moriscos trying to flee the city. The word was, the Crown had put out a decree saying all Moriscos must be ready to depart in twenty days, but already the city was on the move. Zachary began to run.

He met a road block of armed men and was turned back from his usual route, so he grabbed a man passing by, 'What's happening?'

'Murdering bastards! They've looted the Santa Dominica. The priest's dead, and all the windows smashed. They're going to get them off the streets.'

Zachary was already running towards Señor Alvarez's house.

The yard was totally silent. No sign of Señor Alvarez or anyone else. He battered his fists on the kitchen door but Ayamena did not answer. He pushed his shoulder against it but it was locked. He hurried round the back to their yard but saw no sign of life. With growing alarm he wondered if they had already gone.

The first person to appear was Elspet, hurrying in with her eyebrows knit into a frown.

'Bad news. No ships are sailing,' she said. 'There is a mass exodus of people planned and we cannot leave for England for another three weeks.'

He did not answer her, returning to England was the last thing on his mind. He pounded on the door to the training hall, but that too was locked.

Elspet called out, 'The Moriscos have been—'

He shouted back before she can finish, 'I know. Have you seen Ayamena? Or Nicolao?'

'No, I've only just got here. The streets are in chaos. I passed a crowd kneeling in the middle of the street. They are saying if nobody believes they are Christian they might as well be Moors, they'll get expelled anyway. There were children there too, looking completely bewildered. It's terrible, we are turning them back to their heathen ways, not away from them.'

He jumped back down the steps. 'Is that what you think they are? Ayamena and Nicolao? Heathens?'

'They have not embraced the Church of Rome,' she said stiffly. 'And I believe in the Holy Roman Church.'

Anger boiled up in his chest. 'So you don't think it unjust, that they should be torn from their homes and shipped somewhere else on a whim?'

'There must be good reason—' she began.

'What good reason?' he yelled, incensed. 'I'm not even going to argue with you. Have you seen Luisa?'

She had the grace to be abashed. 'No. She's not here. And of course I feel sorry for them. Nobody should be treated this way. This would never happen in England, would it?'

He stared at her, with her hair tied up so neatly in its kerchief. 'Oh, so you think we're so civilized? We, who force our priests to hide in the back of fireplaces, who call people heathens without knowing anything about them, and who dismiss Spain as somehow inferior to England. We are so damned cultured, aren't we? Well, at least Spain has passion! Not like England, with its damp courtesies and cold heart!'

He did not have to look on her shocked face long, for the gate opened then and Señor Alvarez and Nicolao rushed in. Señor Alvarez was supporting Nicolao by the arm.

'Have you seen Luisa?' Nicolao asked, his eyes straining around the yard before he was even properly inside.

'No, I was wondering where everyone was,' Elspet said. 'I was worried that you—'

'You have not seen her?' Señor Alvarez seemed to bring sanity back to the yard.

'I haven't seen anyone,' Elspet said, her face still red as a plum from their altercation.

Nicolao let out a small moan of frustration. 'I hoped she'd come here. Señor Alvarez is going to help us get away to France, to avoid the conscript. But there's been trouble at the Santa Dominica church, and a girl came to tell us they'd seen Luisa there early this morning. They don't know anything else, except there was a fight and many killed – the army were there. We can't find out what's happening and nobody has seen her since.'

'You're saying Luisa was there?' Zachary heard his own urgent voice.

'I'm sure she's safe,' Elspet said, but they all ignored her.

Zachary took a deep breath to try to order his thoughts. 'Did you go to the church?'

'Yes,' said Señor Alvarez, 'I did. The King's militia have been and boarded it up. You can tell something has gone on – broken glass from the windows is all over the street.'

'I can't think where she would go,' said Nicolao, his voice rising. 'Why hasn't she come home? We went to the hospital where they take people like us. One of the women was in there with a gash to the head. She said Luisa had been with them, but then she just disappeared. Ayamena's taken Husain. They're going door to door asking at all our friends' houses, but so many people are moving we're worried we won't find her or . . .' He couldn't finish, but none of them wanted to contemplate the other possibility, that she had been arrested by the King's men.

'Let us keep busy until Ayamena returns.' Señor Alvarez placed a comforting hand on Nicolao's shoulder. 'Come, we'll prepare. We will need to move your family today if you are to leave Seville. It will be harder once they start to round people up from the villages to take them to the embarkation points.'

Zachary took this in. They were going to round people up. A shiver ran through him. He must find Luisa.

'You know we can't go without her.' Nicolao sounded desperate.

The old building. It was worth a try. Zachary spoke loud, to get their attention: 'I know a place she might have gone.' They looked at him doubtfully.

'Where?' Señor Alvarez asked.

'It'll be quicker if I go,' he said. 'Please, just wait here in case she comes back.' He set off at a run.

'Let me come with you,' said Nicolao.

'No, I'll go alone,' he yelled over his shoulder.

Nobody had touched the place since they were last there. The stairs still smelt of dry dust and masonry. He raced up to the top floor, calling out, 'Luisa? Are you there?'

But there was no answer, at the top he looked out through the gap where the balcony jutted over the streets beneath. The sharp northerly wind barely disturbed the view, the scene below was laid out like an illustration. He drew his hands over his eyes to clear them, and looked down, unable to take it in.

My God, the whole river was a mass of boats. He could hardly see a thumb's width of water. All the galleons he had seen out at the point and more. Hundreds of smaller craft bobbing alongside. The loop of the Guadalquivir reminded him of a black noose, the rope writhing through the city and out towards the coast.

He looked to his left. Flanking the river, battalions of men were preparing arms; and on the road a cavalcade of armed men trotted downstream on horseback. As the sun passed momentarily between the clouds it struck needles of light from their helmets. It came to him, with dread certainty, that this was a well-planned operation, not just a notion. He had thought the rumours to be scaremongering. He could not see how the king could move a whole population, yet here was the evidence right before his eyes. A chill rippled up his spine.

He turned his head to stare back into the room; there was the one chair casting its faint shadow on the bare boards. Its presence seemed to point to the emptiness of the room. There was no sign of Luisa.

He was wrong. He had been so sure he would find her here. Bitter disappointment filled his heart, not just because she was not there, but because he thought she might come to him if she was in trouble. That the place would be as special to her as it was to him.

He could not conceive of her and her family being put on to those boats. The idea was unreal; from up here the boats looked like toys. But he had heard the gunfire last night, heard the talk in the streets of the death penalty for Moriscos who remained. Panic seized him. He must try to find Luisa, wherever she was. Nicolao's words, that people had been killed at the church, repeated in his mind.

Perhaps if he could find the priest, he might see if he could find out anything more. He grabbed the handrail and plunged down the stairs, thrusting open the broken door. It bounced back and he heard a sharp cry.

Just behind the door Luisa struggled to her feet holding her nose.

'You fool!' she shouted at him.

'Oh God, I'm sorry.' He tried to take her arm to help her up.

'You've broken my nose. *Mentecato!* She shrugged away from him, holding her face. Her nose was dripping blood.

'I didn't know you were there!'

She rolled her eyes. 'Come in then, before someone sees us, pull the door behind you.'

'Everyone's looking for you. Your parents are out searching for you.'

'You've broken my nose.'

'Everyone's searching for you.'

'More fool them. I told them I'm not going.' She dabbed at her nose with her sleeve.

'Here.' He handed her a kerchief.

'Does it look bad?' she asked.

He went up close and put his hand on her cheek to tilt it to the light. 'I don't think it's broken.'

'No thanks to you.'

He stroked her cheek, and her hairline. 'Oh Luisa. I was worried.'

'I think it's stopped bleeding.' She tucked the kerchief into her waistband, and looked up at him. Her voice cracked with tears. 'They expect me to go with them, the fat-witted fools.'

'Hush, hush,' he said, folding his arms around her. In the brief time before she pushed him away he could feel her trembling.

'Luisa, where've you been? Everyone's half-crazed with worry.'

'I went to the Santa Dominica. I got caught up in some trouble there.'

'I know. Someone saw you. But what happened?'

She folded her arms. 'Please, don't make me talk of it. It was horrible.'

'Luisa, we need to let your parents know you're safe. Shall we walk back together?'

'No. I'm not going with them. I'm Spanish. I believe in the Holy Mother Church. I've spoken my catechism since I was four years old. What happened this morning just made me realize it even more. I'm not like them. They were smashing up the altar like wild animals.

Why should I leave? I don't want to go to Africa, to their primitive life with all its outlandish prohibitions. But Mama and Papa don't understand that. They didn't take the instruction. If they had, they would know their faith is just superstition, Papa doesn't realize, you see. But my mind's made up, I'd rather stay here in a Christian country – whatever the risks – than go with them to Africa.'

'They're not going to Africa.'

'That is what it says on the notices, and Maymona says that's where the ships are bound.'

'No, Señor Alvarez is going to help you get to France and from there onwards to Fez or Tunis, at least that's what he said.'

'Tunis, Africa, what's the difference? Are you saying you want me to go?'

'Of course I'm not. But I want you to be safe. They're killing anyone left behind.'

She shook her head sadly and pulled away from him. 'You are, aren't you? You're telling me you want me to go. I thought . . . I thought that it meant something. That we had . . . Oh never mind.' She turned away from him and went to the window.

'Don't look out there!' he called, but too late.

She was silent a long time staring out of the window, dabbing at her hurt nose with her sleeve. He wound his arms around her from behind.

Finally, she turned, and her eyes were glazed with unshed tears. 'Please, go back to my father. Tell him I will not come. I will take my chances here with you. I would rather live a short life in the Spain I love. If I die, then so be it.'

He caught hold of her. She tried to pull away, but he did not let go. He pressed his lips to hers and felt her answering response. Losing her had suddenly become all too real. He pushed her away to look at her, 'If you are thinking of staying for me then please don't. It is too dangerous. Please, Luisa, come back with me. Just speak to your family. They say they won't go without you and if they don't go today, it might be too late. And if they end up having to go to the embarkation points they will have to leave Husain behind.'

'What?'

'Children under the age of seven who have been brought up Christian will be re-housed. They are to go to holding camps until they can be assigned new families.'

'No.' She pulled away, shaking her head in disbelief.

'It's true. Señor Alvarez is trying to help your family stay together. He risks his own skin to do this, I know.'

'Nobody asked him to. He shouldn't interfere.'

'He is only trying to help,' he sighed in frustration. 'Like all of us.'

'It's my life,' she said quietly, jutting out her chin in defiance. 'Mine, to do with as I please. I had thought I had found someone who would understand me, someone who would let me be free to choose my way of being in the world. To live in Spain and dance and be free, that's all I want.'

'I know. But if you stay, you will be looking over your shoulder the whole time for the neighbour who will betray you or slip a knife into your back. Do you want that? Because I don't. I don't want you to live in fear like that.'

'But at least I will be alive! Not cut off from my land and my people and my God.'

'What about your family?' He walked away from her in frustration, and shouted, 'You have a family who loves you. That is more important than land or religion. For pity's sake, Luisa, you don't know how lucky you are!'

He didn't know how to make her understand.

He paced the floor a moment, then turned to her, 'Listen,' he said, 'I've had no family to love me since I was twelve years old and, what's more, I am such a pathetic man that I had to worm my way into someone else's, just so that I could feel I belonged somewhere. If I die tomorrow, who'll care? No family will mourn me, not a one.' He tasted his own bitterness. 'And if I was lost, nobody would come looking.'

Luisa reached out to touch him. 'I care,' she said.

The touch was like a flame that made him pull her to him. When he could bear to release her he shook her gently. 'Luisa, your whole family are out risking their necks searching for you. Please, I beg you, come back with me. Even if it's just to say goodbye. Think of your mother traipsing Husain round the streets asking everyone if they've seen you. They deserve your love and respect. I heard your father say they won't go without you, and you know what that means – the risk they take.'

A single tear trickled down her cheek.

He carried on, 'Risk your own life if you must, but don't risk theirs. They did nothing wrong except love you. You would condemn them to death for that?'

She held out her arms and they held each other tight.

'I'm scared of losing you, Mr Deane,' she said.

'And I'm scared of losing you.'

'Come with me.' Her voice was a whisper. He did not know if she meant home, or to a new land, but it did not matter. For suddenly he was certain. He would go with her to the ends of the earth if need be.

Chapter 45

Elspet prepared food, though she had scant idea what to do with the ingredients in Señor Alvarez's kitchen. The men arrived for training, all with tales to tell of insurrections and rioting. Señor warned her not to go into the city lest she become caught up in the unrest provoked by the King's declaration.

Alexander said the señor had sent a message to his friends in a small fishing village near Tavira who were prepared to help the Ortega family get away to France. He asked if Elspet could make provisions for the family for the journey, because poor Ayamena was out with Husain searching for Luisa, who had gone missing. Elspet did her best. She had found spelt to make flatbread, and corked up a pot with olive oil and goat's cheese. From all accounts Moriscos were particular about their meat, so she had used only vegetables and cheese.

The talk between the men was of how the city would manage with the loss of so many of its Muslim population. Pedro Gutierrez said it would be like draining the city, that Seville would struggle to subsist without the Morisco artisans, without their farming skills and their craftsmanship. She remembered that Luisa worked at the pottery, and asked him if the people who worked there were all Moriscos.

'It's already empty, the kiln's blowing ash, and cold, like in all the other workshops,' he said sadly.

Señor Alvarez appeared to see how she was faring. She looked down apologetically at her floury skirts. 'There is no bread, today, the bread man has not been.'

'I expect he's left, like most of the traders in this barrio. He will have more important things to worry about than feeding us.'

'How will the city manage without the bakers?'

'I expect it will adapt. People find new habits, like always.' He was staring at her, it made her nervous.

'Your cheek looks a little better,' he said.

'Oh that. I hardly notice it. And it seems a small injury in comparison to what is going on in the city. Such a shock, everywhere in chaos. It's so sad. I don't understand why this exile is necessary.' She went back to mixing dough.

'It was always a threat. Spain has been gradually scrubbing Islam out, but it's folly to try to erase history.' His voice was frustratingly calm.

'That wasn't what I meant. I mean it seems so cruel. People were living together side by side well enough, weren't they?'

'Not well enough, I suppose. It is complicated. The Ottoman Turks have seized our trade routes, and the King fears Moriscos might give them aid. He knows Spain was not always his; that it belonged to the Arab world before him, and the people still remember, the stories are passed from generation to generation.'

'Will he expel them all?'

'It looks that way. He can't risk a rebellion. And he won't forget the story – the last sigh of Boabdil as he surrendered the precious keys of the city to Ferdinand and Isabella. He fights in case it comes full circle.'

'I feel for Ayamena and Nicolao. Do you know, my father said the new king was a holy man, a man of the Church, one of toleration.'

He picked up one of the leathery apples taken from the winter stores and weighed it in his hand. 'Ah yes, the Church.'

It felt like a chastisement. She stopped mixing and went to wash her hands in the bowl by the door to cover her confusion.

'I wish that they could stay, that is all,' she said. 'They could try harder to convert them to our faith. Exile seems so unnecessary.'

'Does a person's religion matter so much to you?'

'Of course it does. The Church has given me so much . . .' She hesitated, something in his reaction made her bite her lip.

He turned his back. There was an awkward pause. 'Mistress Leviston, thank you for your help in the kitchen, I know the Ortegas appreciate it.' He tapped his foot. 'I know it to be selfish, given the circumstances,' he said returning to face her, 'but I am glad you cannot sail for England and I will have the pleasure of your company for another few days. And Mr Deane too, of course.'

She cast him a shy glance and his eyes looked into hers briefly before they dropped away. She could not help it, she still desired him. The tension was palpable and to cover it she wrapped the food in cotton cloths ready for packing in the baskets. He passed the apple from hand to hand before taking a bite from it.

He stood next to her again. 'Shall I help pack these things?' Awkwardly, he put the apple back down on the table. She sensed he was uncomfortable with small conversation. The silence in the room was broken only by the noise of the fire crackling in the wood-fired oven in the corner. She was intensely aware of his slim brown hands folding the cloth, of his presence beside her.

He pointed to the oven. 'I asked Pedro to light it, so you can bake your bread. Best to make plenty, for there will probably be shortages. Everyone needs to eat, whatever goes on in the city.'

'With your appetites I will be baking all day.'

He laughed, and it lightened the atmosphere, like a lick of flame on a dark night. But then his voice became serious again, 'Mistress Leviston, I have to ask. If I can manage to arrange it, would you be willing to accompany me on the journey to Tavira? I would not think it, but now Martha has gone, it would make for less suspicion if Luisa was the maid of an English lady.'

She wanted to please him so she heard herself say, 'If it will help, then of course I will. But I'm not sure I won't be more of a hindrance. And you will have to tell me what to do.'

'Thank you. The Moriscos have twenty days to leave, so I understand. When Zachary returns with Luisa, then we will make plans to leave early next week,' he said, giving her a warm smile and touching her on the shoulder with a brush of his fingers as he left.

The sensation of his touch made her yearn for more. The apple lay on the table where he had left it. She scooped it up and pressed it to her lips where his had been only moments earlier. It was only then she realized she was shaking from head to foot, from passion or terror she could not say. A low moan escaped her. No one must know how she felt about the señor, she could not bear the humiliation if he were to reject her again. What was more, she did not know what frightened her the most, a journey across bandit-ridden Spain, with the King's militia snapping at their heels, or the thought of spending more time alone with Señor Alvarez.

Zachary and Luisa dodged their way through the narrow thoroughfares away from the main streets. Through the intermittent gaps in the houses they saw a throng of people jostling past, shouting slogans. Their hoarse shouts caused Luisa to duck and put her hands over her head to protect herself. Occasionally they pressed themselves under the eaves at the crash of breaking glass or the dull thud of shot. Zachary wrung Luisa's hand in his as they ran, pulled her back against the wall when a group of soldiers ran past the entrance to their alleyway.

At the sign of the Spreadeagled Man they threw the gate open and burst inside. There was not even time to catch their breath before Ayamena was upon them, yelling, 'You selfish girl! What do you think you are doing, worrying your father half to death?' She beat at Luisa with her fists, but Luisa put up her elbows to shield herself from Ayamena's rain of blows. 'You think we've nothing better to do than run after you?' Finally, she stopped, and they looked into one another's faces.

'Oh Mama,' Luisa choked out.

Ayamena clasped her tight and patted her back. 'Your nose. Foolish, foolish girl.' She pushed her to arm's length. 'You will come?' Luisa just nodded.

Zachary repressed the urge to run and embrace her. A great wave of relief coursed through him.

Chapter 46

The men were supposed to be training, but the confusion in the city meant they were reluctant to start, and everyone knew that the Ortega family were even now preparing to pack and sell all their possessions.

'What will Señor Alvarez do after this for help? First Alma and Daria, now Ayamena and Nicolao.' Zachary turned the handle of the grinder. He was using the whetstone kept in the tack room for sharpening their blades.

Alexander said, 'And Luisa. I am not blind, you know.'

'You know, she wasn't going to leave. But I think I persuaded her it would be safer to go with her family.' He said nothing of his own plans to leave with her.

'It will be difficult. Heaven alone knows if there's a way out of Seville for them, except by the King's ships.'

Etienne passed through with a bucket of water for the señor's horses, but stopped to say, 'I'll be glad when it's over. Once it's done there will be less of the trouble, and the people will soon forget, heh?'

Zachary thought of Luisa. 'I don't think so. Moriscos have been part of the fabric of this city for so long, it will be like amputating an arm.'

'It is Don Rodriguez's men at the port,' Etienne said, 'his crack troops.'

'How do you know?' Alexander asked.

Etienne looked from one to the other, his face had turned red. 'Didn't you say you saw them training for something, Deane?'

'Yes, that's right, he did,' Alexander said.

'What does Señor Alvarez intend to do?' Zachary asked. 'Somehow I can't see him joining forces with Don Rodriguez. Nobody's been to ask him for assistance in moving anyone as far as I'm aware.'

Alexander shrugged his shoulders. 'I don't know. I've not seen him. He went straight into his chambers. Do you know, he took the best swords away, and left us with the blunts and a load of rusty rapiers. Said it was good practice. Pedro and the apprentices are hanging around the yard waiting for him to come out and give us some more instructions.'

Zachary and Alexander went back to the yard, where the other men were sheltering under the canopy from the drizzle. A fire had been lit in the Ortegas' quarters, for smoke trickled from the chimney. Elspet was staying with the family to offer her help in packing. What was happening in there, Zachary wondered, what must Luisa be thinking? The yard was quiet, just the dripping from the bare tangle of twigs above their heads.

'What's the matter with you all?' A shout from the top of the stairs. Zachary looked up to see Alvarez glaring down at them. 'Have you nothing useful to do? Have not one of you the wit to unsheath a sword?' His voice descended on the party like a douse of cold water. 'The training must continue, no time for wasteful talk.'

They all looked sheepishly at one another and hurried to pick up arms from the heap in the corner. It was the first time Zachary had heard him yell like that. It gave him an uncomfortable feeling in the pit of the stomach. The other two men jumped to it, and were soon drilling up and down the yard.

Zachary looked at the weapons in disgust. Alvarez had even taken Zachary's own sword from him, but he soon saw the sense in Alvarez's methods. The men were rattled. Thank the Lord we're not using sharps, he thought, because Alexander was clumsy and slow to react, and several times Zachary's button got right to his throat, and Alexander looked mightily surprised to see it appear there.

As soon as they had commenced the drill, Señor Alvarez turned smartly on his heel and went within.

Alexander stopped and looked around to check he had gone. 'Something's not right,' he said, disengaging.

Zachary was impatient with him, 'Do you think I don't know that? The whole city's gone mad. He's a little on edge, that's all. It's not surprising, given what's going on at the quay. Come on, put up your guard.'

'I keep thinking of all those people with no place to go.'

'I know. Please – don't make me think of it,' Zachary snapped, and twitched up his rapier to encourage him, but Alexander wouldn't re-engage. Zachary dropped his own tip down and said, 'I've got to keep moving. Or I won't be able to bear it, that I can't do anything. They'll take Luisa and I can't do a damn thing about it. Even Alvarez can't do anything. You saw all those armed troops.'

Alexander shook his head. 'He'll think of something.'

'They can't hide. They'll kill them if they find them.'

Alexander said, 'Don't. Let's stop. I haven't the heart for it. I keep seeing all their faces, those people from the villages walking to the docks, and thinking that could have been my village. I saw them bringing a group of Moriscos down. There was a woman just like my grandmother, she was limping along with two sticks and you could see every step was an effort. And an injured man, his leg blasted apart, on an old door for a stretcher.'

'Hey, you two. What are you doing standing about?' It was Pedro. 'Don't let Alvarez catch you idling like that, he'll have you standing back in that circle again!'

Zachary clapped Alexander on the shoulder. 'Come on, friend. We can't let it stop us. We must keep up the training, we'll be useless else. That's what the training is for, to help us stay detached. Now, *en garde.*'

Zachary saw the focus come back into Alexander's practice, and gritted his teeth. When life got difficult this had always been his answer, to unsheathe a sword and shadow-play his enemies, though he felt a fraud dispensing advice to Alexander when half of him was desperate to be in the building on the other side of the yard with

Luisa. Damn it, not a soul had been in or out of the Ortegas' quarters for hours. Elspet still had not come out to the training yard. He wondered what old Leviston would make of her now. He should be proud. Not many women would have had the courage to do what she had done, learn to fence and take cuts like a man.

Alexander's tip met the inside of his wrist and jerked him back to attention. They were tiring, but when Alvarez still did not appear, they wordlessly moved into the whip and thrust of the fire technique until the sweat ran down their foreheads.

'Is it nearly time to break?' Alexander panted.

As if he had read their minds, Alvarez appeared on the balcony of the library. Zachary saw him and leapt into the evasive footwork of the air element. It took all his concentration. He and Alexander moved in concert to the tang of metal, the scrape of boots and the slight grunt of each other's breath, exhaled with force. Zachary glanced up to gauge Alvarez's reaction, and was surprised to see him motionless on the balcony, paying them no attention, his eyes staring fixedly over the wall. Something about his watchfulness sent a shiver up Zachary's spine.

Despite the palpable air of tension, the women managed to produce a midday meal. Luisa and Elspet carried the big wooden table out under the canopy. Alexander and Pedro brought chairs from inside. The rain stopped and everything smelled of damp earth. The air threatened a chill but on the table steamed a white bean stew, bread which had been freshly baked and muslin-wrapped cheeses. There was no meat or wine.

Zachary tried to catch Luisa's eye but she would not look at him. Her eyes were cast downwards, and it pierced him to the soul. As if to acknowledge this, Ayamena gave him a brief wan smile. Luisa went to fetch another chair and he tried to take it from her, to help, but she shook her head and carried it herself. When she looked up at him her eyes were pools of pain. 'Don't make me leave without you,' she whispered.

'I won't.' He gripped her arm in reassurance.

They sat. Ayamena and Nicolao with Luisa between them at one side of the table, the men at the other. They left a space at the head of the table for Alvarez, but he did not arrive.

'I'll go and see where he is,' Nicolao said, feeling his way out of his chair.

A few moments later he was back. 'Eat without him, he says.'

Zachary exchanged an enquiring look with Elspet, but she merely shrugged.

Luisa ladled out the stew. He watched how she tipped it carefully into the bowls so as not to waste a drop, tilting the spoon against the edge of the pot, and how she made sure her father's bowl was filled and he had his spoon before she dealt with her own.

'Let us say grace,' said Etienne.

There was a silence. Nobody wanted to invoke anyone's God.

Luisa cut the bread and offered it round. Her hand touched Zachary's as she passed it over, and he felt the intensity of her touch like a bee sting.

Alexander handed Elspet the salt crock. 'Anyone else?' said Elspet.

'Yes, pass it over,' Zachary said, and he and Pedro started to discuss the use of pikes rather too loudly. Etienne scowled and mumbled the Latin grace to himself. Zachary tore off some bread and crammed it into his mouth, tasting the savoury salt-taste of the beans, and the floury texture of the bread. Like the rest, he was hungry and for a moment there was no sound.

He paused, spoon held to lips. A chant from inside, a discordant tone that rose and fell, hardly taking space for breath. The hairs stood up on the back of his arms. The sound of it went on, and he knew it could only be Alvarez yet with all his might he did not want it to be him. He set down his spoon. Everyone else on the table was listening too, though they pretended not to. The sound held them in thrall.

Zachary looked across at Nicolao. Big tears were rolling down his cheeks, Ayamena gripped his hand on the table, her knuckles white with it.

'What? What is it, Papa?' Luisa's voice was cross.

'The midday prayer,' he whispered.

Barely was there time to register this, then there was a disturbance on the street. Dogs barked, followed by the muffled sound of baying voices, the rumble of cartwheels.

'Quick!' shouted Alexander. Everyone stood; Alexander rushed to pick up his sword belt and his buckler. Zachary followed, unsure what was happening. A pounding at the courtyard door. He looked around for Alvarez, but still he did not appear.

An apprentice hurried out of the house, and Nicolao gestured him to the door. More knocking. From outside came the shout of, 'Open this door by proclamation of the King.' In the yard Alvarez's men scurried to gather and put on arms.

'Get into the house!' Zachary shouted to Luisa, but there was no time. The door burst open, breaking the bar like kindling, and the yard filled with armed musketeers. Ayamena grabbed Husain by the hand and dragged him kicking into the kitchen. Elspet took hold of Nicolao's arm to try to steer him into the house, but he would not move, just strained his head to one side to hear what was happening, his heels dug into the ground.

A man dressed in black stepped forward. Behind him was massed a cohort of armoured soldiers. Zachary took stock of them. He knew straight away his button-ended foil would be useless against these men, but still could not let it drop to his side. One of the men arrested his attention. Don Rodriguez, armed with a musket, staring straight at him from beneath his helmet.

The man said, 'There are Moriscos in this domicile, and we are here to take their goods, by order of the King's proclamation.' He rattled off the words as if he had said them many times before. 'I must also advise you that we will be back at dawn to take the livestock if it has not been sold or slaughtered by then.'

'But sir, we were told we were not due to leave for another week,' Nicolao protested. 'You said twenty days. We are not prepared yet, we still have goods to sell.'

'You must have misunderstood,' said the King's man. He turned to look behind him to exchange a complicit look with Don Rodriguez, before stating baldly, 'It is too late for that. The Moriscos of Triana will be moving down to the Port tomorrow. You will leave tomorrow or the next day.'

'Excuse me, sir,' Elspet stepped forward, attempting the voice of reason, 'but can you return later?'

Zachary had to admire her nerve, standing up to this official with his army ranked behind him.

She carried on, 'I will help the family sort their belongings—'

'No. You do not understand. That is not possible. If they are reluctant, then my men will remove their goods by force. Besides, this is a school of fence, is it not?'

Don Rodriguez gave a derisive snort from behind him.

Zachary moved to put himself between Elspet and the men, and put up his foil. 'It is. And a very good one.'

Don Rodriguez ignored the rapier. 'Aha, the hothead Englishman. He seems to want six years in the galley. Well, it won't be a school of fence with no weapons, will it? We have orders to confiscate all arms.' He grinned. 'We'll start with the cutlery. It's probably all these men are fit to wield anyway.'

Zachary sprang forward in indignation, but Alexander took hold of his arm.

'Let me go, you ass!' Zachary twisted to get loose, but Alexander held him firm.

'Don't be a fool,' Alexander hissed, 'we're outnumbered. And you can't fight with that. Wait for Alvarez – he'll give the orders.'

'Leave off!' Zachary struggled, but the bigger man pinned down his sword arm with both hands.

'How many Moriscos live here?' barked the King's man.

Zachary looked at the ground. Nobody answered. When he looked up, Rodriguez had lifted his musket to his shoulder.

'Four,' Etienne replied hurriedly. 'The Ortega family. The father and mother, the girl Luisa, and her brother.'

'Bring those people forward. They're for Barbery. I need to check them on my list to arrange transportation. Four from this house, you say?'

Zachary started to protest, but his voice was drowned by another. 'No, five.'

Zachary turned and gaped.

'Señor –?' Only Alexander spoke, but the words died on his lips.

From the corner of his eye Zachary saw Elspet's stricken face, her hands had jumped to her mouth.

Señor Alvarez seemed somehow even taller. He addressed them all with a deprecating shrug of his arms. 'I will go with the Ortegas. They are my kindred. I would not have them go with no protection.'

Don Rodriguez dropped his musket from his shoulder and walked towards Señor Alvarez. 'Just as I thought, you're a sham. I knew it straight away. Carranza could see it too. That's why he gave his blessing to Pacheco. Dirty blood is always dirty blood.' He turned to Zachary and Alexander who were too shocked to move, 'You stupid, gullible men. The English and Dutch cannot see what's in front of their pointy noses. His sword school is useless. Look at him – you thought to learn the sword from *that*?' He spat at the señor's feet.

Señor Alvarez did not react, except for a slight tightening of his lips.

'You bastard!' Zachary lunged forwards towards Rodriguez but Alexander restrained him by the shoulders.

'Think, man,' Alexander hissed at him. 'Use your intelligence, not your anger.'

Zachary took a few ragged breaths. The señor was talking gently to Ayamena. 'They will not permit me arms. But I have some coin and gold set aside. When the time comes we will travel together. Now go. I will deal with these men. Go gather your warmest clothing, stout footwear. Get provisions for the journey, bread and cheeses. And make sure the little one has his slate.' Ayamena hurried inside, beckoning to Elspet to follow.

Elspet did not move. She looked as if she did not understand what was happening. She walked over to the señor too stiffly, as if she had a rod in her spine. 'Are you telling us you're leaving?'

He smiled gently. 'I'm sorry, Mistress Leviston. It appears I will have no choice.'

'But I—'

He hushed her, and took her hand. He spoke softly, not taking his eyes from her white face. 'There is something rare between us, is there not?' She nodded dumbly. 'Wherever I am, that will still be there. Perhaps we will meet again, eh, who knows?'

He lifted her hand and his lips lingered there a moment. Her face suffused with colour.

Zachary felt the strength of emotion in Elspet and a bolt of recognition pierced his heart. Luisa and Ayamena were still standing half-behind the kitchen door. He swivelled to catch Luisa's eye.

'Search the house.' The order moved the troops into action. Zachary's sword was wrenched from his grasp.

As the men swarmed over the house Luisa rushed to Zachary's side and threw her arms around him. He held her slight frame tightly to his chest, his hand on the soft plait of hair at the back of her head, as if he would weld her presence to him. 'Go inside,' he said, 'go and find your brother. He'll be scared. Don't worry, I won't leave you.'

Soon the yard was full of piles of swords and goods. There was not a damned thing they could do. There were just too many soldiers. Zachary felt the helplessness and anger wash over him just as it had when he was a child, but all he could do was watch and grit his teeth. The yard looked like a giant bonfire with everything hurled there all higgledy-piggledy. The soldiers loaded everything that was not on their persons on to carts. Outside in the street beggars seized upon any oddments that fell to the ground with greedy eyes. Zachary flinched as a basket went by with one of Alvarez's precious books wedged between dripping oil lamps and half-burnt logs from the upstairs fireplace.

'Shall we take this?' One of the men asked, indicating the table.

Rodriguez answered, 'Yes. But we must allow them to eat. Take the knives and bowls and tip the food on the ground. They like to sit on the ground to eat, so I'm told.'

When the yard was empty the guards shouldered their muskets.

'Be ready at noon tomorrow.' The King's man gave the order and the wagons, with their carrion crowd running after, teetered away down the street.

In the middle of the yard the bread lay in the mud, next to the mess of stew emptied from its bowl. The congealed mess had the imprint of a boot pressed into it where someone had trodden in their haste to leave.

Elspet appeared tense-faced at the kitchen door. Señor Alvarez looked as though he might speak to her, but then he shook his head and walked up the stone stairs to the upstairs room.

Zachary saw her whole frame sag. He called to her, 'Elspet!' But she shut the door deliberately.

If he was going to go with Luisa, it was time to tell her the truth.

Chapter 47

Elspet dare not think, did not know what to do, so she set to sweeping. Señor Alvarez was leaving, and she had left it too late. He admired her and it was too late.

'Elspet, have you a moment?' Zachary's voice broke into her thoughts.

'Will it not wait?' Elspet said. The last thing she wanted right now was a conversation with Zachary Deane.

'No. I need to speak with you now. Whilst I have the courage.'

She wiped her hands on her skirts and put down the broom. She attempted to talk, to return to normality, though the words seemed empty. 'I can't believe it's all over. Look at the place. Not a stick of furniture left. Broken pots and mud everywhere. And the Ortegas –'

'Please. Can we go upstairs to the library and talk?'

'If we must.' She hoped he was going to talk of Señor Alvarez, so she followed him up the stairs to the library. Her throat was tight as she saw the familiar balcony, the empty shelves, and realized that soon the señor would be gone from her life. Everything was breaking up. She swallowed, determined that Zachary should not see her cry.

They stood in the bare room, the silence hovering between them. She realized it was the first time she had actually properly looked into Zachary's face. He appeared strained, his sharp features even sharper.

'I don't know how I can break this to you after all this time,' he said, 'but I feel I must. I will be leaving too, with the Ortegas. I can't go on deceiving you any longer. I am not your brother. I am no relation to you at all.'

So he was disowning her completely. She looked at him coldly. 'I know you dislike me, but you do not need to be so cruel. I suppose you will tell me now that you have decided to sell the business after all. Have I not enough to contend with? I have just lost . . .' She struggled to compose herself, her voice came out as a croak – 'everything.' He started to speak again, but she spoke over him, 'I have no time for this, if you are going to dredge up our disagreement again. Ayamena needs me. Excuse me.' She twitched her skirts to the side and rushed headlong towards the door.

'Stop!' He grabbed her by the shoulder; she twisted away to free herself.

'How dare you!'

'I'm sorry.' He let go. 'This wasn't how I meant it to . . . look, I'm sorry.' His apology disarmed her. She paused a moment, and he launched in, 'I've lied to you. I need to ask your forgiveness.'

She turned to face him. She was wary. Why should she trust him? What did he want?

His face was serious, his hands clasped together before his chest. 'You've got to listen. I meant it. I'm not your brother. I have never been any relation to you at all. I lied to you, and I lied to your father.' He repeated, 'Elspet, I'm not your brother.'

'No.' She refused to countenance it. 'I don't believe you. What sort of game is this?' She put her hands up to her forehead, trying to take it in. 'Wait,' she managed, 'wait whilst I get this straight.'

Her thoughts raced. Zachary stood firm, shoulders hunched, as if expecting a blow to come. A cold realization dawned on her. She stared at him as if she had never seen him before. 'But if you are not any relation at all . . . then who are you?'

'Nobody. Just myself, the man you see standing here. The man you've trained alongside these last months. My mother knew your father. She pretended I was his son because – well, because she had no money to support me. Then your father sought me out, and I—'

'I can't listen to this any more.' She backed away towards the stairs. She was almost weeping now with indignation, 'I don't understand. Tell me it's not so.' But his words had the ring of truth about them. Her hands felt for the support of the wall. She whispered, 'It's true. You lying devil, it's true.' His face did not deny it. Rage coursed through her. 'Have you no morals at all? How could you? Pretend all this time, put me through all . . . all of this? And worse, you took my poor father for a fool.' He was trying to speak, but she cried over him, 'You know you've ruined my life.'

'I'm sorry, I—'

'Your mother was a whore, wasn't she? That's what they all said, but I was so naive. I didn't believe my father could have –' She couldn't even finish, it disgusted her.

'She did it for us. For me and my brothers.' He stepped towards her, his hands in a gesture of open supplication. 'Your father was a decent man. Out of all of them, he was the only one she trusted, don't you see?'

She didn't see. The past had broken into fragments. 'All I see is that my father was weak and in thrall to his baser nature. And you and your mother conspired to cheat us. You are a liar and a sham. I can't believe you could sit at table with us knowing all the time . . .' Her voice broke with emotion. 'You deprived me of my father's company in the last months of his life. For that I cannot forgive you.' She grabbed her skirts in her fists and hurried down the stairs, and out into the courtyard, where she stopped, eyes streaming.

She put her hands to her knees and tried to shake away the thoughts that spiralled in her head.

'Mistress Leviston?' It was Alexander. 'Is something the matter?'

'No,' she lied, standing and wiping her eyes with her sleeve. How could she tell him anything? 'No, I'm just tired, that's all.'

He took her arm and led her to the bench in the wall. 'The way the soldiers came, it was not a pleasant experience. Nicolao and his family did not deserve such treatment.' Seeing that she was not responding, he pressed her arm and said, 'Hey, we will all miss our training together, I know. And Señor Alvarez leaving, well, it has been a shock. And I know you will miss him more than most.'

She winced. Had her feelings for Señor Alvarez been that transparent? She must have looked a complete fool. Alexander continued, 'He holds you in high regard; that much I know.' She put on a brave front, and smiled an uncertain smile. 'That's better.' He held out a kerchief and she blew her nose.

'I think I might take a walk,' she said shakily, 'to clear my head.'

'Then I'll accompany you.'

'No, I'd rather go alone, if you don't mind. I won't go far, and not into the city.' She could not wait to get away from under his solicitous gaze.

He frowned but did not insist further.

She blundered past the back doors, the scrubby grass where the goats and pigs foraged, along the dusty donkey track in the opposite direction to the city. It was dusk, but the sky smelt of rain. She let herself run like a child, stumbling along the road, pressing her sleeve to her eyes. At the small white-painted church just on the next corner, she pushed open the heavy wooden door and fell into its darkness and shelter. She inhaled the smell of old tallow and limewash and thanked the Lord it was empty.

A few straw hassocks littered the ground, but when she knelt she found herself unable to pray. Her world was collapsing around her. Her intimations, small though they were, of finding happiness with Señor Alvarez were now as chaff. How stupid she had been to pin her hopes on that. And he was a Muslim. She had never known this most intimate thing about him. It was as though God himself was laughing at her.

She thought of the sword school, empty of furniture like an abandoned ship, and wondered if she had ever really learned anything there. Whilst she was training every day it seemed to mean something, but now it seemed ludicrous, the thought that she might ever be able to fight like a man. She knew that soon she would have to stand by, and watch helpless as her friend Ayamena, who had only tried to heal and cure, was forced into exile with the rest of the Morisco people.

She stood and rubbed the dust from her knees. Her mind skittered around Zachary Deane. She did not know now whether to be glad or sorry that he was no kin of hers. How could he have kept up the pretence for so long? It was beyond belief. And yet there had always been something, some inkling that she had known from the beginning. Perhaps it was because of the señor, seeing his confession, his truth about his faith; maybe that had given Zachary the courage to tell the truth. But that did not make it right, what he had done to her, to come into her life like a storm, riding roughshod over them all. And what of Father? It would have broken his heart to know he was not Zachary's proud parent after all.

She weighed Zachary's words, puzzling over them. He said Father had sought him out, and she would like to know more about why her father had done that. The fact was that if she had known he was not her half-brother, she would have contested the will immediately, and she would still be in West View House in England, walking the dogs, and sitting in the evenings with her embroidery. And David Wilmot would even now be sorting the bales in the warehouses and taking a hackney carriage home to his wife. She recalled his white face, the discs on his eyelids. Poor David.

She walked to the little arched window carved in the wall, and looked out over the bare folds of the landscape. Who would she be if she had never seen Spain? She was a different woman now from the person who left England. She flexed her arms, sinewy now, and interlaced her hands, holding them out before her. They did not feel like embroiderer's or lace-maker's hands. They were strong, the forearms muscled from wielding a sword.

She felt the raised scar on her cheek. She did not need Wilmot to protect her now, she was as well-versed in the sword as he had ever been. There was nobody she was beholden to either. Not her father, not Señor Alvarez, not even Zachary Deane. Even if Zachary kept her fortune, at least she would be in control of her own destiny. Señor Alvarez always said that a person was always free if they chose to be, no matter what the outside circumstances. That freedom was an inner state, a choice, independent of the world.

She leaned her elbows on the sill and let her chin rest on her hands; exhaled. She had learned something in her training after all. Nothing more could be taken from her, yet here she was, at home with herself at last. A great peace descended on her. She took out her rosary beads and ran them through her fingers, wonderingly, not in prayer, but in silent gratitude.

Zachary watched from the back window of the library as Elspet ran out of the back gate, her hands over her face. He cringed. It had not gone well, but then what had he expected? He had not seen her return, and now more signs of unrest were visible all along the city skyline. Plumes of smoke and sudden flashes. The faint sound of shouting and running feet in the streets. He wondered if Elspet had gone back to her lodgings, and what Señor Alvarez would say if she did not come back. Everyone could see he admired her, his eyes lingered on her every time she appeared.

Señor Alvarez had repaired the wooden bars at the front door to the yard. No one could go out or come in that way. A fine drizzle of freezing rain was falling now, causing the roofs to drip. Alvarez had asked to meet the men in the upstairs room. They sat around on the floor, as there were no chairs. With relief he saw the door creak open and Elspet appear quietly, pale and red-eyed, to join the men in the circle. He moved to one side to make room for her, and she lowered herself down between him and Pedro. He saw Alvarez's face lighten at her reappearance.

'I'm afraid the training is at an end,' Señor Alvarez said. 'I will be leaving Spain with my friends the Ortegas. I do not need to say how much I have valued your commitment to the method of *Destreza*. But your allegiance to me is finished. You do not have to stay tonight,' Alvarez said, 'but if you do, then I have a favour to ask.'

Alexander looked to Zachary questioningly, but Zachary shrugged.

'You understand, it is not for me,' he said, 'but for the Ortegas. Nicolao will not stand a chance on the mercenaries' galleys. If the Ortegas go to the port then the authorities will take little Husain and put him to slavery in another family, and Luisa . . .' He paused, unwilling to finish. 'Please, I understand it would be an act of charity if you do this last thing for me. Help us get to Tavira, tonight, to the boats.'

Zachary tried to take it in, that they would be leaving so soon.

'I will help. Nothing has changed. I said before, I do not know if I can be of any use, but I will help you,' Elspet spoke up first.

'Thank you, Mistress Leviston – Elspet – but I'm afraid we cannot do it alone.'

'Did you think I would stay behind?' Zachary said. Elspet turned and looked openly at him.

'Thank you,' she said. It was the first sign of approval she had ever shown him. He was surprised how good it felt that she approved of him.

'I'm sorry, señor, but you cannot stop our training now,' Alexander said. 'We demand one more night of your instruction.'

'Yes, I haven't quite got all the moves on paper,' said Pedro. The men laughed.

'You, Etienne?' Etienne nodded.

'Good. Then I'll show you where I have hidden the best weapons.'

Zachary sorted and checked the blades he'd retrieved from the chimney of the upstairs room where they had been wedged tight. Alvarez had had the foresight to hide them well. It was all very well to say he'd volunteer, they were just words. But now the reality was coming closer his mouth was dry as paper. He had seen the King's troops up close now and a shiver of apprehension caused him to catch his breath. If it came to Luisa's safety, though, he was ready to fight.

Etienne Galen seemed nervous too. In the harness room he grumbled to Alexander and Zachary, 'Why should you put your life at risk for these people? They are servants only, after all. Why do you not refuse? You could leave right now if you wanted.'

'I'm doing it for Señor Alvarez,' Alexander said, pulling down the bridles from the hooks, 'because he is my master. If we don't fight for him as a company, then what was the point of all the training?'

'I paid him, I owe him nothing. The training does not make me his vassal for life.'

'You do what you want,' Zachary said, 'but I'm with Señor Alvarez. I admire him. A man should help his friends. And besides, his friends are mine too.'

Etienne scowled. 'You are a fool. No Morisco is to be trusted. That is why they expel them. And did not Carranza believe in the purity of the blood?'

'Now just a—'

'We are all Alvarez's students, not Carranza's. You lack courage, my friend, that's all,' Alexander said.

Etienne whipped a dagger from his belt, and lunged towards Alexander, but Alexander shot backwards out of reach.

Zachary grabbed Etienne's arm. 'Hey! Hold off now! Either fight with us, or leave. There's strife enough outside that gate without having it inside as well. Are you with us or not?'

At that moment Alvarez reappeared, and Etienne slid out of the stable.

'What's with him?' Zachary whispered.

'Just scared I think,' said Alexander, 'like all of us.'

Zachary strapped the saddlebags on the horses and marvelled at Alvarez's calm. How had Alvarez anticipated yesterday's events? He was lucky to have found someone who would loan them a boat. But then Alvarez had that effect on people – only he could have arranged such a thing in this climate of chaos. Even now, he had persuaded Pedro Gutierrez to go out into the city, to bargain with his relations, and quietly replace the essentials they would need for the journey.

They were to travel in smaller groups rather than in a large obvious convoy. They might slip past the blockades of troops that way. Zachary suspected that it was also so that at least some of the family might make it to the boat alive. He had a bad feeling about this journey. He fingered the lucky piece of Calvary wood that still sat in his pocket, now worn smooth by his fingers.

Pedro Gutierrez arrived from his home with more provisions and warm blankets. 'It is all I could bring without causing suspicion,' he said.

As they packed the scant bags and rolled blankets, Alvarez gave them all specific roles. The whole party was to dodge the embarkation order by riding out that night to the coast, near Tavira, over the border into what used to be Portugal but was now part of Spain. Señor Alvarez had already written to Señor Quevedo in Tavira at the first sign of trouble. Though Catholics, the Quevedo family, like many Portugese, were not enamoured of being a part of Spain, nor of their new King Felipe's methods.

They were to travel openly on the main thoroughfare, as if they had nothing to hide. The King's militia would be expecting fleeing Moriscos to avoid the main roads. Etienne Galen was to scout ahead, to look out for trouble on the road, and come back and warn them of troops ahead.

'Why me?' Etienne asked. 'Surely Pedro has more local knowledge? I would be better bringing up the rear.'

Alvarez explained that Pedro was to travel with Ayamena and Husain. He was the least suspicious-looking of them all, being Spanish born and bred, and it would reassure the woman and child to have a true-blood Spaniard with them. Etienne was to do as requested and act as scout. Etienne finally agreed with a surly expression.

Zachary was nervous that Luisa was to travel first, as Elspet's lady's maid, in a carriage and pair. Alexander would accompany the women, riding alongside, with one of the stable lads driving the carriage. Zachary and Alexander had been sent to procure a carriage and Alvarez had given Zachary coin for the hire of it, and for the journey ahead. He had paid off the driver, telling him he would use his own man, at which Alexander had tipped his hat. Zachary had to suppress a smile. Anyone less like a coachman he could not imagine.

Now he watched Alexander put the two rangy Spanish bays in traces. It had cost a fine cap of gold, that carriage, but it did look well. Truth be told, he was jealous that Alexander was to go with the ladies. He had not had a moment alone with Luisa all evening, only once, when they passed in the corridor of the stable block. He had grabbed her hand as she passed and pressed his lips to it.

'Don't forget to wait for me,' he said.

'I would not go at all, but for you,' she said, snatching an embrace.

Alvarez helped Nicolao load the panniers, though Zachary could tell the señor was doing the bulk of the work, and giving Nicolao the easier tasks. He and Nicolao were to travel together, for Alvarez was the best swordsman and Nicolao's eyesight made him vulnerable. They were to ride on horseback, with a mule carrying small goods and provisions strung behind them. They would wait a few hours after Elspet and Luisa had set off, before departing.

Zachary himself had been put to bringing up the rear, to check the road behind them, and to gallop on to the party ahead to give warning should anything approach from the rear. It was a role he would usually have relished, the chance to take his own time, to lag a little if he felt like it. But not any more, now he wanted to spend every moment he could in sight of Luisa.

When Etienne reappeared, Alvarez handed him a roll of parchment. 'Give this to Señor Quevedo, he knows my signature. We are old friends, and he will give you hospitality until we are all gathered there.'

Etienne nodded, a slight smile on his lips, and tucked the parchment into his bag. He threw the saddle blanket and saddle over his horse and pushed his sword and buckler to the rear.

'God speed. The rest of us will follow after you,' said Alvarez, as Etienne mounted. 'Make sure to come and tell us if there are troops on the road ahead, or anything else to hinder our safe passage. If anyone stops you, tell them you are on your way to relatives in Sines.'

'I will,' Etienne said. He mounted his black horse.

'Good luck,' shouted Alexander, as he and the señor dragged open the big back gates. 'See you in Tavira.'

Etienne spurred on his horse and it galloped out into the dusk.

When all was prepared, the mules loaded, the carriage set and ready to go, they went to fetch Alvarez and found him kneeling in the arms room, checking each blade as though for war. He gave them all a circular metal plate to wear under their soft hats. 'You may wear this if you wish,' he said. 'These good people are under our protection. It is a big responsibility.'

It was sobering. The remaining men glanced at each other and left quietly, carrying the crown protectors in their hands. Zachary noticed they all took a little longer to prime their blades then, and Pedro loaded his firearms while they waited; none of them spoke.

A few hours later as the sun grew low in the sky, he peered into the open carriage. Elspet waited pinch-faced there, dressed in a borrowed black cloak with the hood up to cover her hair and face. Luisa huddled inside too, wearing one of Elspet's gowns. She shrunk back against the leather upholstery.

Zachary held open the door and said, 'Till later. Go safely,' and Luisa looked back at him with eyes full of emotion. A surge of love welled up in his chest. He gripped her hand tightly a moment, and shut the door. 'God speed, be safe,' he repeated through the window, glancing at Elspet, who sat still as an icon, but replied with a nervous smile. She had not mentioned their conversation, but he had felt a heaviness drop from his shoulders like a winter cloak now he had told her. They were free of each other, he realized, but paradoxically it had made him value her more. He sincerely wished her well.

After Alexander had climbed up in front, they rumbled away through the gates. On the horizon he saw the flash of fire over the city. Pray God Alexander would take care of them both.

The waiting was hard. His mind was on Luisa and how she might be faring. Nicolao and Ayamena held fast to each other's hands. Alvarez and Nicolao were to go next. Nicolao called out to Husain to be good, but Husain, seemingly oblivious to the tension in the yard, was still running around, chasing after one of the hens with a pointed stick. Nicolao kissed his wife tenderly. '*Salaam*,' he whispered, and Alvarez helped him mount.

Alvarez and Nicolao and the mules clopped out, with Alvarez leading the way. 'Give us an hour before you leave,' he instructed Pedro.

Ayamena bravely bustled about, loading the cart with a few last-minute items gleaned from the stables that the King's men had not touched – a leather bucket for water, a sack of grain, even the hay nets. 'We'll take anything that's left,' she said. 'Never waste anything. You never know, we might be able to sell it on the way.' Meanwhile, Pedro waited patiently in the driver's seat.

They listened for the cathedral bell, its mournful note made them acutely aware of the passing time. Finally, Zachary mounted and said, 'Come on, Husain, time to go.'

Husain pouted. He was still trying to catch the hen, which was more and more determined not to be caught. 'But she should be inside the hen house with the others. It's raining.'

Zachary put his finger to his lips, 'Quiet!' A noise of shouting close by, out on the street. He tried to remain calm, 'She'll be all right. Leave her be now, and climb up.'

'No.'

More urgently now; 'Come on, or we'll go without you.'

A hammering on the front gate. Shouts from outside of 'Moros, moros!'

'Sounds like more trouble,' shouted Pedro, 'Let's move!'

Zachary's voice cut through the noise. 'Señora Ortega, call Husain!'

Pedro stood up to look over the wall at what was happening. 'Go ! Go!' he yelled, cracking the whip. The horse startled and leapt forward, with Ayamena Ortega clinging to hold on as it lurched away. She turned her head and bawled 'Husain!'

Husain was transfixed by the commotion at the front, standing there with the stick in his hand, his mouth open. Ayamena stood up and bellowed at him again. She was still screaming for her son as the cart careered out of the back gates.

The door in the wall rattled and there was a great thud. The wooden planks bowed as if under a great force. Another thud, and another. A crack of splintering wood and the door burst open. A mob of angry people surged into the yard. Townsmen with cudgels and the King's armoured swordsmen, spiked bucklers in their hands. Bristling behind them, the butts and barrels of soldiers' muskets glinted in the remains of the light.

Husain appeared to shrink. He quailed a moment, then ran, but his legs wouldn't carry him quick enough.

Zachary was shouting but it was as if Husain had been overtaken by a great tide. The rain slashed down from the sky. The yard filled with men and the smell of damp leather and metal. Husain stumbled and disappeared under the sea of people, his stick waving before it was dragged out of sight.

Zachary turned his horse and plunged back into the crowd. Some cleared to give him space but most were intent on breaking into the buildings; they trampled over the splintered wood and swarmed in through the doors. He couldn't see Husain.

He pulled his horse around, frantically searching the crowd, but there was no sign of him. He leapt off and ran into the kitchen, shouting: 'Husain!'

People were everywhere, blocking his view. Outside the gate a crowd was chanting, repeating the same phrase over and over, like the roar of bullfight. 'Moros! Moros!'

Zachary craned his head over the forest of heads and helmets. A man in dripping plate armour rose up in front of him, his great back blocking his path. He turned to him and said, 'Dirty bastards. Looks like they've gone. You seen them?' Zachary shook his head. A musket butt dug into his back as someone turned.

He still could not see Husain. Where was he? Using his elbows to clear breathing space Zachary pushed his way through the damp backs upstairs towards the training hall, but did not get far for the crush of people coming in the opposite direction.

They forced him back down into the yard where his horse was still loose. A man was hitting the poor beast with a switch to move it away, but it neighed and churned in the centre of the milling crowd. All was confusion. The leaders of the mob, satisfied the building was empty, pressed out through the back gates, but seeing nothing out there flooded back through the yard and into the street. The sheer force of momentum dragged Zachary with them. Almost lifted off his feet, he struggled to keep his footing, thought he might be trampled in the crowd.

Then he saw Husain. It was just a glimpse, between the backs of the men in front. A man in full plate armour and helmet had him gripped tightly by one skinny arm.

Zachary tried to squeeze his way forward but could not move far, he was impeded by the backs of the taller men in front. He was stuck, but even from there he could see the street was already full of terrified people, most half-dressed, presumably Moriscos dragged from their beds and guarded by the angry rabble of townspeople and the King's musketeers. They were herded together in a knot like beasts.

'Mama!' Husain cried, searching vainly amongst the faces of the crowd. Zachary shoved harder, but could make no headway. The soldier dragged Husain into the corral of Moriscos, where a woman who looked as though she wanted to be kind took hold of his shoulder. Husain flinched away and cowered, whimpering, unsure who to trust. A gash on his forehead trickled blood down on to his nose. He had lost a sandal, and had one bare foot. His hand still clung to the broken remnants of his stick. Zachary's heart sank. Around the small group of Moriscos seethed an impenetrable wall of armour and guns.

Zachary was crushed on all sides. There was no room to draw a sword, even a dagger. He shouted, 'Husain!' again, but it was no use, the crowd were moving away up the road. For a few moments he was dragged, stumbling, with them.

With a huge effort he turned round, the blood pounding in his ears. He dodged and weaved through the thinning crowd and leapt through the broken gate back into the yard. His horse shied away from him, snorting, the whites of its eyes flashing. Curse the bloody animal. He caught hold of the slippery reins, but the beast was spooked and would not stand still or let him mount. When he finally managed to wedge a toe in the stirrup the horse bucked, trying to unseat him, but he clung tight, clapping his heels against its sides. As he pointed its nose out of the back gates, Pedro ran in.

'I told her to wait further up the road,' he panted. 'Where's Husain?'

'They've taken him. I couldn't –' Zachary was still wrestling with his side-stepping horse.

'Oh God in heaven. What will we tell Ayamena?'

Zachary did not answer but helped Pedro mount behind him and kicked his horse on. A hen squawked and flustered out of the way of his galloping hooves. As they pounded out through the gates he spied a small straw sandal trodden into the mud.

Ayamena was already clambering down from the wagon when they skidded to a stop. Her face was stricken. She looked from one to the other. 'Where is he?' Pedro slid down, but she had seen the answer from his face. 'We will go back,' she said. 'Turn the wagon.'

Pedro put his hand on her shoulder and said gently, 'There is no point. They will take your son to the children's camp. All the Morisco children are to be held there until they can be rehoused with Christian families. If you go back they will send you somewhere else from your son anyway.'

'No,' she protested, her voice rising, 'I'm going back for him. I'm going back!' She began to run down the road, manto flapping, but Pedro was too quick and reached to catch her, struggling, in his big arms. She sank to her knees in the mud.

Zachary dropped to his knees beside her. He caught hold of her hand, 'I'm sorry. I could do nothing to stop them. But I swear by Our Lady and all that's holy, I will go back and find out what I can, once you are safely away from here.' He put his arm across her shoulder.

She wept into his chest. 'But he's all alone. What will I tell Nicolao? We should have gone together. It will be no life if we are not together.'

'Hush,' said Pedro, stiffening. They listened. There was a faint sound in the distance. 'Get back on the wagon,' he shouted. 'Stick to the plan. We will be no use to Husain if they take us, they will shoot us if they think we are – how do you say? – resistance.'

Zachary pushed the grieving Ayamena back on to the wagon. 'You will be safe with Pedro,' Zachary said, 'he will take care of you. I'd trust him with my life.'

Pedro looked surprised. He was not used to compliments from Zachary, but it worked. 'Get up here,' Pedro said gruffly. 'We will go and find your husband and daughter. Zachary will find out where your son is, and see what can be done. That's right, isn't it?'

'Yes,' Zachary said.

Ayamena was dragged away by Pedro in a bear-like grip, and the wagon jogged off.

Zachary looked back at the city of Seville, the black silhouettes of the buildings lit up by blasts of gunfire. Bells were ringing all over the city. His heart was torn. In the village near Tavira, Luisa would be looking out for him. Waiting to get on that boat. He had promised her. But how could he go to her, and tell her her brother had been taken, and it was all his fault?

The city looked like a black fortress. Somewhere in there, a six-year-old boy was terrified and looking for his mother. He remembered being a boy, and the misery of being suddenly alone. He remembered the butt of his brothers' boots and the certainty that nobody cared enough to help him.

Zachary turned his horse, dug in his heels, and galloped back towards Seville.

Etienne struggled to release himself from the guards' grip, but they would not let go. The grand house had been emptied of furniture but was full of men in full plate armour. As he was dragged upstairs the only portrait still hanging on the wall was of Felipe III, and the face had obviously been used for target practice. Perhaps it had not been such a good idea after all, to come to Don Rodriguez.

'He says he has news of a rebellion. In Portugal – Tavira.' The guards dropped him to his knees before Don Rodriguez.

'Is this true?' The big man loomed over him.

'Yes. Alvarez and his men.' He staggered to his feet.

'Alvarez the fencing master?'

'He has a party of swordsmen with him, and a group of Moriscos ready to stir up trouble in the villages.'

'You said they would cause no trouble.'

'I thought—'

'Where is this? And how do I know this is reliable information this time?'

Etienne took the scroll he was supposed to deliver to the Quevedo family and passed it over. Rodriguez took a moment to read it through narrowed eyes. 'And just what's in it for you?'

'For me?' Etienne swallowed.

'Yes. Why are you telling me this?'

Etienne felt a squirm of fear. 'Because you pay me to keep you informed about what Alvarez is doing. How he trains. And because

I'm a good Christian. Why else? It's our duty to report these things to the authorities, and—'

'You are an untrustworthy little shit, aren't you? Do you mean it's because you were afraid to be caught with them? You're a coward, Galen. Men I can't trust are no use to me. Take him away, have him sent to the San Jorge. A spell in there should help him to know his own mind.'

Etienne cried out, 'No, not that! Not the San Jorge! I've done nothing wrong. Only what you asked, what any good man should—' But the guards had already seized him and were hauling him away. He saw the ornamental tiled floor with its gilded *olembrillas* pass under his eyes. 'Wait,' he cried, 'I'll do anything!'

Don Rodriguez watched him go. The grovelling Frenchman's report had the aura of truth about it. It seemed more than likely that Alvarez could be negotiating with Moriscos from the Portuguese villages. Alvarez was capable of mustering men, but it might take time – after all, he had no readily available army behind him, no discipline. Alvarez tried to keep his men as individuals, and that was fine for duelling, but too unpredictable for war. Only one thing made a man obey orders, and that was if the fear of disobeying orders was equal to, or greater than, his fear of the enemy.

Alvarez had never been able to see that. Now he knew why; the man was just Morisco shit like all the other vermin they were moving out of this city. Good thing Carranza was dead; he would have been horrified to see how Alvarez had debased his art.

But if Galen was right . . . Rodriguez read the paper again. It seemed genuine enough, and promotion was in the air, he could smell it. He thought how fine it would look to the King if he quelled such an uprising. He strode from the chamber and called for his sergeant.

Chapter 48

Elspet peered out from the hood draped to hide the scar on her cheek. Next to her lay two razor-edged daggers. The hilt of the sword dug into her hip bone as the carriage jolted down the road. She glanced at Luisa, and wondered if her stomach too was churning with fear.

She remembered Etienne asking her if she would fight. She shivered involuntarily. Pray God it would not come to that. Luisa stayed grim and silent in the seat opposite her. Elspet could think of nothing comforting to say.

Near the city gate she heard a low murmur, and looked out to see the glint of armour, and white steam rising from a long snake of people – Moriscos from the neighbouring towns on their way to the embarkation points. Trepidation filled her. Just outside the gates she felt the inevitable slowing of the wheels as Alexander tried to pull off to the side of the road.

Luisa seemed unperturbed, her oval face pale, the knit of her brows hardly changed, but Elspet wondered what she could be thinking. These were her people. She imagined Nicolao and Señor Alvarez following in their wake and hoped they were close behind. There had been no sign of Etienne, though, he had not been back to warn them of this blockage on the road.

'Are you ready?' Elspet asked.

'Yes,' said Luisa. 'Don't worry.'

'Just keep quiet, don't say a word.'

The tramping of soldiers boots. A man in a plated helmet and breastplate jutted his head through the window. 'Where are you going?'

Alexander appeared behind him. 'I am Dutch. Here are my papers. I am escorting this English lady to Sines. This is her maid. When we heard the proclamation we were trying to get out of the city. We wanted to get out of Seville and to her brother's before you brought in the Moors, but we see we left it too late.'

'You shouldn't be on this road at all. We've two thousand Moriscos to bring down to the port. You'll have to turn back.'

'He advises we turn back,' Alexander said to her.

'Quite impossible,' she said in her best English. 'I have to be in Sines by the end of the week for my brother's wedding. Tell him to move his people off the road.'

Alexander widened his eyes as if she had taken leave of her senses, but the guard smiled. 'Women!' he said. 'I think the señorita would not thank you, if you continue on this road,' he said. The two men laughed, complicitly. 'I am sorry, señor, but you must move. No one goes out of the city today. The road ahead will be blocked too. Wait until we pass, then return home. Tell the womenfolk to come out and stand off to the side.' He gestured them out of the carriage with the point of his musket.

They stood in the drizzle by the side of the road, which was already a thin slime of yellow mud. Alexander and the boy dragged the pair of horses off to the side of the road, the carriage spattering them with water from the wheels. She caught Alexander's eye and they exchanged worried glances. His face was taut and drawn, and despite his height he struggled to control the horses which trampled over his feet. Finally, he had them standing quietly.

'You are armed,' said the guard. He had found her daggers in the carriage and now eyed her sword-belt.

'Would you have a lady travel abroad without some protection?' she retorted. 'I have had to leave my Moorish servants, and now I have only this stupid Dutch woman. And she's been dumb since birth. What else was I to do?'

He grunted. Luisa stood, head bowed, thankfully still silent. The guard's eyes shifted to the procession coming towards them. Four or five armoured men marched in front; columns of soldiers were ranked to the side with muskets and pikes. Boxed in by them shuffled a wretched bunch of people with barely any baggage, only sagging haversacks and tied bundles. They looked to be wearing all the clothes they possessed, but their backs were sodden with wet, their hems dripped, the men's hair and beards hung in rat's tails.

Elspet could do nothing but stare. There were women there, nursing mothers and children. Old people who limped with a stick and shivered, despite the fact that others were steaming with the exertion of walking. Many were barefoot. As they passed, their feet made footprints in the mud, but these were quickly blotted out by the people walking behind. As they walked, the women sang mournfully in an ululating lilt. They paid no heed to Luisa and Elspet standing there as they passed, their eyes were blank, or fixed on the city ahead.

The sound of the women singing had a creaking quality as if it had been long buried. When Elspet looked at Luisa she saw her cheeks were wet with rain. That was until Luisa brought her sleeve up to wipe her eyes, and Elspet realized with a jolt it was tears. She dare not go to comfort her, it would look too intimate to behave so with a servant.

'Wait a while after we pass,' shouted the guard. 'We move slow, no point in you being right on our tail.'

'Yes, sir, we will,' called Alexander.

It took perhaps one quarter-hour for the procession to pass. The guard trotted to catch up with the back of the party, and as the rain fell dark and heavy, Elspet watched them grow smaller as they headed to the city.

Alexander put the horses back in traces.

'We go on,' he said. 'Not back, as the soldier ordered. You all right?'

She nodded and they waited as he hauled the horses and carriage back on to the track. They climbed inside, wet running from their shoulders. Elspet reached out to Luisa.

'Don't worry,' she said. 'Señor Alvarez and his students will look after your family.'

'I hope Mama doesn't see that,' she said.

To her surprise, Luisa did not pull her hand away but gripped it tight as the carriage moved off again. Eventually she said, 'Those soldiers, do you think they'll let them pass?'

'Señor Alvarez trained his men well. Your family could not be in better hands. Never fear, they'll get to Tavira somehow.'

They had to make a detour into a derelict farmstead as Alexander saw yet another smaller group of Moriscos on the road, and they held their breath as they passed. But as night fell there were no more hold-ups and the roads became rutted and uneven. They travelled through the blur of rain until they could no longer make out any trace of Seville on the horizon. Finally, the lights of a small fishing port twinkled in the distance. The carriage stopped by a group of gnarled olive trees; the branches rattled in the wind.

'I'm going to walk on ahead,' Alexander said to them through the window. 'Etienne was supposed to meet us to show us the way, but there's been no sign of him. Perhaps I've missed him somehow. Wait here until I come back for you. I'll go and find the Quevedo family and check it's safe.'

He disappeared into the darkness. From here they could hear the moan of the wind, and the crash of waves breaking against rocks.

'Are you afraid?' Elspet asked into the black cave of the carriage.

'No.' A short laugh. 'I am angry, that is all. I am Spanish and a good Catholic. I am being made to flee my homeland for no good reason. What sort of a man is he, that would do this to his people?'

'I don't know. In England our king will not allow us to worship in the Roman Church. Señor Alvarez says it is easy to have an opinion when you have no power, but when you have power, when you are a king, then your opinion will uphold some and exclude others. Señor Alvarez says it is better not to have opinions at all.'

'Huh.' The voice was disparaging. A short silence and then, 'I don't understand what you are doing in Spain. Why do you wait for Zachary Deane before you go home to England? He is not interested in you, that much I know.'

Elspet laughed. 'I know he's not interested in any sort of suit with me, nor I with him. He probably despises me. It's complicated. I thought he was my half-brother, but now . . . I'm not sure what he is.' It was the first time she had admitted the truth. 'But I think I am financially reliant upon him. We are tied together through my father.'

'How?' Luisa's voice was curious.

Elspet told Luisa the truth. And telling her, she found she was not nearly so emotive about it as she had been before. Next to these people who had already been stripped of their possessions and were fleeing for their lives, her own concerns seemed petty and insubstantial.

At the end of her tale, Luisa said, 'So I think you do not want to marry Mr Deane?'

Elspet laughed. 'He would be the last person on this earth I would choose. Besides, I have a feeling he has his heart set on someone else.'

Luisa was silent.

Elspet listened to the wind rattle the branches, the rain smatter down on the carriage roof.

At length Luisa said, 'You need not have helped me and you did. You have changed. When you came to fetch my mother to your English friend I thought you were just another lazy white woman with too few skills and not enough common sense.' Elspet opened her mouth in indignation; she did not know whether to be flattered or insulted, but Luisa went on, 'I saw how you trained in the yard with the men. I was wrong. You are not afraid of hard work. I don't know how things will turn out, but I won't forget your kindness.' And from the dark a thin, cold hand found her, and she found herself pulled into a tight embrace.

When Alexander returned he said, 'Bad news. Etienne never got there and Señora Quevedo is not expecting us until next week. I told her the situation and I think I've persuaded her not to turn us away.'

He drove them to a group of small farm cottages up an unmade track. The wind was even fiercer here, and the noise of the sea closer.

A boy was standing there with a palely glowing lantern at the only cottage that looked habitable. Señora Quevedo, a leather-skinned woman of about forty years, beckoned them inside under the low beams and sat them to steam before the fire.

Luisa thanked her for their hospitality and shyly told the señora of the crowds on the route. Alexander said if they did not mind he would leave the women at the farm and ride back to show the others the way, since there was still no sign of Etienne Galen. Elspet hoped Galen was all right. Though she had never liked him, she could not help but hope he was lost somewhere and not dead at the side of the road.

'You must eat,' said the señora, 'and then I will take you to join the others.'

'Others?' Luisa said. 'But my family are behind us.'

'The others who will take the boats. We are all waiting for the early tide. Six boats. My husband's too. Eat first, then Bento will show you.'

Elspet needed no encouragement to eat and drink for she was hungry and tired and eating seemed a form of normality. The woman served up mutton broth with a kind of sourdough bread. All three women ate in silence. Afterwards, with the help of the boy, Bento, they unloaded the few bags from the carriage to the covered porch around the front of the building. The señora looked at Elspet strangely as she buckled on her sword and stowed her daggers in her belt.

'Do not worry, señora. Señor Alvarez has trained her,' Luisa said, as if that explained everything.

In the end, restlessness drove them out on to the porch despite the wind. Every small noise made Luisa look up the road, until at last the sound of hoofbeats announced the arrival of Nicolao Ortega and Señor Alvarez.

'They're here! Thanks be to God.' Luisa ran to embrace her father and ply him with questions as he fumbled to tie up his horse and hand Bento the reins of the mule. Señor Alvarez sprang down and greeted Señora Quevedo with a peck to each cheek. Elspet suppressed a twinge of jealousy that he could be so easy with her.

After exchanging formalities, the señora said, 'Come, now the ladies are dry, Bento will take you to the others, and show you where you can wait. There are too many of you for my small casa.'

Bento went ahead with the little globe of the lantern and pushed open the door of the next cottage.

Elspet drew in her breath. The room was completely full, with not a hair's breadth of space remaining. Not a floorboard could be seen, except where water trickled through a gash in the roof to make a dark stain on the floor below. Every stick of broken furniture had a person perched there, people crowded against the walls and people leaned on the windowsills and in the doorways. Some had strings of shoes hung around their necks, or the tools of their trade. Crammed in every square inch of space were solemn-eyed children, livestock, tied cloth bundles, cages of poultry. The room smelt of sweat and damp and fear. The people gathered there looked up at the newcomers with silent hostility.

Señor Alvarez was clearly taken aback. He exchanged a look with Elspet and ushered her backwards out of the door. 'Are all these waiting for the next tide?' he asked.

'Yes, sir,' Bento said.

'Where have they all come from?'

'The people from the vineyards in the village. They did not want to leave their children. Christians came in the night with knives to loot their houses. One ran to us for help, and then another, and then more. So many people.' He sucked in his lips and shook his head. 'Word spread somehow. Father can't turn them away. We've sent a few hundred already, yesterday and the day before.' He laughed. 'Mother thought we had finished, but more keep coming. Like you. The people going today, well, some of their husbands or brothers own the boats you will sail in.'

Alvarez walked past Elspet on to the porch and stood for a moment, deep in thought. Rain dripped from holes in the awning on to his shoulders.

'What is the matter?' asked Alexander.

'Too many of us,' she heard Señor Alvarez say. 'A fleet of boats at anchor is an easier target than a single boat. Moving a hundred people to the boats is much more obvious than moving only a few. And the more people, the more often it has gone on, the greater the chance the authorities will want to stop us. Others in the village might not be as sympathetic as Señor Quevedo. Did he tell you when the next ebb tide is?'

'No,' Elspet said. 'We haven't seen him, he is out preparing the boats with the other men. But I guess soon.'

'I asked the boy,' Alexander said. 'It's at five bells. Only a few hours.'

'How far behind were Ayamena and Husain?' Elspet asked.

'I said to leave it two hours,' Señor Alvarez said, in a worried tone. 'We weren't expecting to go today. It wasn't what we planned.

We planned for next week; the tide was later then.' 'Then they'll be cutting it fine,' Alexander said.

Chapter 49

In the distance, thunder rumbled and Zachary ran down the back streets dragging his trotting horse behind, glad that the buildings were high enough to afford some shelter. He threw the reins over the fence at the sword school, and sprinted to the quay. A sense of unreality hung over him. How would he find Husain? It would be like looking for a single straw in a thatch. His only hope would be to intercept him before he reached the holding house.

At the quay it was even worse than he thought. Hundreds of angry people were waiting to embark, caged between ranks of soldiers, like wild dogs ready to turn and bite at any moment. Mercenaries searched the assembled people for arms and prised their belongings from them with threats and beatings. A scuffle broke out right in front of him, but the soldiers bludgeoned the Morisco man with the end of a pike until he handed over his gold.

Around the cordon, half of Seville seemed to be there; to barter and haggle over trinkets and coin, and watch the spectacle of the people being driven on to the ships. Further down the road Moriscos covered their heads as a rain of stones fell on to them from the jeering crowd. He couldn't see any children.

He approached one of the onlookers politely, trying not to appear desperate, 'Excuse me, where are these people from?'

'From Carmona and Estepa, and some from Triana.'

'Where do they take the children?' Zachary said.

The man took him in with an appraising look. 'The tobacco factory. The warehouses of Martin de Vérez. But they've blocked the road at both ends. It's crazy mad with screaming women. Some are frantic, trying to get their babies and children out, but there's even more begging them to take their older ones in. There's a rumour they will all be –' He mimed slitting his throat and glanced sideways at Zachary to gauge his reaction. 'The poor beggars are not sure if they're all going to be dumped at sea.' He sucked in his breath and then whispered, 'If you're looking for your child, my son, they will not let you have him. They want the children for servants and slaves. Trained of course, to be good Christians and hate the race of their fathers and mothers.'

His bitterness was like a canker. And there was some sort of enjoyment in his words too, as though he relished delivering this news.

A crack and a flash, and they both fell to the ground, covering their heads. Another rumble and the sky lit up. But it was only lightning, splitting the sky with its ragged scrawl.

They stood up sheepishly, brushed the wet from their knees as another bolt came from nowhere right overhead. The hot poker of light attached itself to one of the pikemen and they saw him stutter and fall. A sudden hush, and even from where they stood, they caught the smell of burning. Simultaneously a cheer broke out from the assembled Moriscos and a cry of 'Allah!' Everyone surged forward to see what was happening.

Zachary shuddered. It was a sign from heaven. God's wrath released on those responsible for these terrible events. He had a feeling of being caught in something momentous.

'Lord have mercy,' he cried, and sent up a silent prayer for help as he took advantage of the diversion and set off at a run towards the warehouses by the river.

As the old man had told him, the road was closed off. The street had a barricade of upturned tobacco barrels with pikemen and musketeers lined up behind to keep back the men and women who were trying to find their children.

He cut round to the other side of the building where the soldiers were bringing in children they had separated from their families at the port. They were escorted in gaggles of five to ten. Between the great armoured beetles of pikemen, they looked so small and lost. At this side too, women wailed, clamouring for their babies, alongside male elders who hurled insults and shook their fists. Here too, they were held back by the well-disciplined ranks. In the gathering dark the children's gazes combed the faces behind the soldiers, searching for someone they knew.

Zachary observed for a moment from a distance. He took a breath to remember his training. All his senses were alert – a deer listening for the hunter. If a chance came to get through he would be ready. He moved himself in a leisurely walk, down to the part where the troops were most sparse, alongside the river, following a few other well-dressed civilians in wide-brimmed hats. He scanned the line of troops. There was a gap in the barricade there, guarded by four men.

Zachary joined the tail of the merchant party and saw one of the civilians hold out a paper to the nearest guard. The guard gave it a cursory glance and waved them through. Zachary hurried to stick close to the moustachioed man in front. As he passed through he let out his breath. He still could not see any children, but he cast his eyes about for a door to the warehouse.

'Hey! Get back. We were here before you.'

It was only then he realized he was in a queue of about eight men, all well-dressed in Walloon ruffs and with the obligatory long tucks, their swords, hanging from their belts. Their cloaks and embroidered hose marked them out as wealthy men. The line ended at a peeling, iron-red door set into the factory wall. He apologized and stepped to the end of the queue, hoping to blend in with the other men he had come in with, who were just joining the queue. Thunder rumbled again as he craned over the heads of the soldiers in front, to try and catch a glimpse of Husain.

'I expect there'll be a bigger queue soon. The terms are not bad, eh? Just give them bed and board and we get twenty-five years of work out of them at least before they have to be released. The Crown will give a gift of grain and shoes too. My wife wants a girl, for the laundry.'

But Zachary wasn't listening, he had spotted a line of carts, heavily guarded by pikemen, trundling towards the warehouse. As each one passed he stood on tiptoes to look at the children inside. The wagons stopped. A bare-headed woman had made it through the barrier and was trying to climb up to reach her child, but a soldier clubbed her over the head and dragged her like a carcass out of the wagon's path. The crying children fell solemn and silent, and just at that moment the rain began to pelt from the sky. Great bouncing drops, that made the children bow their heads and squint against its impact.

There, between two other boys, was Husain, clinging white-faced to the rails. A toddler, grubby tear-stains in vertical stripes down his cheeks, gripped tight on to Husain's arm as the cart jerked its way towards the doors. But Husain's eyes still searched the crowd. Zachary turned his head quickly away. He did not want him to recognize him and shout out.

He moved himself closer to the armed convoy but could see no way through, the soldiers were two deep all around it, the rain splattering off their helmets. The cart set off again towards the open doors. But just as it did, the iron-red door in the wall opened and the queue of men, shuffling closer to be out of the rain, pressed towards it. Zachary ran to join them. A sharp dry smell of snuff met his nostrils.

He heard the portly merchant at the front of the line say, 'We are members of Don Rodriguez's confraternity. Here are the papers. Pérez said if we came down early we could have the pick of them.'

The soldier by the door said, 'More of you, eh? Ten reales.'

'Hey! Nobody mentioned anything about paying. You should be paying us. We've got to keep the vermin, haven't we?'

'No fee, no entry. It's a favour we're doing you.'

There was much grumbling and fumbling in purses from the assembled men, who had not anticipated being asked for payment.

Zachary shifted from foot to foot. He wished they would hurry. He still had to get Husain away, and time was passing. Luisa would be wondering where they were, and at the thought of her an intense longing flooded his chest.

The men were still protesting. It was soon apparent that the man in front of Zachary did not have ten reales. He continued to complain, screwing up his wizened face. Zachary's purse was full. Alvarez had supplied each of them with enough money to pay passage if it was needed.

'Look, I'll loan you it,' Zachary said, anxious to speed up the process. 'We'll go in together. Here – enough for the both of us.' He took the purse from his belt pouch and thrust it into the man's hand.

'I'll pay you back,' the man said. 'It's very good of you. My name's Rincón, by the way.' Zachary did not volunteer his name. By this time they were at the door and the elderly Rincón handed over the money.

'Twenty, for me and my friend,' he said, 'But I still think it's robbery. Don Rodriguez never said anything about payment.'

Zachary kept his head low as he passed. He had actually got inside the building. One step nearer. Now they were in the factory, the sound of crying rose and fell.

Ahead of him in the gloom of the warehouse the would-be buyers were searched and their weapons laid aside on a bench near the door. Damn. He watched as they searched Rincón methodically and removed his tuck to a side table. Zachary thought quickly. Never leave yourself unarmed – the first rule of the streets. He put his elbow up to his face and feigned a sneeze, opening his mouth. His paring knife, folded and sheathed into its bone handle, dropped out of his sleeve to rest on his tongue. He closed his mouth tight.

He submitted to the search, and the soldier took his buckler and signalled to him to remove his sword-hanger and sword. The soldier felt the front of Zachary's doublet and his sleeves, before moving to the side to open his pouch and feel under his cloak for concealed weapons. Zachary caught sight of the hilt of a dagger nestled against the soldier's thigh.

Very well. If the soldier was to take Zachary's sword, he would have himself something in exchange. As the soldier patted down his back Zachary coughed and raised his hand to his mouth. The paring knife fell neatly into his hand. In one deft movement he flicked the blade open and with a quick chop relieved the man of his military dagger, complete with its leather scabbard.

He raised his arm as if to assist the man feeling down his back behind him, and let the dagger slide down his sleeve until it rested under his armpit. Then he clamped down his arm to keep his prize. He re-sleeved his paring knife to its usual place.

The man had finished searching. 'Next,' he called, and slapped Zachary on the back to move him forward.

Shafts of dim light through the closed shutters and some feebly burning lanterns illuminated air thick with tobacco dust. The children cowered away in the darkest corner of the vast building, behind the gritstone grinding mills, and the packed earth where the horses trod in circles to turn them. One of the men who had gone in earlier had already chosen a small boy and was attempting to tie his hands together. The boy howled and twisted and struggled until a soldier helped the merchant to force the boy still by holding him by the hair. Zachary looked around for Husain. He rubbed his hand across his brow. How would he ever find him? There were so many children, all crying or screaming. The air reeked of tobacco and terror.

He waded his way into the throng of children like a man stepping into the sea. Another man in front of him picked up a babe and examined him for defects before bundling him under the arm like a sack of grain.

'Where are the older ones?' Zachary asked.

The man wagged his head behind him. 'Over there.'

A touch on his arm made Zachary spin round. 'Here. You'll need this.' Rincón passed him a metal collar with a pin-lock and chain and a leather leash attached.

'Oh, no need,' he said, feeling the weight of the contraption in his hands with revulsion.

'I insist,' Rincón said. 'I'm only after a baby. My wife fancies something to train from the beginning. You'll have more need of this, if you're after something older.'

A hand fastened itself around his wrist. He looked down meaning to shake it off, but suddenly found himself looking into familiar eyes.

'Mr Deane?' Husain whispered, his bottom lip trembling.

It was all Zachary could do not to sweep him up and hug him.

But he musn't arouse suspicion. Zachary put his hand to his lips in a gesture of quiet. Husain's brown eyes never left his own.

'He doesn't look very strong,' Rincón said, approaching, pursing his lips. 'What about that one over there? He looks more sturdy.' He pointed to where another thick-set lad was hitting a smaller boy with his fists. Husain's grip tightened on his wrist.

'No, this is the one for me. I don't want trouble.'

'Well, if you're sure. I'll help you get the collar on him.'

Rincón showed Zachary how to click the lock closed and turn the key. Husain let them do it without protest. 'Wait for me outside my friend,' Rincón said, handing him his purse. 'I won't be long.'

'I will,' shouted Zachary, but he was already guiding Husain back to the light of the door. At the other end of the warehouse more distraught children were arriving. Husain's eyes kept straying to where they tipped them off the back of the cart like sheaves of tobacco.

'Husain,' Zachary whispered, 'I'll get you out of here. Just keep quiet, and do as I ask. Your mama is waiting, but you must be good. Understand?'

He nodded trustingly. Zachary led him by the leash towards the door. Almost there. Zachary resisted the urge to run, and strolled with him towards the light.

Just before the door a table had been set up where two soldiers were waiting to sign out the Morisco slaves.

'Ten reales,' said the soldier nearest to him. 'Name?' These men were helmetless, fully armed, but in civilian clothes. The nearest one was poised with a quill in his hand.

'But I paid it already, when I came in.' His heart began to pound in his chest.

'Well it's another ten to take him out. The blockade will not let you pass without a valid paper of sale. Even those who are friends of Don Rodriguez.'

'Wait a moment whilst I find change.'

The sound of the foreign accent made the other soldier turn in curiosity. He frowned as if solving a puzzle, before his mouth opened. 'Hey!'

It was Fabian, Don Rodriguez's man.

'Quick,' Zachary said, hoisting Husain by his skinny arm towards the door.

'Stop!' Fabian's command made a momentary silence.

The soldier behind the table stood up, hands on the table, but he was not quick enough. The concealed dagger was already finding its way down Zachary's sleeve to his hand. Zachary flicked the sheath to the ground and thrust the tongue of the blade down hard into the soldier's sleeve. The soldier was pinned there, slumped over the table.

'Now,' he shouted, pushing Husain into motion. He swept up his sword and hanger from the table by the door as he passed, yelling, 'Run!'

They pelted down the quay, Zachary stumbling after the fleet-footed Husain. Behind them, the thud of footsteps, but he dare not turn. His sword straps trailed on the ground. Past the crowd of indignant merchants, now swelled to about a dozen. One of them put a hand out to stop them, but it was a half-hearted attempt, they kept on running. The blockade was ahead; a black and silver castle wall, where armed pikemen and arquebusiers were holding back the crowd, preventing children from entering or leaving. A flying stone from the crowd beyond narrowly missed their heads.

Before Zachary had time to think, the terrified Husain dodged left away from the barriers down a narrow side street. He had no choice but to follow. He sprinted panting after him. Husain veered back and forth, through the pelting rain, looking for a way out, but it was no use. The only way out was on to the main boulevard again and the blockade.

Hussain stopped in the middle of the street. It was a dead end.

'Get into that doorway,' shouted Zachary, frantically trying to buckle on his sword. Husain dodged sideways.

Fabian rounded the corner, sword in hand, and stopped. His eyes scanned the street, and with a sinking sensation Zachary saw the lead trailing from the doorway. Too late. Fabian pounced on it, jerked hard and Husain was dragged trembling into the open.

'Still after a slave boy for nothing. You don't give up easily, do you? My orders are that those resisting transportation are to be killed.

I'm afraid you are about to lose your boy again.'

Zachary bounded forward, but Fabian made a sudden thrust towards Husain with his sword. Husain screamed with all his might but he was nimble and jumped to the side, out of range. Fabian's weapon was a slender iron point designed to pierce through armour.

Fabian looked surprised that it had missed but raised it with both hands to bring the weight of it down on to Husain's head.

Zachary sprang at him and let his sword fly to counter it. Fabian prepared to riposte but he was still clinging to the leash with his other hand, and Husain's screams were distracting as he struggled to pull the leash from his grasp.

Fabian thrust at Zachary with the lethal point, but Husain jerked him off-balance and the reach of it was just short. Zachary felt the whisper of it brush against the buttons of his doublet. Too close for comfort.

He made a rapid sweep to Fabian's legs. He missed, but Fabian was forced to let go of Husain to step away.

'Get out of the way!' yelled Zachary. Husain ran, head down, to the side.

Zachary felt all his training come into play. His sword swooped like a swallow but Fabian parried it every time. He forged forwards like a ploughshare.

'Mr Deane!' Husain's panicky voice cried out.

Fabian jabbed hard and strong down his centre line. Zachary was forced to retreat, beaten back until he was almost up against the shuttered windows of the building behind him. Water from the eaves poured down on his head.

Fabian loomed over him. Zachary saw the glint of triumph in his eyes. Luisa's serious face flashed into his mind and in the same instant he recalled Alvarez's training with the cloak. He hooked the tip of his sword through the cord and the wet cloak dropped heavy as a grain sack on to his arm. Holding the collar he cast it out like a net. It curled around Fabian's throat and twitched him sideways off target.

Fabian cursed. But Zachary withdrew the cloak and was already flicking it out again just as the bigger man grunted and put his weight behind his sword. The cloak wrapped around Fabian's neck and tightened, fouling his sword. Fabian's free hand reached up to free himself, but in that moment Zachary struck.

Fabian staggered back, blood pouring from his chest.

Zachary did not wait to see if he was dead. He simply scooped Husain up on to his hip and ran out of the alley, back on to the main thoroughfare. They'd have to risk the barricade.

He slowed to get his bearings, and Husain whimpered, 'Where's Mama? I want Mama.'

'Get down now,' he said, 'and keep quiet. She's waiting further up the road.'

Husain jumped down, and Zachary caught the end of the leash. It didn't feel good holding him like a dog, but he didn't want to lose him. The sun was almost down and dark shadows lay across their path. They walked warily towards the barricade. The ground was wet after the downpour, their feet splashed in the wheel ruts, now filled with water. Husain walked in his one sandal, with his head down as if expecting a blow at any moment.

'Papers, please.'

Zachary hoped to stall him. He started to search his pouch.

'They are here somewhere, I had them only a moment ago.' The guard paused to listen as a piercing wail rent the air.

'It's Maghrib,' Husain whispered, 'the sunset prayer.' He dropped to his knees in the mud and touched his forehead to the ground.

On the other side of the barricade, the belligerent crowd fell silent. Men and women dropped to their knees where they stood. The guards turned to look at the sudden quiet. The sound of the imam was the only sound, 'Allahu akbar,' he chanted.

'They did this earlier,' said the guard. 'A full quarter bell, it lasted. We threatened to fire on them if they didn't get up, but Don Rodriguez sent orders that we're to keep it peaceable.' He shook his head. 'Can't understand it at all, going down into the filth. Best get your boy up. You'll soon beat that nonsense out of him. You can go through now, it will be easier for us whilst they're occupied.'

He did not ask for papers. Zachary forcibly dragged Husain to his feet, and hustled him forward. The guards parted to let them past. When they got to the other side of the barricade he saw the whole street was lined with men and women all kneeling in neat rows facing the same direction.

Husain stopped, and even though Zachary pulled on his arm he would not move. 'I want to pray with my papa,' Husain said. 'Where is he? You said you'd take me to him.'

'Come on, Husain, we've got to get to the sword school. My horse is there, and then we can find your mama.'

'No,' he said, 'you said she'd be here. You said. Where is she?' His voice broke with tears.

'She's waiting outside the town.'

'Don't believe you,' he sobbed. 'You said she'd be here and I can't see her.' He began to shout, 'Mama! Mama!'

'Be quiet!'

'Mama!' Husain's wails reached a crescendo. A guard turned to look. There was nothing else for it. Zachary picked him up and ran with him down the streets, it was twilight now and Husain pummelled and screamed for Ayamena all the way. When they got to the sword school Husain calmed a little at the sight of a familiar place, but when he saw no sign of his parents he refused to be put on the horse.

Zachary tried to lift him up into the saddle, but he screeched and punched and drummed his heels and would not let go of his arms. Finally, Zachary stopped trying.

'For God's sake, Husain. Help me. It's hard enough, but you have to help me.' He held tightly on to him as if swaddling him until the boy seemed to have tired himself out. Time was running out and he did not know if he could make it to Tavira. He sank down against the wall and stroked Husain's hair.

'Look, Husain,' he cajoled, 'you have to trust me. Your mama and papa have gone to the boat. You remember your papa talking about the boat, don't you? Well, they are waiting for us there. If we get on to the horse we'll get there quicker. Your mama will be there, and your papa and Señor Alvarez; they have your slate and chalk with them. And your sister Luisa . . .' He felt a lump come to his throat.

'And if I get on the horse Mama will be there?'

'If we're quick.'

'Promise?'

He made the sign of the cross. 'Please, Husain. If we don't go soon we might miss them.'

'Mr Deane?'

'Yes?'

'I'm afraid of the horse. And I'm hungry.'

'Well, there's a bit of bread in my pouch. Will that do, until we get there?'

He nodded solemnly and held out his hand for the bread.

'There's a good boy,' Zachary said, as Husain crammed the bread into his mouth.

Zachary unlocked the collar and leash and threw it away to the corner of the yard. He squeezed Husain tight and kissed the top of his head. Pray God they'd be in time.

Chapter 50

The arrival of Ayamena without Husain had shaken them all. Nicolao leaned against the wall, one arm around his wife, his hand on Luisa's head, as if to reassure himself she at least was there. Luisa, in turn, had Nicolao's wrinkled hand in hers, but stared up at the night sky, at the streaky moon disappearing behind scudding pewter-coloured clouds. Ayamena's eyes were fixed on the track from the main road.

Elspet did not know how she could be of comfort, except to stay with them. She did not really think Zachary could find Husain, or that he could do anything at all against the might of the King's militia. And now she was surprised to find herself concerned for his safety too. He had been family for so long, she could not suddenly think of him as none of her kin.

The small group waited outside under the awning on the covered porch. There was no room in the derelict cottage with the other refugees anyway. Pedro and Alexander stood out in the road, their pipes lit now that the rain had stopped. Elspet watched Señor Alvarez's profile, and he turned and caught her eye. It was as if the rest of the world disappeared. To hide her confusion she knelt to speak to Ayamena. 'Would you like anything? You've not eaten, and Luisa and I had soup –'

'No. Nothing at all. Just my son.' And Ayamena twisted the corner of her robe in her hands. 'Quiet,' Ayamena whispered, suddenly still. Everyone listened. A muffled noise of footsteps, whispers, the clanking of metal and wood, the bleat of a kid. The people in the cottages were moving down to the harbour.

'They're leaving,' Elspet said.

'I won't go without him,' Ayamena said.

'Let's get ready anyway, my love.' Nicolao prompted her by struggling to his feet. 'Then when he comes we won't miss the tide.'

'Let me carry something,' Elspet said.

'I'll manage. Please,' said Ayamena, 'won't one of you go to see if there's any sign of them?'

'I'll go,' Pedro said. 'Poor old Alexander's done enough galloping for one day. He can walk down with Señor Alvarez, escort you to the boats.'

A man whistled softly from the track below, a penetrating sound like the shriek of an owl. 'My husband,' said Señora Quevedo. 'It's time.'

'Thank you,' Alvarez said and bowed to her. Elspet saw the flash of his scabbard beneath his cloak, and realized that he, too, was armed.

'God speed,' whispered Señora Quevedo, crossing herself firmly.

They followed the sound down towards the beach. Señor Alvarez took hold of Nicolao's arm and Luisa took Ayamena's.

'Maybe they're already waiting at the boat, Mama,' she heard Luisa whisper. Luisa, too, was pretending that Zachary and Husain would come; how much harder it must be for her.

They could see nothing for there were no lamps, not a single candle. The wind would have guttered them anyway. But Elspet followed the shuffle of footsteps and the rustle of clothing, the jangle of coins and the clanking of buckets, in the hope of a moment to say farewell to Señor Alvarez and wish him safe passage.

They followed in the tracks of those in front towards the sea, down a steep stony track ravaged by streams of running water. The moon was just setting, three-quarters full, beneath it the tide ballooned dark and menacing. Against a makeshift jetty several small rowing boats dipped and swayed, and further out the dark hulks of bigger fishing smacks could just be seen rising and sinking with the swell. As the group picked their way down the track they were overtaken by more people, all in a hurry to get to the boats, jostling and pushing past with their burdens on their heads.

But Ayamena and Nicolao hung back, looking over their shoulders for any sign of Zachary or Husain. Elspet wished Señor Alvarez and the Ortegas would hurry and get on board. The first boats had already departed and the others were filling fast.

'You should go with Señor Alvarez now, Mama,' Luisa said.

'Take Papa and get on board. I'll wait for Zachary and Husain.'

'Yes, Ayamena, time to go.' Señor Alvarez pressed her arm.

'No. Look what happened last time. This time we stay together. We go as a family or not at all.'

'But señora, look at the jetty. Those rocks couldn't be seen before. The tide has turned and soon the boats will not be able to take you.' Alexander pleaded with Nicolao, 'Please, señor, I'll help you into the next boat.'

But Nicolao shook his head. Elspet looked out to sea, two of the rowing boats were halfway out, the others were over-full already and launching perilously from the jetty. The sandy part of the shore was littered with bags and chattels. The goat was still with them, on its tether, wrapped around the wrist of a lanky youth. Elspet made a count. There were about twenty more people left on the shore besides the Ortegas. Señor Alvarez and her friends would go in the next boat. It was time for farewells.

She touched Señor Alvarez on the shoulder and he turned. 'He isn't coming,' she said.

'I know,' he said.

'Ayamena will break her heart.'

'At least he tried. Here,' he pulled out a rolled parchment from a bag slung over his shoulder and passed it over to her. She made to open it, but he closed his hand over hers. 'Not now. There's no time. It is personal. It is for your future – a letter of love.' His dark eyes were serious but tender.

She blinked back tears; she found she could not speak. He pulled her into his arms and pressed his lips on her forehead. She clung to him, feeling his warm back beneath his cloak.

A volley of shot whisked over the tops of their heads. The blast was deafening. Señor Alvarez unsheathed his sword.

'Get down!' he shouted.

Elspet was disorientated, but stowed the parchment in her bodice and turned to look to her right. A company of horsemen had appeared on the cliffs. From here, now a pale flush of dawn light had appeared, she could just make out their silhouettes. The upright muskets at their shoulders and the shape of their helmets announced they were armed soldiers.

She fought the urge to run. 'Señor! Get into the boat!' she shouted. 'For God's sake, get into the boat!'

Over to her left she saw another dark rabble of men pouring down the track. Alexander and Pedro had seen them too and had put themselves between the mob and the fleeing Moriscos.

Her two companions were managing to hold the path, but more people edged around them to the sides. It took a moment before Elspet realized that these others were not militia but looters after the possessions left on the shore. Baskets and bags, sacks and barrels, they were all disappearing into grasping hands, snatched into the blackness. A soft thud behind her. With horror she saw a woman fall, and the man who had clubbed her drag her bundle from her arms. Elspet drew her sword and ran after him, but he scrambled away, out of the reach of her blade.

When she looked again at the shore the youth was tugging at the goat's halter, whilst a man with a scarf tied over his face was on the other end trying to wrestle it free.

'Leave it!' she cried to the youth, 'Just get aboard!' The last row boat was now sliding up to the jetty.

'What's happening?' she heard Nicolao cry out. 'Is it Zachary?'

Señor Alvarez took his shoulder to guide him on to the boat. 'We are leaving. Don't worry. Ayamena and Luisa are just behind us.'

The others on the shore panicked as more looters poured on to the beach, and they began to run for the jetty. A man stumbled to carry his injured wife to the boat. What had been an orderly procession was now all confusion.

Elspet saw Luisa drag Ayamena on to the landing stage. 'Please,

Mama,' Luisa said. 'Papa's on the boat. You have to leave now or he'll be all alone.'

A dark figure grabbed Luisa's bag and tried to rip it from her shoulder. Elspet saw him lift a lump of wood as if to strike but Elspet leapt up to him, drew her sword and pushed her blade to his throat.

'Leave her,' she spat. The man slunk away. Elspet shoved Ayamena hard from behind. 'Now go!' Luisa used the force of Elspet's push to drag her mother towards the jetty.

Señor Alvarez was standing up in the boat. She could see his white hair, he was shouting and gesticulating and pointing. The two men with the oars were about to push off, when he suddenly dropped down into the boat. Moments later he was back up again pointing.

She heard the clatter of hooves on the path and the looters scattered. Alexander and Pedro pelted down the track towards her.

'Horses,' Alexander panted. 'I think it's the army. For God's sake get them on board.'

'She won't go,' shouted Elspet, 'She's waiting for Husain.'

'Then we'll have to make her. Come on.' The men helped Luisa drag the protesting Ayamena to the boat.

Luisa climbed in first, and took her father's arm. 'Help me, Papa,' she cried.

Alexander and Pedro lifted her in where Luisa and Nicolao and the señor were ready to receive her. But she was fighting all the way, clawing and beating at them.

When Nicolao and Luisa finally had their arms locked around her, she still struggled. 'Husain,' she sobbed, attempting to clamber out, 'my little one, I haven't abandoned you. I'll make them come back for you.'

The oarsman lifted the oar and pushed against the jetty. The boat slid away slowly. Alvarez had his hand lifted in farewell, his gaze fixed on Elspet's face. Elspet lifted her hand to her mouth intending to blow a kiss, but found that she could not, she saw Luisa's stricken face, and Ayamena, still reaching for the shore, her mouth open in anguish.

Chapter 51

Husain's fingers dug into Zachary's ribs. The horse was tiring, and Zachary's hands were numb from riding into the rain and wind. Both were unused to the saddle and in the end Zachary had to prop Husain between his arms instead of him riding pillion, so he could support him upright.

They lost the route to Tavira and had to double back, but when they finally clattered up to the house and the señora said the boats had left, that they were too late, Husain turned grey and silent.

'Don't give up yet, little soldier,' Zachary said. He pictured Luisa's face. He had made a promise. He gritted his teeth and hoisted Husain back up again and galloped towards the shore. From the cliffs he heard gunfire, and its flash lit up the sky.

Trouble. He spurred his horse on, only slowing as he came to the steep stony track to the harbour. Below him the lights of large fishing vessels keeled at anchor in the distance, but a fishing smack nearer to the shore caught his eye. By the jetty a rowing boat was pushing off, rocking on the swell. There were still dark shapes of people on the jetty milling about, some men, and a woman. He clapped his legs hard against the horse's sides.

On the way down the horse shied and sidestepped to avoid people running up, carrying bundles and bags, and a man dragging a young goat behind him. He wasn't sure who these people were and searched their faces, but they put their heads down and scurried past. As he arrived on the shore with Husain, the horse floundered as the stony surface suddenly gave way to soft sand.

'Mama!' Husain's thin voice cried. He seemed to have come to life.

Zachary tried to hold the squirming boy still. A shot rang out and he lost control of his horse, which bucked and stumbled sideways. From behind him, another shot – this time the retort too close for comfort. The horse bolted forwards into the sand. Zachary clutched tight to Husain, the reins flapped loose. A jerk, and a foreleg gave way under the horse and it fell, pitching them both on to the ground. By instinct his body wrapped round Husain as they hit the ground. They rolled over and over. A stone cracked against his ear, dirt and sand filled his mouth. He must shield Husain, from the timing of the shots, there must be at least two arquebusiers.

But Husain slipped from his grip like a rabbit and ran towards the boat, screaming again 'Mama!' Zachary's ears were buzzing but he thought he heard someone cry: 'Husain!'

Husain ran down the sand. A shot exploded in the dirt behind him, but he leapt forward and kept running pell-mell towards the boat, arms flailing.

Zachary scrambled to his feet to look over his shoulder for the source of the shot. Amid a cloud of white smoke, five armed militia men were bearing down on them from the bank. Another ball slammed into the ground, just at Husain's heels, sending a shower of sand into the air.

He'd never make it. Zachary launched himself after Husain, ran as if a fuse had been lit inside him. His feet turfed up wedges of sand. He stretched out his hands to scoop up the terrified boy. He heard another crack and felt a searing pain in his left shoulder.

But they were only yards from the jetty. The boat was just off shore. Everyone on board was shouting, he could see their mouths open and close. His legs were slowing but he was aware of the tall whitehaired figure of Alvarez, standing in the stern waving. He fixed his eyes on Ayamena, her arms reaching out for her son. Her mouth was shouting too, but her words were lost in the wind and the noise of hooves behind him.

'Help us!' he yelled, holding the boy beneath the armpits.

The figures on the jetty dived off to take cover. Another shot, and this time he felt the shot graze past his temple as if in some other slower time, the flesh of his ear tearing from his scalp as the red-hot metal seared its path towards the boat.

The force of its passage spun him to his knees. Instinctively, he put his hand to his head and felt blood and bone. A splash. Husain whimpered on the jetty before him, his eyes wide with shock. Zachary staggered upright and with the last of his strength lifted Husain to the edge. In his blurred vision he saw hands paddling frantically over the edge of the boat. They were coming back for him. The scene before him began to swim.

He made an almighty effort and thrust Husain forward into his mother's arms. He thought he caught a glimpse of Luisa stretching out to him, when nausea engulfed him. His knees hit the deck with a crack. He rolled off the jetty into the soft sand, and moaned in pain. The sky was black now, the moon eclipsed by clouds. He heard shouting from behind, and the soft plash of oars. He hoped to God they would make it. God speed, Luisa, he thought, I'm sorry I let you down.

He could not fight any more. He was as good as a corpse lying there. And as he watched, the sky slowly turned white as snow.

Elspet felt the thud of her own heart beating. She dare not come out from under cover. Zachary was injured on the planks above, that much she knew. A blast of fire and suddenly he toppled into the sand beside her, groaning in pain. His face was a mass of grazes, the side of his head seemed to be pouring blood. He rolled over and lay still. She scrambled round to see the wound in his shoulder and saw with relief it was only a flesh wound.

'Zachary.' She shook him. A hiss through the air and then a splash. So they were still firing at the boat. She sent up a silent prayer.

Another splash, but then silence.

Zachary came to, his face gaunt with pain. 'Luisa? Is she…?'

She waited, straining for the sound of another shot. When it did not come she said, 'They all made the boat, Zachary. You did it.' She shook him by the shoulder.

'The whole family?'

'All on that last boat.'

She turned his head, and saw his ear was mostly gone, from which the dark seep of blood dripped through his hair and on to the grey sand. She remembered Sister Josefa, the Barefoot Beata, and tried to stay calm.

'The soldiers?' his voice was thick.

'Hush, I need to listen.' It fell ominously silent then, except for the suck and swell of the sea. She did not know if the soldiers had gone or not. Somewhere a horse neighed and then she saw it – it was riderless, trotting down the beach, reins flapping. Shock set in. Her teeth chattered with fear. 'Oh Mother Mary,' she said under her breath. 'Oh Mother Mary.' Over and over, as if it would help. She thought she heard another shout, but could not be certain. Her hands shook.

She peered out from under the jetty. A helmeted soldier holding an arquebus out before him approached. Dread enveloped her. He saw her movement and stopped warily in his tracks, paused to reload his weapon.

'Get under cover,' she hissed to Zachary, but her words sounded weak and he did not respond. 'Please, try to move.' She tried to pull him further under the shelter of the jetty, but he was heavy and she only managed to drag him a few inches. She saw the shaky flare of the flint light up the metal breastplate and the soldier lift the gun to his shoulder to take aim.

A blast and a bright white light. She threw herself to the ground, hands over her head, as shrapnel fell from the sky. The echo ricocheted round the harbour, splinters of metal rained on to the planks above them. When the noise died away she raised her head. In place of the soldier was a standing cloud of foul-smelling smoke.

There was a dark shape lying on the sand surrounded by debris. What was it? She could not see the soldier any more. Just empty space. It was a moment before she realized – his gun must have clogged and exploded.

A second soldier ran towards the body through the smoke, but stopped short, staring. He looked up to the sky, and crossed himself.

In a panic in case he should see them, she tried to drag Zachary away from that place, but he was too heavy and he groaned in pain.

'Leave me,' he moaned, 'hide somewhere. Save yourself.'

The second soldier turned and ran back towards the horses. She tracked his direction and saw that over by the wall Alexander and Pedro had taken on the rest of the militia men, who had abandoned the arquebus, and were fighting on foot. The clash of their weapons reminded her with sudden poignancy of the training yard.

There were three still fighting. Another lay motionless on the ground near the horses. The fifth soldier's distorted shape was like a boulder in the sand. Beyond him she could see Pedro was struggling against his adversary. He was a smaller man than the soldier, and the soldier wore a metal breastplate. Pedro was tiring, his cuts had little effect on the metal, and now he was backed up against the harbour wall. She took a dagger from her belt. Señor Alvarez was gone. Zachary would probably bleed to death. If Pedro and Alexander were killed, then she had no doubt they would kill her too — or worse.

She ran along the edge of the harbour wall, head down, until she was behind the soldier. Pedro saw her approach and she caught his eye. In this small moment of communication they understood each other. He paused in his attack for a fraction. She waited until the soldier raised his arm for his final cut and then she thrust hard and deep under his arm. She retreated; the dagger was still stuck there, its hilt sticking from under his arm.

The soldier blundered backwards, confused, and her sword flew like a bird from her scabbard. He turned to face her, eyes wild as a stuck bull. She engaged his weapon and he relaxed momentarily, seeing a woman standing there. Nimbly, she stepped around his blade and made a strike to the neck.

Taken aback he parried her blade clumsily to the side, before making a swipe for her head. Only now did it occur to her that she was fighting for her life. The thought hit her like an arrow and made her legs buckle under her; her skirts tangled in her feet as she struggled to move away.

The man grinned and raised his sword to smite downwards. Over his shoulder she saw Pedro lunge, bring his blade around from behind and pull sharply back. The sword glinted against his neck as the soldier's blade faltered in mid-air then dropped from his grasp.

Pedro let the body slump into the sand and sprinted away. Elspet stood over it, unsure what to do. Pedro was running towards Alexander, who was just holding his own against the other two men, by dancing out of their range. Their weapons were shorter and heavier, but there were two of them and they were herding Alexander backwards into a corner. The shorter one heard something and looked behind where Pedro was approaching, but she saw his eyes taken by something behind her.

'Watch out!' he yelled to his thick-set companion.

She swivelled to look.

Zachary had rolled over and was hauling himself with his one good arm over the sand to reach an arquebus where it had fallen. The soldier sprang towards them but Pedro was nearer and leapt into his path.

The man was heavily built and powerful. He fought off Pedro's blows until Pedro was forced to back away.

'Pedro!' Even as she shouted, she knew she was too late. The beach was still littered with the remnants of Morisco possessions. Pedro stepped back into a mis-shapen bundle and toppled. She saw his legs fly up, heard the thud as his back hit the sand, the rattle of his sword belt. He grunted as he fell, but the soldier did not pause. He thrust his blade hard down, straight into Pedro's chest.

Elspet backed away. It was so quick. Pedro did not even cry out. She knew with certainty her friend would never stand again. The thought incensed her. The soldier was still coming towards her, she ran for the gun but as she picked it up, she realized she did not know how to use it. She threw it towards Zachary, but he was too weak to handle it. He was on his knees, trying to stand, his sword in his left hand. The soldier saw Zachary and laughed.

'The piss-pants Englishman who can't fight,' he said, 'in the dirt again.' It was only then that Elspet remembered she'd seen this man before. The day the soldiers looted the yard.

'Rodriguez,' Zachary said, rising shakily to his feet.

But Rodriguez had already drawn back his sword and made to thrust it into Zachary's chest.

'Don't you dare touch him!' Elspet leapt in from the side and engaged his blade with hers.

'Get out of my way,' he growled, trying to move her blade.

She stood firm despite his pressure. 'I said, don't touch him.'

He stabbed at her then, and the speed of his attack gave her no time to think. Her blade slid around his like water. Her edge cut upwards into his cheek. He swore and stepped back out of range. His hand came up to his cheek, and he felt the blood, slick between his fingers and thumb, his expression amazed.

'Vixen,' he said, as he drew back to launch another thrust to Zachary's chest.

You will have to kill me first, Elspet thought, lunging forward with the tip of her sword.

Rodriguez parried her easily, laughing. 'Come on, little lady. He's finished anyway. Why bother? What's he to you?'

'He's my brother,' she pressed her blade towards him, 'keep away.'

He clashed hard against it to force her away. She imagined the circle. Felt it live inside her. It calmed her. She extended all her senses, reaching out in her heart to the señor. Rodriguez stood with his sword outstretched, his breath rang in her ears. She looked into his face and a slight narrowing of his eyes gave away his moment of attack. He propelled his sword forward and she stepped round the circle to the side. But he was too quick, his weapon shot round after her and she felt hers fly upwards from her grasp. She let out a cry, but kept her eyes fixed on her adversary.

Before her sword even hit the ground Zachary was waving his. She grabbed it. Just in time she rolled away to the side in a flurry of sand and the big man's blade missed her by a flea's width. It pierced her skirts and stuck into the ground.

The slight delay as he struggled to withdraw it was all the time she needed. Zachary's sword was light and strong and familiar in her hand. She deflected easily as Rodriguez made another strike and slid it upwards to his wrist. I have you, she thought, but then just in time he turned his guard and pushed her away.

She saw the change in him.

He paused too, gathered himself. That she was a danger had just penetrated his awareness. He ignored Zachary, who had sunk back gasping to his knees and was no threat to him. He walked towards her, eyes like a snake about to strike.

His slow approach made her stomach curdle. If she did not prevail then Zachary would stand no chance. She backed away and leapt up on to the jetty to give herself more height. With both hands she brought the blade slicing fast towards his neck. He saw it and leapt to the side. A powerful spring and he was on the jetty with her, pressing forward with a series of shattering blows. His force vibrated up her arm.

She tried to stave him off. He was bigger and stronger and relentless. But her mind was agile and as he made a last cut towards her face she sprang sideways off the edge like a cat into the shallows. She turned quickly at a sound behind her. Alexander was running to help her. She angled a penetrating strike upwards and succeeded in making a deep cut to the soldier's knee. He let out a groan of pain and Alexander ran up the jetty and pounced, about to engage him.

'Curse you!' Rodriguez yelled, hobbling, staggering back. Alexander followed him and drove in his blade. She saw Rodriguez lose balance, and the panic in his eyes as he fought to regain it, arms flailing.

Slowly, so slowly, he fell into nothingness. A splash.

Alexander and Elspet moved cautiously along the jetty to see what had become of him. He thrashed in the water, his face gasping at the surface, struggling for air, his weighty armour dragging him under. 'He can't swim,' said Alexander.

Elspet looked away. She could not watch.

When she looked back he floated face-up, a pale blurred outline just under the water, like a lump of wreckage moving back and forth with the waves.

A noise of galloping hooves told them that the remaining soldier was leaving. Elspet let Zachary's sword drop from her grasp.

She cast her eyes out to sea. In the distance she made out the small black dot of the boat still moving against the light of the sky, and further still a fishing smack waiting at anchor in the deeps.

Alexander followed her gaze, before turning to look at the fallen figure of Pedro. 'So they made it. Lucky for some,' he said sadly.

Chapter 52

It was strange to be back in Seville. It looked like a different place, a city bereaved. The stones in the city walls must have been witness to so many conquests, so many lives lived and lost, every empire built on the ruins of another. Elspet took out the letter from Señor Alvarez, and sat at one of the taverns at the side of the road. It was the first private moment she had taken for herself since she had gone to Tavira. After the night the Moriscos left, Alexander had begged Señora Quevedo for help, and she had mustered men from the village to help carry the dead from the beach, and then sent them on to another safe house.

Together, she and Alexander travelled back to Seville in a hired wagon, with Pedro's body laid out in a sheet, and Zachary groaning in the back. Fortunately, they had encountered no one en route. The other Moriscos from the villages must be already gathered at the port by now or long gone. She shuddered at the thought of it, imagined the Ortegas and dear Señor Alvarez out in the vastness of the sea. She tried to quell the yearning of her heart.

She had asked to be dropped here, at a tavern just inside the city walls. Alexander would fetch a physician for Zachary, and then return to the same spot later to meet with her. She weighed the roll of parchment in her hand. She had been too busy dealing with the dead and the wounded to open it.

A love letter, the señor had said. She was not sure she could bear words of affection now he was gone. She ordered some tea and some raisin and apple cakes, but left them untouched on the table. Slowly she unrolled the parchment and began to read.

At first she could not fathom it. She turned it over, looking for something else. But then she understood.

'Oh señor,' she said. She began to laugh, and laugh. Tears rolled down her face. She opened it again, ran her finger over where he had signed his name in expansive letters, put her lips to his name and kissed it. He had told her he loved her, but not in words. She would have liked words, but this was better. The feeling in her chest swelled to bursting. Only he could have thought of something like this.

Pray God everything would knit well and not turn putrid, Zachary thought. He was lucky to be alive. The physician had dressed his shoulder, and sewed up the remains of his ear, but even after a week he was still deaf in that side, with a ringing in his head that would not stop.

The sun was out though it was bitter cold, and the sharp shadows of clouds danced over his balcony. On the side table next to the bed lay his mother's letter where he had left it, still open and lifting slightly in the breeze. He picked it up to fold it and put it away, but could not resist reading it one more time. Her voice, her slight Spanish burr, echoed in his mind.

25th Day of September, 1599
Dearest Zack,

By the time you read this I will be gone and you will have to face the future without me. Pray do not grieve too long – life is short and precious and the world will be a worse place without your sunny smile. You must listen to your Mama now.

I have written to Uncle Leviston – he will come to find you, and you must take his instruction – and then you will grow up to be the fine, educated gentleman I know you can be.

God forgive me, I deceived the poor man all these years,

told him you were born early, that you were his son. I owe him much, for it is he who paid for your lessons, kept you in shoes, bought bread for our table. So don't you forget it. Your blood father – well, let's just say he came but once, and never again. So what was I to do, with three hungry mouths to feed and no business? Oh Zack, I am not asking for forgiveness, only understanding.

Uncle Leviston has grown to love you, of that I am sure. So do this last little thing for me, my peppercorn – keep our secret. For I fear your brothers will not prove kind, and they are already set on a dangerous life. And above all, I can rest easy if I know you will be safe in the care of such an English gentleman.

Though I may be gone and life may deal you bitter blows, you must never give up hope for better things . . .'

Her last farewells always threatened to bring a lump to his throat, not because of the words themselves but because they were her last and brought back the pain of those first lost days without her. So he closed the letter into its well-worn square and thought how she would raise her brows if she could see him here, if she could know what a life with Uncle Leviston had led to. He laughed at the sheer irony of it; that the safe, respectable life she imagined for him had never existed.

Do parents always hold out these false hopes for their children, he wondered? In some ways he felt she had not known him at all, yet in other ways, since being in Spain, he had grown mysteriously more like her, more at home in his own skin. He inhaled deeply and smiled.

⌒

Gabriel had been to visit and give him news of the expulsion. They had lost three men from Guido's workshop, but Gabriel himself had become indispensable. And Elspet had come every day, with Alexander. They sat on his bed, and made crumbs with their offerings of honey cakes and dates.

451

Zachary had asked her if she believed in destiny.

'I don't know,' she had said. 'I believe in something, some force that moves us through life. Perhaps it's just the feeling, the sensation of being alive. I put my trust in nature more than I ever did, and I'm grateful for small things like the sun coming up and shining every day.'

'It's just that now I can't imagine that I might never have known you,' he said. 'And it was one chance in a million that I picked up your father's notice. It seemed like a wind from the gods.'

'I know what you mean. When I came to Señor Alvarez, I fancied that Agrippa was talking to me. I was scared of it, but fascinated; I really thought he had written his books especially for me.' Zachary raised his eyebrows. 'I know. It seems a foolish notion now, but it made me want to stay, to know more. Like a guidance. Do you think that is fanciful?'

'Look,' he brought out the piece of Calvary wood from his pocket, 'my mother gave me this. Said it was a piece of Christ's Cross. I've carried it all these years, thinking it would protect me, like a talisman. Is it superstition, or has it kept me safe? Would that soldier still have blown himself up if I had not carried it? I don't know.' He slipped it back in his pocket. 'We all have our interior lives, I suppose. Some hook to hang up the things we can't explain.'

She nodded.

'Do you know, Elspet, though I wanted it so badly, I fought the señor's instruction. And your father, and you. All of life. Until I realized that it was myself I was really fighting. Alvarez taught me that I do not have to be the same person I lived with and hated for so long – the thief, the liar and the man who dare not open his heart. That I could let all that go.'

She sighed, and her voice choked. 'I miss them so much. I miss the training with señor, the smell of Ayamena's cooking. I can't believe it is all over, that I will never hear him call "Mistress Leviston" again.'

'He was something special to you, wasn't he?'

She swallowed, twisted her hands in her lap.

'Luisa too,' he said. 'I promised I'd go with her. I hope . . .'

She quietened him by placing her hand on his. 'She saw, and she will understand.' So they had sat together then, each with their own thoughts and longings.

Today the dizziness and blurred vision had subsided enough for him to walk unaided to the fencing school, and as he walked gingerly down the streets he saw every third house was boarded up, the street-front stalls closed, and there was refuse building up on the highway. Seville was only just beginning to count the cost of losing its Moorish population.

Luisa was ever in his thoughts, and his heart ached for news of her. He paused a moment, closed his eyes tight and sent out his intent to her that she should be safe and well. He hoped she might be thinking of him. Praise be, there was a swordsman such as Señor Alvarez with them, and they were bound for Morocco and Fez, and not Oran. Whilst he was laid up in bed Alexander had brought news of more atrocities against the Moriscos when they reached Oran. That the men had been robbed and killed, and the women and children raped or sold as slaves. The thought troubled him like a sore that would not heal.

Though he was physically weak, and the injuries were still raw, it was these other wounds that hurt more. To love and lose. To fear for your love's safety and not know where she might be, or whether she was still alive. It made every moment feel unbearably fragile, the sheer delicacy of human life.

When he arrived at the Spreadeagled Man the sight of the new yard door brought a lump to his throat. He remembered the sound of it splintering, and little Husain's terrified face. And worse, he could still see Luisa in his mind's eye. Every place was a place she would have trod, with her light dancing step. At his knock, Alexander himself opened up.

'Ah, the English Terror,' he said, laughing. 'How do you fare, my friend?'

'Better, now that I don't have to listen to your Dutch nonsense with both ears,' he said, rallying himself.

He looked around. The yard was clean and tidy; a new tilt post stood in the centre, with wooden arms on a swivel.

'We have been waiting for you. We could not start training without you,' Alexander said.

'Steady! It might be a few more days before I can beat you again,' he said.

Elspet appeared from the kitchen. She was wearing her old yellow gown and smiling. She hurried over and he made a one-armed bow with a flourish, 'Oh it's good to see you on your feet,' she said, and her warmth was infectious.

He grinned at her. 'What's this? What were you doing in the kitchen? Surely after all this time you've not decided to do women's work? Gird yourself, woman, and get out here with the men.'

'I can see the injury's done nothing to improve you, still the same old Zachary.' She flapped him away with a dishcloth.

'Enough of your jesting now, they will be here to see the papers any moment,' said Alexander.

Zachary took in at a glance that Alexander was dressed tidily, with his beard trimmed and his shoes polished. 'What?' he said.

Alexander dropped his smile and shook his head morosely, 'All Morisco property is to be confiscated and reclaimed by the King. I spoke to the notary yesterday. Don Rodriguez's sergeant-at-arms wants to take this place on and use the yard to stable his horses. Can you imagine? The King's commissioner and his notary are coming here today with the requisition order.'

'Is this true?' Zachary asked.

Elspet nodded, her lips pressed together, and bowed her head. 'Bastards.'

'Come up to the library,' Alexander said. 'There are chairs up there and you can sit whilst we wait. You are still a little weak and—'

'Damn you. I don't want to sit. I can't bear the thought of any of Don Rodriguez's men in this yard. It is disrespectful to the señor.' They were moving upstairs, so he had no alternative but to follow. He kept talking as he went. 'And it's so unjust. How long have we got before they come?'

When he got inside the library there were new chairs and a new olive-wood table. In the middle of its polished surface was a document held open by four lead weights.

'Tell him, Elspet,' Alexander said, suppressing a smile.

She pointed to the document, 'They can't take it.' She beamed at him. 'It's quite in order,' she said, 'take a look.'

He did not understand.

'They won't be able to take the building because it does not belong to a Morisco, it belongs to me.'

'To you?' He was baffled. 'But how?'

'Señor Alvarez had the deeds made out to me and pre-dated them before the embarkation order. It is signed and sealed by a lawyer and by Girard Thibault. He gave me the copy of the document just before he got on the boat.'

Alexander leaned over to talk to him, 'He was clever, Zachary. It is just perfect. He knew it was what you might want most in the world.'

'Me? What do you mean?'

'We think he was giving you the opportunity to trade property with Elspet. He knew you were the one to take over his school in Spain. She wants the lace business you own, isn't that right? You have what she wants, and she has what you want, see?'

'You mean he meant us to exchange?'

'It certainly looks like it to me,' Alexander said.

He could not take it in. 'But we can't know that. You can't be serious. And Elspet,' he protested, 'you know full well I'm not your brother. I have no legal entitlement to any of your goods.'

'Señor Alvarez did not know about that when he made me the bequest,' Elspet said, picking up the parchment and holding it out to him. 'He thought we were kin, and simply saw a way to show his regard for us both. You heard him say over and over that tradition is important, that the school must not die, and you are the best of all of us, everyone knows it.'

'Perhaps it might sound sentimental, but we are all brothers here, those that trained with the señor,' Alexander said. 'You know it is so.'

Zachary was staggered. He could only open and close his mouth, no words would come.

She placed the document in his hand, and her hand over his, and said gently, 'I'm telling you that between us we own both my father's lace business and this school. We can decide between us as a brother and sister might, where best our respective skills might be employed.' She paused, her face flushed with emotion.

He took hold of the paper.

'That is, if you are willing,' she said. 'I'm not saying it will be easy.' She walked to the window and he saw her look out. The winter sun just tinged the curls of her hair in a silvery light. 'I'm not sure where my future lies now,' she said. 'The lace business might be too small for me now I have seen Spain. I enjoyed the fencing more than a woman should. And I have a yearning to see more of the world, to visit the cathedral cities of France, the Vatican in Rome, and oh – so much more.'

'A Grand Tour?'

'Yes.'

'I hope it is longer than mine, then.'

She laughed.

Zachary said, 'I will be happy to share with you, Elspet, if it is what you want, but it is far, far more than I deserve.'

'I want to make up for lost time. I have no other family except my sister Joan and she's a nun. You have all been my family. And I didn't really try to know you as a brother before, I was jealous of you, and resented you taking Father's attention. But I think it would please him to see both our names on one document.'

'I'm hardly the kind of brother a girl might have wanted. And I have a past I cannot change. But I will try to be the sort of son your father could be proud of.'

'Zack, you risked your life for a six-year-old boy. Anyone would be proud.'

'Whatever you do, it is important the school remains,' Alexander said, 'so that you can pass on what you know. And so that when the dust settles, those who love you know where you are to be found.'

Zachary could not speak. The memory of Luisa's face filled his vision.

Señor Alvarez's apprentice poked his head into the room. 'Excuse me, Mistress Leviston, but three men are in the yard asking after you.'

'Then I suppose we'd better go down,' Elspet said.

And Zachary looked back at her and held out his arm.

The swallow swooped low over the coastline of Morocco; the sand unravelling beneath her like a cloth of gold. On the beach a boat was unloading; the people a line of ants carrying their burdens ashore. The swallow did not stop to watch the people inch their way across the landscape. She flew onwards – onwards to where the pools in the reed beds reflected the blue of the sky, and the feathered plumes of the reeds released their seeds to float on the wind.

Afterword

After Felipe III of Spain signed an edict in 1609, the entire Muslim population, along with anyone who had converted from Islam to Christianity, was ordered to leave Spain on threat of death. By 1613, it is estimated that 400,000 people had been forcibly removed in this mass expulsion from Spanish territory.

Girard Thibault won first prize in a fencing Tournament in Rotterdam in 1611. His book, *Academy of the Sword – The Mystery of the Spanish Circle in Swordsmanship and Esoteric Arts*, was published in 1630 and is still available today in a translation by John Michael Greer, complete with Thibault's original engravings of the practice of *La Verdadera Destreza*.

Brief Historical Background

England

England in 1609 was ruled by the Protestant James I, who was James VI of Scotland. In 1603, he succeeded Elizabeth I, the last Tudor monarch of England and Ireland, who died without an heir. James continued to reign over all three kingdoms for twenty-two years, a period known as the Jacobean era, until his death in 1625.

During James's reign, Catholics were forbidden to practise their faith openly. This stemmed from a series of Catholic uprisings during the reign of his predecessor, Elizabeth. Those who refused to attend Anglican services were called 'recusants' from the Latin *recusare* – to refuse, and were pronounced guilty of high treason. The recusancy laws were in force from the reigns of Elizabeth I to that of George III, though they were not always enforced with equal intensity.

After the failed Gunpowder Plot of 1605, in which Catholics, led by Robert Catesby and Guy Fawkes, attempted to assassinate the King by blowing up the House of Lords, James I sanctioned even harsher measures against recusants. Parliament passed the Popish Recusants Act in which the recusant was to be fined £60, or to forfeit two-thirds of his land, if he did not receive the sacrament of the Lord's Supper (Holy Communion) at least once a year in his Church of England parish church. The Act could also require any citizen to take an Oath of Allegiance which denied the Pope and the Catholic faith and swore allegiance only to the King.

In Catholic homes, for fear of persecution, Masses were said secretly. Priests, often Jesuits, struggled to keep their presence hidden from the authorities. Catholic worship often took place in secluded parts of the house, perhaps in the cellar or roof space, and nearby there would be a hiding place to provide a space where missals, vestments, sacred vessels, and altar furniture could be stored at a moment's notice. These spaces were also used as bolt-holes for the officiating priests in the event of an emergency.

Many such 'priest-holes' are attributed to a Jesuit lay brother, Nicholas Owen, who devoted the greater part of his life to constructing them. They were sometimes built as an offshoot from a chimney, as at East Riddlesden Hall, or set behind panelling as in Ripley Castle in Yorkshire. I like to think that someone like Nicholas Owen would have constructed the priest-hole at West View House.

Catholics were not the only religious faith to which James I found he was in opposition. On his accession, the Puritan clergy, intent on a more rigorous service, demanded among other things, the abolition of wedding rings, the term 'priest', and asked that the wearing of cap and surplice should become optional. However, the King was strict in advocating conformity, inducing a sense of persecution amongst many Puritans as well as Catholics.

As a result of these religious divisions, the King commissioned a new translation of approved books of the Bible to resolve difficulties with all the different versions then being used. The Authorised King James Version, as it came to be known, was completed in 1611 and is considered a masterpiece of Jacobean prose And of course it is still in widespread use today.

Spain

Whereas in England Catholicism was repressed, in Spain Catholics were the ruling majority. To understand the climate of oppression for religious minorities in Spain in 1609, one must look back a few centuries to 1248, when Seville, formerly a Moorish city, fell to Christian armies.

For the following centuries after conquest Christians were

determined to expand their dominion over Spain, and on 2 January 1492 Muslim Granada fell – a momentous day for Christian Europe, a day of rejoicing, but for the Maghreb it became a day of eternal sorrow. Just as the day is marked by celebrations in Spain, in Morocco black flags are hung out to indicate loss and mourning. Some descendants of those expelled still retain the original fifteenth-century keys of their Andalusian homes as a symbol of their lost culture.

After the conquest of Granada by Christians the Jewish population was driven out, whilst tolerance was promised to its Moorish citizens. So by the seventeenth century the Moors had become indelibly Spanish. Some were genuine Christian converts, and many, like Sancho Panza's neighbour Ricote (in Cervantes' novel *Don Quixote*), and Luisa in my novel, thought of themselves as '*más cristiano que moro*'.

The Spanish Inquisition is associated with the persecution of the Jews but it is not common knowledge that Muslims were also tried and tortured by this institution and that they too were the victims of a raging anti-Semitic ideology. During my research trip to Seville, I visited the remains of the San Jorge Castle and saw chilling evidence of this persecution, which the Inquisition applied not only to rival faiths to Catholicism but also to mystics of their own faith.

A short period of relatively peaceful co-existence was shattered when the Archbishop of Granada, Hernando de Talavera, was replaced by the fanatic Cardinal Cisneros, and Muslim religious leaders were persuaded to hand over more than five thousand priceless books with ornamental bindings, which were then consigned to bonfires. Only a few books on medicine were spared the flames. Unsurprisingly, this event led to an armed response from Muslims in the First Rebellion of the Alpujarras in 1499. By 1502, the monarchy had rescinded the treaty of tolerance and Muslims in Andalusia were forced to convert or leave. Those who converted were called Moriscos, which means 'little Moors'.

Many Moriscos professed their allegiance to Christianity while practising Islam in secret. Every aspect of the Islamic way of life, including the Arabic language, dress and social customs, was condemned as uncivilized and pagan. A person who refused to drink wine or eat pork, or who cooked meat on a Friday might be denounced as a Muslim to the Inquisition. Even practices such as buying couscous, using henna, throwing sweets at a wedding or dancing to the sound of Berber music were un-Christian activities for which a person might be reported to the Inquisition by his neighbour, and obliged to do penance.

Further repression of the Moriscos resulted in a second Rebellion. Fearing the rebels were conspiring with the Turks of the Ottoman Empire, the uprising was brutally suppressed by Don John of Austria. In a spate of atrocities the town of Galera, to the east of Granada, was razed to the ground and sprinkled with salt, after the slaughter of 2,500 people including 400 women and children. Some 80,000 Moriscos in Granada were forcibly dispersed to other parts of Spain, including Seville. Christians from northern Spain were settled on their empty lands. Ayamena and Nicolao in my novel were displaced from Granada before settling in Seville.

As early as the sixteenth century, The Council of State proposed expulsion as a solution to the on-going Morisco 'problem', for which the previous exile of the Jews provided a legal precedent. However, the action was delayed because of Spain's pressing political concerns abroad and because of the drawbacks of losing so many skilled Muslim labourers from the Spanish working population.

Juan de Ribera, the ageing Archbishop of Valencia, who had initially been a firm believer in missionary work, and the conversion of the Moorish population to Christianity, became in his declining years the chief partisan of expulsion. In a sermon preached on 27 September 1609, he said that Spanish land would never become fertile again until these heretics (the Moriscos) were expelled. The Duke of Lerma, the corrupt chief minister, agreed with him. The new king, Felipe III, known as Philip the Pious for his religious zeal, finally acquiesced to their political pressure and the expulsions began. The embarkation order was read out in Seville on 10 January 1610.

Further Reading

Amberger, Christophe J., *The Secret History of the Sword*, Multi-Media Books, Canada, 1999

Carr, Matthew, *Blood and Faith: The Purging of Muslim Spain*, New Press, New York, 2009.

Cervantes, Miguel de, *Don Quixote*, Penguin, 2003.

Cohen, Richard, *By the Sword*, Macmillan, 2002

Cressy, David, *Birth Marriage and Death: Ritual, Religion and the Life Cycle in Tudor and Stuart England*, Oxford University Press, 1997.

Edwards, Gwynne and Haas, Ken, *Flamenco*, Thames & Hudson, 2000.

Fraser, Antonia, *The Gunpowder Plot: Terror and Faith in 1605*, Weidenfeld & Nicolson, 1996.

Green, Toby, *Inquisition*, Pan Macmillan, 2007.

Hutton, Alfred, *The Sword and the Centuries*, Wren's Park Publishing, 2003.

Loades, Mike, *Swords and Swordsmen*, Pen and Sword Military, 2010.

Perry, Mary Elizabeth, *Gender and Disorder in Early Modern Seville*, Princeton University Press, 1990.

Perry, Mary Elizabeth, *The Handless Maiden: Moriscos and the Politics of Religion in Early Modern Spain*, Princeton University Press, 2005.

Pike, Ruth, *Aristocrats and Traders: Sevillian Society in the Sixteenth Century*, Cornell University Press, 1972 (and the Library of Iberian Resources online)

Worden, Blair, *Stuart England*, Phaidon Press, 1986.

Destreza Translation Project: www.destreza.us

Martinez Academy of Arms www.martinez-destreza.com

Acknowledgements

I would like to thank in particular Mary and Puck Curtis of the Destreza Translation and Research Project, who answered my questions and supplied me with many leads and suggestions from which to research Carranza and La Destreza. Those interested in the Spanish Art of Defence, can find a valuable resource – both practical and theoretical – on their website www.destreza.us.

Finally, thanks to my agent Annette Green, my editors Jenny Geras and Natasha Harding and all at Pan Macmillan who originally published this book.

About Deborah Swift

Deborah used to be a set and costume designer for the theatre and for the BBC. She is the author of ten historical novels, and lives on the edge of the English Lake District, close to the mountains and the sea. Her books have been shortlisted for many awards including the Impress Prize (UK) and the BookViral Millennium Award (US)

You can find out more about her research and writing process on her website www.deborahswift.com

Sign up for Deborah's newsletter for book chat and special offers.

Deborah is always happy to chat to readers on Twitter @swiftstory

Meanwhile, why not try one of Deborah's other books

The Lady's Slipper
The Gilded Lily
The Highway Trilogy for Teens
Pleasing Mr Pepys
A Plague on Mr Pepys
Entertaining Mr Pepys
Past Encounters

Thank you for reading.
If you have enjoyed this book,
an online review would be much appreciated.

Discussion Questions for Reading Groups – A Divided Inheritance

1. Did you like Elspet and Zachary at the beginning of the book? Did your opinions of them change, and if so what were the moments that caused you to reassess them?

2. Were you surprised by the journey that Elspet took during the course of the novel? How much did her outer journey broaden her inner perception of the world?

3. Does Elspet inherit any of her father's traits? How much is Zachary a product of his poor upbringing? Discuss whether you inherit your major character traits, or are conditioned into them.

4. The expulsion of the Moorish population of Spain is seen through the eyes of the Ortega family. Discuss the romance between Zachary and Luisa, and how it was left at the end of the novel. Did you find this ending satisfying and realistic?

5. Discuss the difference between how Catholics were treated in England and Spain as portrayed in the book. Is religion cultural rather than spiritual?

6. Zachary is obsessed by sword fighting, and later Elspet becomes interested in learning this skill. Discuss the education the men receive at the fencing school and what Elspet learns about herself by taking part in it.

7. Elspet and Zachary become 'family.' What do you think is the true meaning of family for you, and how does this relate to A Divided Inheritance?

8. Senor Alvarez has a hold over both Elspet and Zachary through his character. Discuss what his presence brings to the novel.

9. Persistence plays a big part in the unfolding of the plot. Discuss instances where persistence paid dividends for Elspet and Zachary.

10. What do you think happens after the novel is finished? Do Zachary and Elspet work together or does Elspet go on her Grand Tour? Do you think they meet any of the Moriscos again?

11. What makes a good historical novel? Did you learn something about history from reading A Divided Inheritance? Are accuracy and historical facts important, or is the story paramount?

Printed in Poland
by Amazon Fulfillment
Poland Sp. z o.o., Wrocław

55891489R00284